Aru Shah
AND THE END OF TIME
THE GRAPHIC NOVEL

ADAPTED BY **JOE CARAMAGNA**
ILLUSTRATED BY **ANU CHOUHAN**
LETTERING BY **STEF PURENINS**

BASED ON THE NOVEL BY **ROSHANI CHOKSHI**

RICK RIORDAN PRESENTS
DISNEY • HYPERION   LOS ANGELES   NEW YORK

For Steph, Rick, and Seale, whose
brilliance, humor, and efforts gave this
series a home in the hearts of many
—R. C.

For my wife, Amy, and our kids: Julia,
Lily, and Joey—J. C.

For Chloe and Neve—A. C.

Text copyright © 2022 by Roshani Chokshi
Illustrations copyright © 2022 by Disney Enterprises, Inc.

First Edition, April 2022
10 9 8 7 6 5 4 3 2
FAC-034274-22090
Printed in the United States of America

Designed by Joann Hill

Library of Congress Control Number: 2021949482
Hardcover ISBN 978-1-368-07436-0
Paperback ISBN 978-1-368-07505-3
Reinforced binding
Visit www.DisneyBooks.com
Follow @ReadRiordan

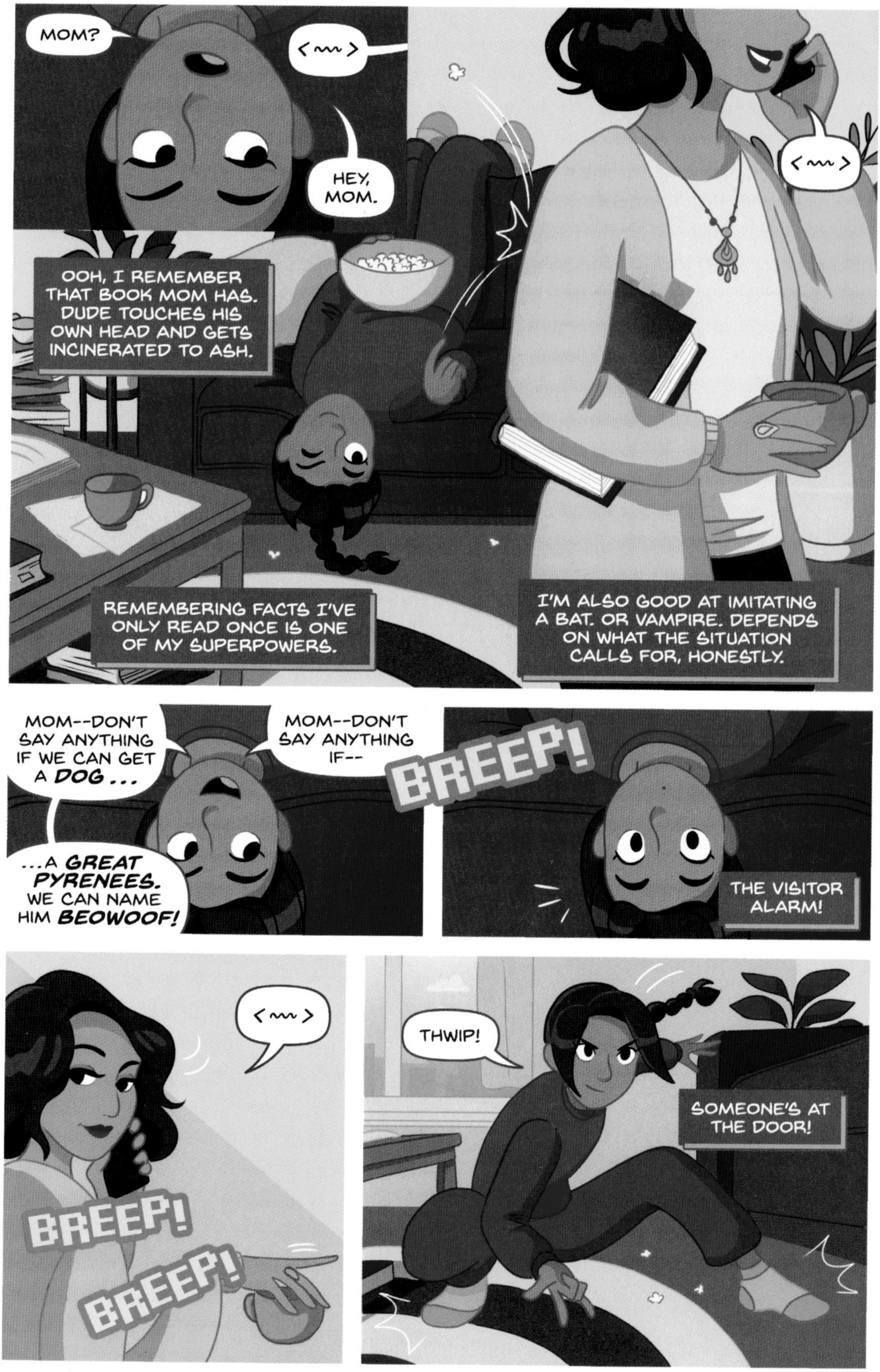
MOM?
<~~>
HEY, MOM.
<~~>
OOH, I REMEMBER THAT BOOK MOM HAS. DUDE TOUCHES HIS OWN HEAD AND GETS INCINERATED TO ASH.
REMEMBERING FACTS I'VE ONLY READ ONCE IS ONE OF MY SUPERPOWERS.
I'M ALSO GOOD AT IMITATING A BAT. OR VAMPIRE. DEPENDS ON WHAT THE SITUATION CALLS FOR, HONESTLY.
MOM--DON'T SAY ANYTHING IF WE CAN GET A DOG . . .
. . . A GREAT PYRENEES. WE CAN NAME HIM BEOWOOF!
MOM--DON'T SAY ANYTHING IF--
BREEP!
THE VISITOR ALARM!
<~~>
BREEP!
BREEP!
THWIP!
SOMEONE'S AT THE DOOR!

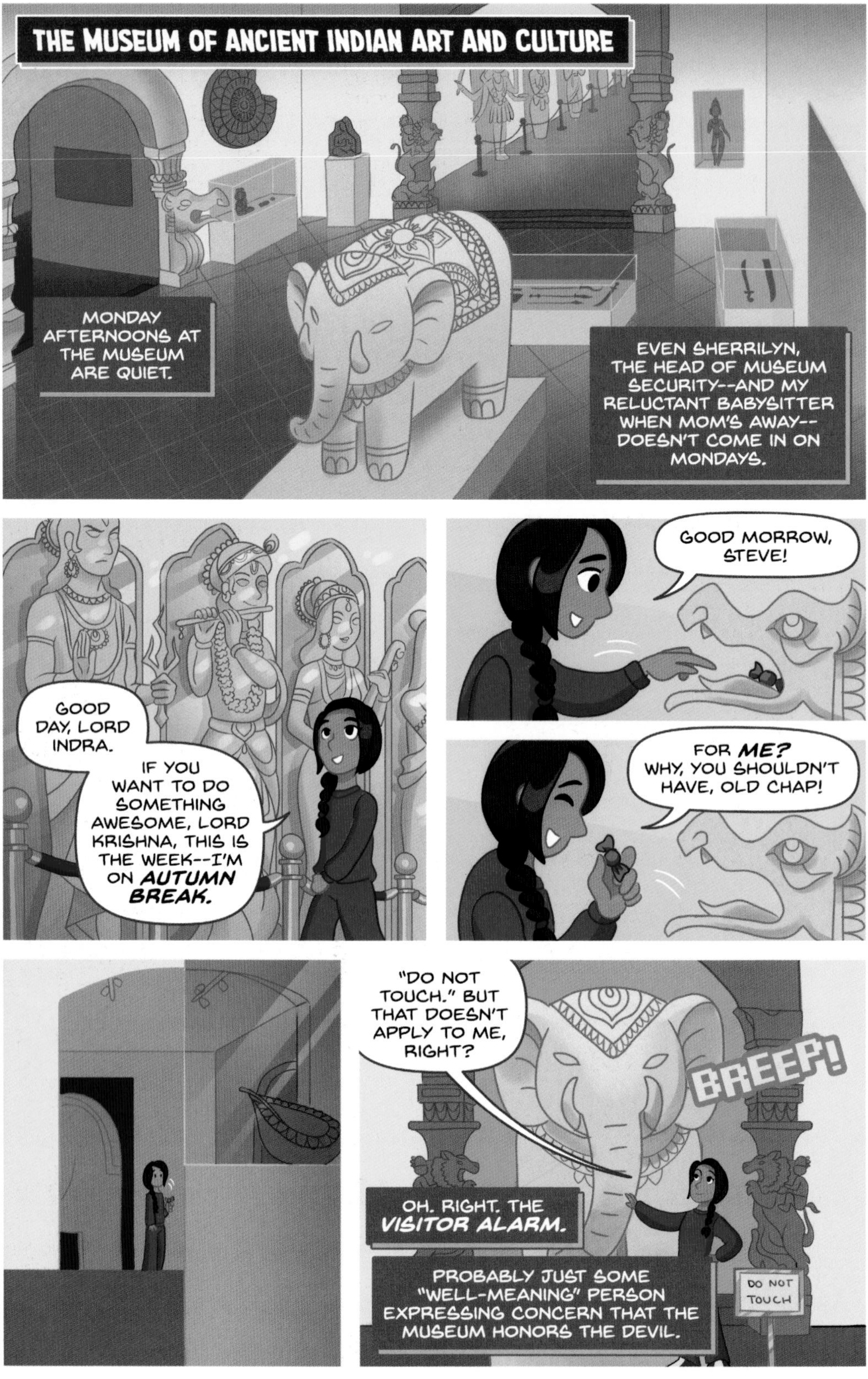
THE MUSEUM OF ANCIENT INDIAN ART AND CULTURE
MONDAY AFTERNOONS AT THE MUSEUM ARE QUIET.
EVEN SHERRILYN, THE HEAD OF MUSEUM SECURITY--AND MY RELUCTANT BABYSITTER WHEN MOM'S AWAY--DOESN'T COME IN ON MONDAYS.
GOOD DAY, LORD INDRA.
IF YOU WANT TO DO SOMETHING AWESOME, LORD KRISHNA, THIS IS THE WEEK--I'M ON AUTUMN BREAK.
GOOD MORROW, STEVE!
FOR ME? WHY, YOU SHOULDN'T HAVE, OLD CHAP!
"DO NOT TOUCH." BUT THAT DOESN'T APPLY TO ME, RIGHT?
BREEP!
OH. RIGHT. THE VISITOR ALARM.
PROBABLY JUST SOME "WELL-MEANING" PERSON EXPRESSING CONCERN THAT THE MUSEUM HONORS THE DEVIL.
DO NOT TOUCH

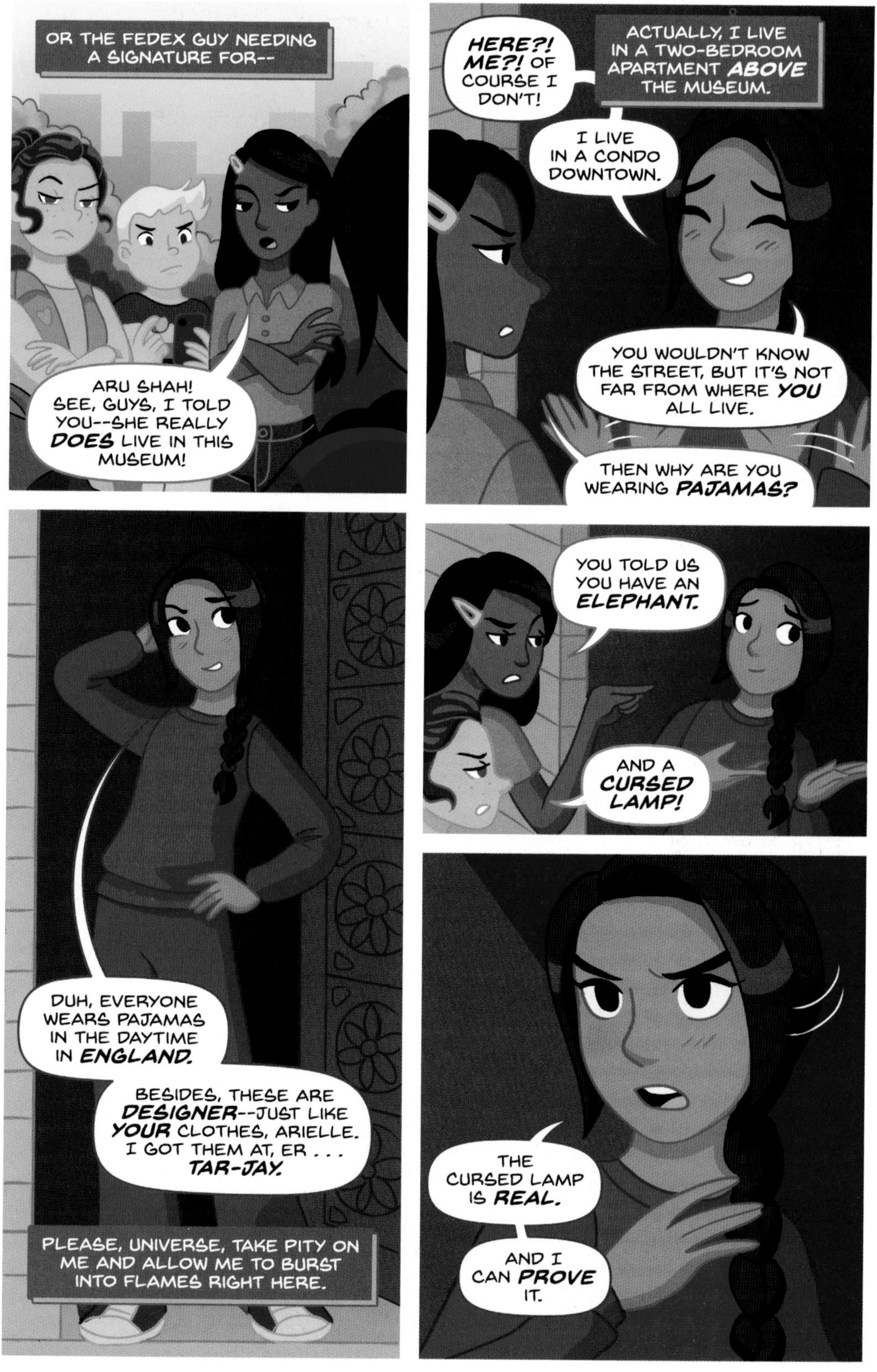
OR THE FEDEX GUY NEEDING A SIGNATURE FOR--
ARU SHAH! SEE, GUYS, I TOLD YOU--SHE REALLY DOES LIVE IN THIS MUSEUM!
HERE?! ME?! OF COURSE I DON'T!
ACTUALLY, I LIVE IN A TWO-BEDROOM APARTMENT ABOVE THE MUSEUM.
I LIVE IN A CONDO DOWNTOWN.
YOU WOULDN'T KNOW THE STREET, BUT IT'S NOT FAR FROM WHERE YOU ALL LIVE.
THEN WHY ARE YOU WEARING PAJAMAS?
DUH, EVERYONE WEARS PAJAMAS IN THE DAYTIME IN ENGLAND.
BESIDES, THESE ARE DESIGNER--JUST LIKE YOUR CLOTHES, ARIELLE. I GOT THEM AT, ER . . . TAR-JAY.
PLEASE, UNIVERSE, TAKE PITY ON ME AND ALLOW ME TO BURST INTO FLAMES RIGHT HERE.
YOU TOLD US YOU HAVE AN ELEPHANT.
AND A CURSED LAMP!
THE CURSED LAMP IS REAL.
AND I CAN PROVE IT.

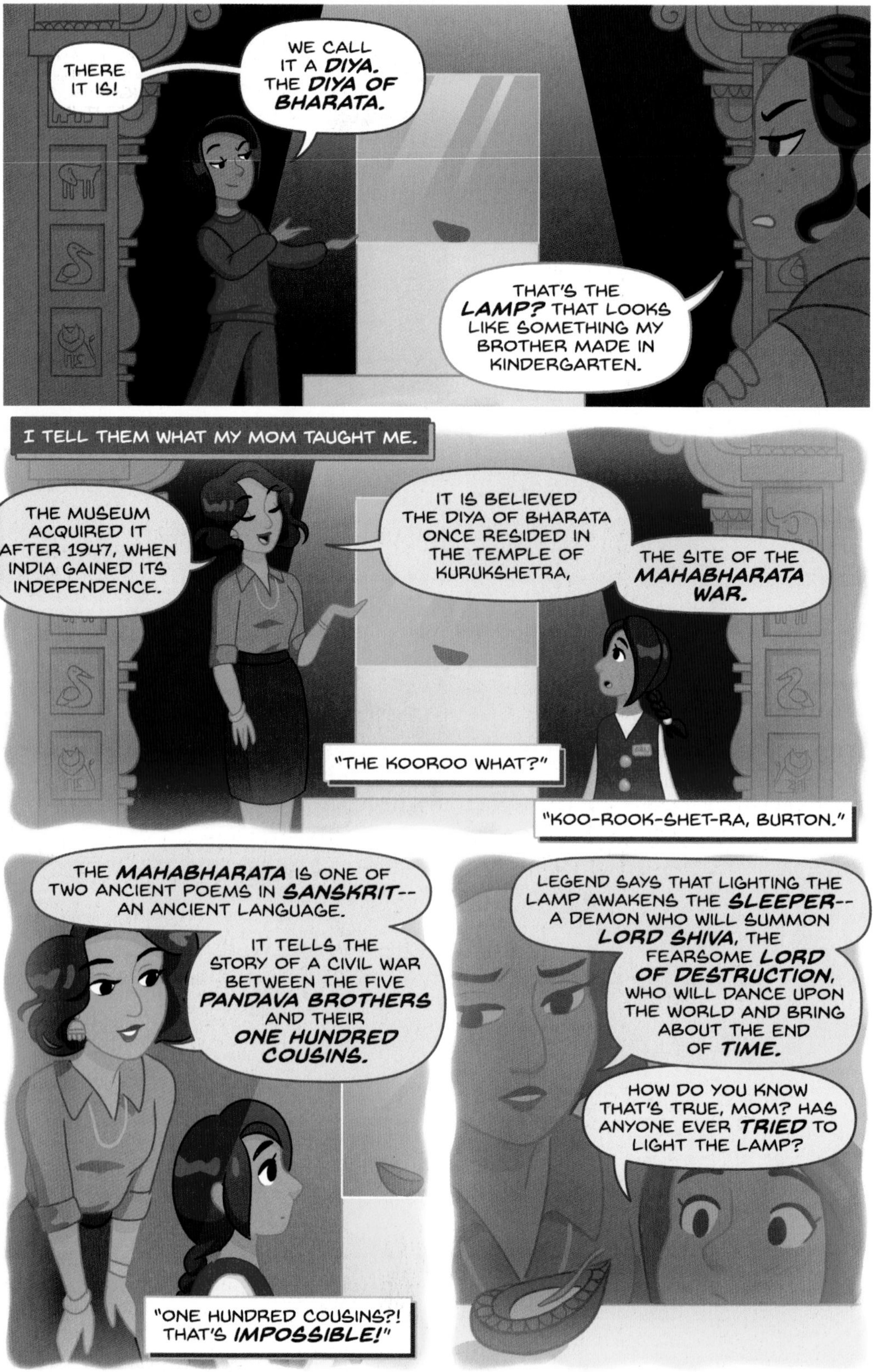
THERE IT IS!
WE CALL IT A DIYA. THE DIYA OF BHARATA.
THAT'S THE LAMP? THAT LOOKS LIKE SOMETHING MY BROTHER MADE IN KINDERGARTEN.
I TELL THEM WHAT MY MOM TAUGHT ME.
THE MUSEUM ACQUIRED IT AFTER 1947, WHEN INDIA GAINED ITS INDEPENDENCE.
IT IS BELIEVED THE DIYA OF BHARATA ONCE RESIDED IN THE TEMPLE OF KURUKSHETRA,
THE SITE OF THE MAHABHARATA WAR.
"THE KOOROO WHAT?"
"KOO-ROOK-SHET-RA, BURTON."
THE MAHABHARATA IS ONE OF TWO ANCIENT POEMS IN SANSKRIT-- AN ANCIENT LANGUAGE.
IT TELLS THE STORY OF A CIVIL WAR BETWEEN THE FIVE PANDAVA BROTHERS AND THEIR ONE HUNDRED COUSINS.
"ONE HUNDRED COUSINS?! THAT'S IMPOSSIBLE!"
LEGEND SAYS THAT LIGHTING THE LAMP AWAKENS THE SLEEPER-- A DEMON WHO WILL SUMMON LORD SHIVA, THE FEARSOME LORD OF DESTRUCTION, WHO WILL DANCE UPON THE WORLD AND BRING ABOUT THE END OF TIME.
HOW DO YOU KNOW THAT'S TRUE, MOM? HAS ANYONE EVER TRIED TO LIGHT THE LAMP?

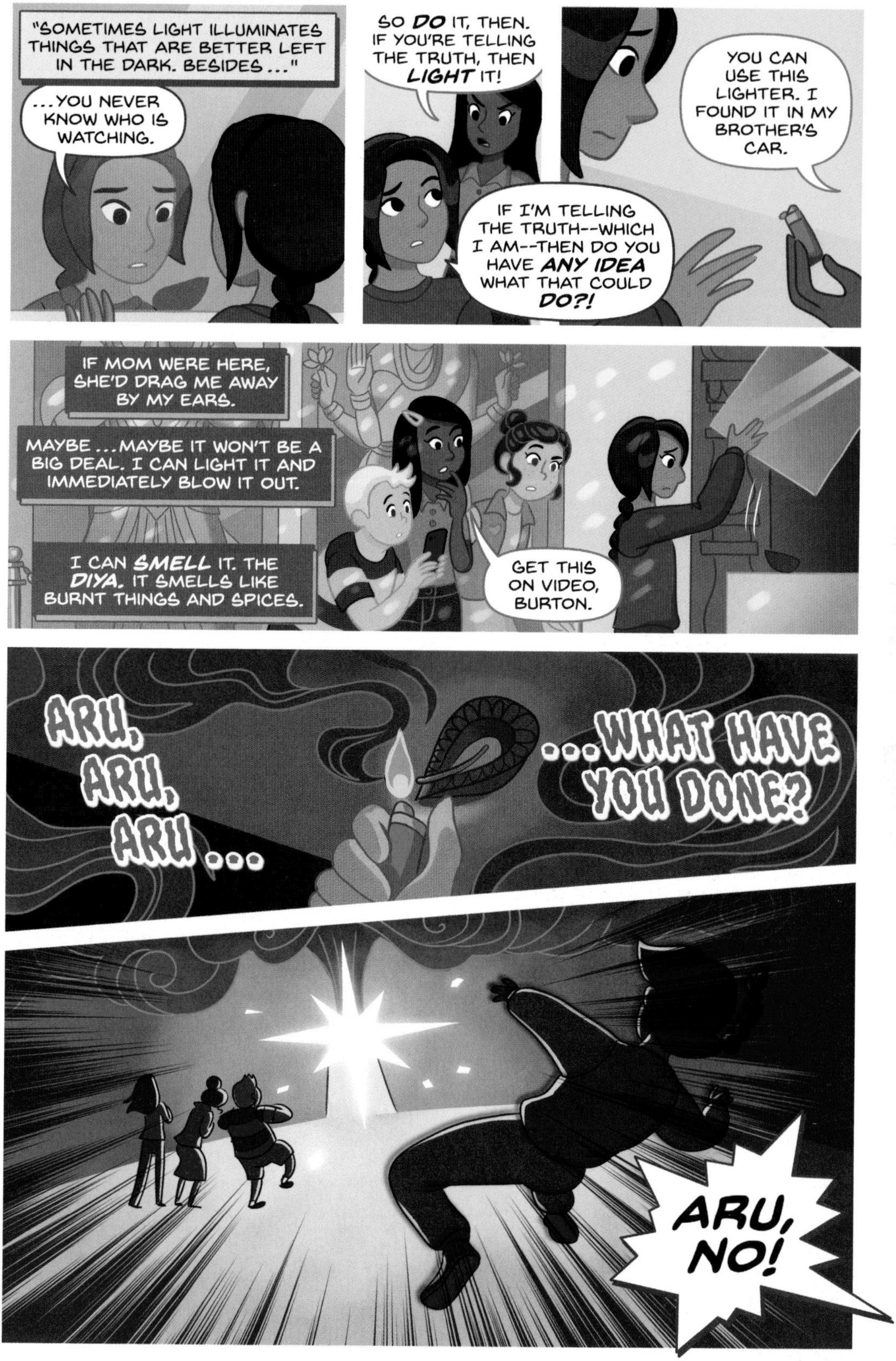
"SOMETIMES LIGHT ILLUMINATES THINGS THAT ARE BETTER LEFT IN THE DARK. BESIDES ..."
...YOU NEVER KNOW WHO IS WATCHING.
SO DO IT, THEN. IF YOU'RE TELLING THE TRUTH, THEN LIGHT IT!
IF I'M TELLING THE TRUTH--WHICH I AM--THEN DO YOU HAVE ANY IDEA WHAT THAT COULD DO?!
YOU CAN USE THIS LIGHTER. I FOUND IT IN MY BROTHER'S CAR.
IF MOM WERE HERE, SHE'D DRAG ME AWAY BY MY EARS.
MAYBE ... MAYBE IT WON'T BE A BIG DEAL. I CAN LIGHT IT AND IMMEDIATELY BLOW IT OUT.
I CAN SMELL IT. THE DIYA. IT SMELLS LIKE BURNT THINGS AND SPICES.
GET THIS ON VIDEO, BURTON.
ARU, ARU, ARU ...
...WHAT HAVE YOU DONE?
ARU, NO!

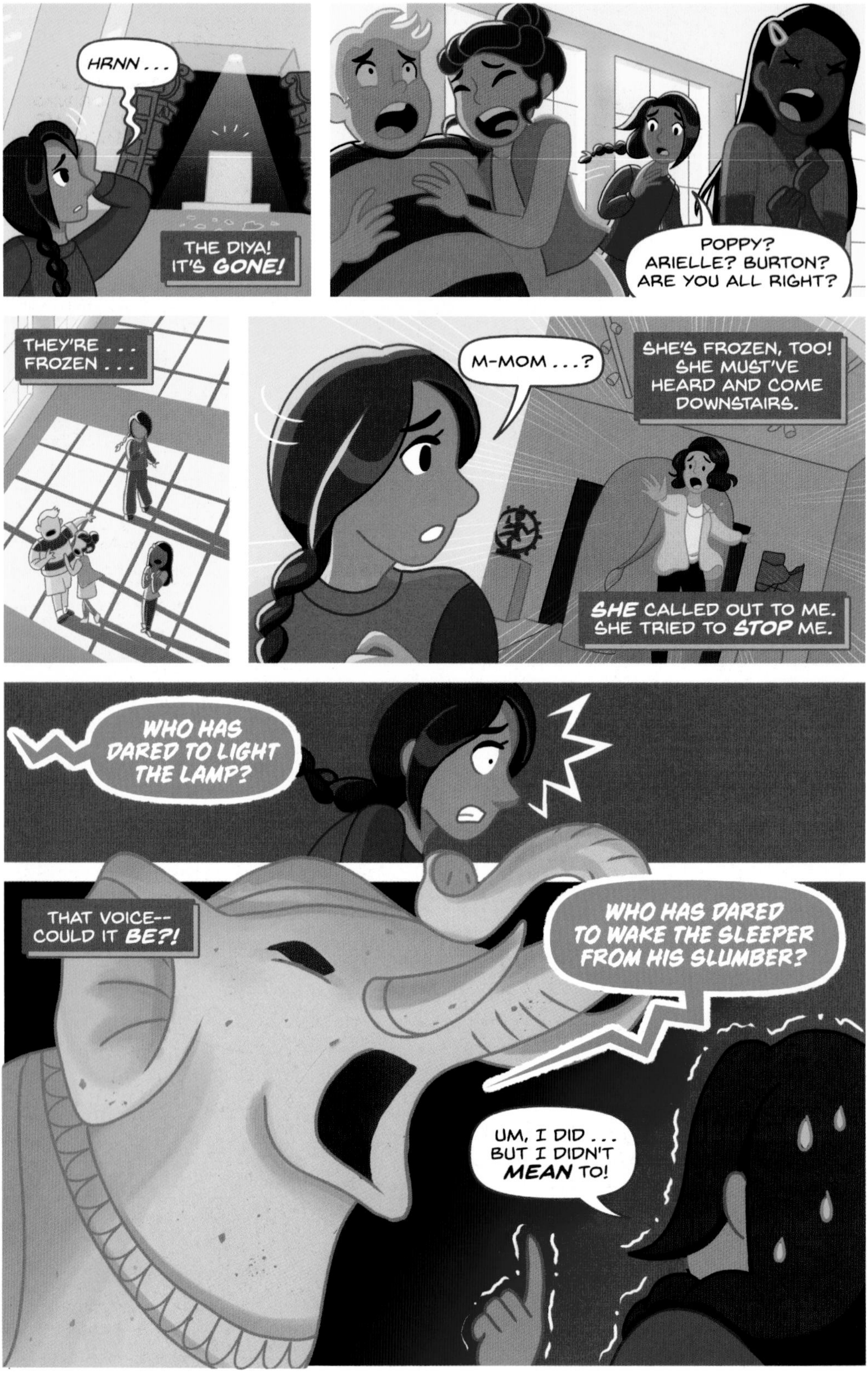
HRNN . . .
THE DIYA! IT'S GONE!
POPPY? ARIELLE? BURTON? ARE YOU ALL RIGHT?
THEY'RE . . . FROZEN . . .
M-MOM . . .?
SHE'S FROZEN, TOO! SHE MUST'VE HEARD AND COME DOWNSTAIRS.
SHE CALLED OUT TO ME. SHE TRIED TO STOP ME.
WHO HAS DARED TO LIGHT THE LAMP?
THAT VOICE-- COULD IT BE?!
WHO HAS DARED TO WAKE THE SLEEPER FROM HIS SLUMBER?
UM, I DID . . . BUT I DIDN'T MEAN TO!

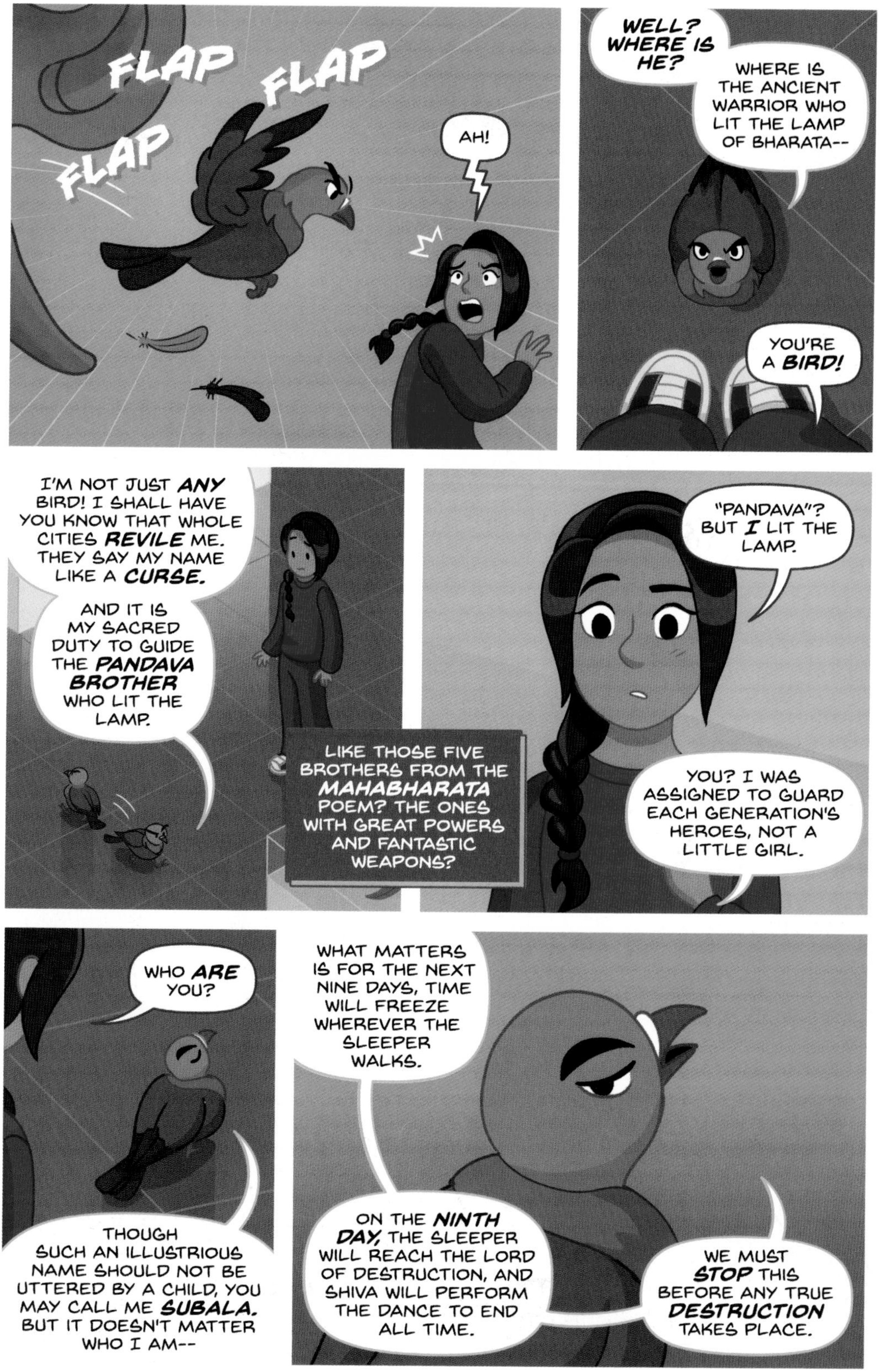
FLAP
FLAP
FLAP
AH!
WELL? WHERE IS HE?
WHERE IS THE ANCIENT WARRIOR WHO LIT THE LAMP OF BHARATA--
YOU'RE A BIRD!
I'M NOT JUST ANY BIRD! I SHALL HAVE YOU KNOW THAT WHOLE CITIES REVILE ME. THEY SAY MY NAME LIKE A CURSE.
AND IT IS MY SACRED DUTY TO GUIDE THE PANDAVA BROTHER WHO LIT THE LAMP.
LIKE THOSE FIVE BROTHERS FROM THE MAHABHARATA POEM? THE ONES WITH GREAT POWERS AND FANTASTIC WEAPONS?
"PANDAVA"? BUT I LIT THE LAMP.
YOU? I WAS ASSIGNED TO GUARD EACH GENERATION'S HEROES, NOT A LITTLE GIRL.
WHO ARE YOU?
THOUGH SUCH AN ILLUSTRIOUS NAME SHOULD NOT BE UTTERED BY A CHILD, YOU MAY CALL ME SUBALA. BUT IT DOESN'T MATTER WHO I AM--
WHAT MATTERS IS FOR THE NEXT NINE DAYS, TIME WILL FREEZE WHEREVER THE SLEEPER WALKS.
ON THE NINTH DAY, THE SLEEPER WILL REACH THE LORD OF DESTRUCTION, AND SHIVA WILL PERFORM THE DANCE TO END ALL TIME.
WE MUST STOP THIS BEFORE ANY TRUE DESTRUCTION TAKES PLACE.

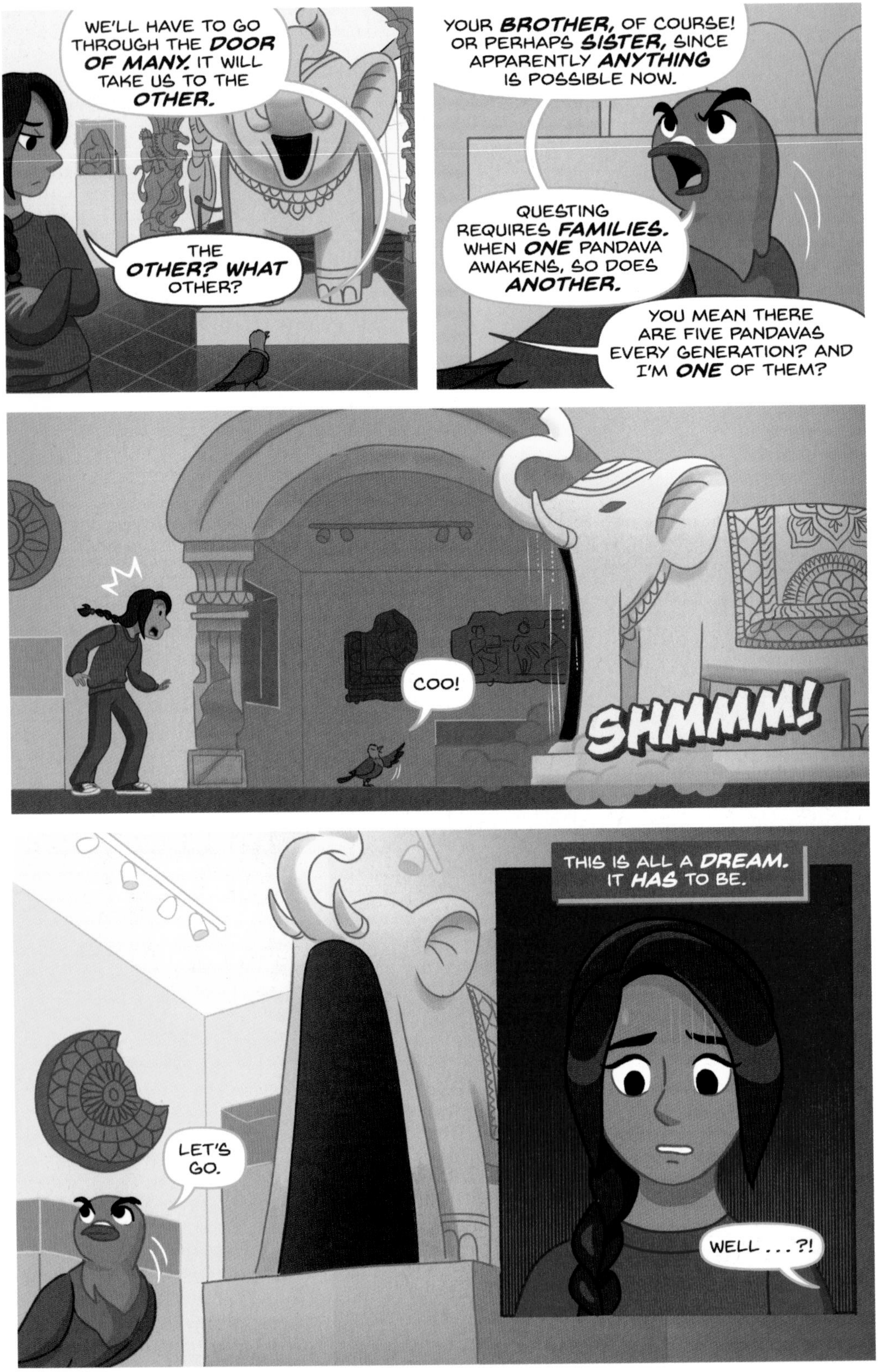
WE'LL HAVE TO GO THROUGH THE DOOR OF MANY. IT WILL TAKE US TO THE OTHER.
THE OTHER? WHAT OTHER?
YOUR BROTHER, OF COURSE! OR PERHAPS SISTER, SINCE APPARENTLY ANYTHING IS POSSIBLE NOW.
QUESTING REQUIRES FAMILIES. WHEN ONE PANDAVA AWAKENS, SO DOES ANOTHER.
YOU MEAN THERE ARE FIVE PANDAVAS EVERY GENERATION? AND I'M ONE OF THEM?
COO!
SHMMM!
THIS IS ALL A DREAM. IT HAS TO BE.
LET'S GO.
WELL . . . ?!

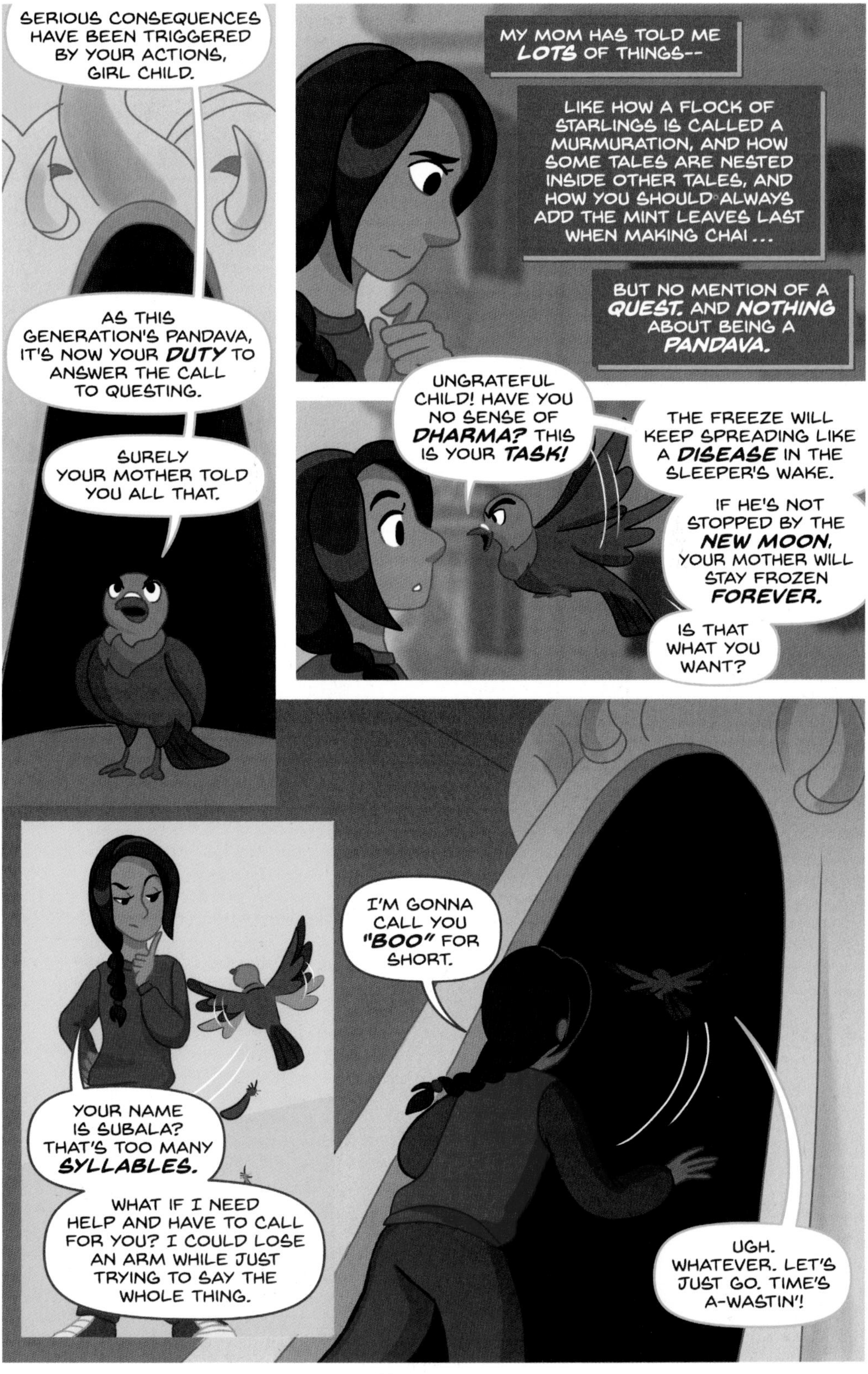
SERIOUS CONSEQUENCES HAVE BEEN TRIGGERED BY YOUR ACTIONS, GIRL CHILD.
AS THIS GENERATION'S PANDAVA, IT'S NOW YOUR *DUTY* TO ANSWER THE CALL TO QUESTING.
SURELY YOUR MOTHER TOLD YOU ALL THAT.
MY MOM HAS TOLD ME *LOTS* OF THINGS--
LIKE HOW A FLOCK OF STARLINGS IS CALLED A MURMURATION, AND HOW SOME TALES ARE NESTED INSIDE OTHER TALES, AND HOW YOU SHOULD ALWAYS ADD THE MINT LEAVES LAST WHEN MAKING CHAI...
BUT NO MENTION OF A *QUEST.* AND *NOTHING* ABOUT BEING A *PANDAVA.*
UNGRATEFUL CHILD! HAVE YOU NO SENSE OF *DHARMA?* THIS IS YOUR *TASK!*
THE FREEZE WILL KEEP SPREADING LIKE A *DISEASE* IN THE SLEEPER'S WAKE.
IF HE'S NOT STOPPED BY THE *NEW MOON,* YOUR MOTHER WILL STAY FROZEN *FOREVER.*
IS THAT WHAT YOU WANT?
YOUR NAME IS SUBALA? THAT'S TOO MANY *SYLLABLES.*
WHAT IF I NEED HELP AND HAVE TO CALL FOR YOU? I COULD LOSE AN ARM WHILE JUST TRYING TO SAY THE WHOLE THING.
I'M GONNA CALL YOU *"BOO"* FOR SHORT.
UGH. WHATEVER. LET'S JUST GO. TIME'S A-WASTIN'!

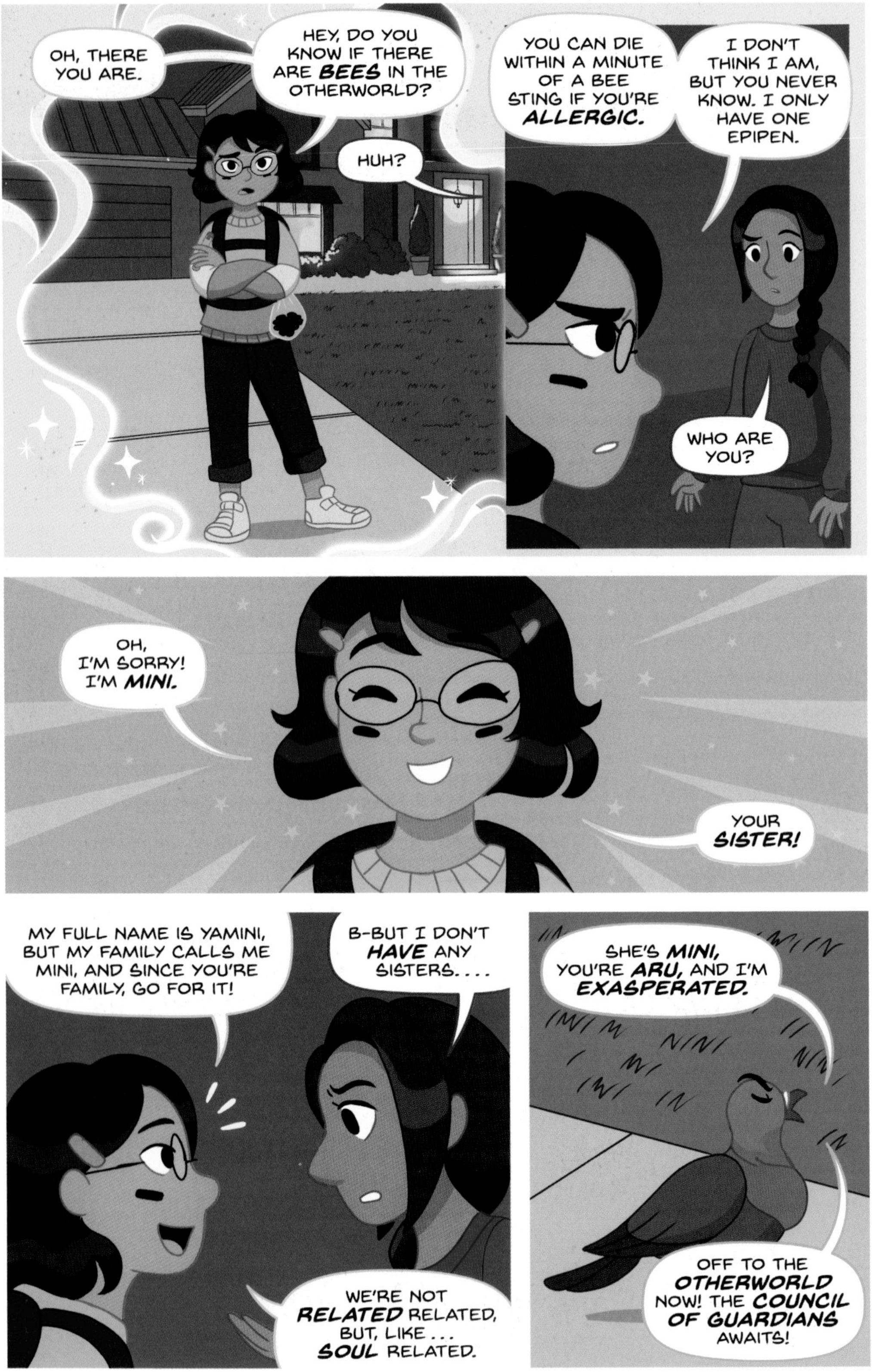
OH, THERE YOU ARE.
HEY, DO YOU KNOW IF THERE ARE **BEES** IN THE OTHERWORLD?
HUH?
YOU CAN DIE WITHIN A MINUTE OF A BEE STING IF YOU'RE **ALLERGIC.**
I DON'T THINK I AM, BUT YOU NEVER KNOW. I ONLY HAVE ONE EPIPEN.
WHO ARE YOU?
OH, I'M SORRY! I'M **MINI.**
YOUR **SISTER!**
MY FULL NAME IS YAMINI, BUT MY FAMILY CALLS ME MINI, AND SINCE YOU'RE FAMILY, GO FOR IT!
B-BUT I DON'T **HAVE** ANY SISTERS. . . .
WE'RE NOT **RELATED** RELATED, BUT, LIKE . . . **SOUL** RELATED.
SHE'S **MINI,** YOU'RE **ARU,** AND I'M **EXASPERATED.**
OFF TO THE **OTHERWORLD** NOW! THE **COUNCIL OF GUARDIANS** AWAITS!

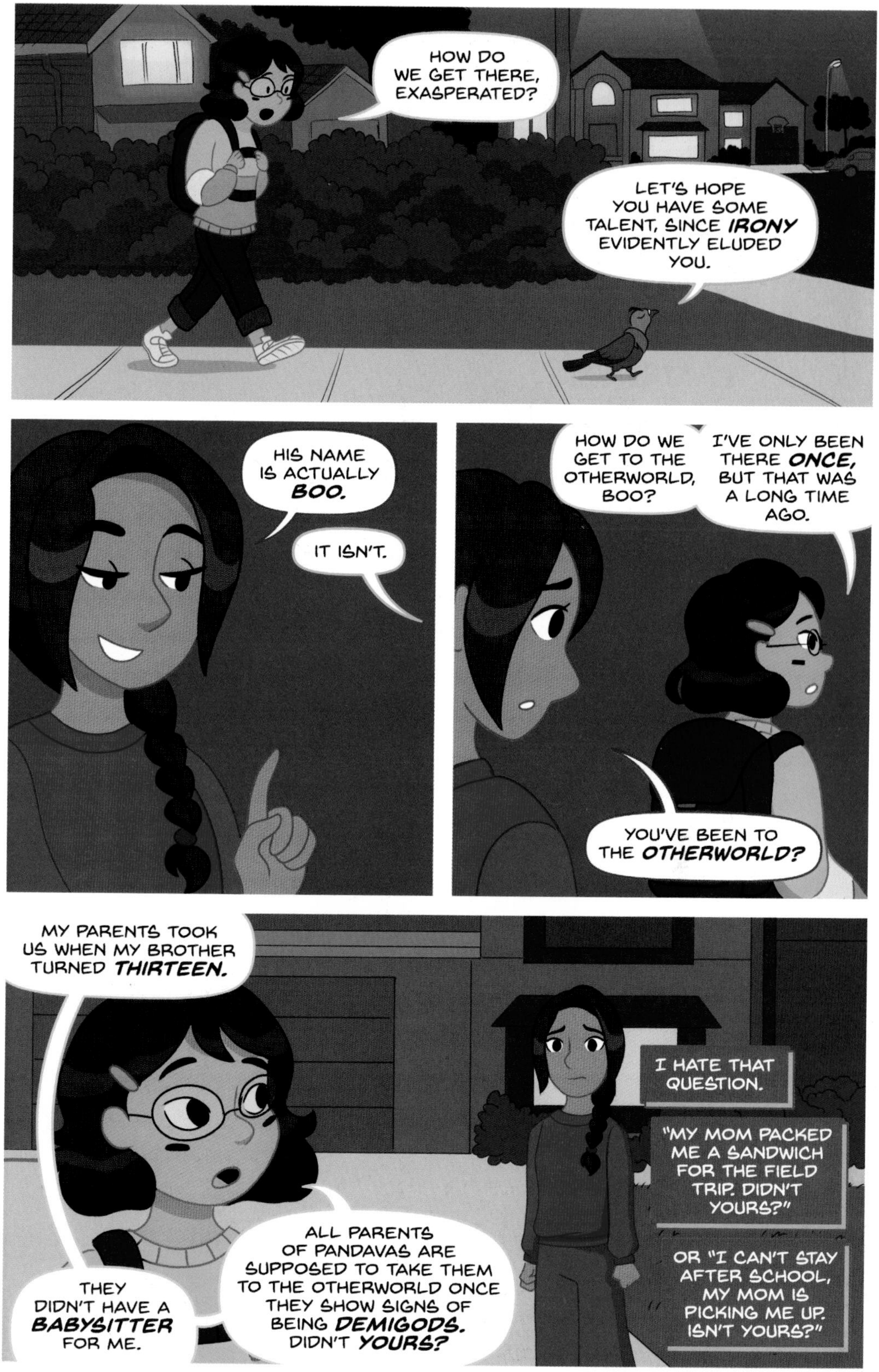
HOW DO WE GET THERE, EXASPERATED?
LET'S HOPE YOU HAVE SOME TALENT, SINCE IRONY EVIDENTLY ELUDED YOU.
HIS NAME IS ACTUALLY BOO.
IT ISN'T.
HOW DO WE GET TO THE OTHERWORLD, BOO?
I'VE ONLY BEEN THERE ONCE, BUT THAT WAS A LONG TIME AGO.
YOU'VE BEEN TO THE OTHERWORLD?
MY PARENTS TOOK US WHEN MY BROTHER TURNED THIRTEEN.
THEY DIDN'T HAVE A BABYSITTER FOR ME.
ALL PARENTS OF PANDAVAS ARE SUPPOSED TO TAKE THEM TO THE OTHERWORLD ONCE THEY SHOW SIGNS OF BEING DEMIGODS. DIDN'T YOURS?
I HATE THAT QUESTION.
"MY MOM PACKED ME A SANDWICH FOR THE FIELD TRIP. DIDN'T YOURS?"
OR "I CAN'T STAY AFTER SCHOOL, MY MOM IS PICKING ME UP. ISN'T YOURS?"

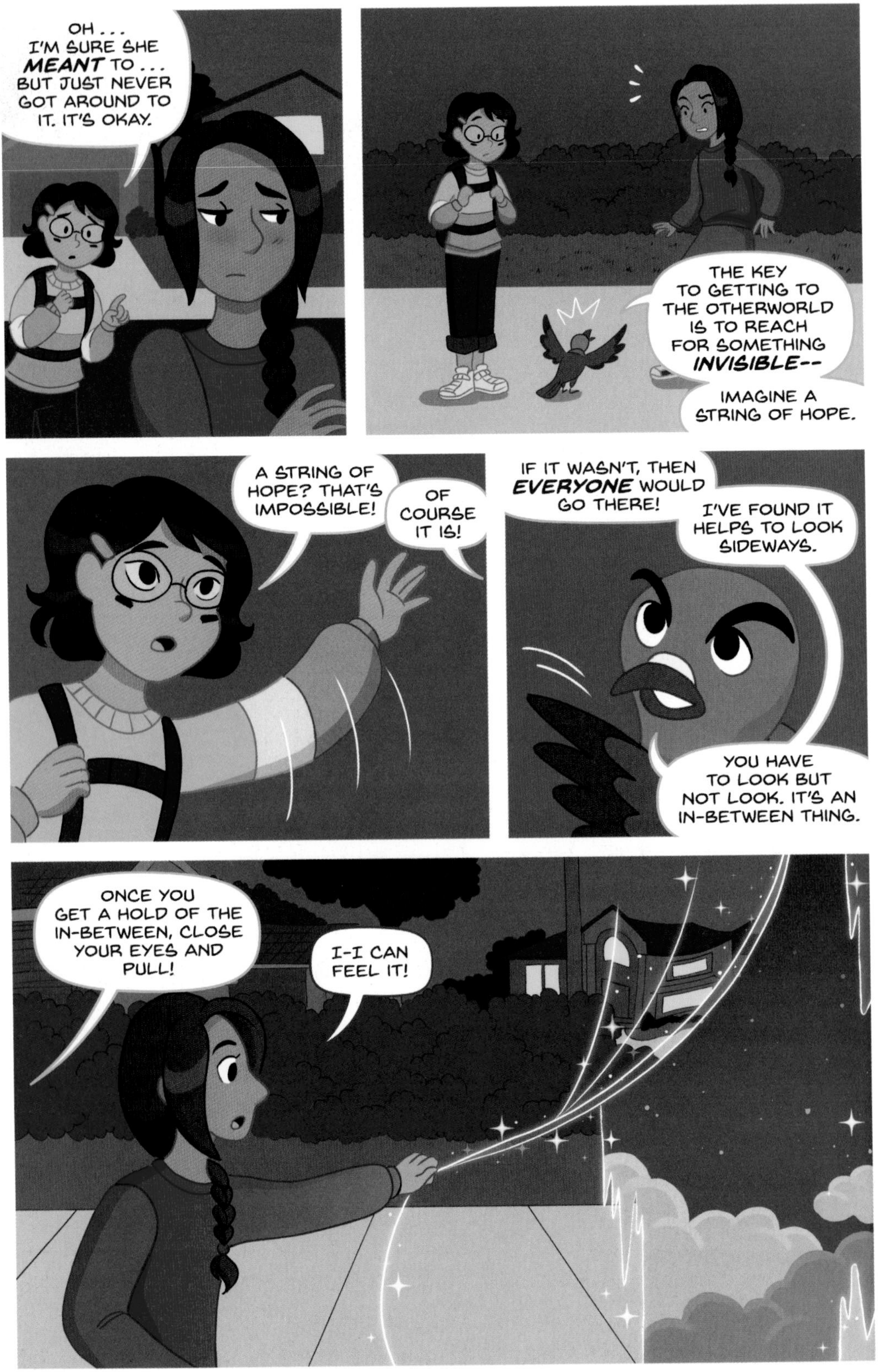
OH . . .
I'M SURE SHE **MEANT** TO . . . BUT JUST NEVER GOT AROUND TO IT. IT'S OKAY.
THE KEY TO GETTING TO THE OTHERWORLD IS TO REACH FOR SOMETHING ***INVISIBLE--***
IMAGINE A STRING OF HOPE.
A STRING OF HOPE? THAT'S IMPOSSIBLE!
OF COURSE IT IS!
IF IT WASN'T, THEN ***EVERYONE*** WOULD GO THERE!
I'VE FOUND IT HELPS TO LOOK SIDEWAYS.
YOU HAVE TO LOOK BUT NOT LOOK. IT'S AN IN-BETWEEN THING.
ONCE YOU GET A HOLD OF THE IN-BETWEEN, CLOSE YOUR EYES AND PULL!
I-I CAN FEEL IT!

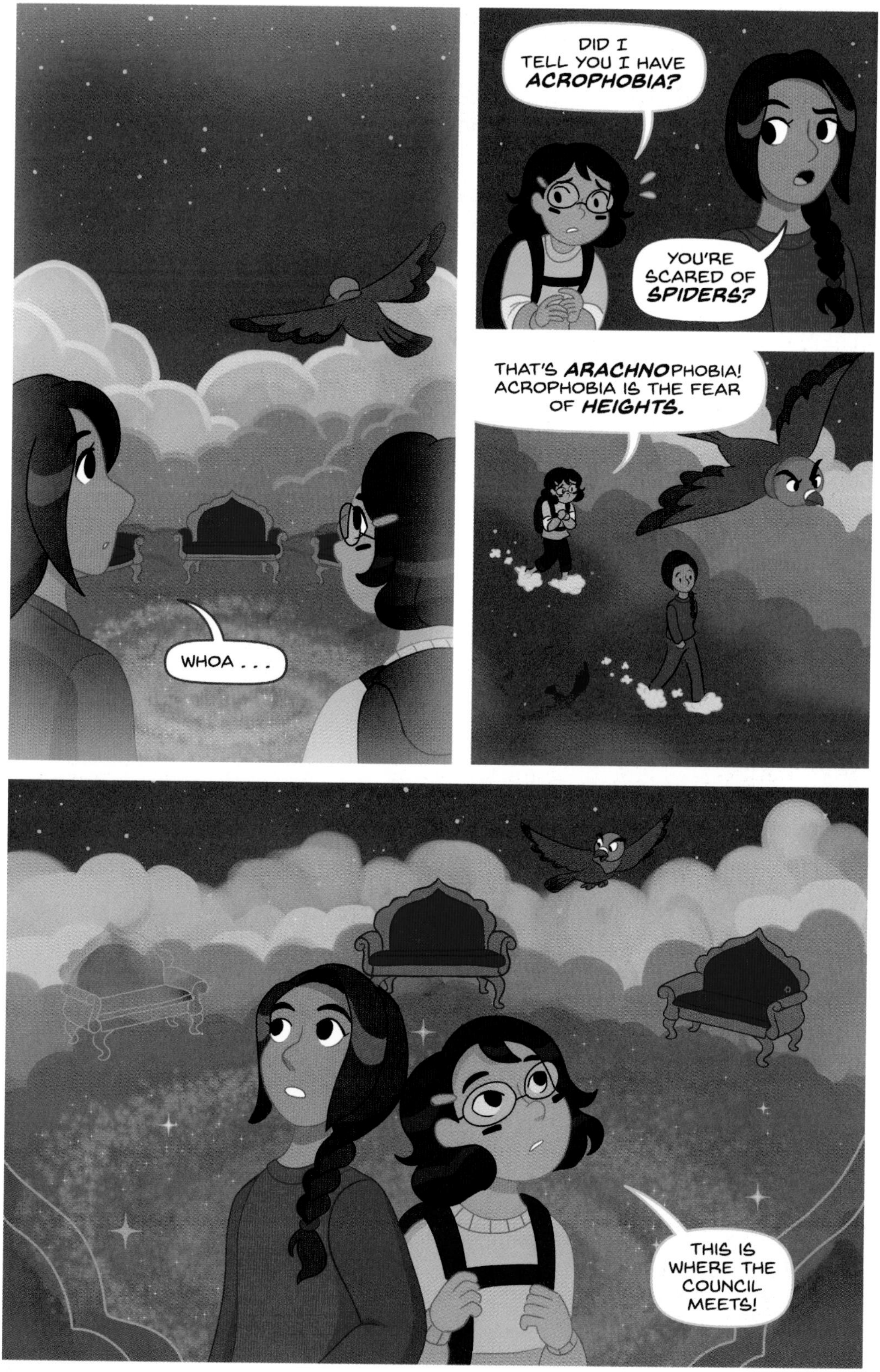
WHOA . . .
DID I TELL YOU I HAVE ACROPHOBIA?
YOU'RE SCARED OF SPIDERS?
THAT'S ARACHNOPHOBIA! ACROPHOBIA IS THE FEAR OF HEIGHTS.
THIS IS WHERE THE COUNCIL MEETS!

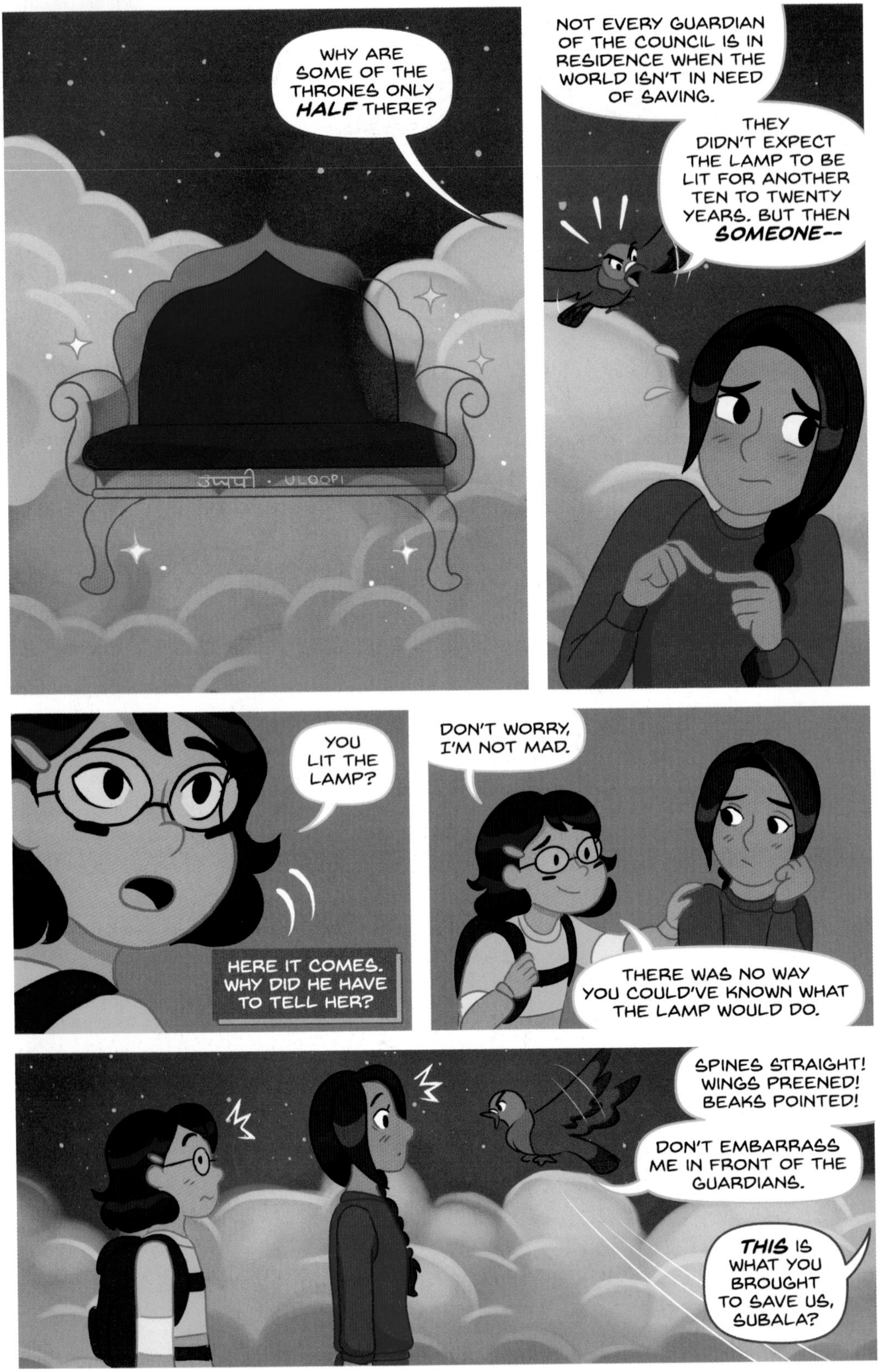
WHY ARE SOME OF THE THRONES ONLY *HALF* THERE?
उलूपी · ULOOPI
NOT EVERY GUARDIAN OF THE COUNCIL IS IN RESIDENCE WHEN THE WORLD ISN'T IN NEED OF SAVING.
THEY DIDN'T EXPECT THE LAMP TO BE LIT FOR ANOTHER TEN TO TWENTY YEARS. BUT THEN *SOMEONE--*
YOU LIT THE LAMP?
HERE IT COMES. WHY DID HE HAVE TO TELL HER?
DON'T WORRY, I'M NOT MAD.
THERE WAS NO WAY YOU COULD'VE KNOWN WHAT THE LAMP WOULD DO.
SPINES STRAIGHT! WINGS PREENED! BEAKS POINTED!
DON'T EMBARRASS ME IN FRONT OF THE GUARDIANS.
THIS IS WHAT YOU BROUGHT TO SAVE US, SUBALA?

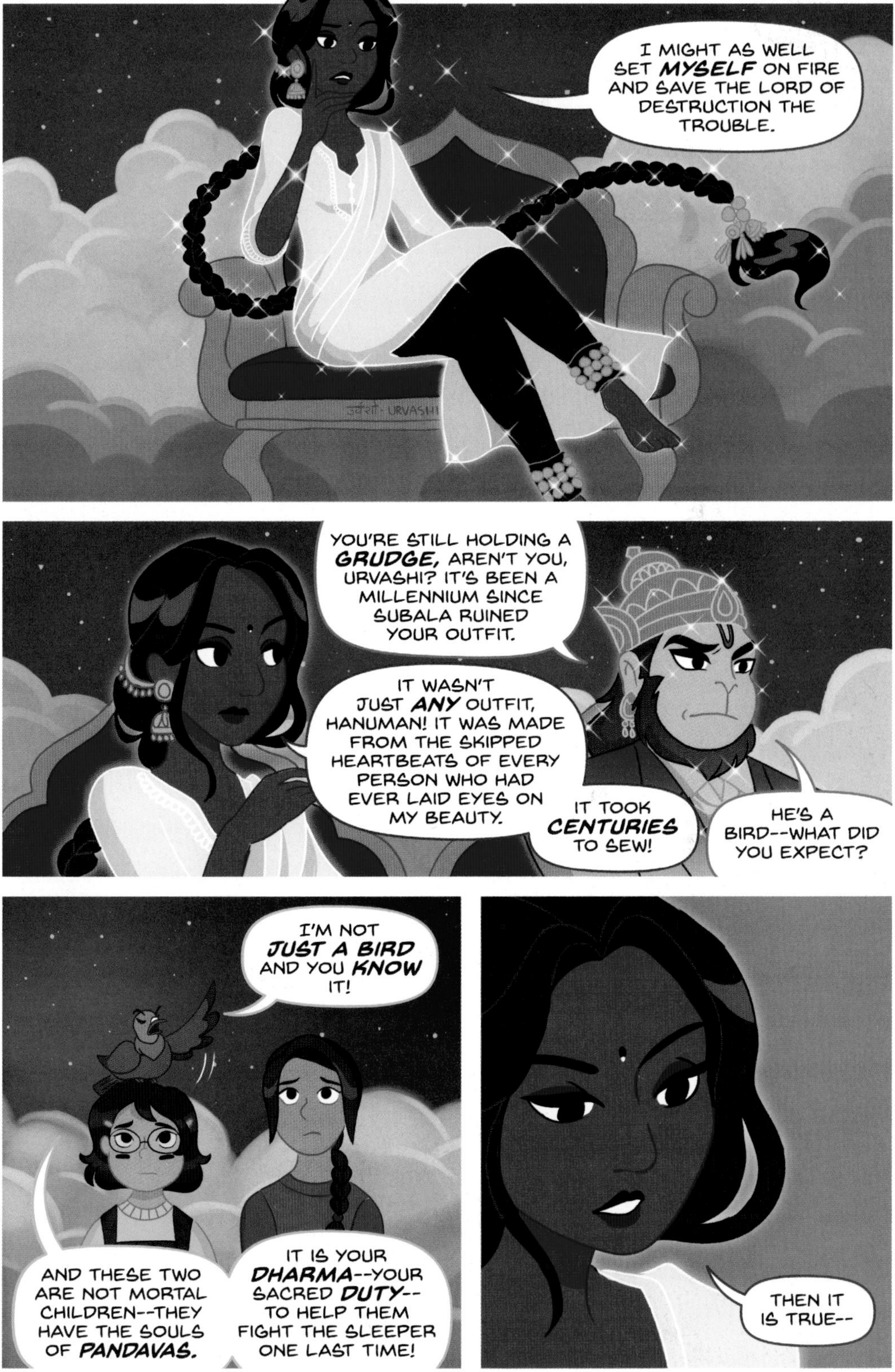

I MIGHT AS WELL SET **MYSELF** ON FIRE AND SAVE THE LORD OF DESTRUCTION THE TROUBLE.
YOU'RE STILL HOLDING A **GRUDGE,** AREN'T YOU, URVASHI? IT'S BEEN A MILLENNIUM SINCE SUBALA RUINED YOUR OUTFIT.
IT WASN'T JUST **ANY** OUTFIT, HANUMAN! IT WAS MADE FROM THE SKIPPED HEARTBEATS OF EVERY PERSON WHO HAD EVER LAID EYES ON MY BEAUTY.
IT TOOK **CENTURIES** TO SEW!
HE'S A BIRD--WHAT DID YOU EXPECT?
I'M NOT **JUST A BIRD** AND YOU **KNOW** IT!
AND THESE TWO ARE NOT MORTAL CHILDREN--THEY HAVE THE SOULS OF **PANDAVAS.**
IT IS YOUR **DHARMA**--YOUR SACRED **DUTY**--TO HELP THEM FIGHT THE SLEEPER ONE LAST TIME!
THEN IT IS TRUE--

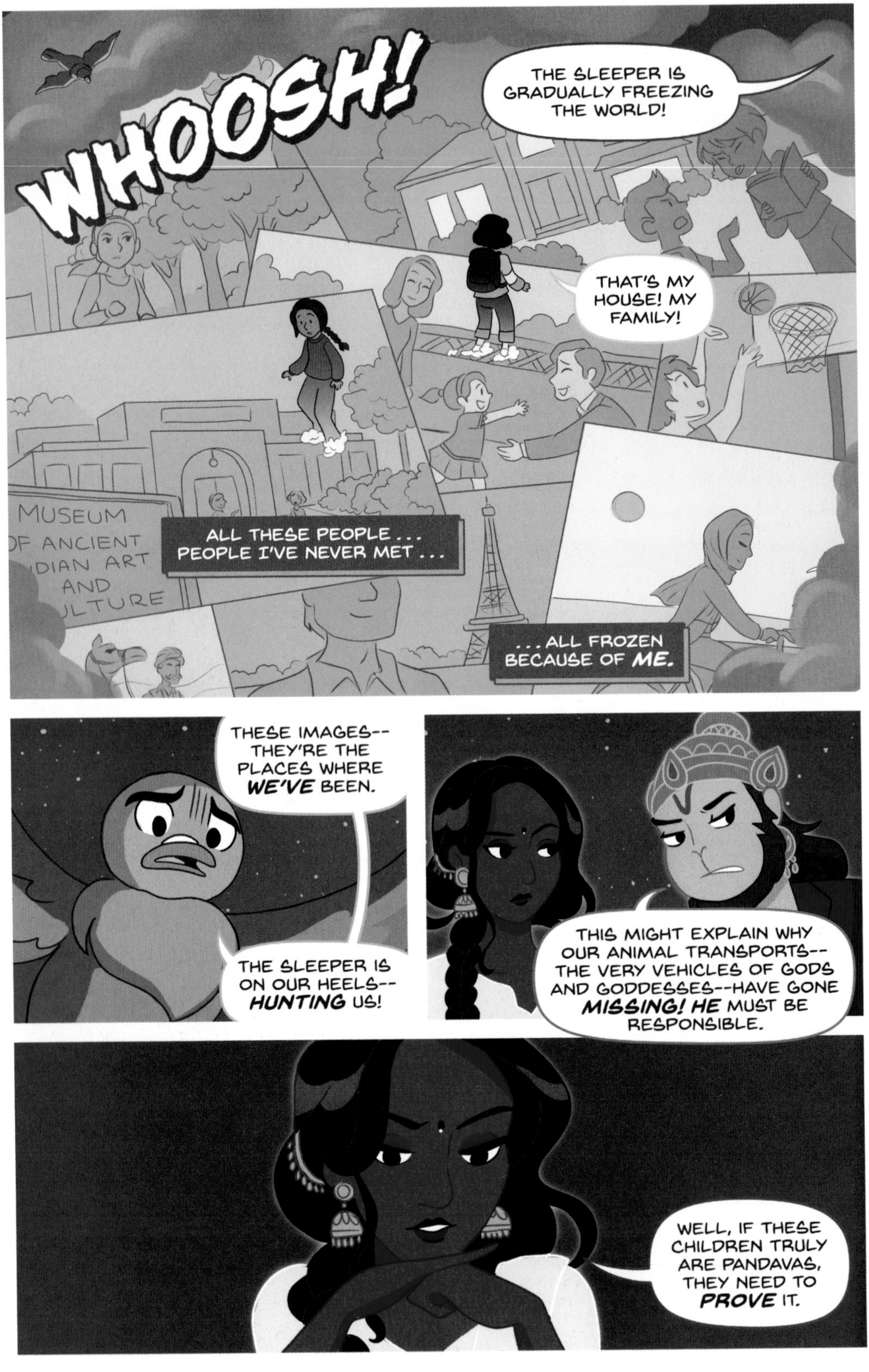
WHOOSH!
THE SLEEPER IS GRADUALLY FREEZING THE WORLD!
THAT'S MY HOUSE! MY FAMILY!
MUSEUM OF ANCIENT DIAN ART AND LTURE
ALL THESE PEOPLE . . . PEOPLE I'VE NEVER MET . . .
. . . ALL FROZEN BECAUSE OF *ME.*
THESE IMAGES-- THEY'RE THE PLACES WHERE *WE'VE* BEEN.
THE SLEEPER IS ON OUR HEELS-- *HUNTING* US!
THIS MIGHT EXPLAIN WHY OUR ANIMAL TRANSPORTS-- THE VERY VEHICLES OF GODS AND GODDESSES--HAVE GONE *MISSING! HE* MUST BE RESPONSIBLE.
WELL, IF THESE CHILDREN TRULY ARE PANDAVAS, THEY NEED TO *PROVE* IT.

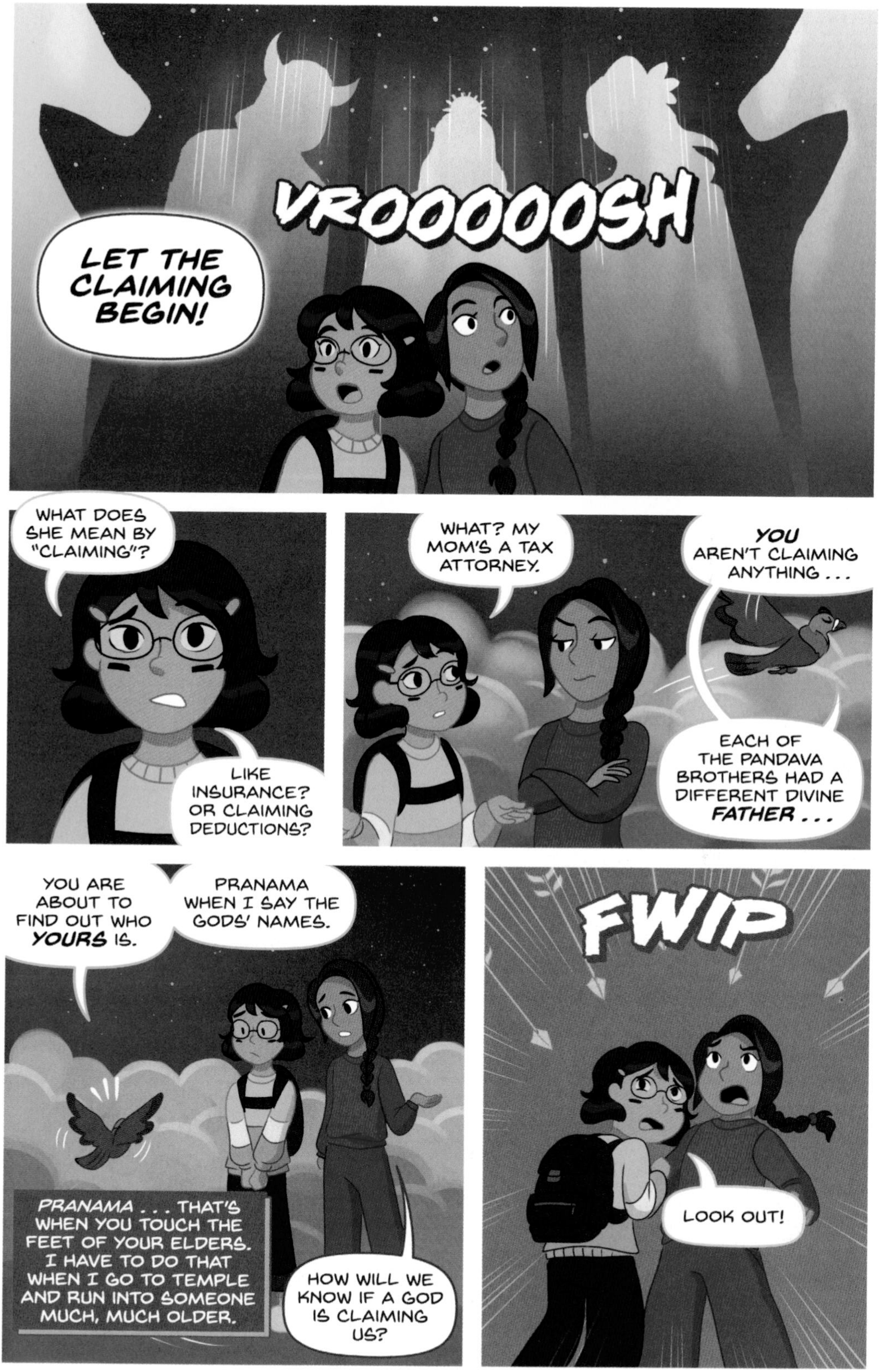
VROOOOOOSH
LET THE CLAIMING BEGIN!
WHAT DOES SHE MEAN BY "CLAIMING"?
LIKE INSURANCE? OR CLAIMING DEDUCTIONS?
WHAT? MY MOM'S A TAX ATTORNEY.
YOU AREN'T CLAIMING ANYTHING . . .
EACH OF THE PANDAVA BROTHERS HAD A DIFFERENT DIVINE *FATHER* . . .
YOU ARE ABOUT TO FIND OUT WHO *YOURS* IS.
PRANAMA WHEN I SAY THE GODS' NAMES.
PRANAMA . . . THAT'S WHEN YOU TOUCH THE FEET OF YOUR ELDERS. I HAVE TO DO THAT WHEN I GO TO TEMPLE AND RUN INTO SOMEONE MUCH, MUCH OLDER.
HOW WILL WE KNOW IF A GOD IS CLAIMING US?
FWIP
LOOK OUT!

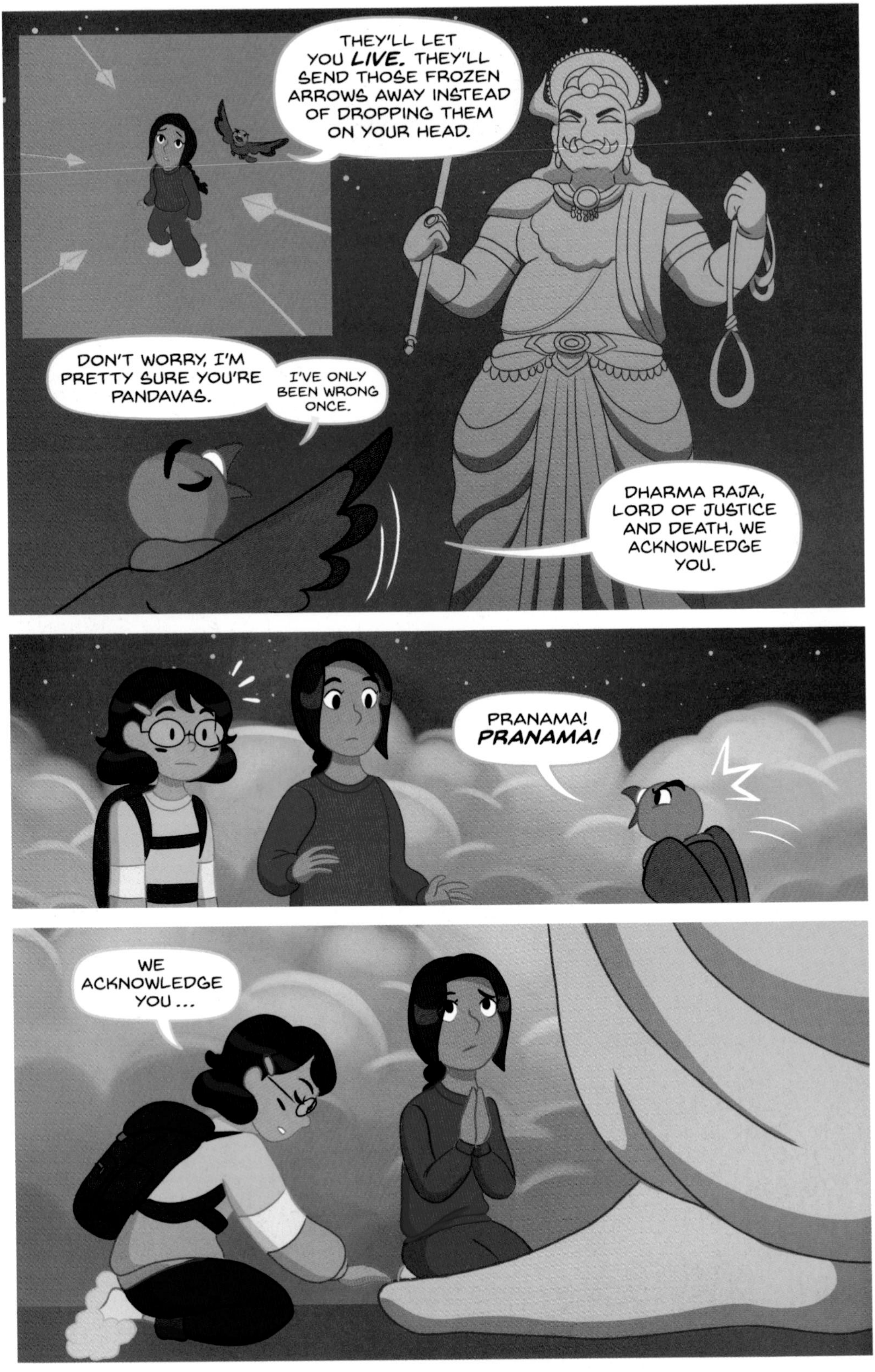
THEY'LL LET YOU LIVE. THEY'LL SEND THOSE FROZEN ARROWS AWAY INSTEAD OF DROPPING THEM ON YOUR HEAD.
DON'T WORRY, I'M PRETTY SURE YOU'RE PANDAVAS.
I'VE ONLY BEEN WRONG ONCE.
DHARMA RAJA, LORD OF JUSTICE AND DEATH, WE ACKNOWLEDGE YOU.
PRANAMA! PRANAMA!
WE ACKNOWLEDGE YOU...

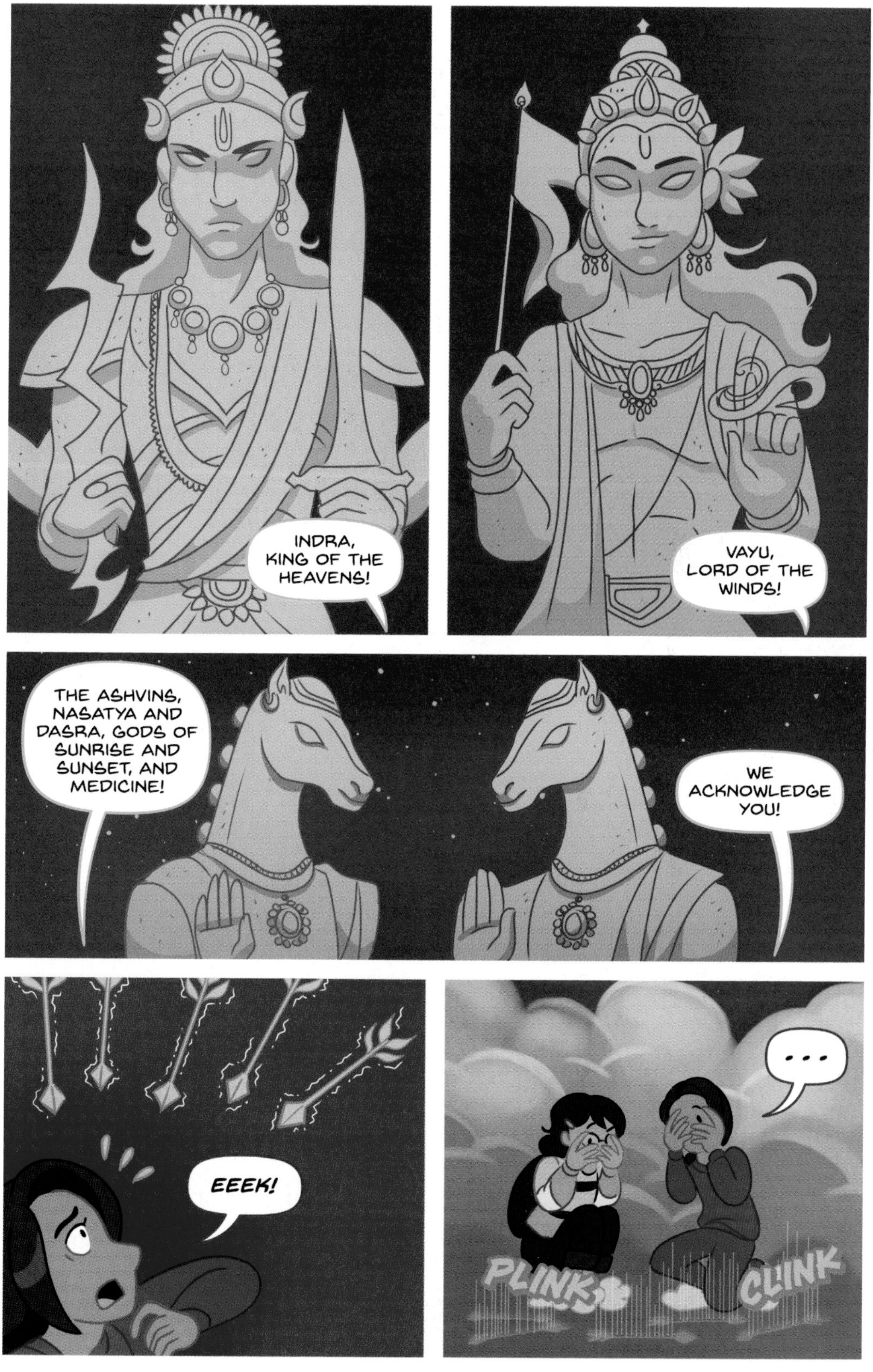
INDRA, KING OF THE HEAVENS!
VAYU, LORD OF THE WINDS!
THE ASHVINS, NASATYA AND DASRA, GODS OF SUNRISE AND SUNSET, AND MEDICINE!
WE ACKNOWLEDGE YOU!
EEEK!
...
PLINK
CLINK

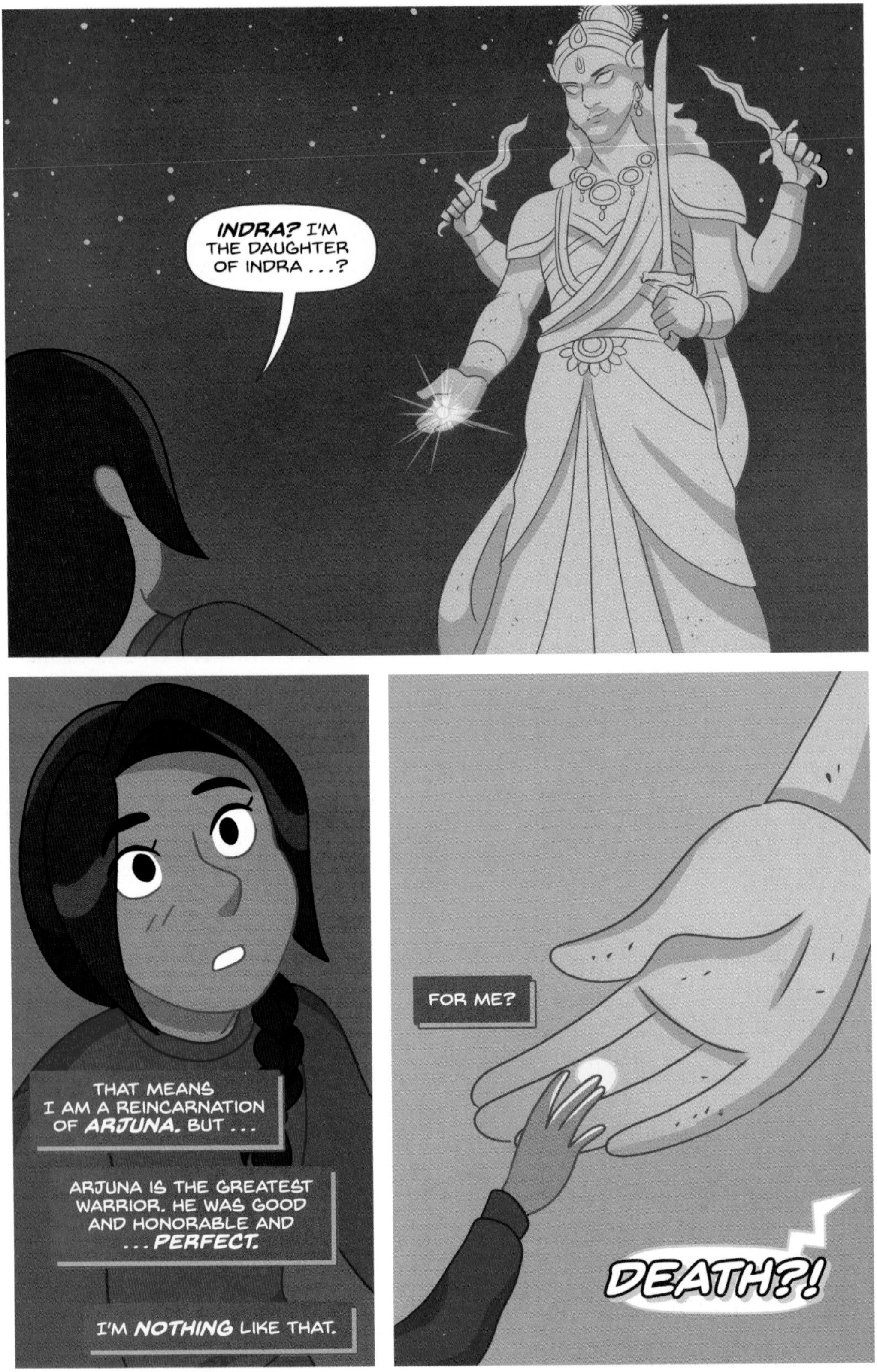
INDRA? I'M THE DAUGHTER OF INDRA . . .?
THAT MEANS I AM A REINCARNATION OF ARJUNA. BUT . . .
ARJUNA IS THE GREATEST WARRIOR. HE WAS GOOD AND HONORABLE AND . . . PERFECT.
I'M NOTHING LIKE THAT.
FOR ME?
DEATH?!

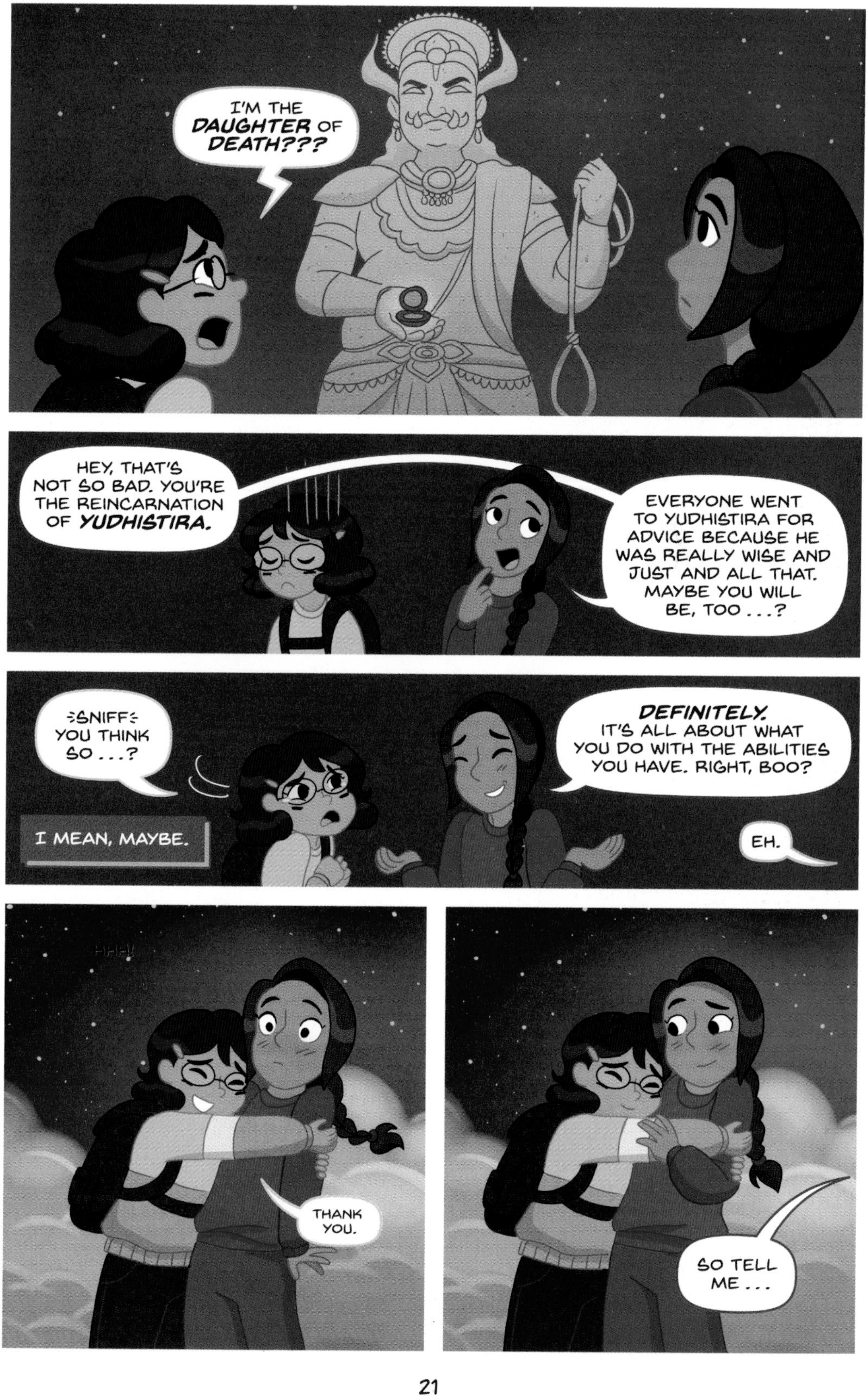
I'M THE DAUGHTER OF DEATH???
HEY, THAT'S NOT SO BAD. YOU'RE THE REINCARNATION OF YUDHISTIRA.
EVERYONE WENT TO YUDHISTIRA FOR ADVICE BECAUSE HE WAS REALLY WISE AND JUST AND ALL THAT. MAYBE YOU WILL BE, TOO . . .?
SNIFF YOU THINK SO . . .?
I MEAN, MAYBE.
DEFINITELY. IT'S ALL ABOUT WHAT YOU DO WITH THE ABILITIES YOU HAVE. RIGHT, BOO?
EH.
HHH!
THANK YOU.
SO TELL ME . . .

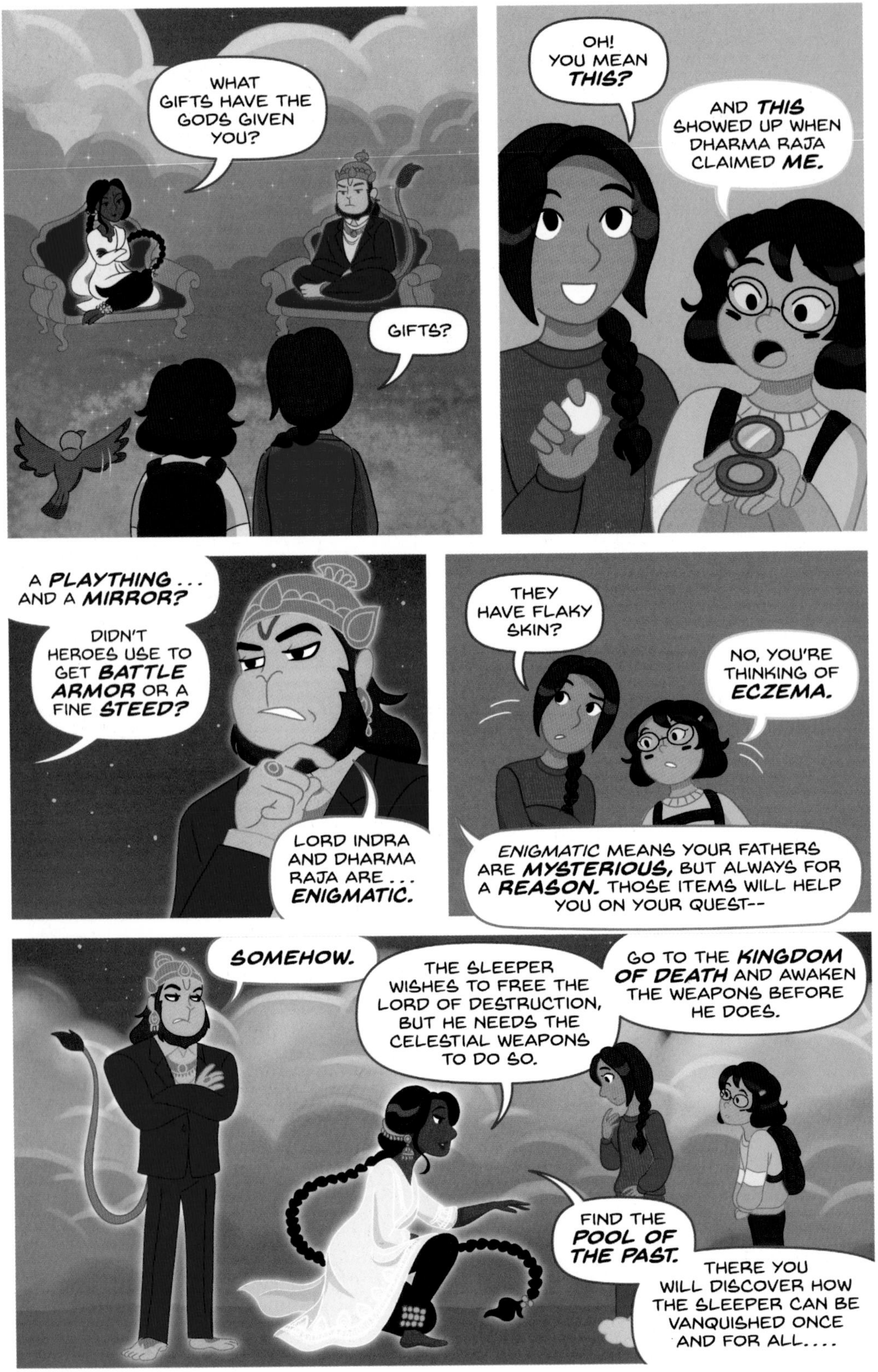
WHAT GIFTS HAVE THE GODS GIVEN YOU?
GIFTS?
OH! YOU MEAN THIS?
AND THIS SHOWED UP WHEN DHARMA RAJA CLAIMED ME.
A PLAYTHING . . . AND A MIRROR?
DIDN'T HEROES USE TO GET BATTLE ARMOR OR A FINE STEED?
LORD INDRA AND DHARMA RAJA ARE . . . ENIGMATIC.
THEY HAVE FLAKY SKIN?
NO, YOU'RE THINKING OF ECZEMA.
ENIGMATIC MEANS YOUR FATHERS ARE MYSTERIOUS, BUT ALWAYS FOR A REASON. THOSE ITEMS WILL HELP YOU ON YOUR QUEST--
SOMEHOW.
THE SLEEPER WISHES TO FREE THE LORD OF DESTRUCTION, BUT HE NEEDS THE CELESTIAL WEAPONS TO DO SO.
GO TO THE KINGDOM OF DEATH AND AWAKEN THE WEAPONS BEFORE HE DOES.
FIND THE POOL OF THE PAST.
THERE YOU WILL DISCOVER HOW THE SLEEPER CAN BE VANQUISHED ONCE AND FOR ALL. . . .

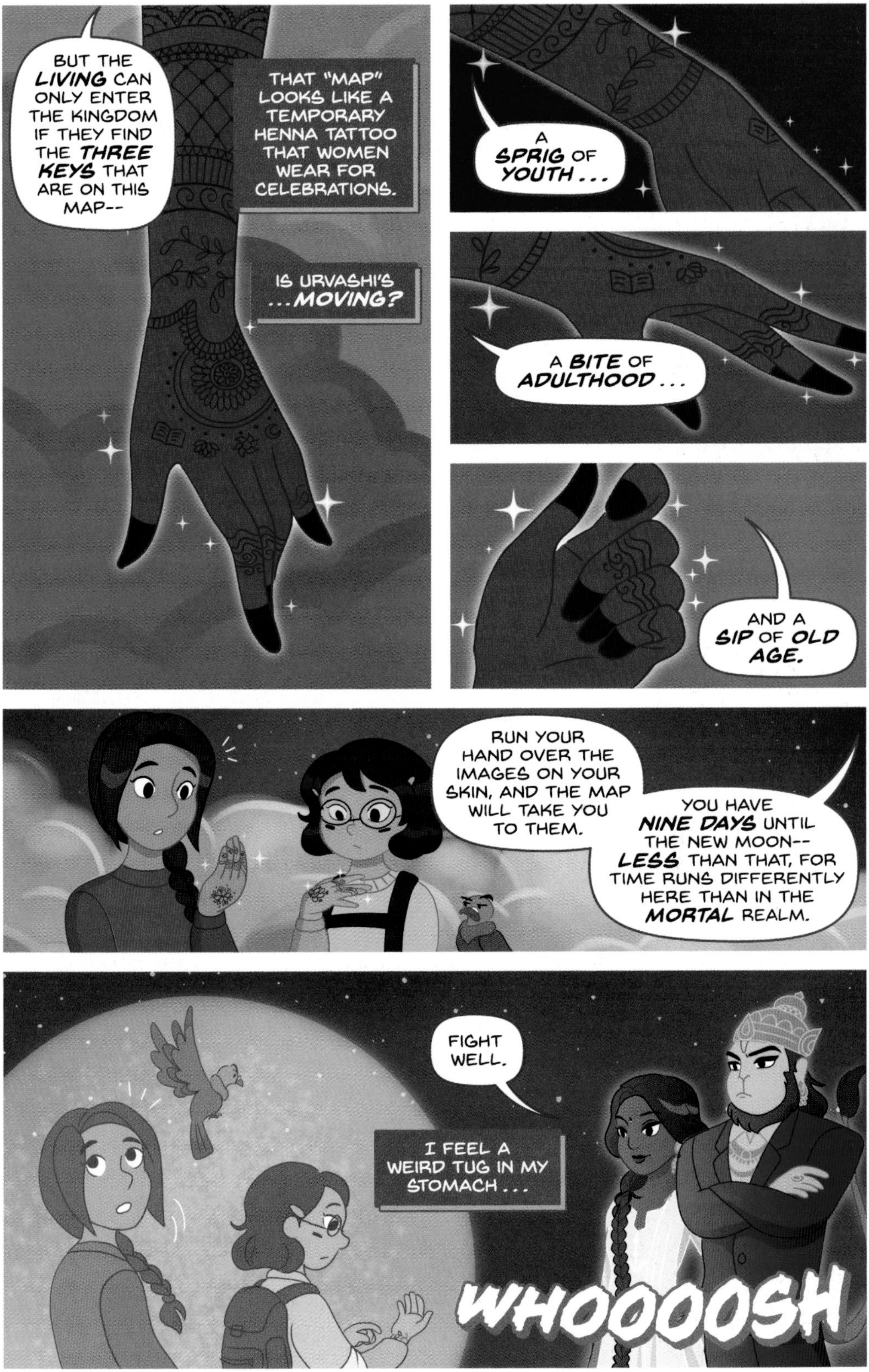
BUT THE LIVING CAN ONLY ENTER THE KINGDOM IF THEY FIND THE THREE KEYS THAT ARE ON THIS MAP--
THAT "MAP" LOOKS LIKE A TEMPORARY HENNA TATTOO THAT WOMEN WEAR FOR CELEBRATIONS.
IS URVASHI'S ...MOVING?
A SPRIG OF YOUTH...
A BITE OF ADULTHOOD...
AND A SIP OF OLD AGE.
RUN YOUR HAND OVER THE IMAGES ON YOUR SKIN, AND THE MAP WILL TAKE YOU TO THEM.
YOU HAVE NINE DAYS UNTIL THE NEW MOON-- LESS THAN THAT, FOR TIME RUNS DIFFERENTLY HERE THAN IN THE MORTAL REALM.
FIGHT WELL.
I FEEL A WEIRD TUG IN MY STOMACH...
WHOOOOOSH

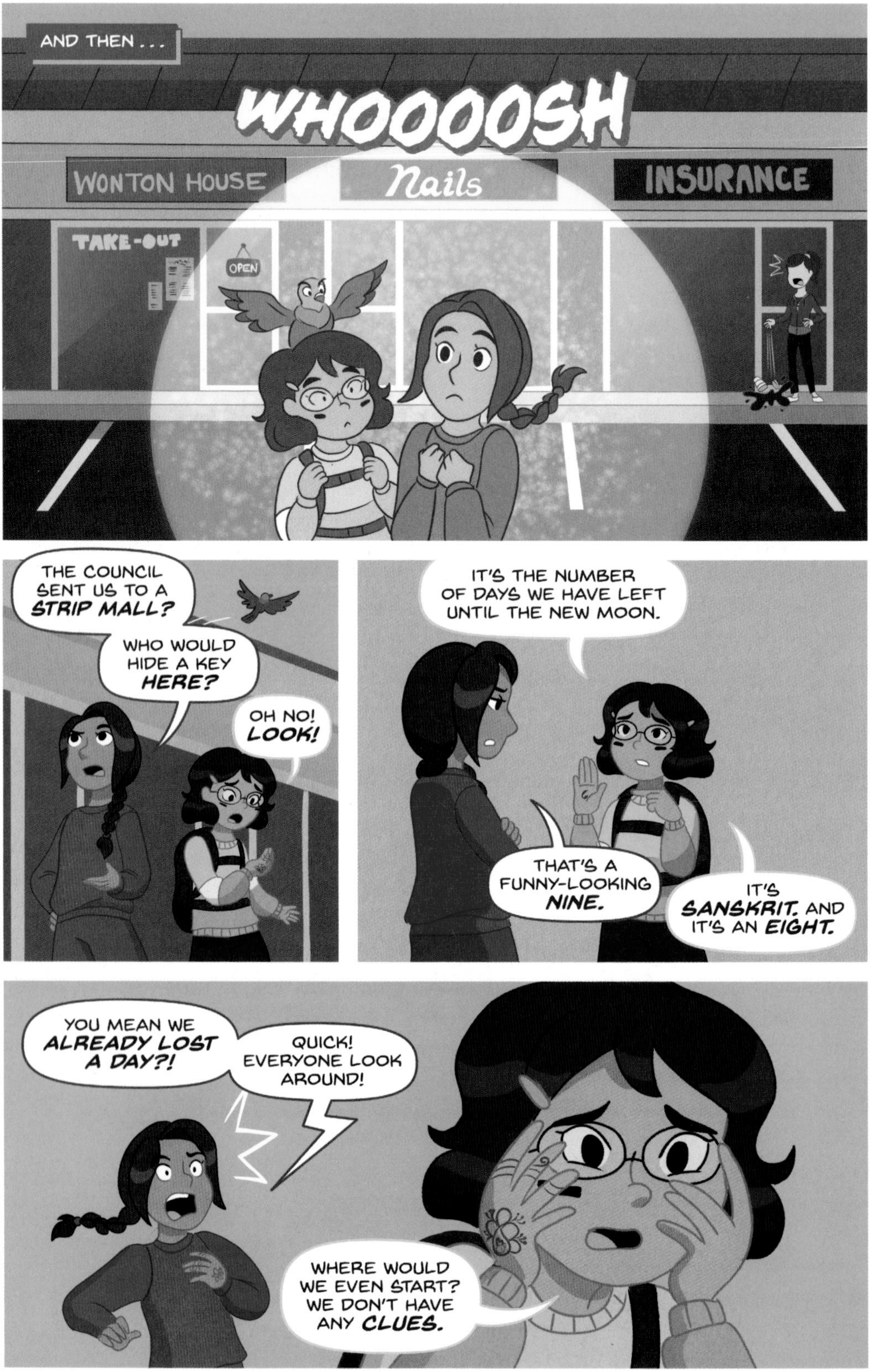
AND THEN . . .
WHOOOOSH
WONTON HOUSE
Nails
INSURANCE
TAKE-OUT
OPEN
THE COUNCIL SENT US TO A STRIP MALL?
WHO WOULD HIDE A KEY HERE?
OH NO! LOOK!
IT'S THE NUMBER OF DAYS WE HAVE LEFT UNTIL THE NEW MOON.
THAT'S A FUNNY-LOOKING NINE.
IT'S SANSKRIT. AND IT'S AN EIGHT.
YOU MEAN WE ALREADY LOST A DAY?!
QUICK! EVERYONE LOOK AROUND!
WHERE WOULD WE EVEN START? WE DON'T HAVE ANY CLUES.

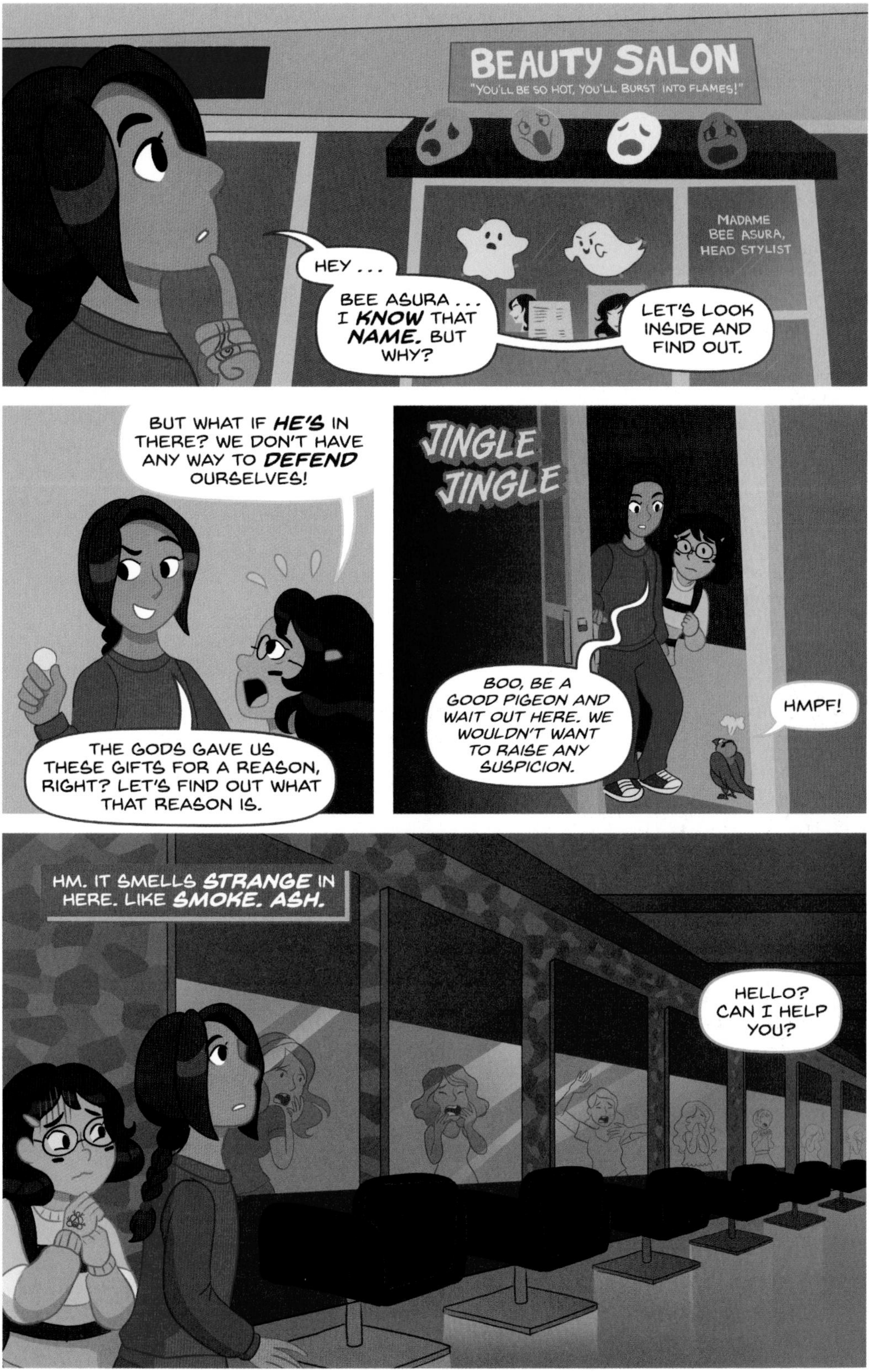
BEAUTY SALON
"YOU'LL BE SO HOT, YOU'LL BURST INTO FLAMES!"
MADAME BEE ASURA, HEAD STYLIST
HEY . . .
BEE ASURA . . . I KNOW THAT NAME. BUT WHY?
LET'S LOOK INSIDE AND FIND OUT.
BUT WHAT IF HE'S IN THERE? WE DON'T HAVE ANY WAY TO DEFEND OURSELVES!
THE GODS GAVE US THESE GIFTS FOR A REASON, RIGHT? LET'S FIND OUT WHAT THAT REASON IS.
JINGLE JINGLE
BOO, BE A GOOD PIGEON AND WAIT OUT HERE. WE WOULDN'T WANT TO RAISE ANY SUSPICION.
HMPF!
HM. IT SMELLS STRANGE IN HERE. LIKE SMOKE. ASH.
HELLO? CAN I HELP YOU?

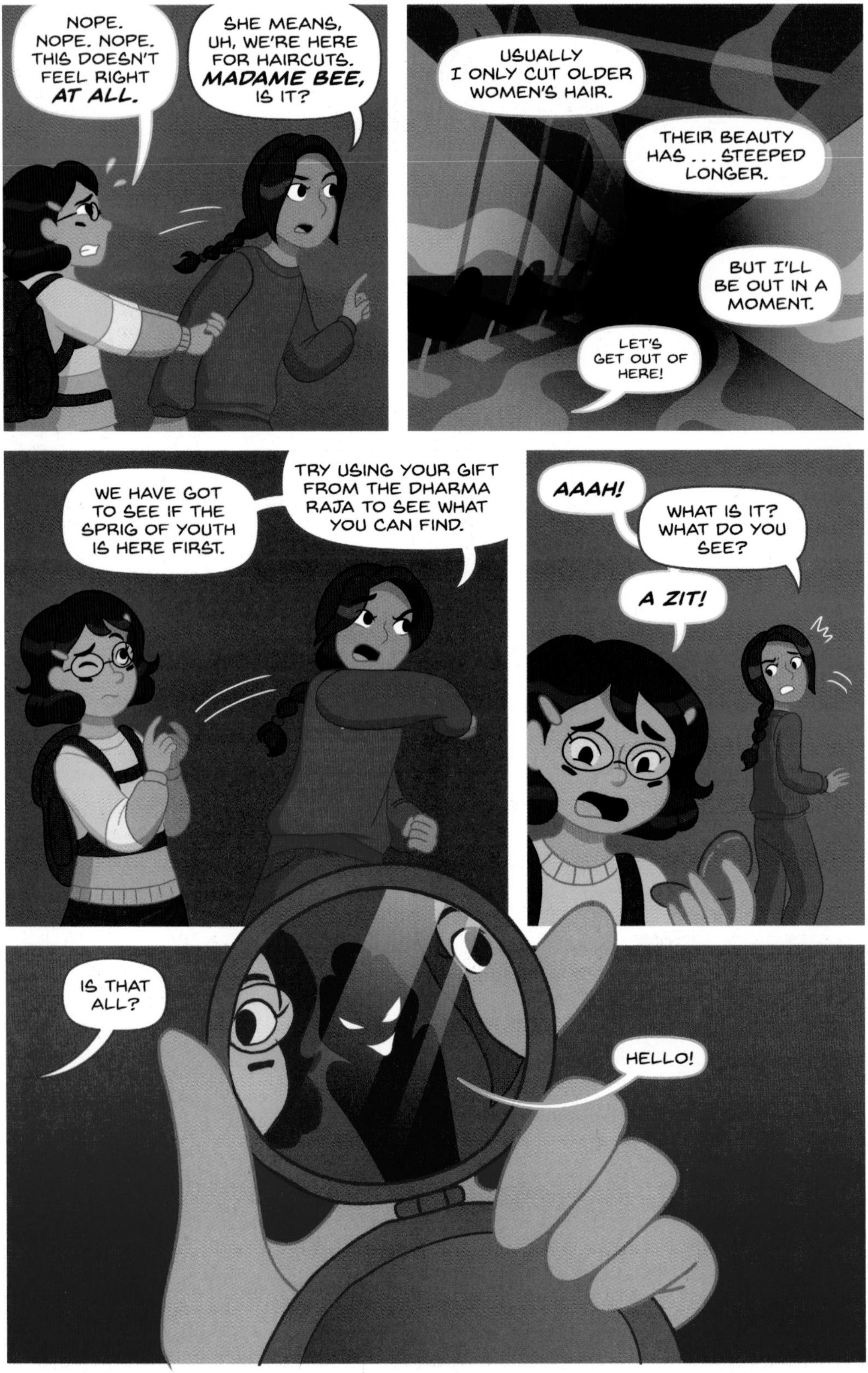
NOPE. NOPE. NOPE. THIS DOESN'T FEEL RIGHT **AT ALL.**
SHE MEANS, UH, WE'RE HERE FOR HAIRCUTS. ***MADAME BEE,*** IS IT?
USUALLY I ONLY CUT OLDER WOMEN'S HAIR.
THEIR BEAUTY HAS . . . STEEPED LONGER.
BUT I'LL BE OUT IN A MOMENT.
LET'S GET OUT OF HERE!
WE HAVE GOT TO SEE IF THE SPRIG OF YOUTH IS HERE FIRST.
TRY USING YOUR GIFT FROM THE DHARMA RAJA TO SEE WHAT YOU CAN FIND.
AAAH!
WHAT IS IT? WHAT DO YOU SEE?
A ZIT!
IS THAT ALL?
HELLO!

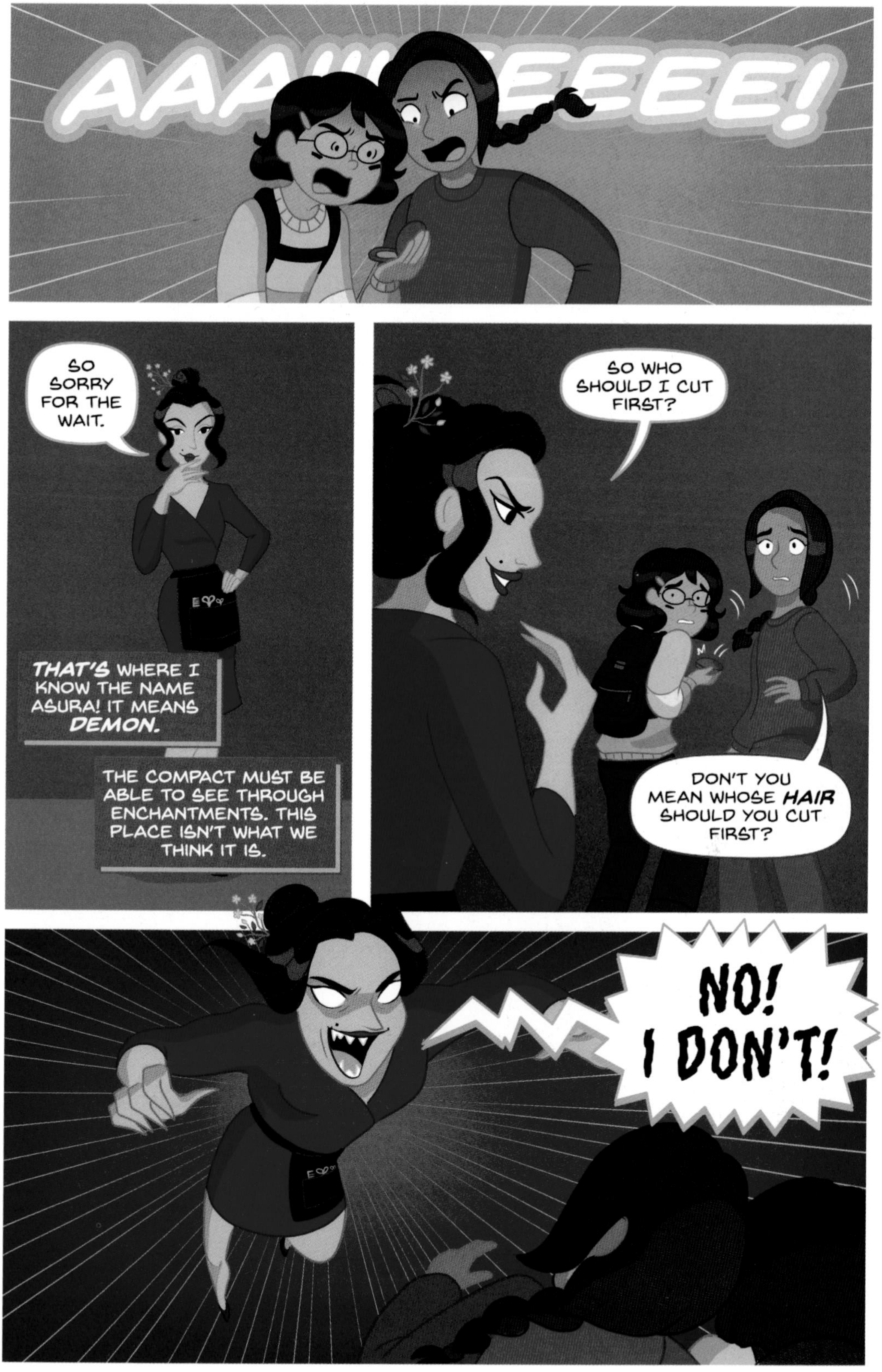
AAAIIIEEEEE!
SO SORRY FOR THE WAIT.
THAT'S WHERE I KNOW THE NAME ASURA! IT MEANS DEMON.
THE COMPACT MUST BE ABLE TO SEE THROUGH ENCHANTMENTS. THIS PLACE ISN'T WHAT WE THINK IT IS.
SO WHO SHOULD I CUT FIRST?
DON'T YOU MEAN WHOSE HAIR SHOULD YOU CUT FIRST?
NO! I DON'T!

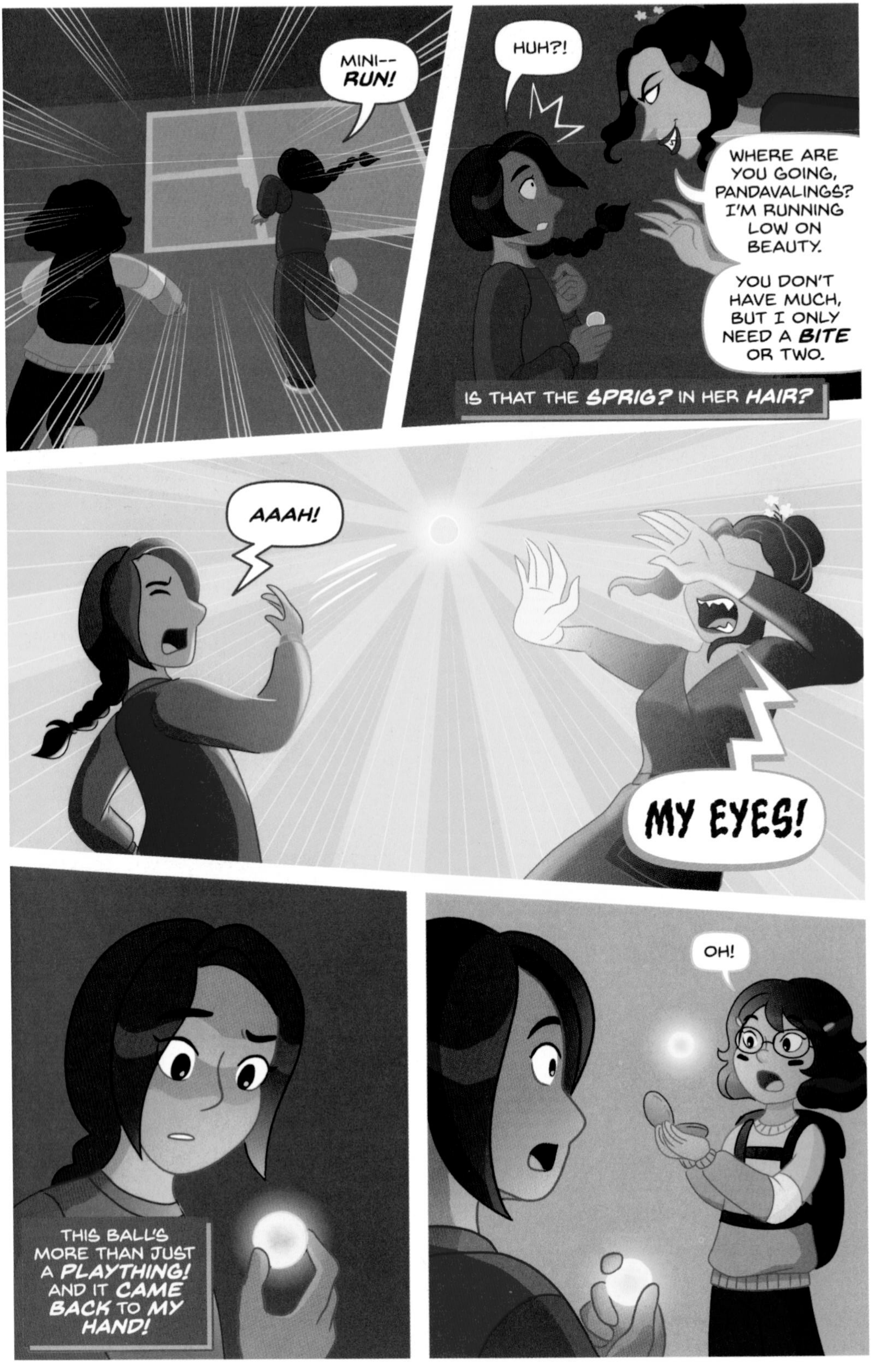
MINI-- RUN!
HUH?!
WHERE ARE YOU GOING, PANDAVALINGS? I'M RUNNING LOW ON BEAUTY.
YOU DON'T HAVE MUCH, BUT I ONLY NEED A BITE OR TWO.
IS THAT THE SPRIG? IN HER HAIR?
AAAH!
MY EYES!
THIS BALL'S MORE THAN JUST A PLAYTHING! AND IT CAME BACK TO MY HAND!
OH!

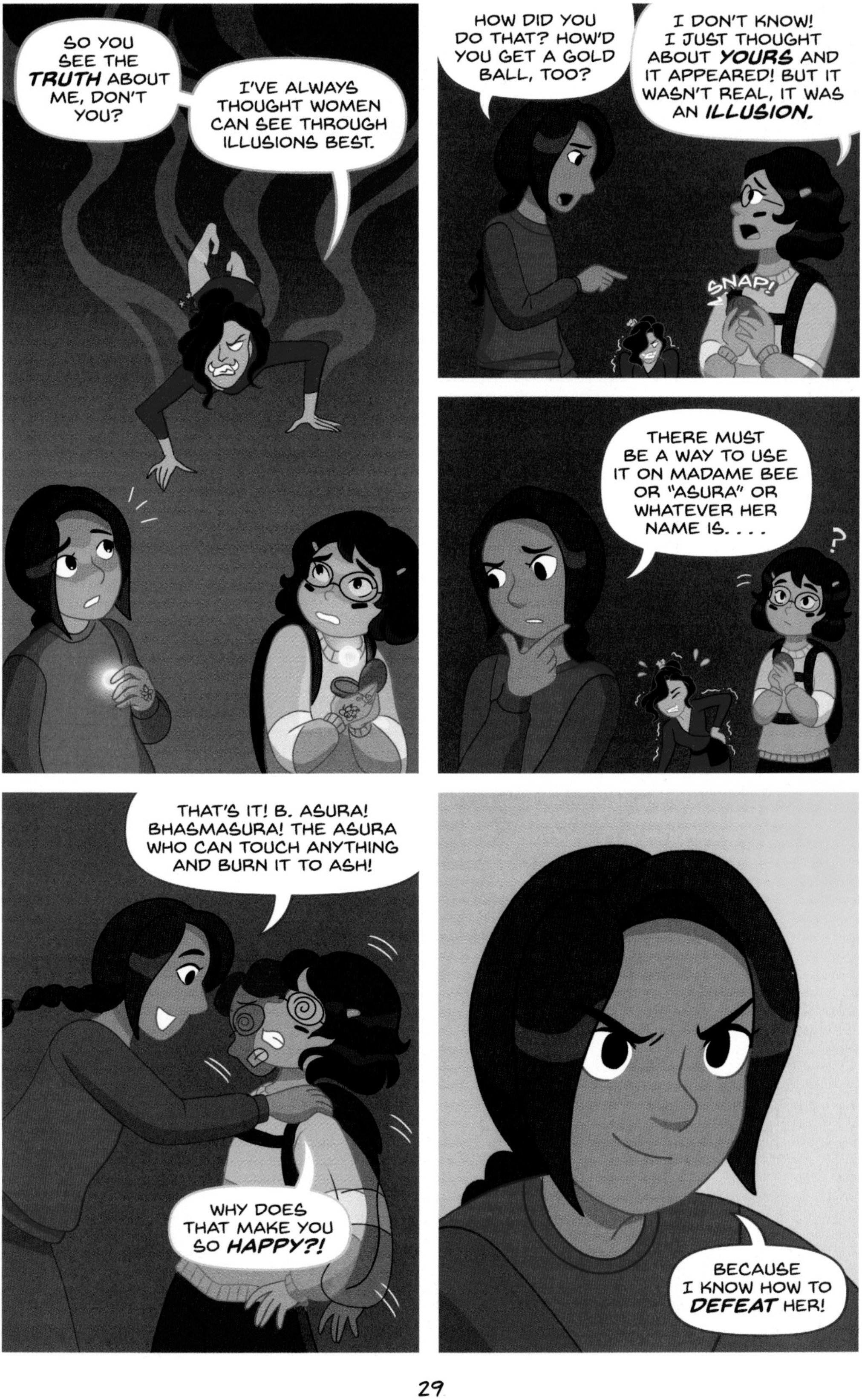
SO YOU SEE THE TRUTH ABOUT ME, DON'T YOU?
I'VE ALWAYS THOUGHT WOMEN CAN SEE THROUGH ILLUSIONS BEST.
HOW DID YOU DO THAT? HOW'D YOU GET A GOLD BALL, TOO?
I DON'T KNOW! I JUST THOUGHT ABOUT YOURS AND IT APPEARED! BUT IT WASN'T REAL, IT WAS AN ILLUSION.
SNAP!
THERE MUST BE A WAY TO USE IT ON MADAME BEE OR "ASURA" OR WHATEVER HER NAME IS. . . .
?
THAT'S IT! B. ASURA! BHASMASURA! THE ASURA WHO CAN TOUCH ANYTHING AND BURN IT TO ASH!
WHY DOES THAT MAKE YOU SO HAPPY?!
BECAUSE I KNOW HOW TO DEFEAT HER!

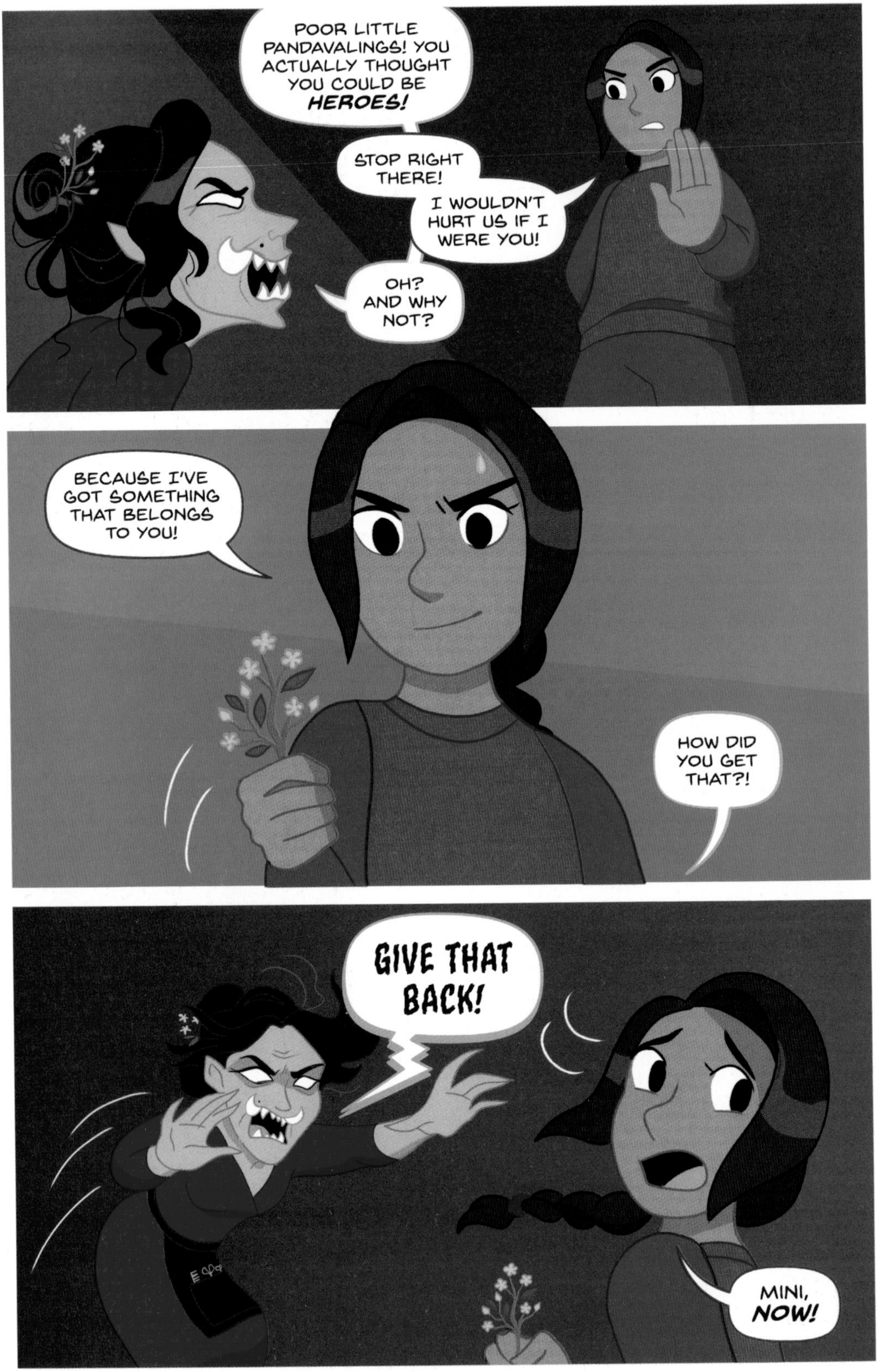
POOR LITTLE PANDAVALINGS! YOU ACTUALLY THOUGHT YOU COULD BE HEROES!
STOP RIGHT THERE!
I WOULDN'T HURT US IF I WERE YOU!
OH? AND WHY NOT?
BECAUSE I'VE GOT SOMETHING THAT BELONGS TO YOU!
HOW DID YOU GET THAT?!
GIVE THAT BACK!
MINI, NOW!

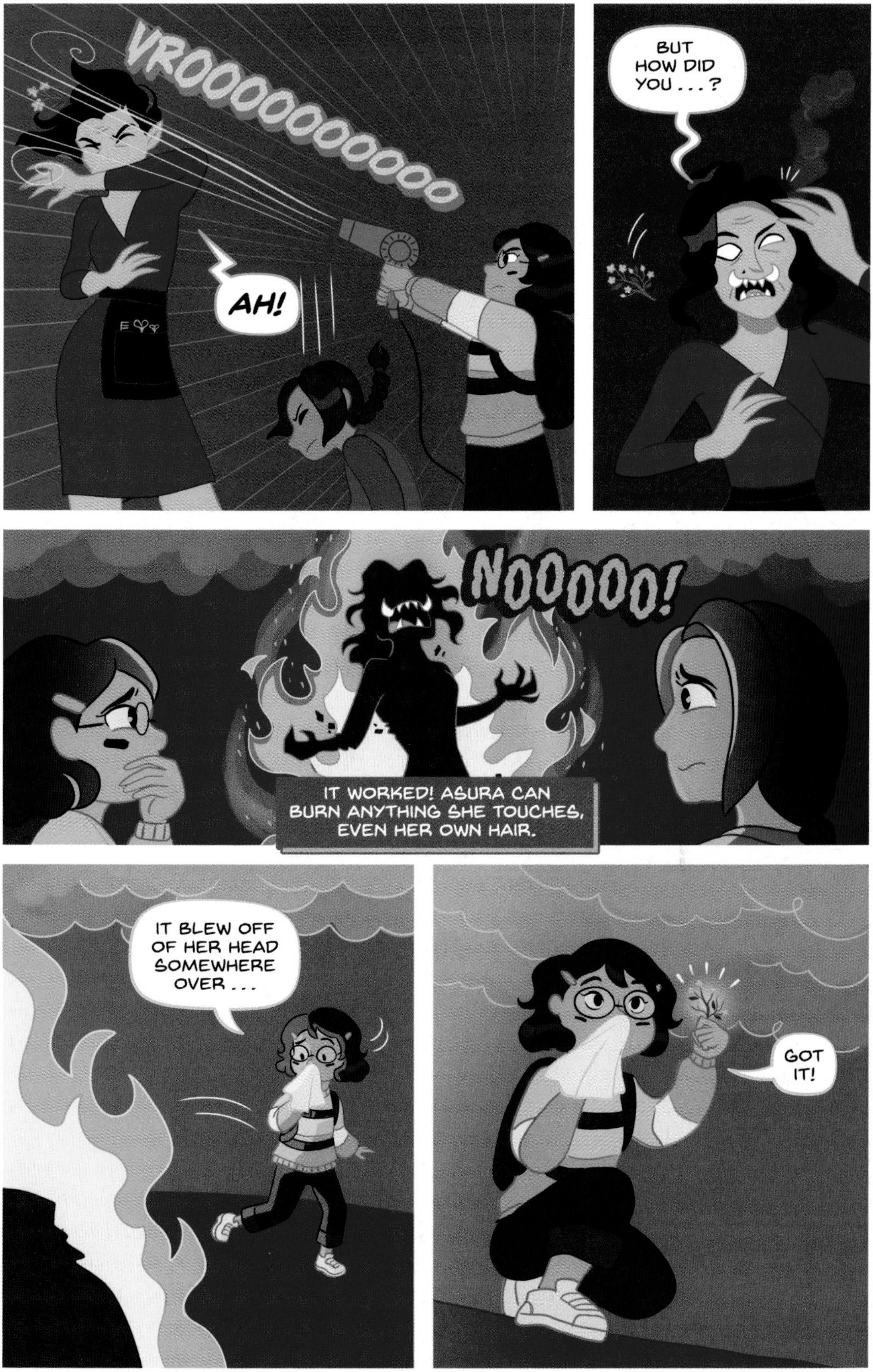
VROOOOOOOOOOO
AH!
BUT HOW DID YOU . . . ?
NOOOOO!
IT WORKED! ASURA CAN BURN ANYTHING SHE TOUCHES, EVEN HER OWN HAIR.
IT BLEW OFF OF HER HEAD SOMEWHERE OVER . . .
GOT IT!

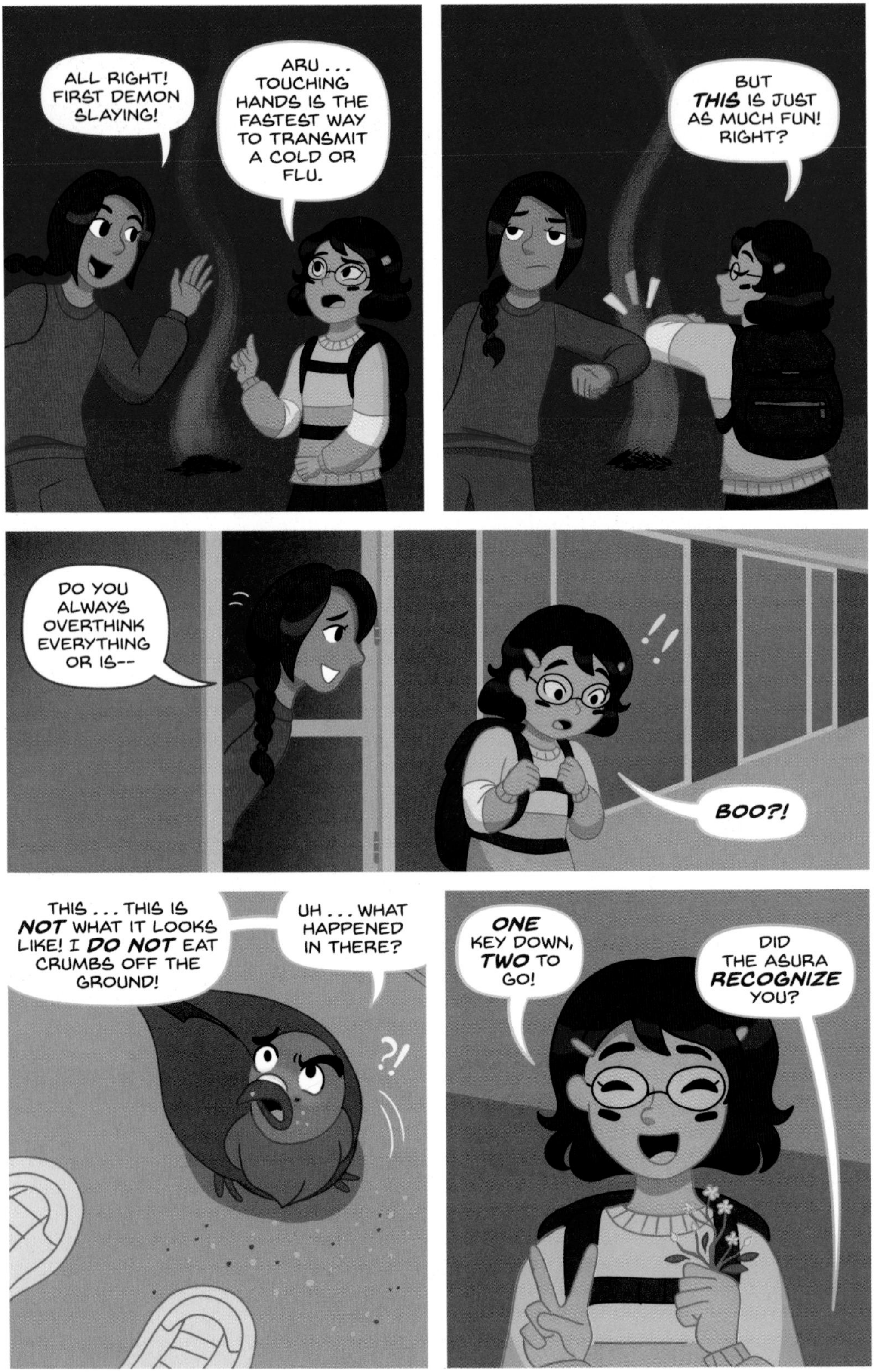
ALL RIGHT! FIRST DEMON SLAYING!
ARU . . . TOUCHING HANDS IS THE FASTEST WAY TO TRANSMIT A COLD OR FLU.
BUT THIS IS JUST AS MUCH FUN! RIGHT?
DO YOU ALWAYS OVERTHINK EVERYTHING OR IS--
BOO?!
THIS . . . THIS IS NOT WHAT IT LOOKS LIKE! I DO NOT EAT CRUMBS OFF THE GROUND!
UH . . . WHAT HAPPENED IN THERE?
?!
ONE KEY DOWN, TWO TO GO!
DID THE ASURA RECOGNIZE YOU?

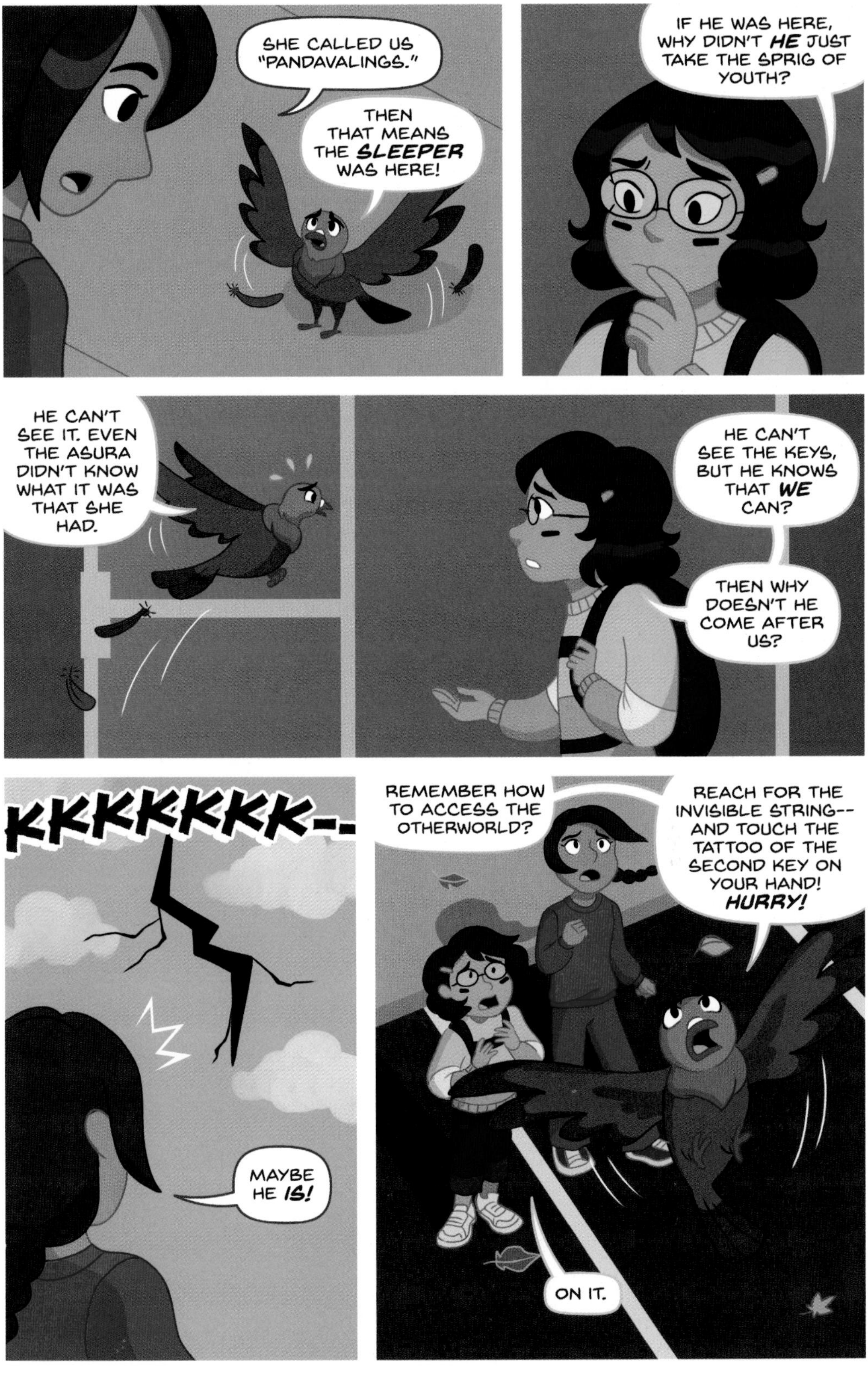
SHE CALLED US "PANDAVALINGS."
THEN THAT MEANS THE *SLEEPER* WAS HERE!
IF HE WAS HERE, WHY DIDN'T *HE* JUST TAKE THE SPRIG OF YOUTH?
HE CAN'T SEE IT. EVEN THE ASURA DIDN'T KNOW WHAT IT WAS THAT SHE HAD.
HE CAN'T SEE THE KEYS, BUT HE KNOWS THAT *WE* CAN?
THEN WHY DOESN'T HE COME AFTER US?
KKKKKKK--
MAYBE HE *IS!*
REMEMBER HOW TO ACCESS THE OTHERWORLD?
REACH FOR THE INVISIBLE STRING-- AND TOUCH THE TATTOO OF THE SECOND KEY ON YOUR HAND! *HURRY!*
ON IT.

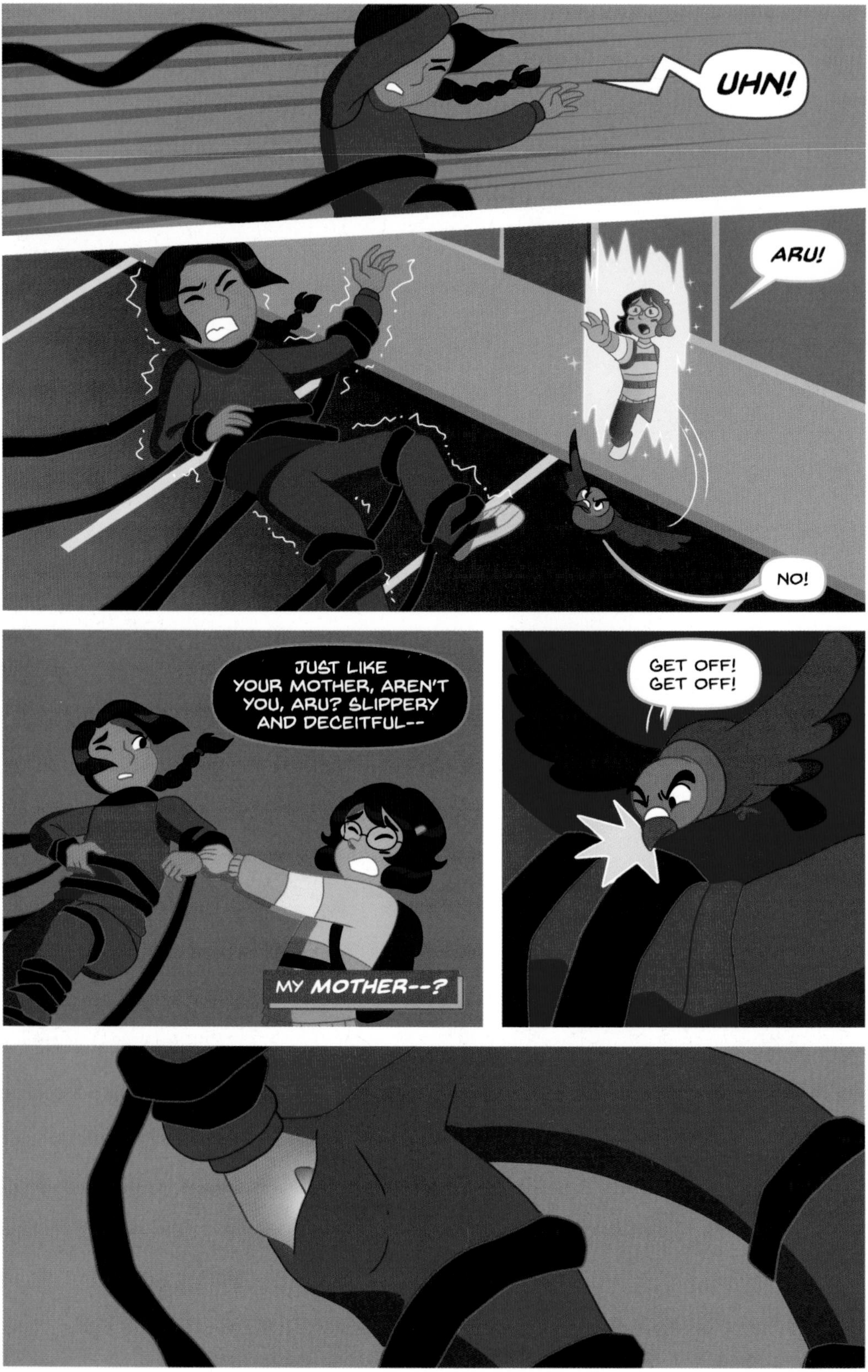
UHN!
ARU!
NO!
JUST LIKE YOUR MOTHER, AREN'T YOU, ARU? SLIPPERY AND DECEITFUL--
MY MOTHER--?
GET OFF! GET OFF!

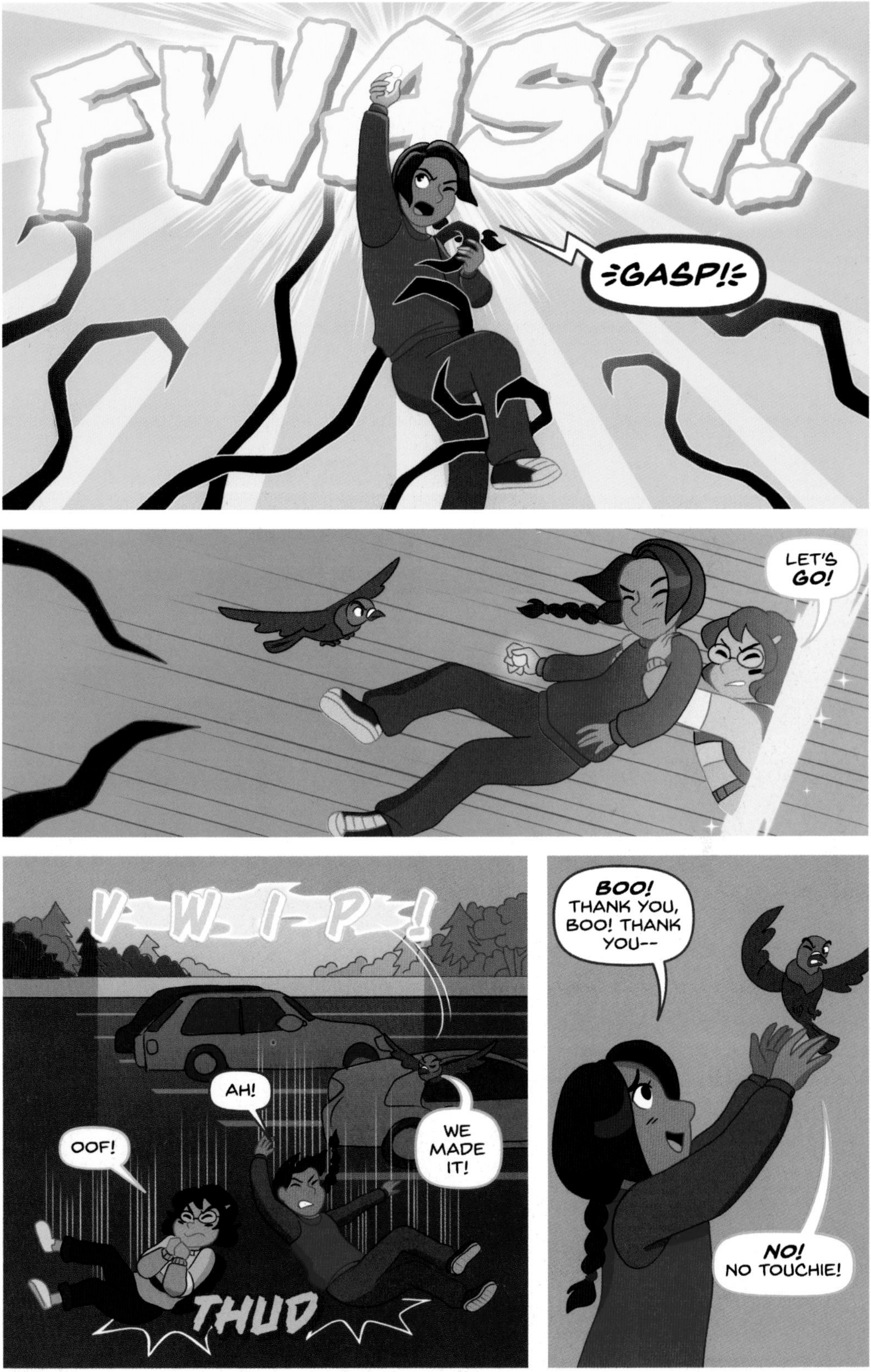
FWASH!
GASP!
LET'S GO!
VWIP!
AH!
OOF!
WE MADE IT!
THUD
BOO! THANK YOU, BOO! THANK YOU--
NO! NO TOUCHIE!

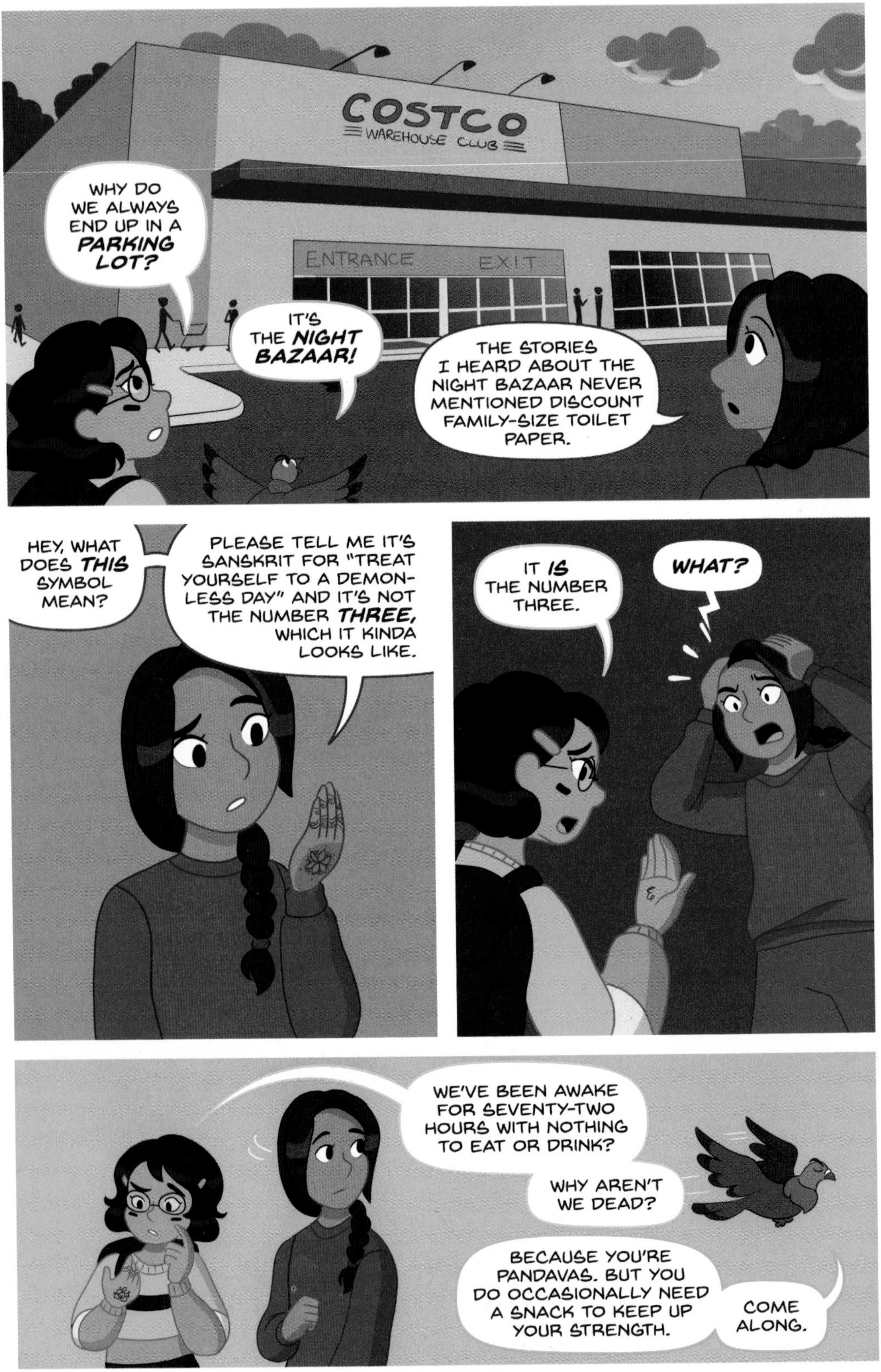
COSTCO
WAREHOUSE CLUB
WHY DO WE ALWAYS END UP IN A PARKING LOT?
ENTRANCE
EXIT
IT'S THE NIGHT BAZAAR!
THE STORIES I HEARD ABOUT THE NIGHT BAZAAR NEVER MENTIONED DISCOUNT FAMILY-SIZE TOILET PAPER.
HEY, WHAT DOES THIS SYMBOL MEAN?
PLEASE TELL ME IT'S SANSKRIT FOR "TREAT YOURSELF TO A DEMON-LESS DAY" AND IT'S NOT THE NUMBER THREE, WHICH IT KINDA LOOKS LIKE.
IT IS THE NUMBER THREE.
WHAT?
WE'VE BEEN AWAKE FOR SEVENTY-TWO HOURS WITH NOTHING TO EAT OR DRINK?
WHY AREN'T WE DEAD?
BECAUSE YOU'RE PANDAVAS. BUT YOU DO OCCASIONALLY NEED A SNACK TO KEEP UP YOUR STRENGTH.
COME ALONG.

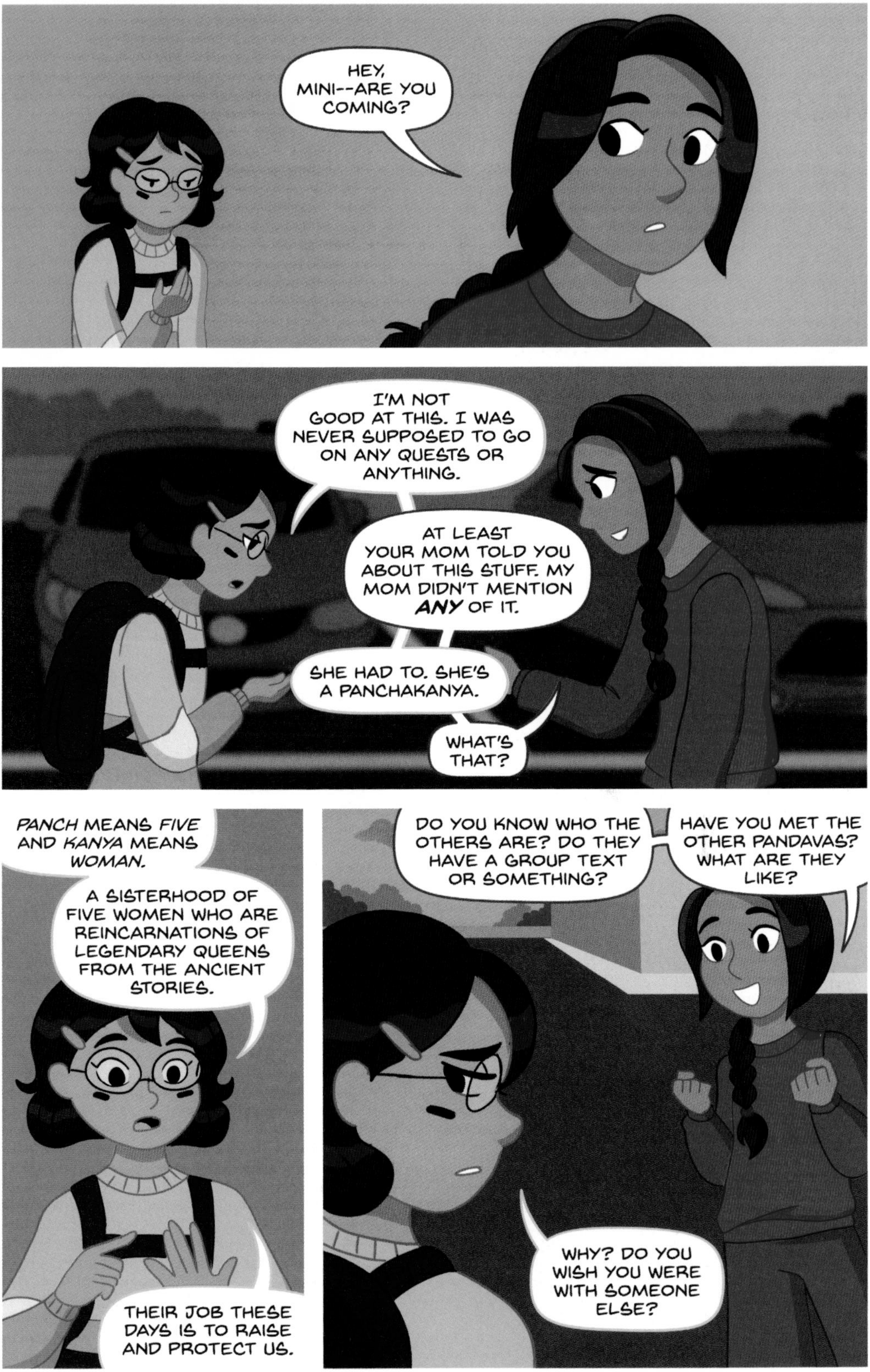
HEY, MINI--ARE YOU COMING?
I'M NOT GOOD AT THIS. I WAS NEVER SUPPOSED TO GO ON ANY QUESTS OR ANYTHING.
AT LEAST YOUR MOM TOLD YOU ABOUT THIS STUFF. MY MOM DIDN'T MENTION ***ANY*** OF IT.
SHE HAD TO. SHE'S A PANCHAKANYA.
WHAT'S THAT?
PANCH MEANS *FIVE* AND *KANYA* MEANS *WOMAN.*
A SISTERHOOD OF FIVE WOMEN WHO ARE REINCARNATIONS OF LEGENDARY QUEENS FROM THE ANCIENT STORIES.
THEIR JOB THESE DAYS IS TO RAISE AND PROTECT US.
DO YOU KNOW WHO THE OTHERS ARE? DO THEY HAVE A GROUP TEXT OR SOMETHING?
HAVE YOU MET THE OTHER PANDAVAS? WHAT ARE THEY LIKE?
WHY? DO YOU WISH YOU WERE WITH SOMEONE ELSE?

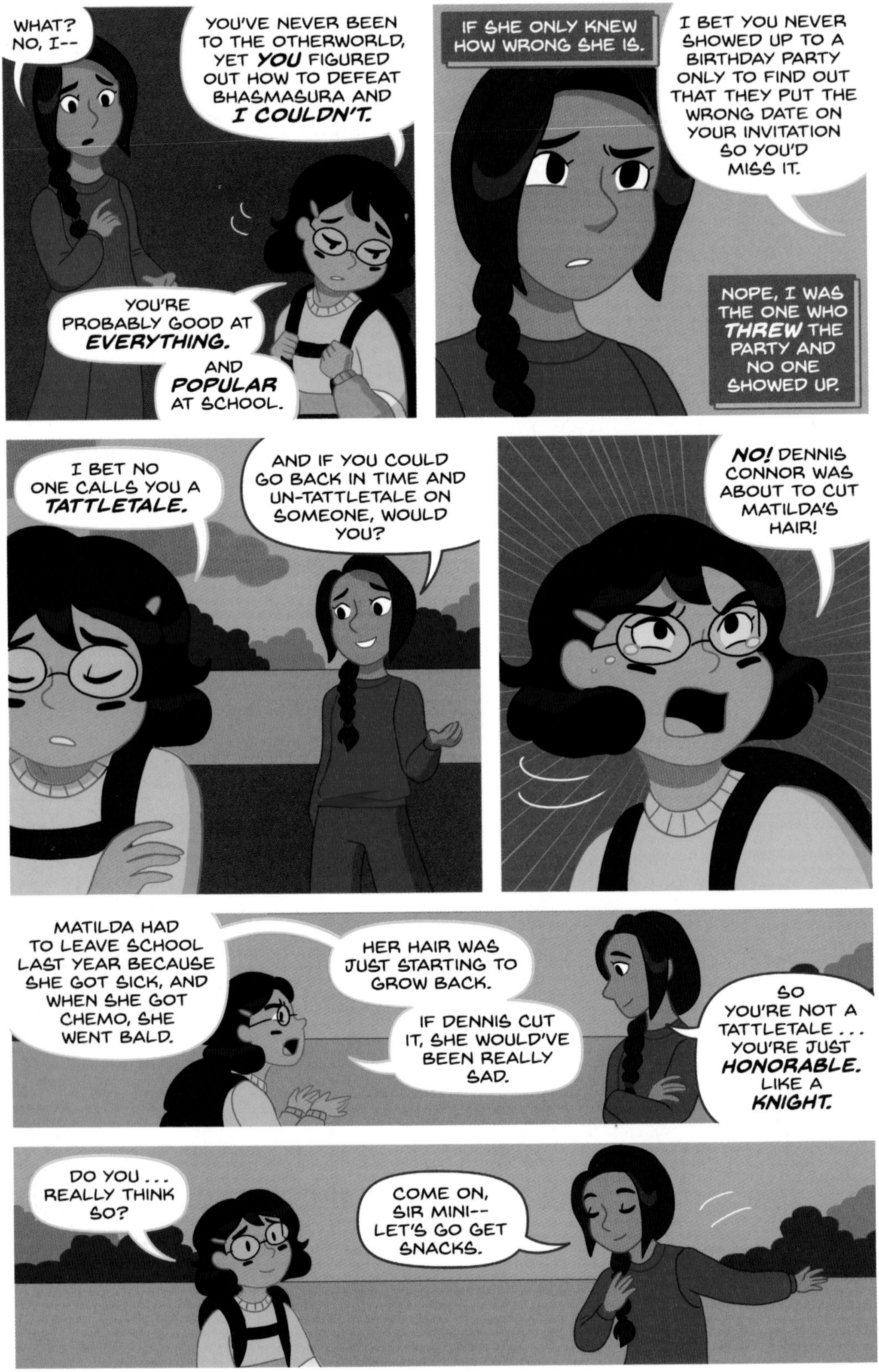
WHAT? NO, I--
YOU'VE NEVER BEEN TO THE OTHERWORLD, YET YOU FIGURED OUT HOW TO DEFEAT BHASMASURA AND I COULDN'T.
YOU'RE PROBABLY GOOD AT EVERYTHING.
AND POPULAR AT SCHOOL.
IF SHE ONLY KNEW HOW WRONG SHE IS.
I BET YOU NEVER SHOWED UP TO A BIRTHDAY PARTY ONLY TO FIND OUT THAT THEY PUT THE WRONG DATE ON YOUR INVITATION SO YOU'D MISS IT.
NOPE, I WAS THE ONE WHO THREW THE PARTY AND NO ONE SHOWED UP.
I BET NO ONE CALLS YOU A TATTLETALE.
AND IF YOU COULD GO BACK IN TIME AND UN-TATTLETALE ON SOMEONE, WOULD YOU?
NO! DENNIS CONNOR WAS ABOUT TO CUT MATILDA'S HAIR!
MATILDA HAD TO LEAVE SCHOOL LAST YEAR BECAUSE SHE GOT SICK, AND WHEN SHE GOT CHEMO, SHE WENT BALD.
HER HAIR WAS JUST STARTING TO GROW BACK.
IF DENNIS CUT IT, SHE WOULD'VE BEEN REALLY SAD.
SO YOU'RE NOT A TATTLETALE . . . YOU'RE JUST HONORABLE. LIKE A KNIGHT.
DO YOU . . . REALLY THINK SO?
COME ON, SIR MINI-- LET'S GO GET SNACKS.

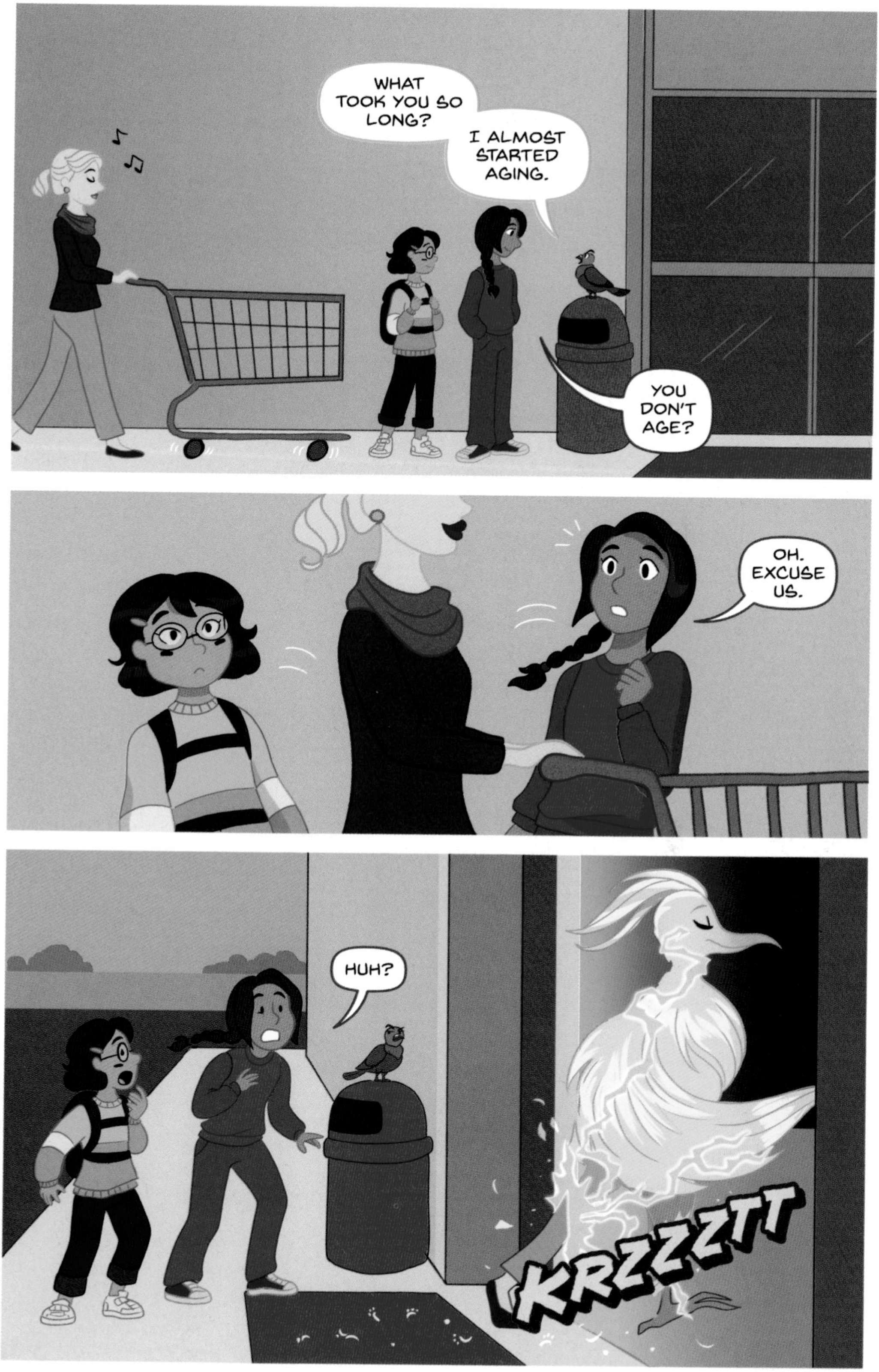
WHAT TOOK YOU SO LONG?
I ALMOST STARTED AGING.
YOU DON'T AGE?
OH. EXCUSE US.
HUH?
KRZZZZTT

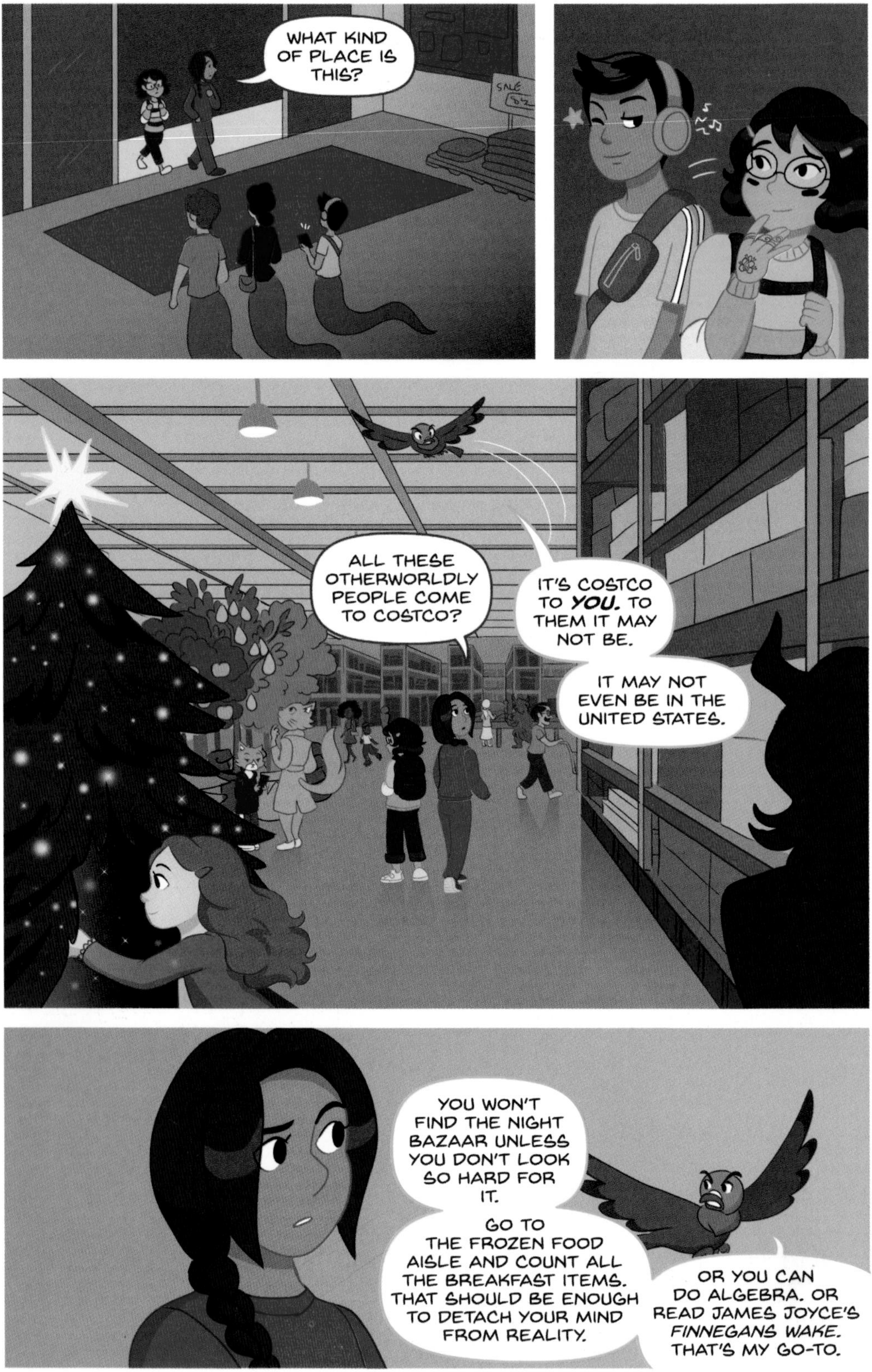
WHAT KIND OF PLACE IS THIS?
ALL THESE OTHERWORLDLY PEOPLE COME TO COSTCO?
IT'S COSTCO TO *YOU.* TO THEM IT MAY NOT BE.
IT MAY NOT EVEN BE IN THE UNITED STATES.
YOU WON'T FIND THE NIGHT BAZAAR UNLESS YOU DON'T LOOK SO HARD FOR IT.
GO TO THE FROZEN FOOD AISLE AND COUNT ALL THE BREAKFAST ITEMS. THAT SHOULD BE ENOUGH TO DETACH YOUR MIND FROM REALITY.
OR YOU CAN DO ALGEBRA. OR READ JAMES JOYCE'S *FINNEGANS WAKE.* THAT'S MY GO-TO.

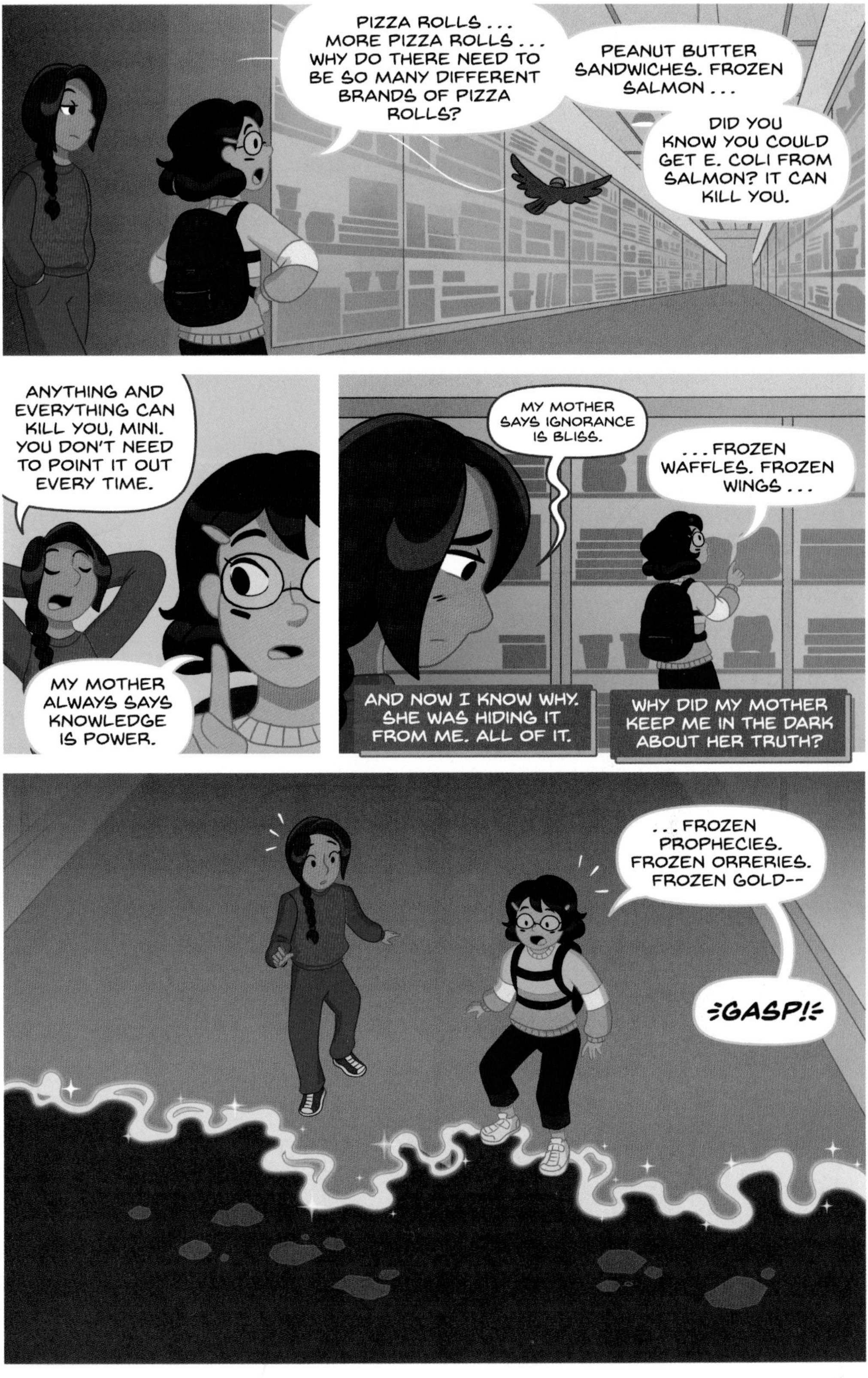

PIZZA ROLLS . . . MORE PIZZA ROLLS . . . WHY DO THERE NEED TO BE SO MANY DIFFERENT BRANDS OF PIZZA ROLLS?
PEANUT BUTTER SANDWICHES. FROZEN SALMON . . .
DID YOU KNOW YOU COULD GET E. COLI FROM SALMON? IT CAN KILL YOU.
ANYTHING AND EVERYTHING CAN KILL YOU, MINI. YOU DON'T NEED TO POINT IT OUT EVERY TIME.
MY MOTHER ALWAYS SAYS KNOWLEDGE IS POWER.
MY MOTHER SAYS IGNORANCE IS BLISS.
. . . FROZEN WAFFLES. FROZEN WINGS . . .
AND NOW I KNOW WHY. SHE WAS HIDING IT FROM ME. ALL OF IT.
WHY DID MY MOTHER KEEP ME IN THE DARK ABOUT HER TRUTH?
. . . FROZEN PROPHECIES. FROZEN ORRERIES. FROZEN GOLD--
GASP!

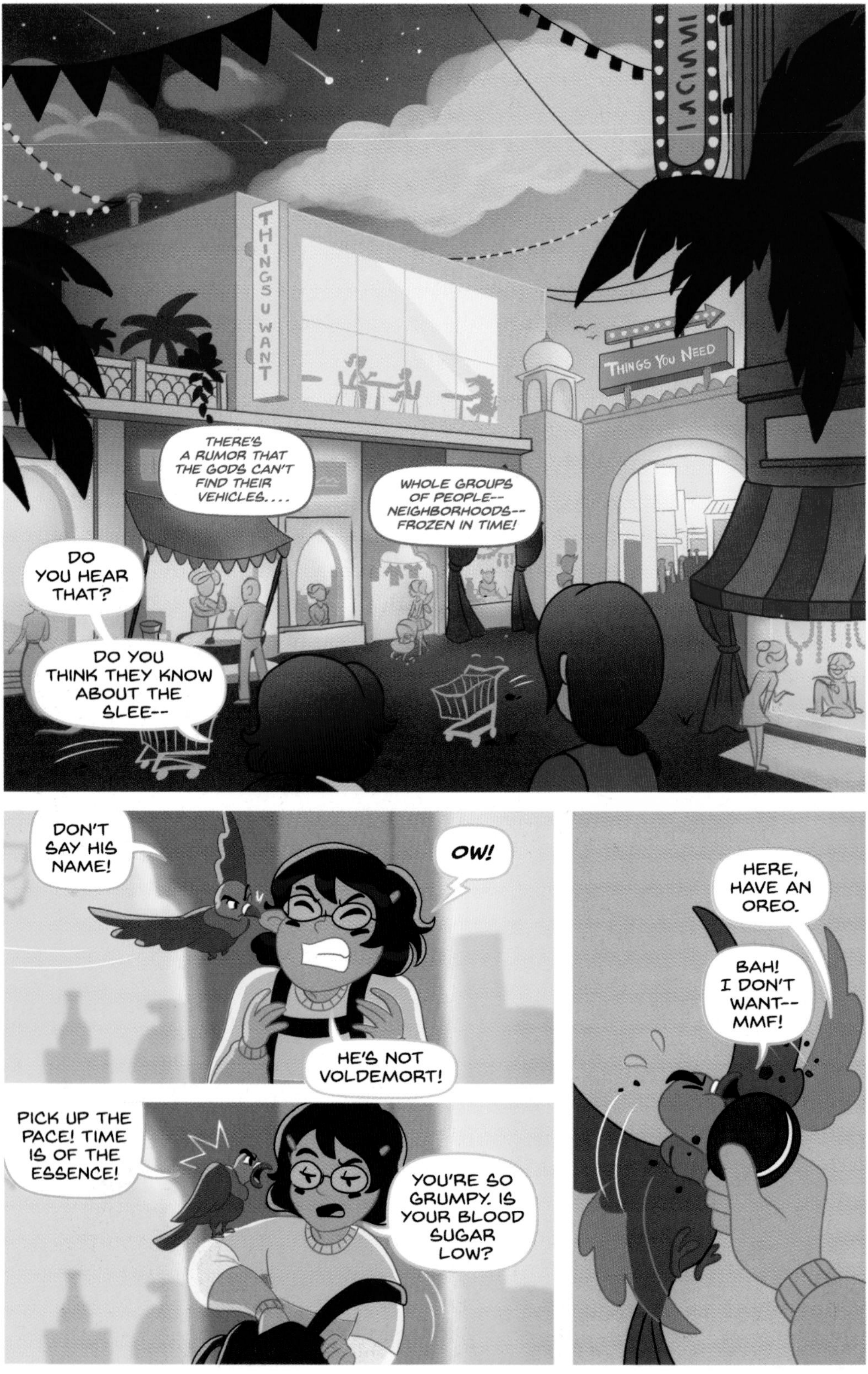
THINGS U WANT
THINGS YOU NEED
THERE'S A RUMOR THAT THE GODS CAN'T FIND THEIR VEHICLES....
WHOLE GROUPS OF PEOPLE-- NEIGHBORHOODS-- FROZEN IN TIME!
DO YOU HEAR THAT?
DO YOU THINK THEY KNOW ABOUT THE SLEE--
DON'T SAY HIS NAME!
OW!
HE'S NOT VOLDEMORT!
PICK UP THE PACE! TIME IS OF THE ESSENCE!
YOU'RE SO GRUMPY. IS YOUR BLOOD SUGAR LOW?
HERE, HAVE AN OREO.
BAH! I DON'T WANT-- MMF!

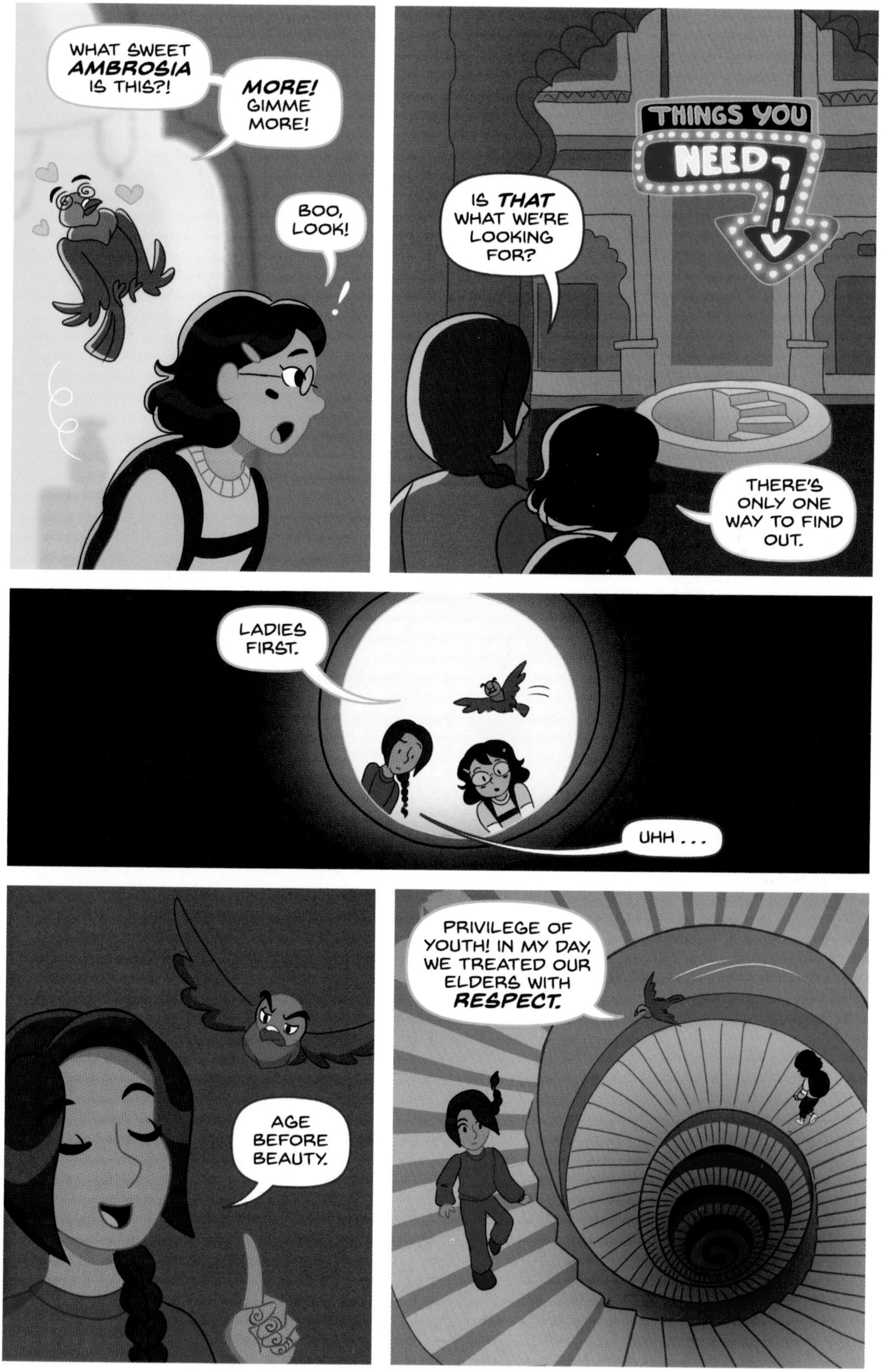
WHAT SWEET AMBROSIA IS THIS?!
MORE! GIMME MORE!
BOO, LOOK!
!
IS THAT WHAT WE'RE LOOKING FOR?
THINGS YOU NEED
THERE'S ONLY ONE WAY TO FIND OUT.
LADIES FIRST.
UHH . . .
AGE BEFORE BEAUTY.
PRIVILEGE OF YOUTH! IN MY DAY, WE TREATED OUR ELDERS WITH RESPECT.

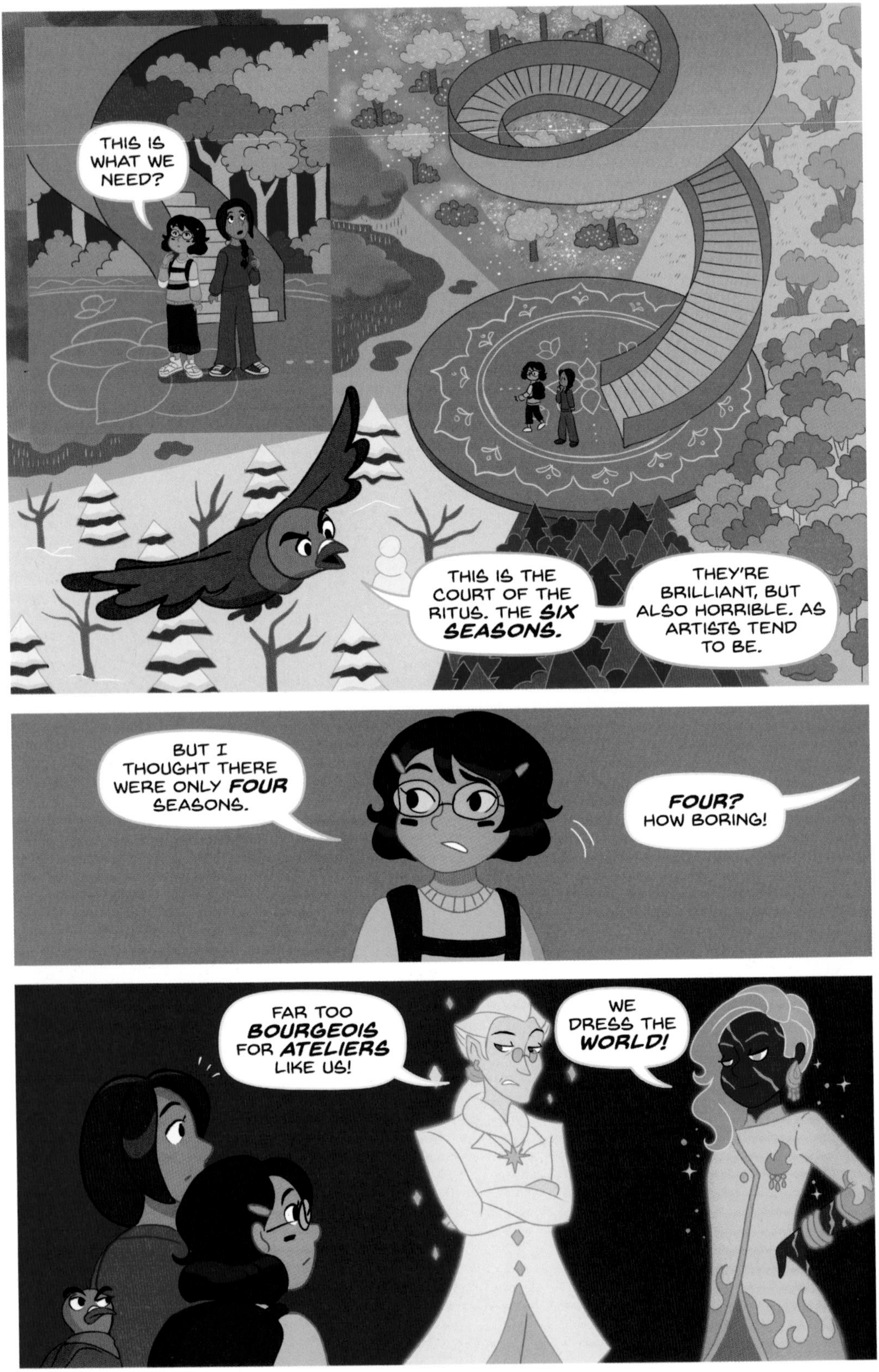
THIS IS WHAT WE NEED?
THIS IS THE COURT OF THE RITUS. THE **SIX SEASONS.**
THEY'RE BRILLIANT, BUT ALSO HORRIBLE. AS ARTISTS TEND TO BE.
BUT I THOUGHT THERE WERE ONLY **FOUR** SEASONS.
FOUR? HOW BORING!
FAR TOO **BOURGEOIS** FOR **ATELIERS** LIKE US!
WE DRESS THE **WORLD!**

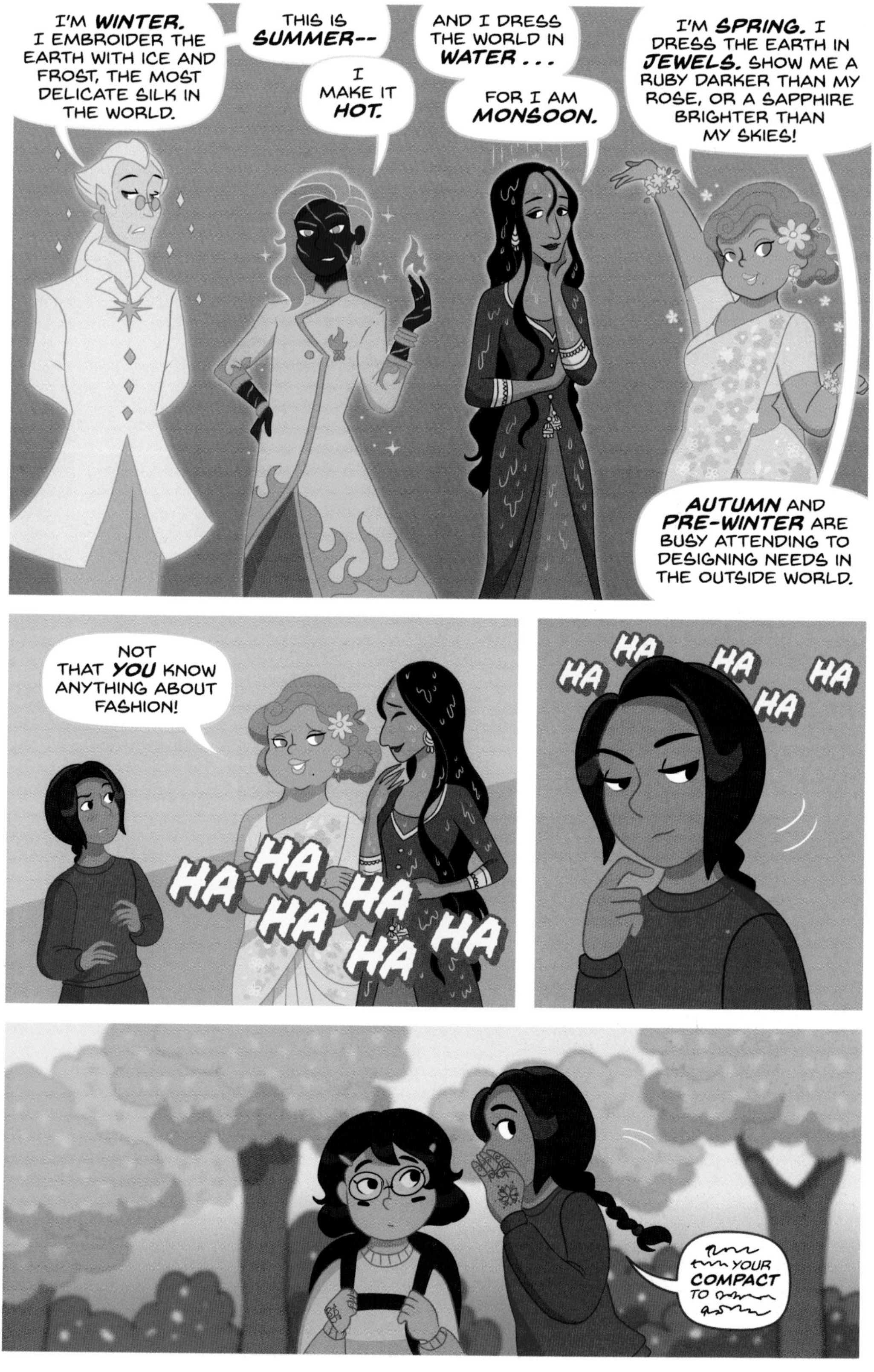

I'M WINTER. I EMBROIDER THE EARTH WITH ICE AND FROST, THE MOST DELICATE SILK IN THE WORLD.
THIS IS SUMMER--
I MAKE IT HOT.
AND I DRESS THE WORLD IN WATER . . .
FOR I AM MONSOON.
I'M SPRING. I DRESS THE EARTH IN JEWELS. SHOW ME A RUBY DARKER THAN MY ROSE, OR A SAPPHIRE BRIGHTER THAN MY SKIES!
AUTUMN AND PRE-WINTER ARE BUSY ATTENDING TO DESIGNING NEEDS IN THE OUTSIDE WORLD.
NOT THAT YOU KNOW ANYTHING ABOUT FASHION!
HA HA HA HA HA HA HA
HA HA HA HA HA
YOUR COMPACT TO

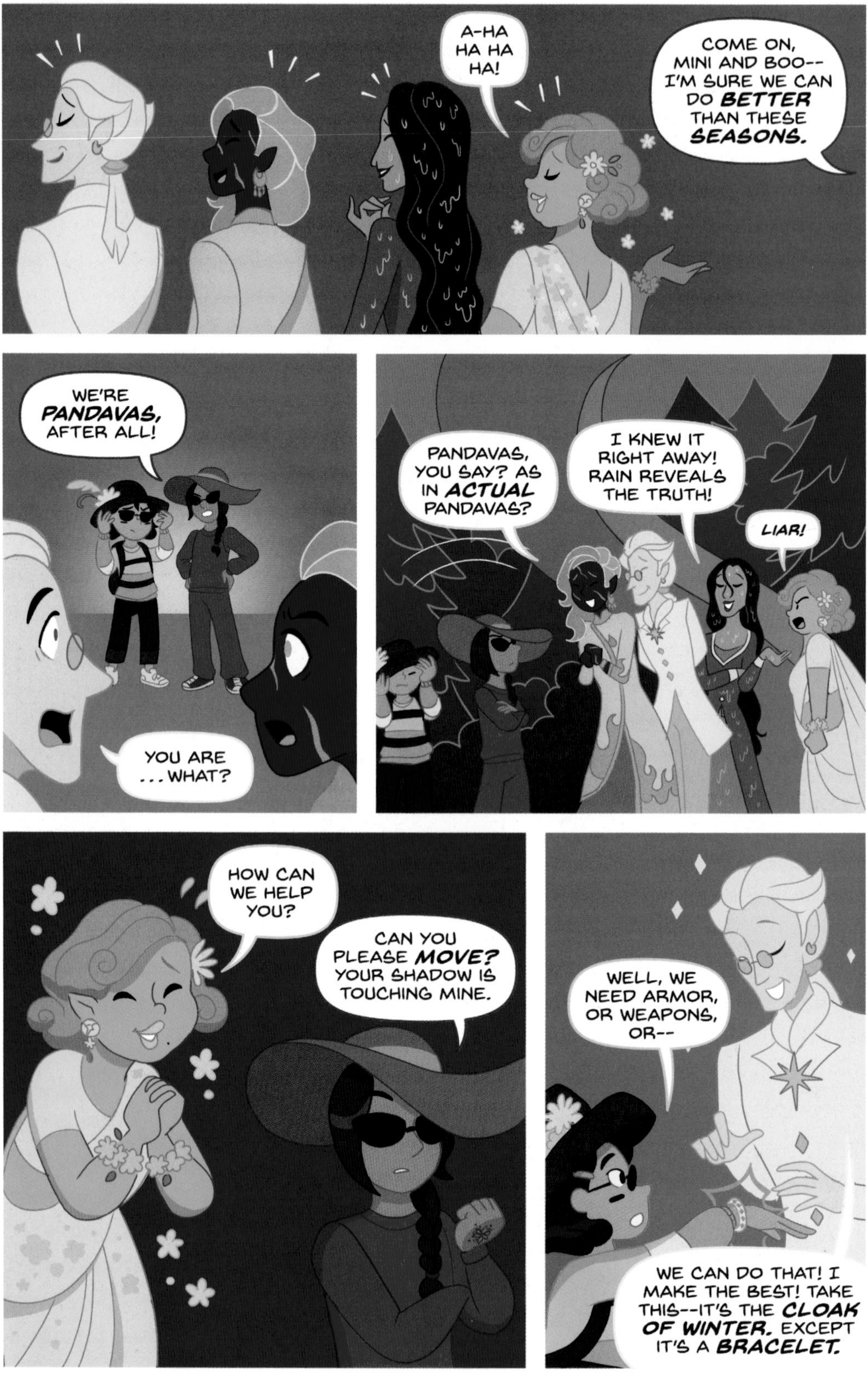
A-HA HA HA HA!
COME ON, MINI AND BOO-- I'M SURE WE CAN DO **BETTER** THAN THESE **SEASONS.**
WE'RE **PANDAVAS,** AFTER ALL!
YOU ARE ...WHAT?
PANDAVAS, YOU SAY? AS IN **ACTUAL** PANDAVAS?
I KNEW IT RIGHT AWAY! RAIN REVEALS THE TRUTH!
LIAR!
HOW CAN WE HELP YOU?
CAN YOU PLEASE **MOVE?** YOUR SHADOW IS TOUCHING MINE.
WELL, WE NEED ARMOR, OR WEAPONS, OR--
WE CAN DO THAT! I MAKE THE BEST! TAKE THIS--IT'S THE **CLOAK OF WINTER.** EXCEPT IT'S A **BRACELET.**

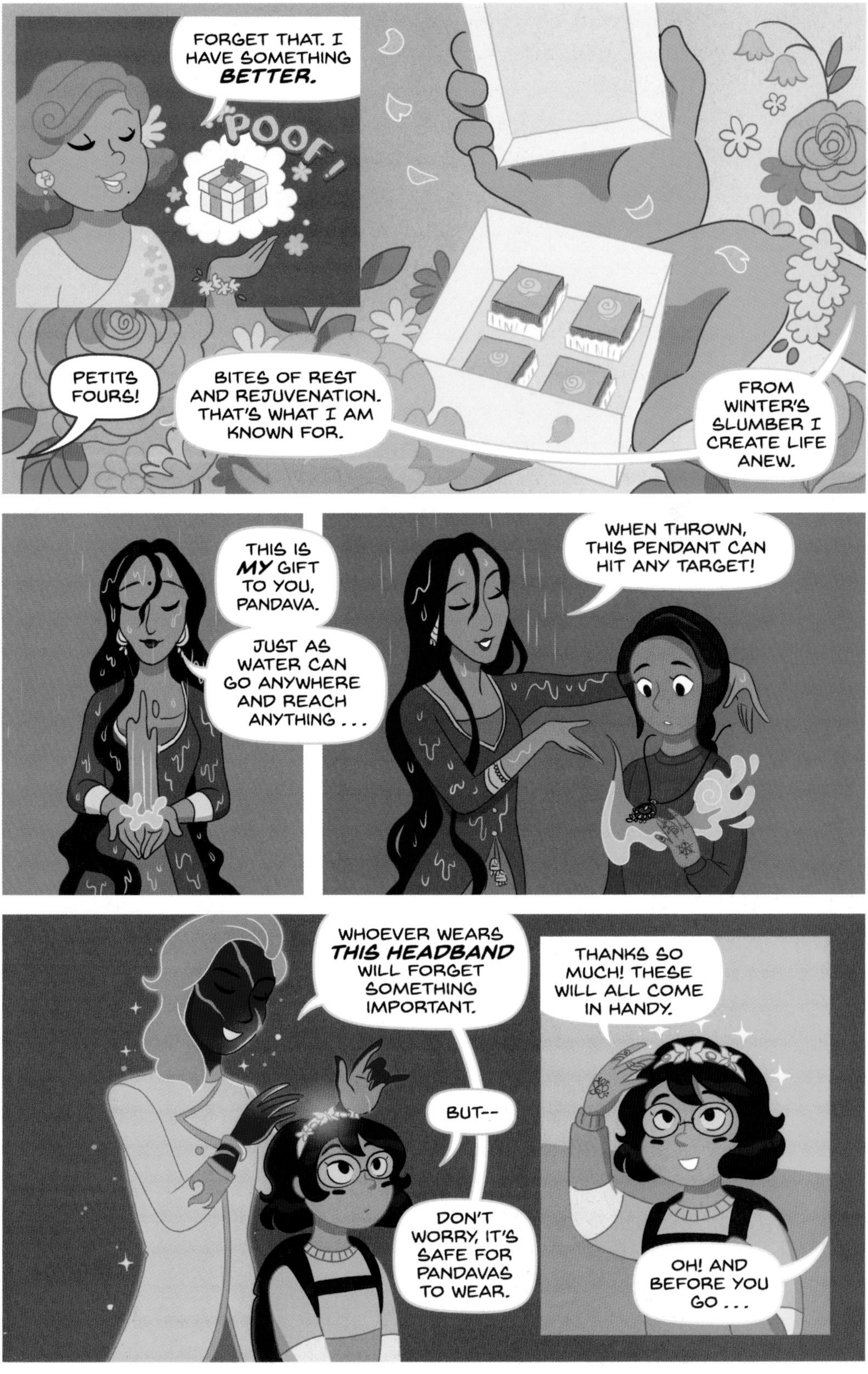
FORGET THAT. I HAVE SOMETHING *BETTER.*
POOF!
PETITS FOURS!
BITES OF REST AND REJUVENATION. THAT'S WHAT I AM KNOWN FOR.
FROM WINTER'S SLUMBER I CREATE LIFE ANEW.
THIS IS *MY* GIFT TO YOU, PANDAVA.
JUST AS WATER CAN GO ANYWHERE AND REACH ANYTHING . . .
WHEN THROWN, THIS PENDANT CAN HIT ANY TARGET!
WHOEVER WEARS ***THIS HEADBAND*** WILL FORGET SOMETHING IMPORTANT.
BUT--
DON'T WORRY, IT'S SAFE FOR PANDAVAS TO WEAR.
THANKS SO MUCH! THESE WILL ALL COME IN HANDY.
OH! AND BEFORE YOU GO . . .

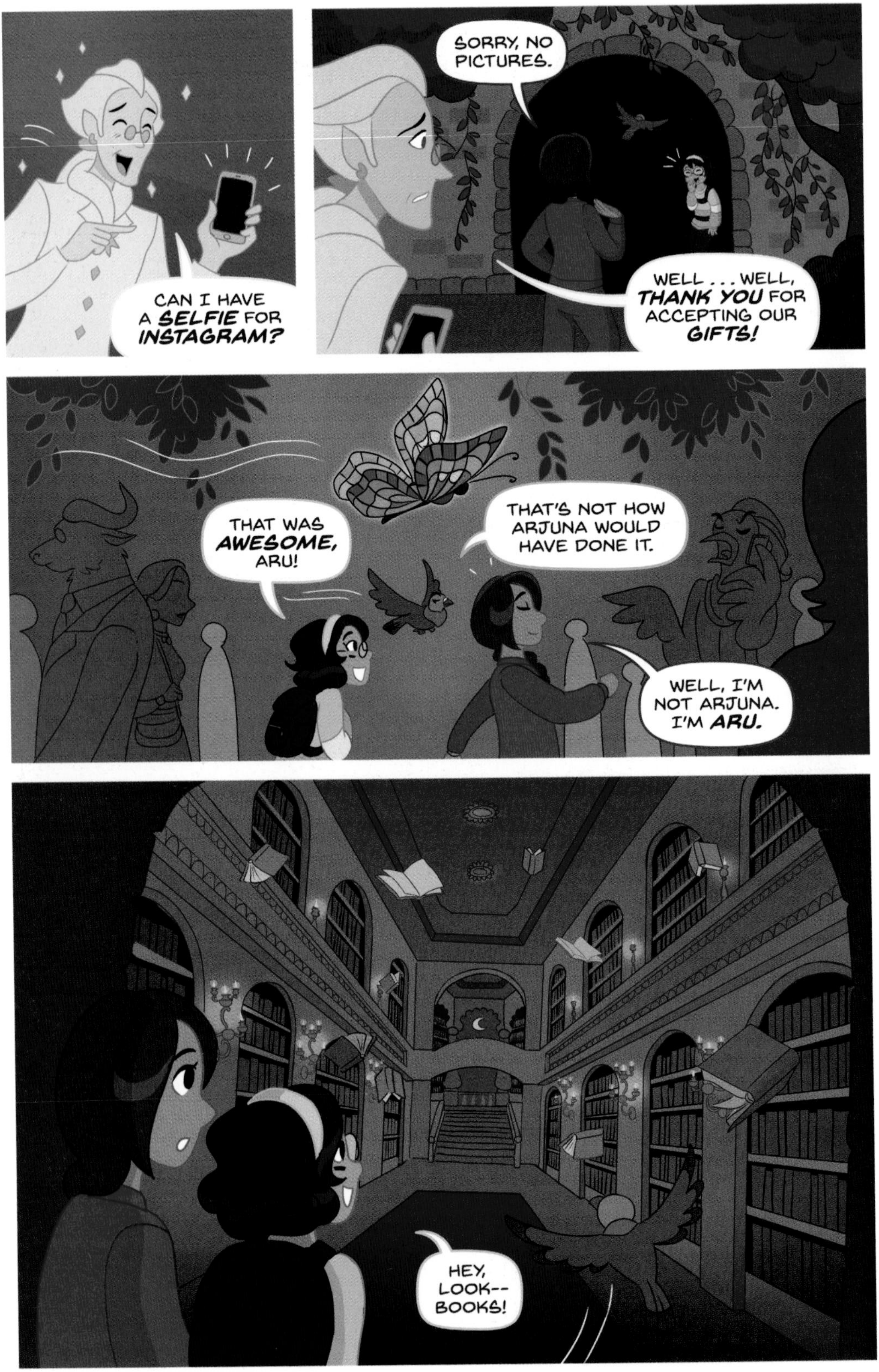
CAN I HAVE A SELFIE FOR INSTAGRAM?
SORRY, NO PICTURES.
WELL . . . WELL, THANK YOU FOR ACCEPTING OUR GIFTS!
THAT WAS AWESOME, ARU!
THAT'S NOT HOW ARJUNA WOULD HAVE DONE IT.
WELL, I'M NOT ARJUNA. I'M ARU.
HEY, LOOK-- BOOKS!

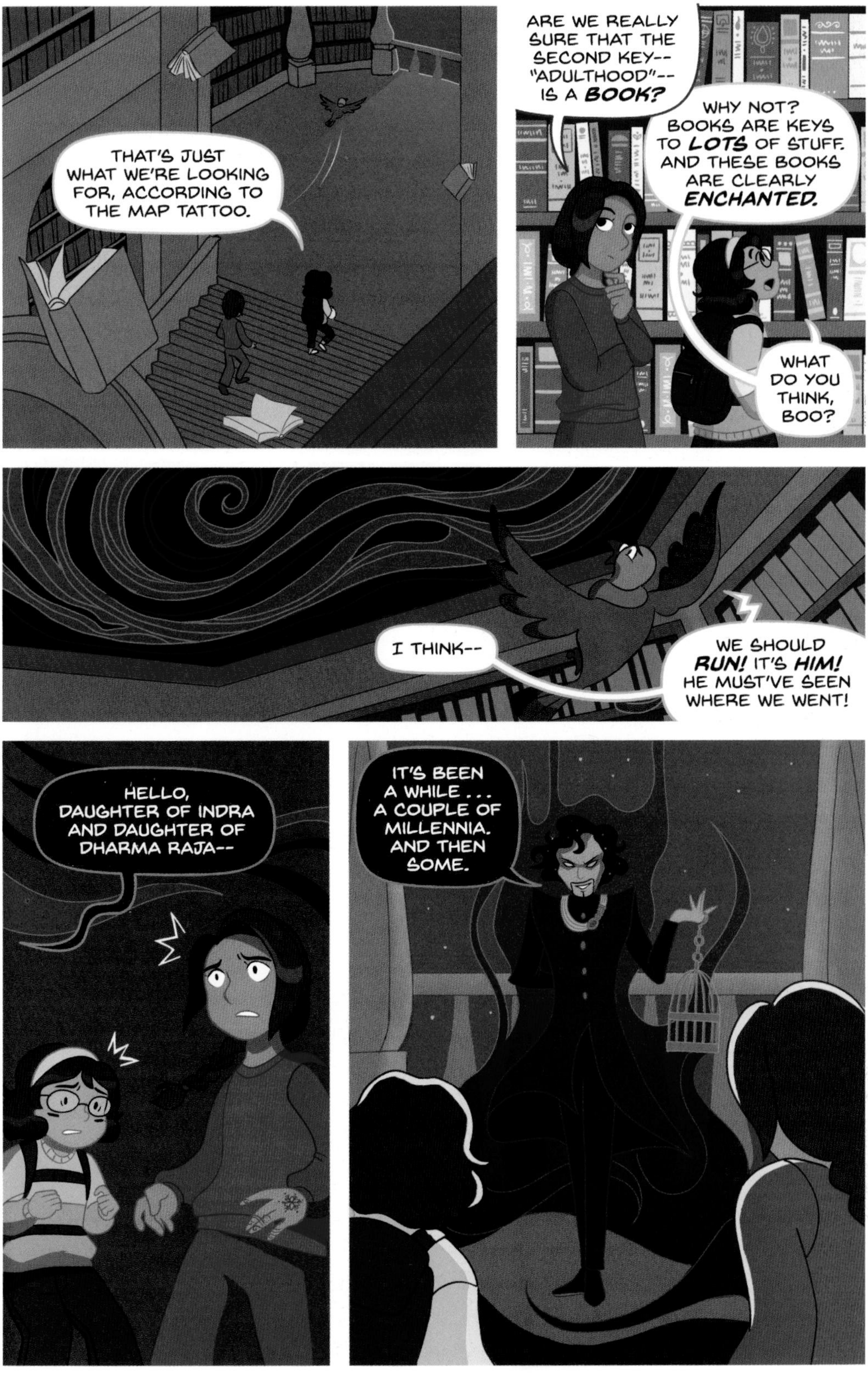
THAT'S JUST WHAT WE'RE LOOKING FOR, ACCORDING TO THE MAP TATTOO.
ARE WE REALLY SURE THAT THE SECOND KEY-- "ADULTHOOD"-- IS A BOOK?
WHY NOT? BOOKS ARE KEYS TO LOTS OF STUFF. AND THESE BOOKS ARE CLEARLY ENCHANTED.
WHAT DO YOU THINK, BOO?
I THINK--
WE SHOULD RUN! IT'S HIM! HE MUST'VE SEEN WHERE WE WENT!
HELLO, DAUGHTER OF INDRA AND DAUGHTER OF DHARMA RAJA--
IT'S BEEN A WHILE . . . A COUPLE OF MILLENNIA. AND THEN SOME.

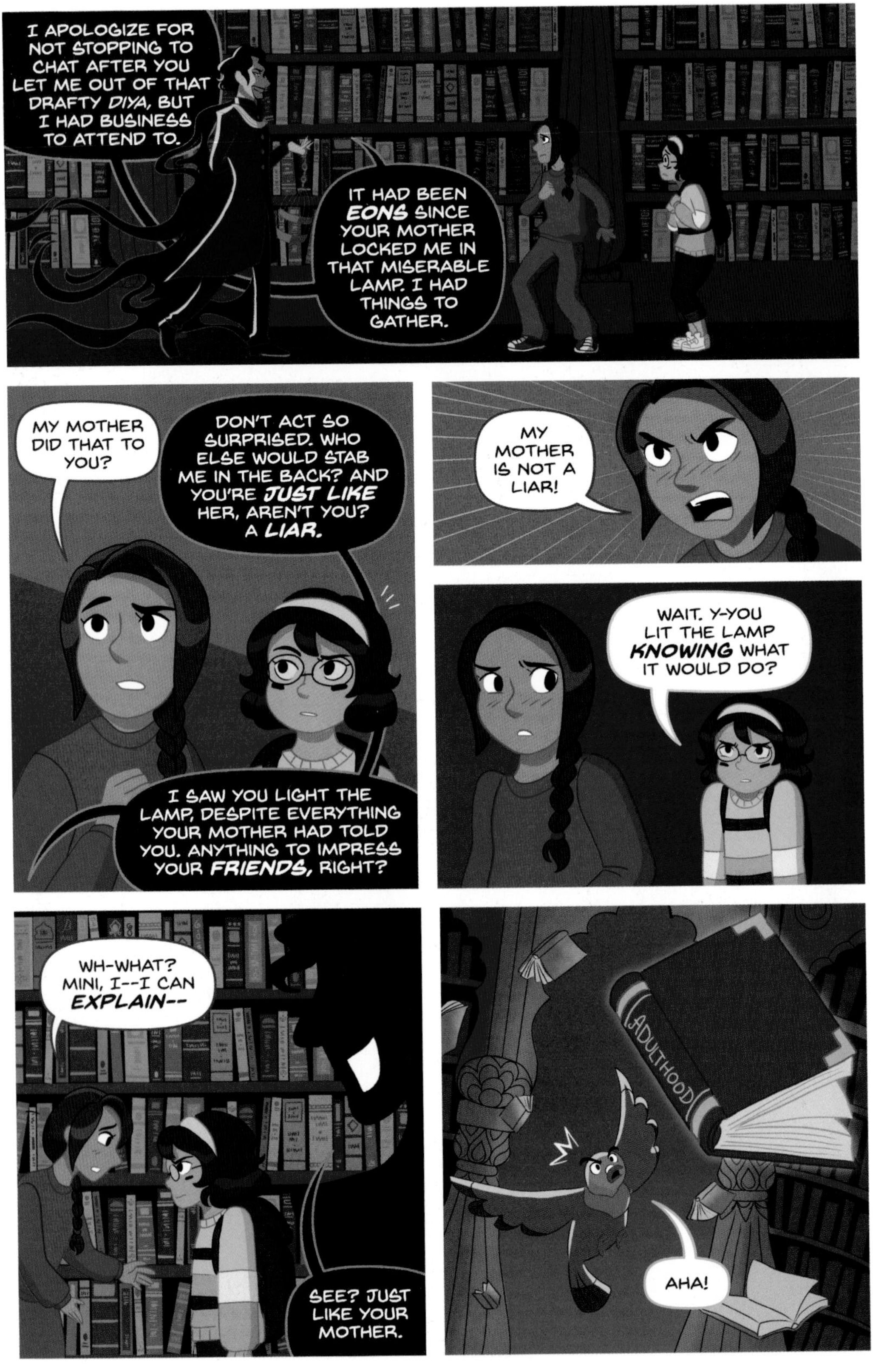
I APOLOGIZE FOR NOT STOPPING TO CHAT AFTER YOU LET ME OUT OF THAT DRAFTY *DIYA*, BUT I HAD BUSINESS TO ATTEND TO.
IT HAD BEEN **EONS** SINCE YOUR MOTHER LOCKED ME IN THAT MISERABLE LAMP. I HAD THINGS TO GATHER.
MY MOTHER DID THAT TO YOU?
DON'T ACT SO SURPRISED. WHO ELSE WOULD STAB ME IN THE BACK? AND YOU'RE ***JUST LIKE*** HER, AREN'T YOU? A ***LIAR.***
I SAW YOU LIGHT THE LAMP, DESPITE EVERYTHING YOUR MOTHER HAD TOLD YOU. ANYTHING TO IMPRESS YOUR ***FRIENDS,*** RIGHT?
MY MOTHER IS NOT A LIAR!
WAIT. Y-YOU LIT THE LAMP ***KNOWING*** WHAT IT WOULD DO?
WH-WHAT? MINI, I--I CAN ***EXPLAIN--***
SEE? JUST LIKE YOUR MOTHER.
ADULTHOOD
AHA!

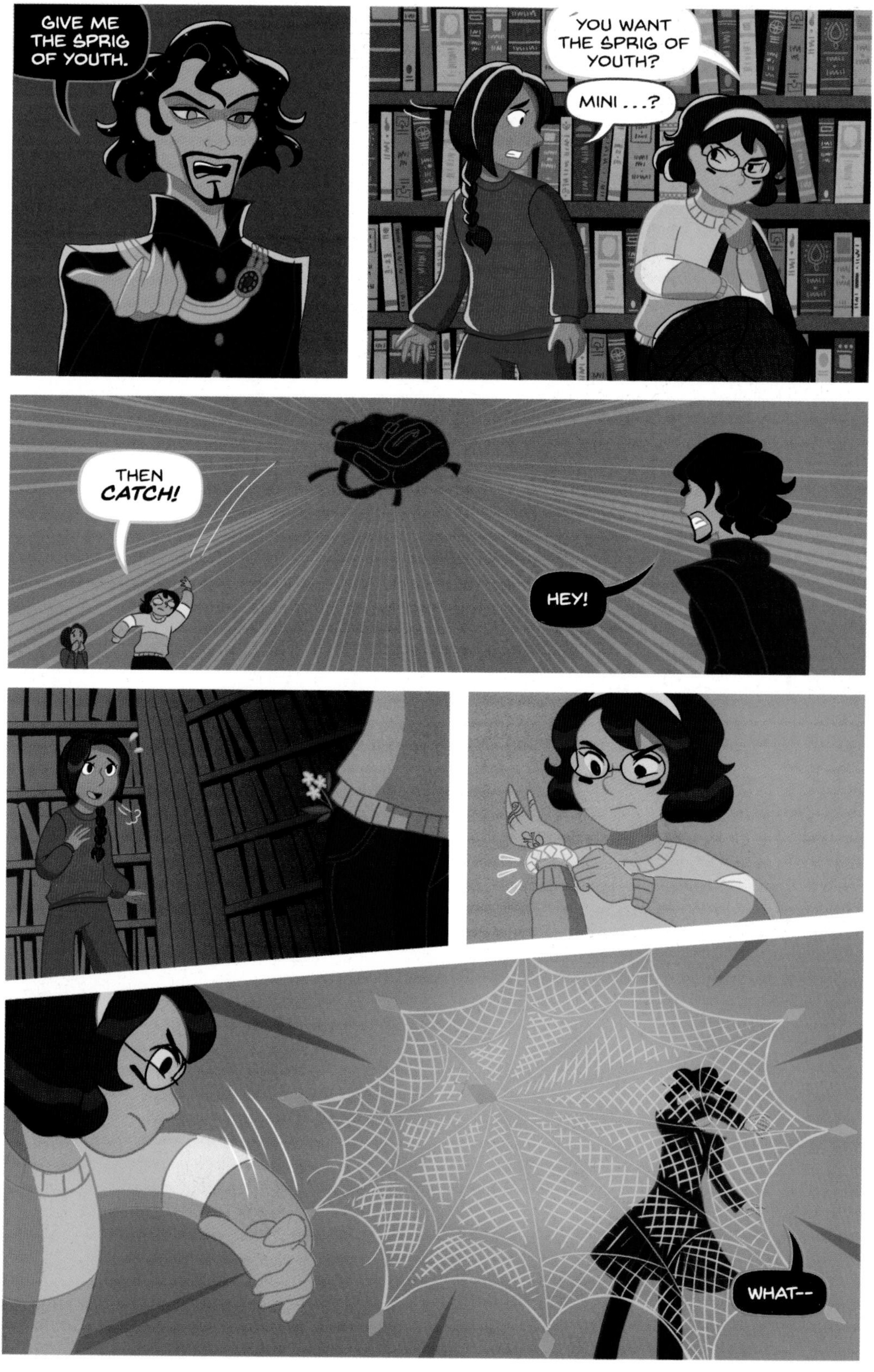
GIVE ME THE SPRIG OF YOUTH.
YOU WANT THE SPRIG OF YOUTH?
MINI . . .?
THEN CATCH!
HEY!
WHAT--

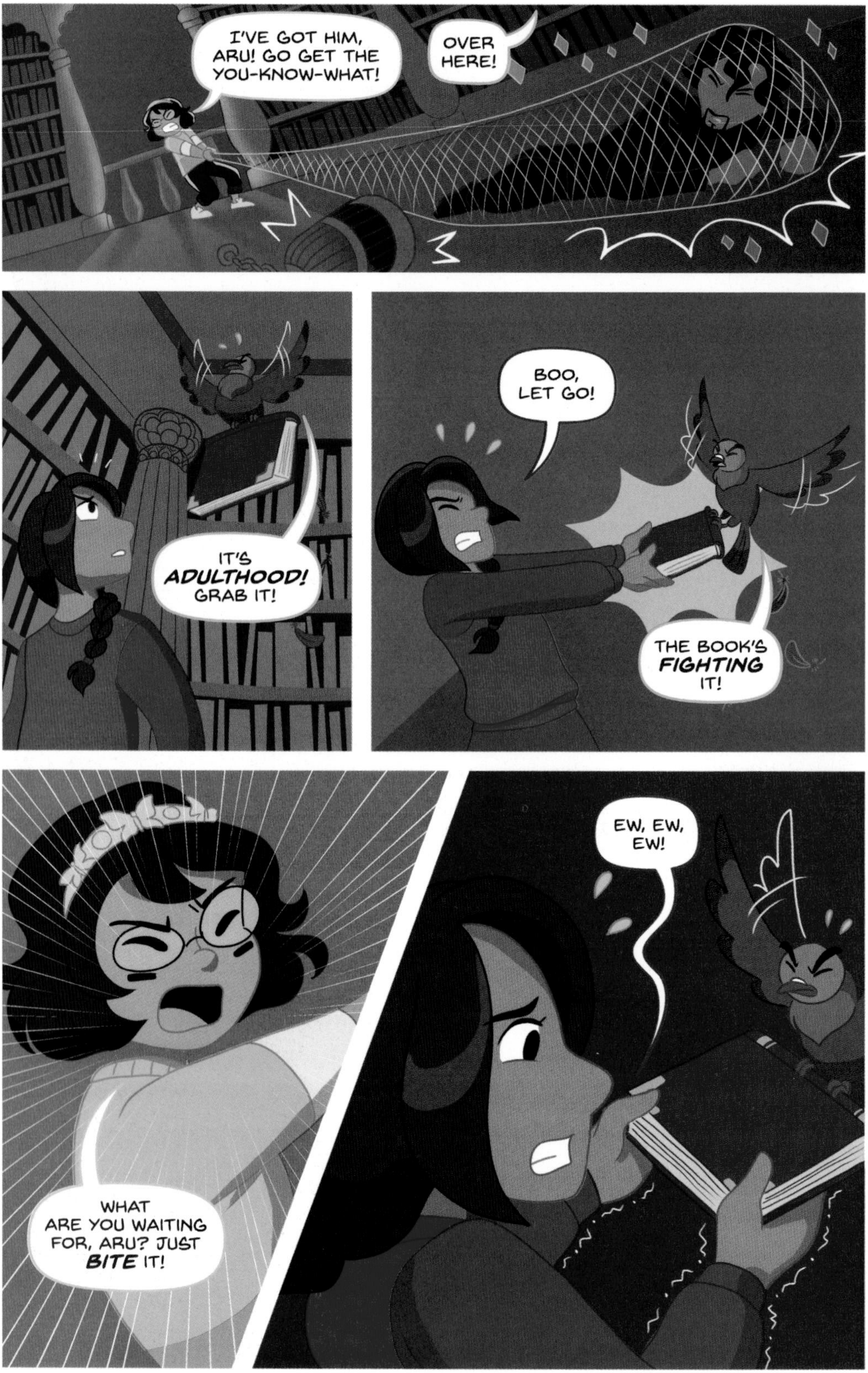
I'VE GOT HIM, ARU! GO GET THE YOU-KNOW-WHAT!
OVER HERE!
IT'S **ADULTHOOD!** GRAB IT!
BOO, LET GO!
THE BOOK'S **FIGHTING** IT!
WHAT ARE YOU WAITING FOR, ARU? JUST **BITE** IT!
EW, EW, EW!

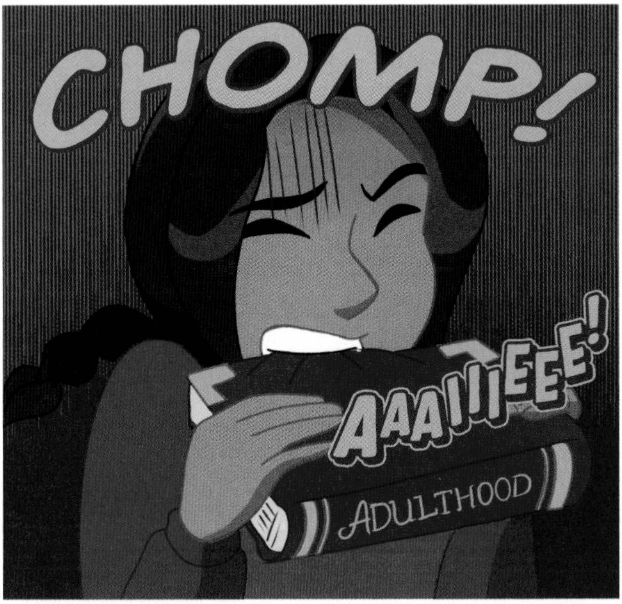
CHOMP!
AAAIIIEEE!
ADULTHOOD

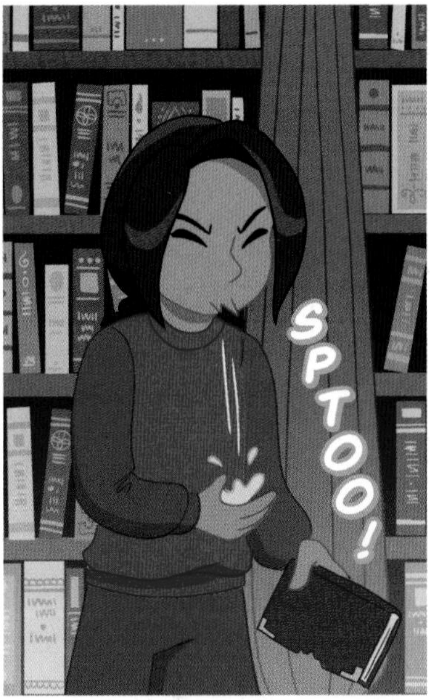
SPTOOO!

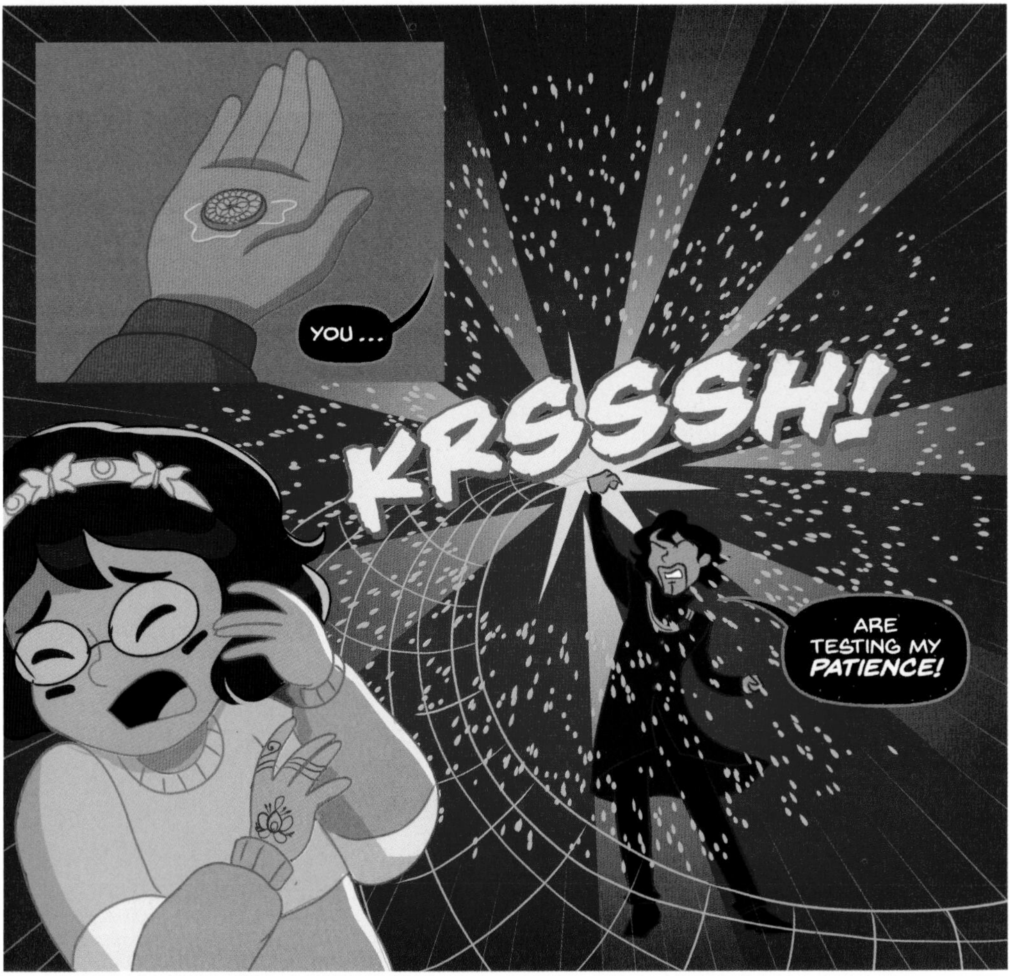
YOU...
KRSSSH!
ARE TESTING MY PATIENCE!

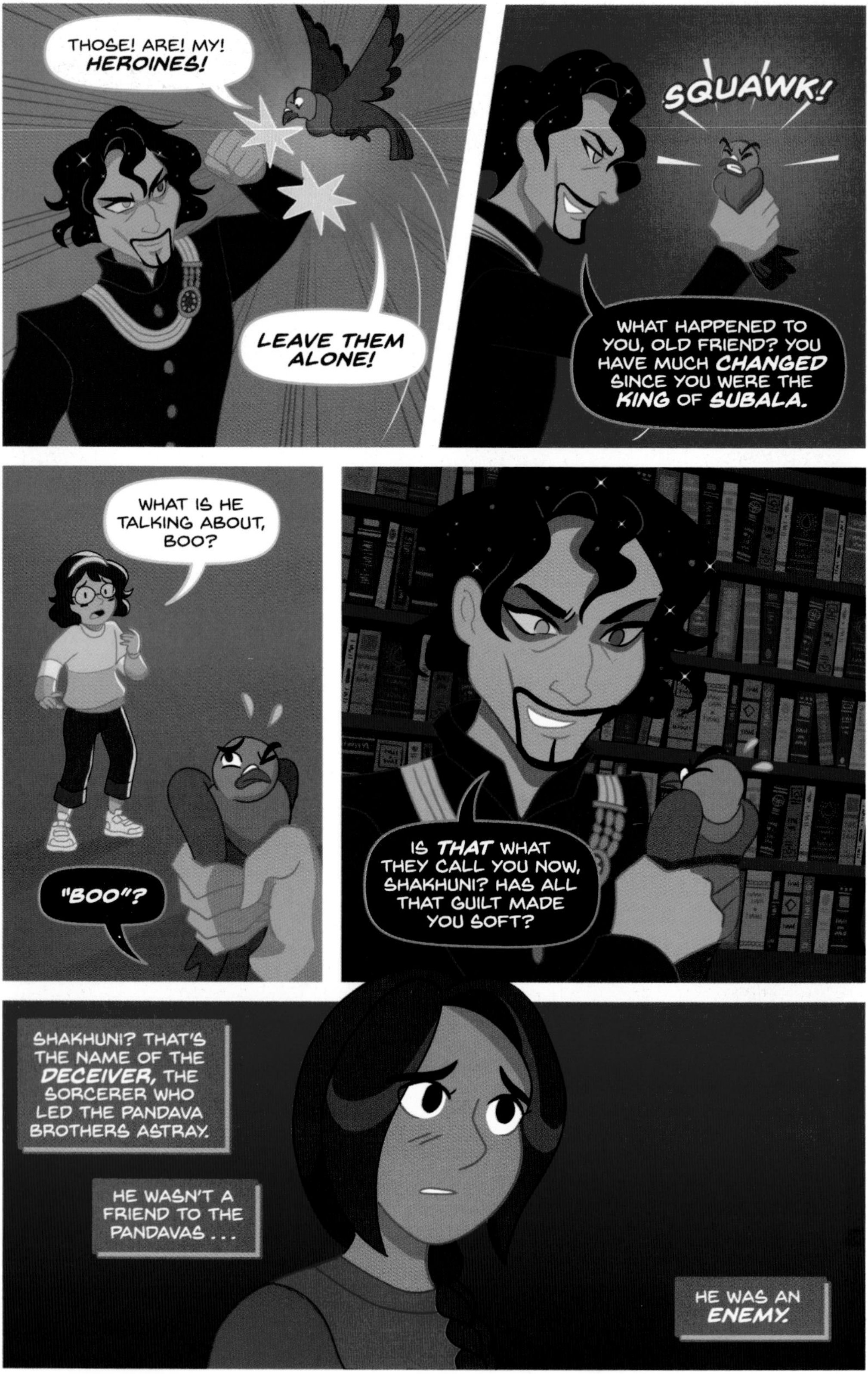
THOSE! ARE! MY! HEROINES!
LEAVE THEM ALONE!
SQUAWK!
WHAT HAPPENED TO YOU, OLD FRIEND? YOU HAVE MUCH CHANGED SINCE YOU WERE THE KING OF SUBALA.
WHAT IS HE TALKING ABOUT, BOO?
"BOO"?
IS THAT WHAT THEY CALL YOU NOW, SHAKHUNI? HAS ALL THAT GUILT MADE YOU SOFT?
SHAKHUNI? THAT'S THE NAME OF THE DECEIVER, THE SORCERER WHO LED THE PANDAVA BROTHERS ASTRAY.
HE WASN'T A FRIEND TO THE PANDAVAS . . .
HE WAS AN ENEMY.

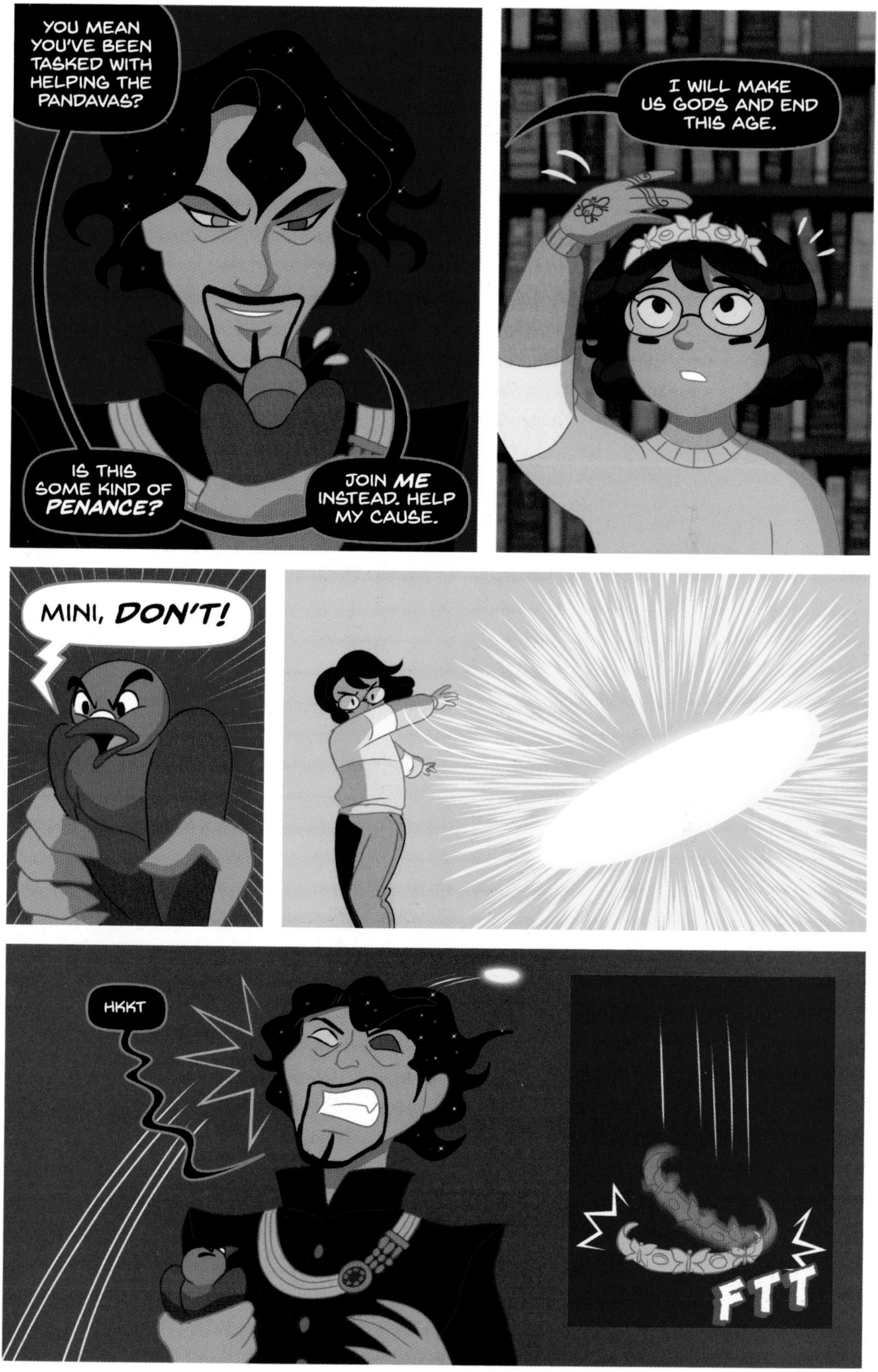
YOU MEAN YOU'VE BEEN TASKED WITH HELPING THE PANDAVAS?
IS THIS SOME KIND OF PENANCE?
JOIN ME INSTEAD. HELP MY CAUSE.
I WILL MAKE US GODS AND END THIS AGE.
MINI, DON'T!
HKKT
FTT

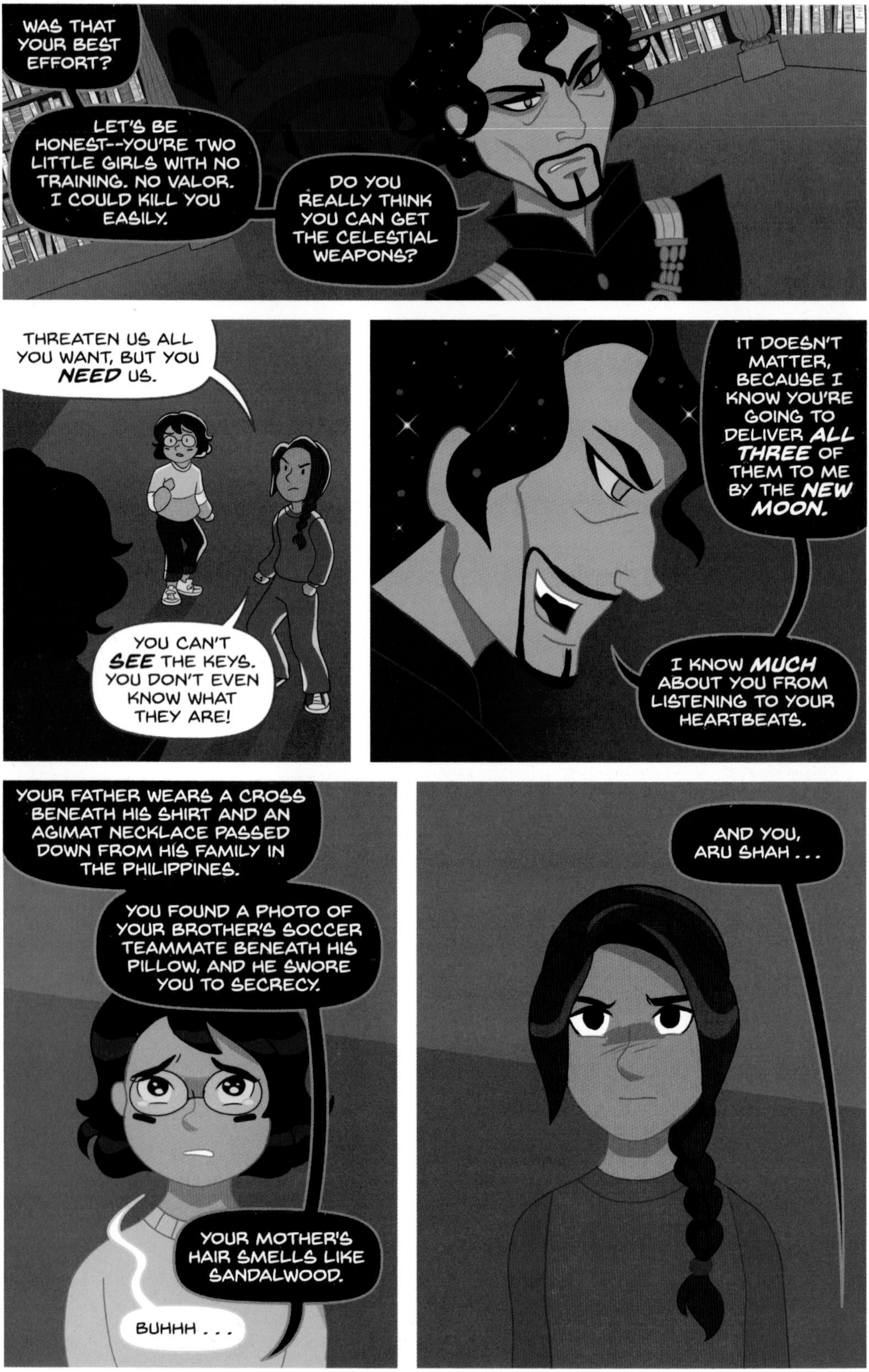
WAS THAT YOUR BEST EFFORT?
LET'S BE HONEST--YOU'RE TWO LITTLE GIRLS WITH NO TRAINING. NO VALOR. I COULD KILL YOU EASILY.
DO YOU REALLY THINK YOU CAN GET THE CELESTIAL WEAPONS?
THREATEN US ALL YOU WANT, BUT YOU NEED US.
YOU CAN'T SEE THE KEYS. YOU DON'T EVEN KNOW WHAT THEY ARE!
IT DOESN'T MATTER, BECAUSE I KNOW YOU'RE GOING TO DELIVER ALL THREE OF THEM TO ME BY THE NEW MOON.
I KNOW MUCH ABOUT YOU FROM LISTENING TO YOUR HEARTBEATS.
YOUR FATHER WEARS A CROSS BENEATH HIS SHIRT AND AN AGIMAT NECKLACE PASSED DOWN FROM HIS FAMILY IN THE PHILIPPINES.
YOU FOUND A PHOTO OF YOUR BROTHER'S SOCCER TEAMMATE BENEATH HIS PILLOW, AND HE SWORE YOU TO SECRECY.
YOUR MOTHER'S HAIR SMELLS LIKE SANDALWOOD.
BUHHH . . .
AND YOU, ARU SHAH . . .

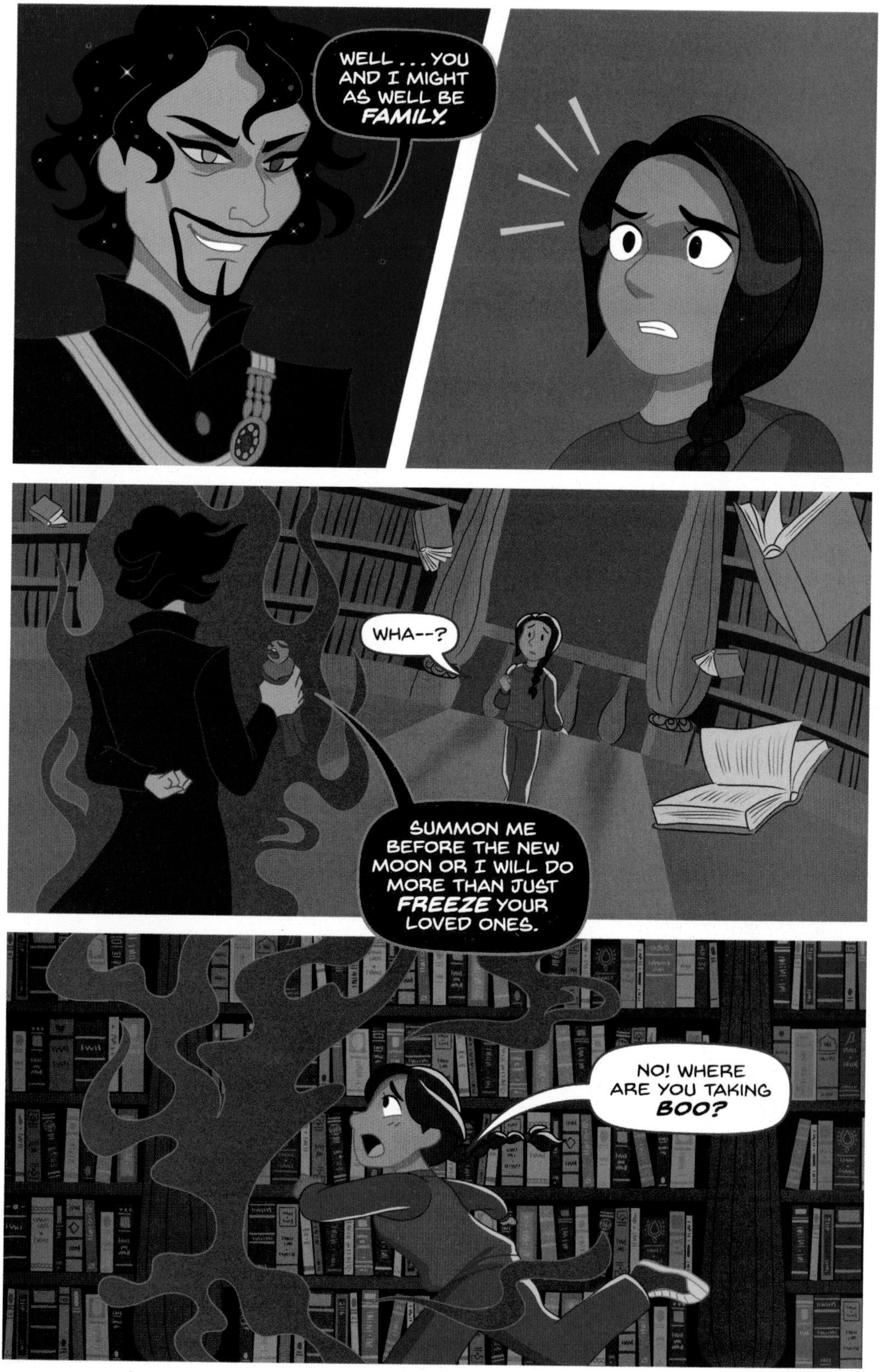
WELL . . . YOU AND I MIGHT AS WELL BE FAMILY.
WHA--?
SUMMON ME BEFORE THE NEW MOON OR I WILL DO MORE THAN JUST FREEZE YOUR LOVED ONES.
NO! WHERE ARE YOU TAKING BOO?

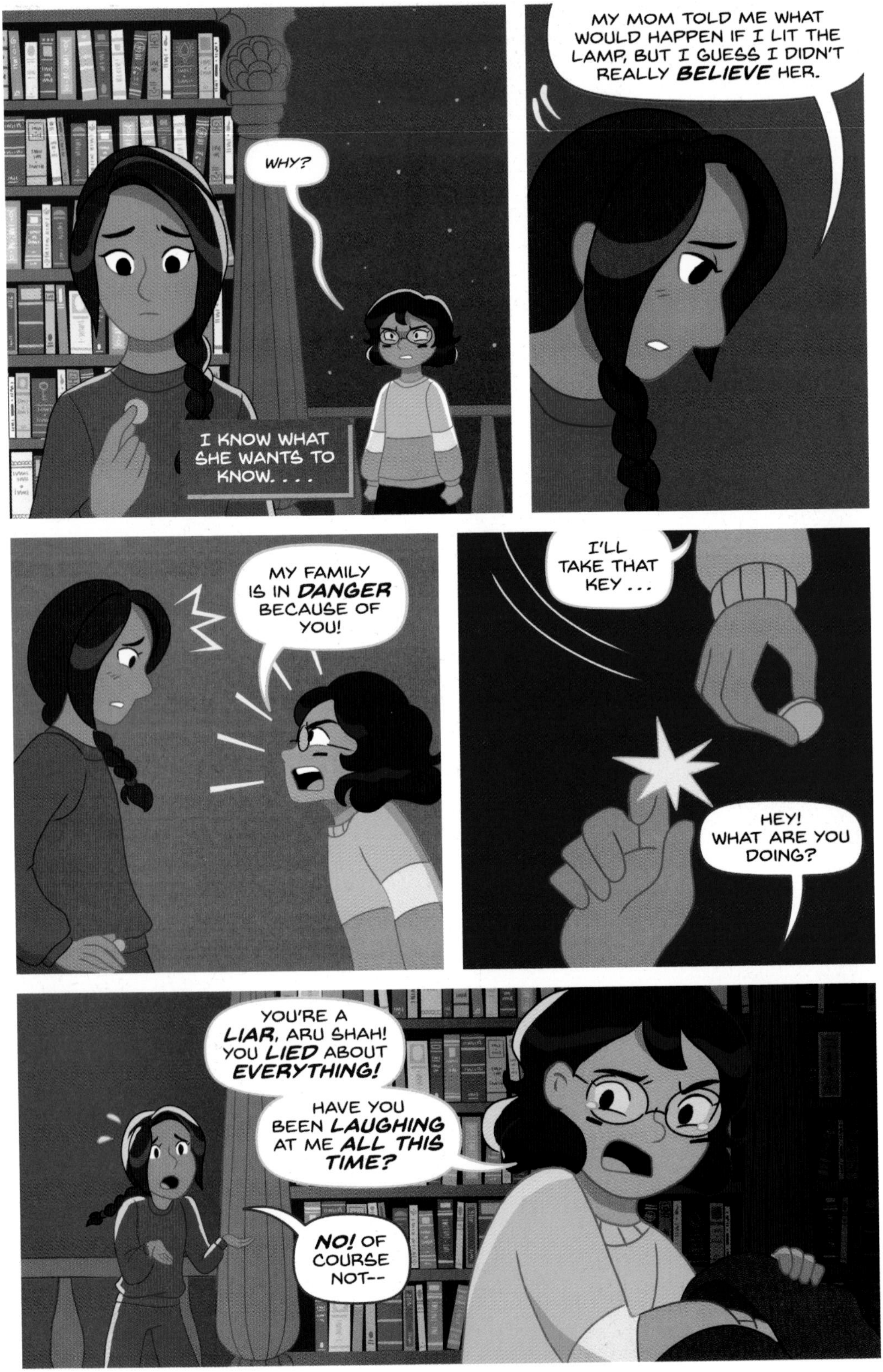
WHY?
I KNOW WHAT SHE WANTS TO KNOW. . . .
MY MOM TOLD ME WHAT WOULD HAPPEN IF I LIT THE LAMP, BUT I GUESS I DIDN'T REALLY BELIEVE HER.
MY FAMILY IS IN DANGER BECAUSE OF YOU!
I'LL TAKE THAT KEY . . .
HEY! WHAT ARE YOU DOING?
YOU'RE A LIAR, ARU SHAH! YOU LIED ABOUT EVERYTHING!
HAVE YOU BEEN LAUGHING AT ME ALL THIS TIME?
NO! OF COURSE NOT--

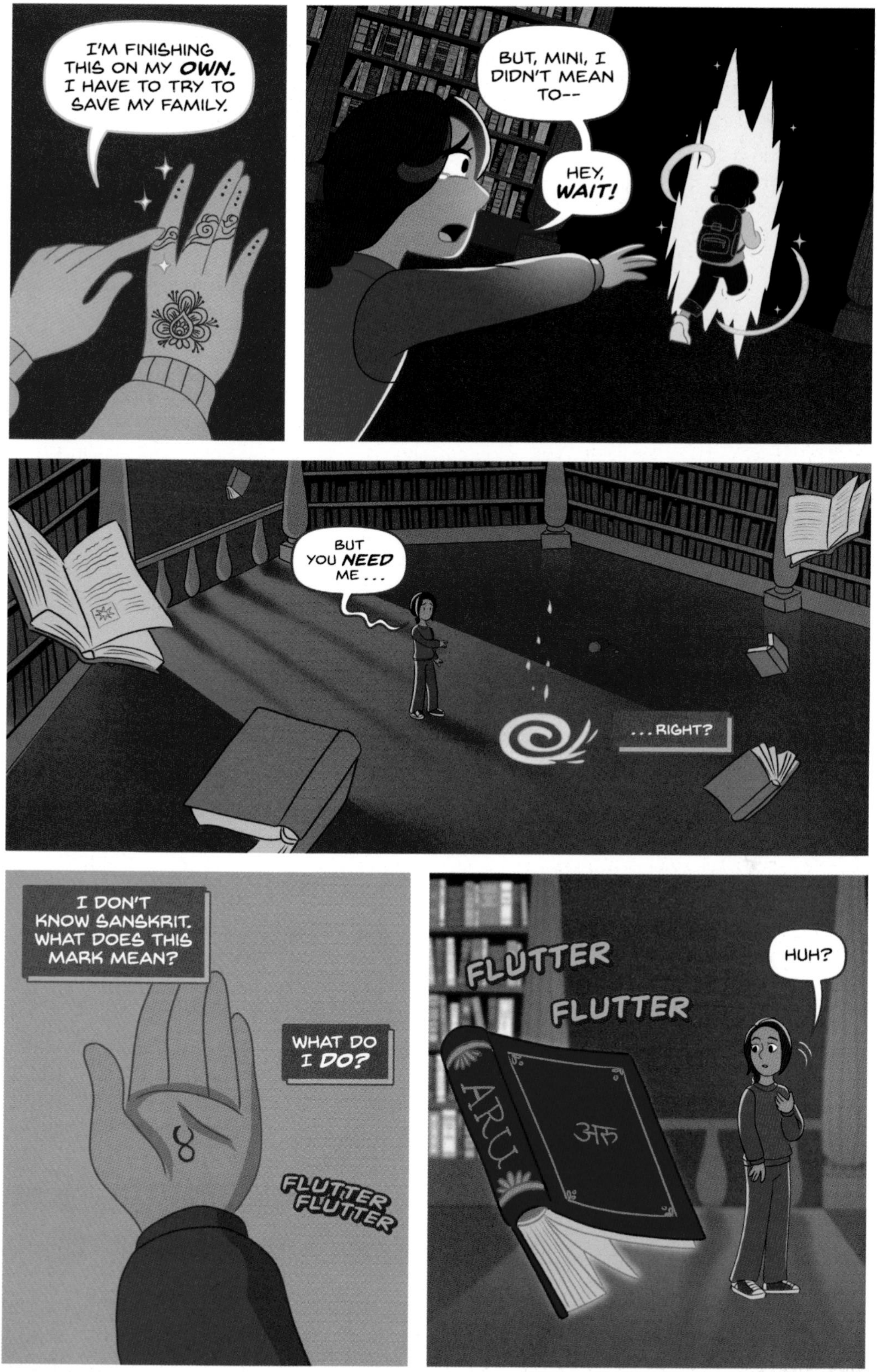
I'M FINISHING THIS ON MY OWN. I HAVE TO TRY TO SAVE MY FAMILY.
BUT, MINI, I DIDN'T MEAN TO--
HEY, WAIT!
BUT YOU NEED ME . . .
. . . RIGHT?
I DON'T KNOW SANSKRIT. WHAT DOES THIS MARK MEAN?
WHAT DO I DO?
FLUTTER FLUTTER
FLUTTER
FLUTTER
HUH?
ARU
अरु

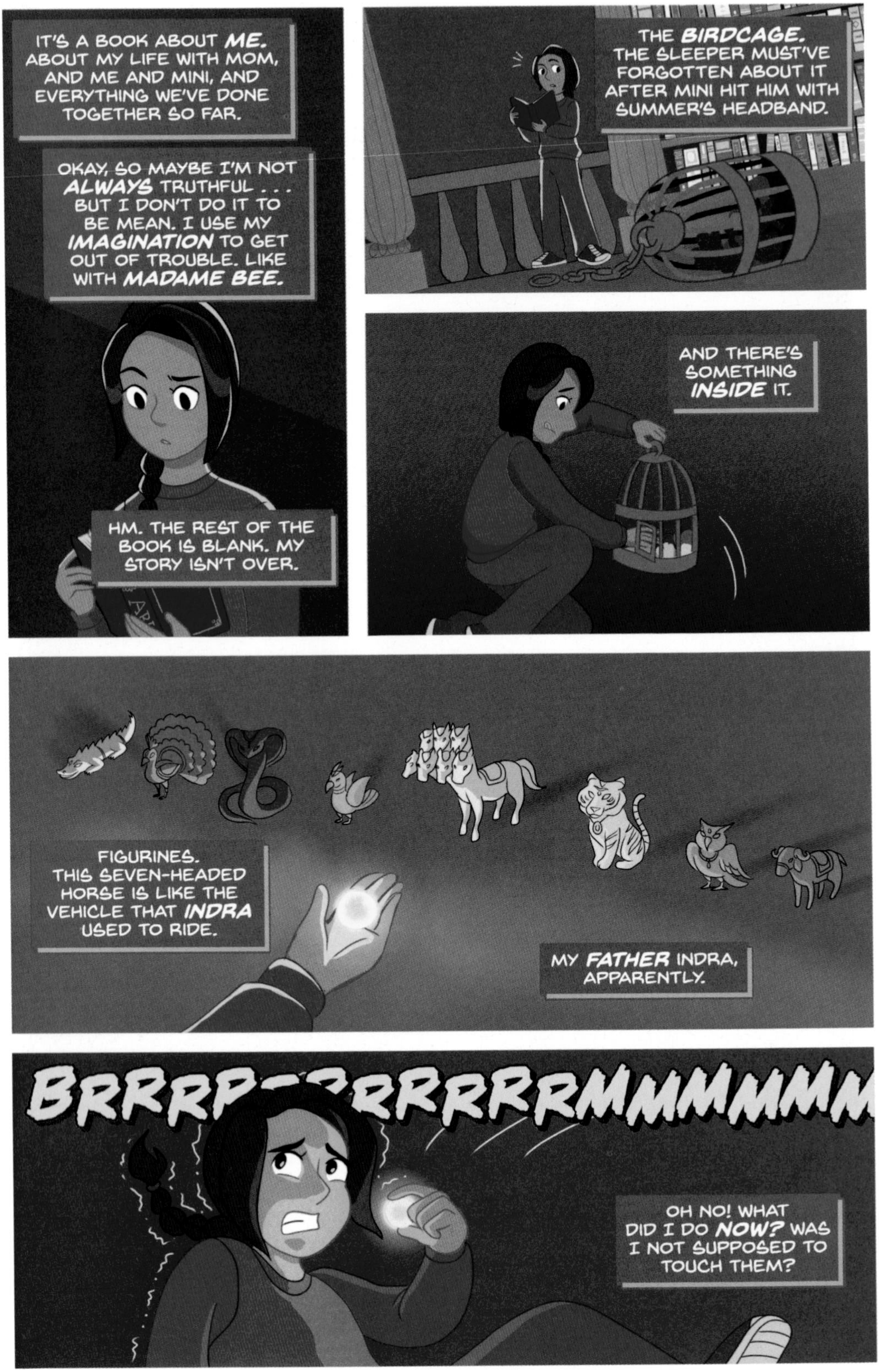
IT'S A BOOK ABOUT ME. ABOUT MY LIFE WITH MOM, AND ME AND MINI, AND EVERYTHING WE'VE DONE TOGETHER SO FAR.
OKAY, SO MAYBE I'M NOT ALWAYS TRUTHFUL . . . BUT I DON'T DO IT TO BE MEAN. I USE MY IMAGINATION TO GET OUT OF TROUBLE. LIKE WITH MADAME BEE.
HM. THE REST OF THE BOOK IS BLANK. MY STORY ISN'T OVER.
THE BIRDCAGE. THE SLEEPER MUST'VE FORGOTTEN ABOUT IT AFTER MINI HIT HIM WITH SUMMER'S HEADBAND.
AND THERE'S SOMETHING INSIDE IT.
FIGURINES. THIS SEVEN-HEADED HORSE IS LIKE THE VEHICLE THAT INDRA USED TO RIDE.
MY FATHER INDRA, APPARENTLY.
BRRRP—RRRRRRRMMMMMM
OH NO! WHAT DID I DO NOW? WAS I NOT SUPPOSED TO TOUCH THEM?

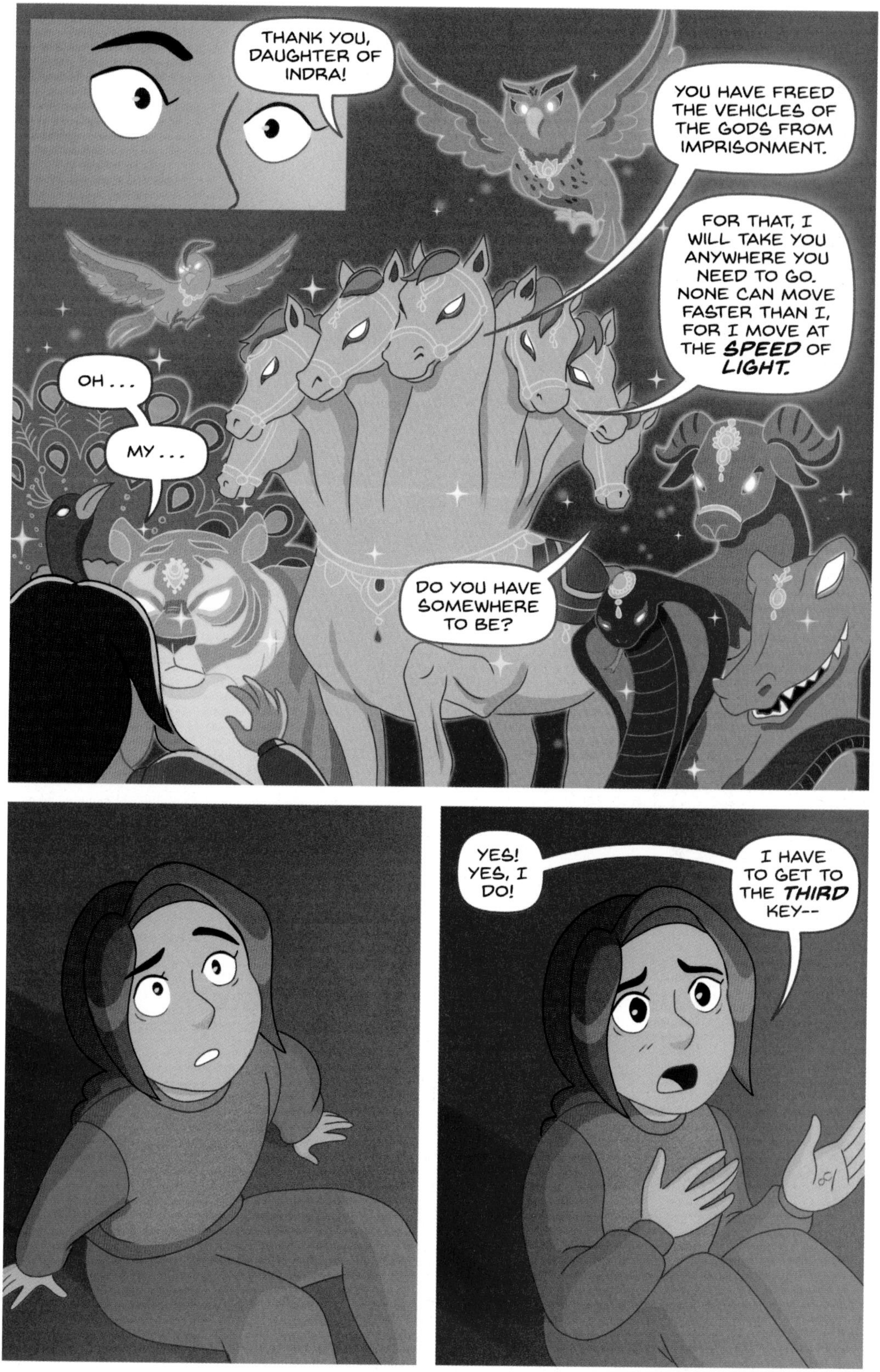
THANK YOU, DAUGHTER OF INDRA!
YOU HAVE FREED THE VEHICLES OF THE GODS FROM IMPRISONMENT.
FOR THAT, I WILL TAKE YOU ANYWHERE YOU NEED TO GO. NONE CAN MOVE FASTER THAN I, FOR I MOVE AT THE SPEED OF LIGHT.
OH . . .
MY . . .
DO YOU HAVE SOMEWHERE TO BE?
YES! YES, I DO!
I HAVE TO GET TO THE THIRD KEY--

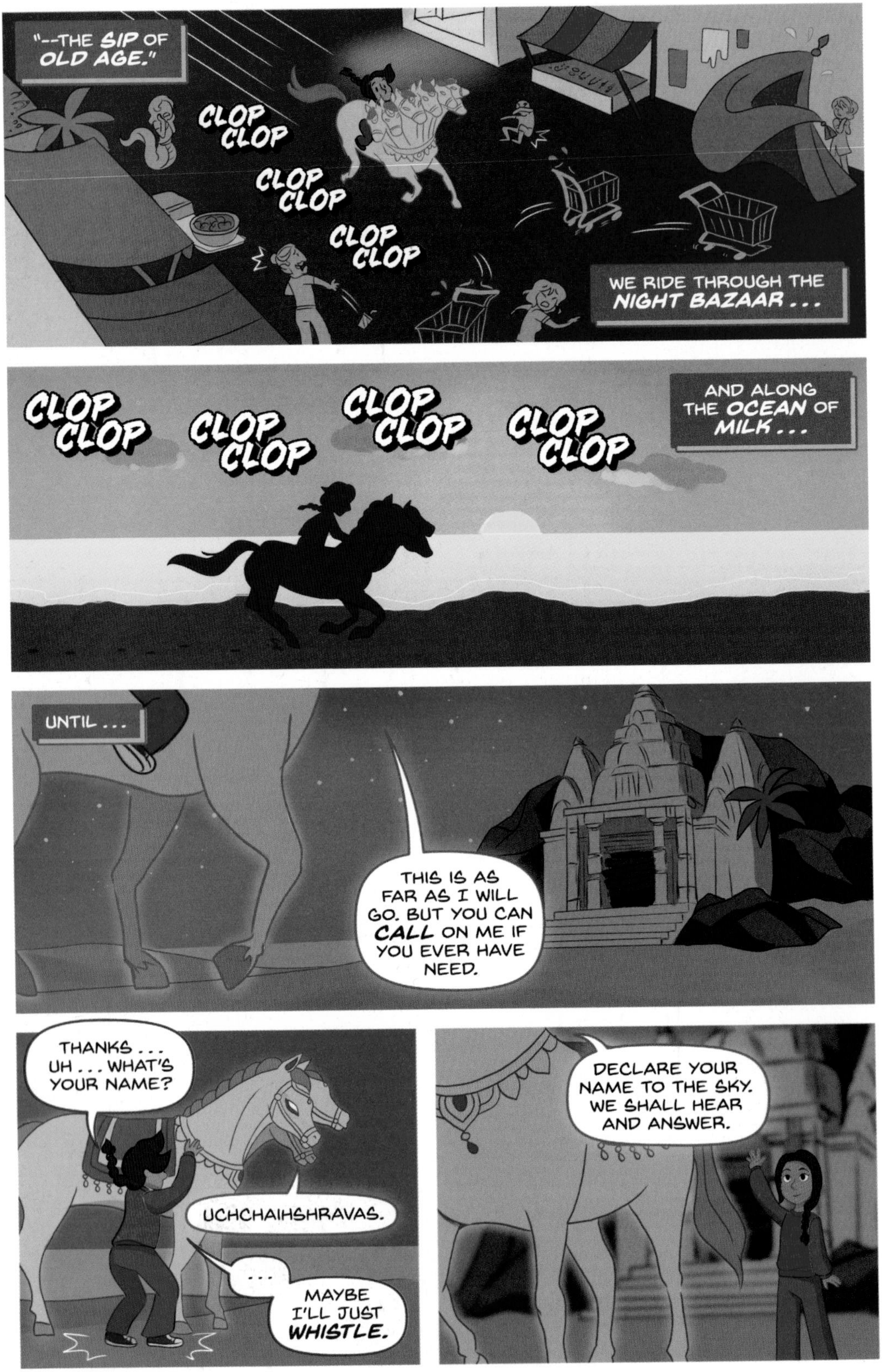
"--THE SIP OF OLD AGE."
CLOP CLOP
CLOP CLOP
CLOP CLOP
WE RIDE THROUGH THE NIGHT BAZAAR . . .
CLOP CLOP
CLOP CLOP
CLOP CLOP
CLOP CLOP
AND ALONG THE OCEAN OF MILK . . .
UNTIL . . .
THIS IS AS FAR AS I WILL GO. BUT YOU CAN CALL ON ME IF YOU EVER HAVE NEED.
THANKS . . . UH . . . WHAT'S YOUR NAME?
UCHCHAIHSHRAVAS.
. . .
MAYBE I'LL JUST WHISTLE.
DECLARE YOUR NAME TO THE SKY. WE SHALL HEAR AND ANSWER.

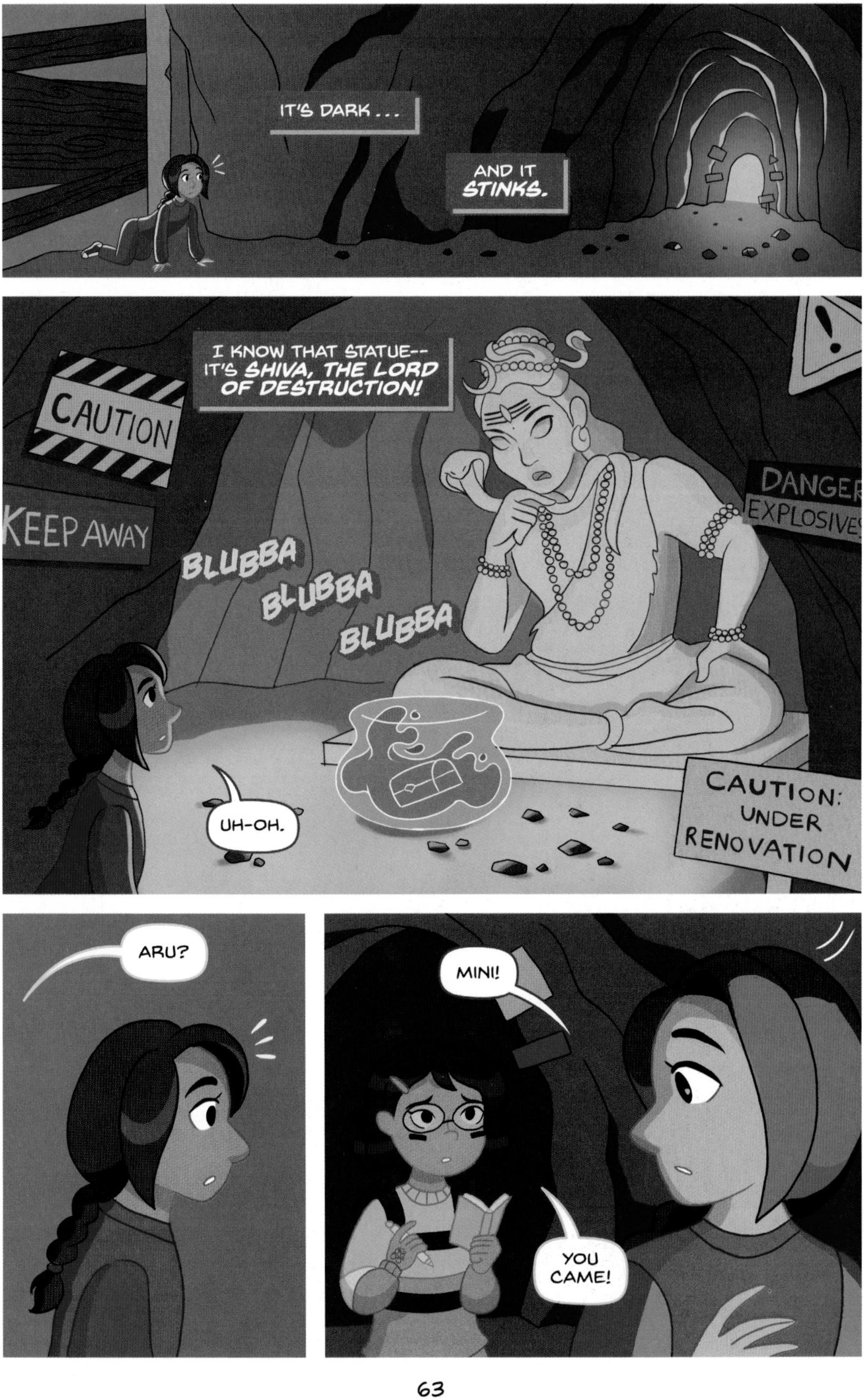
IT'S DARK . . .
AND IT STINKS.
I KNOW THAT STATUE-- IT'S SHIVA, THE LORD OF DESTRUCTION!
CAUTION
KEEP AWAY
DANGER EXPLOSIVES
BLUBBA
BLUBBA
BLUBBA
UH-OH.
CAUTION: UNDER RENOVATION
ARU?
MINI!
YOU CAME!

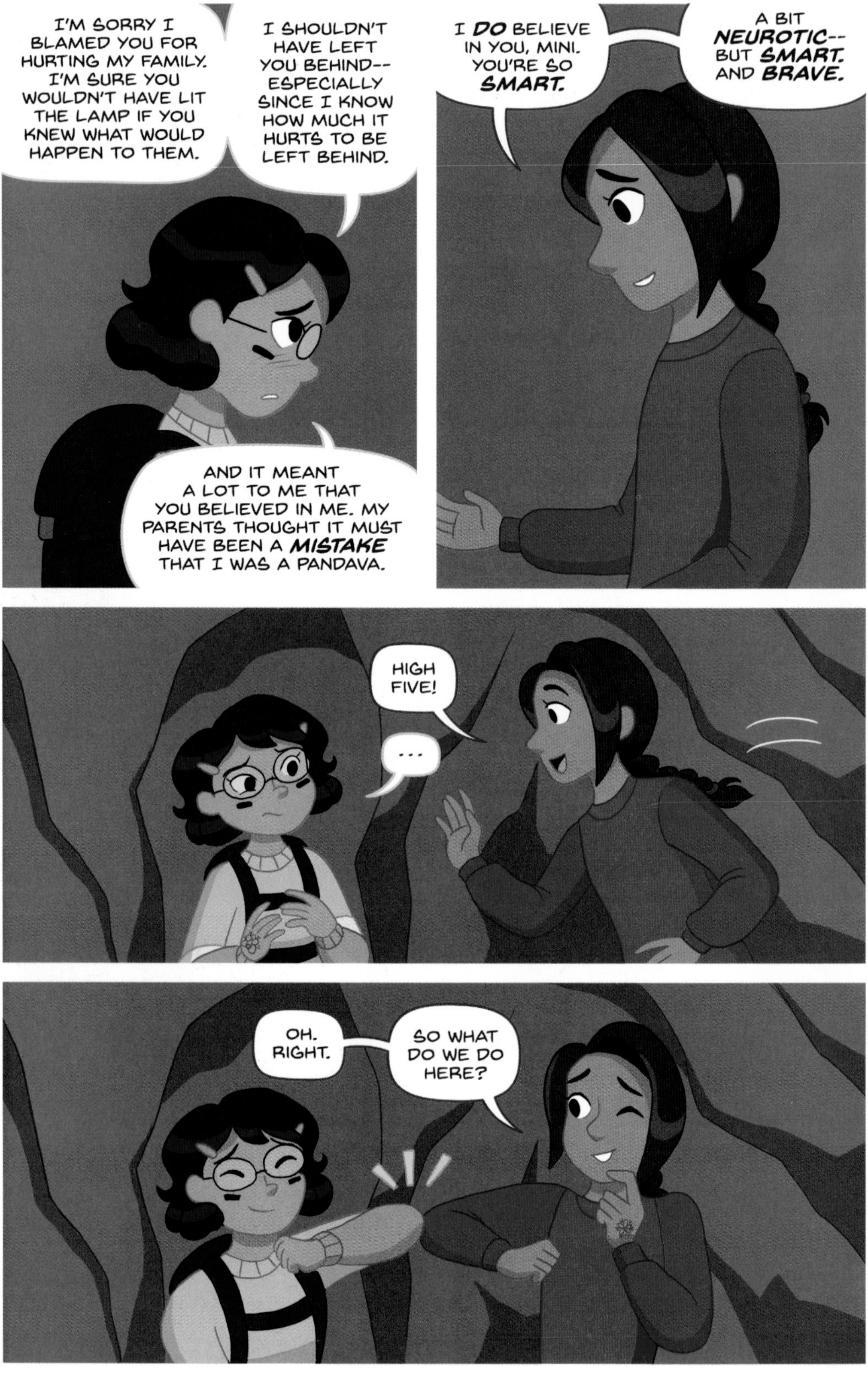
I'M SORRY I BLAMED YOU FOR HURTING MY FAMILY. I'M SURE YOU WOULDN'T HAVE LIT THE LAMP IF YOU KNEW WHAT WOULD HAPPEN TO THEM.
I SHOULDN'T HAVE LEFT YOU BEHIND--ESPECIALLY SINCE I KNOW HOW MUCH IT HURTS TO BE LEFT BEHIND.
AND IT MEANT A LOT TO ME THAT YOU BELIEVED IN ME. MY PARENTS THOUGHT IT MUST HAVE BEEN A MISTAKE THAT I WAS A PANDAVA.
I DO BELIEVE IN YOU, MINI. YOU'RE SO SMART.
A BIT NEUROTIC--BUT SMART. AND BRAVE.
HIGH FIVE!
...
OH. RIGHT.
SO WHAT DO WE DO HERE?

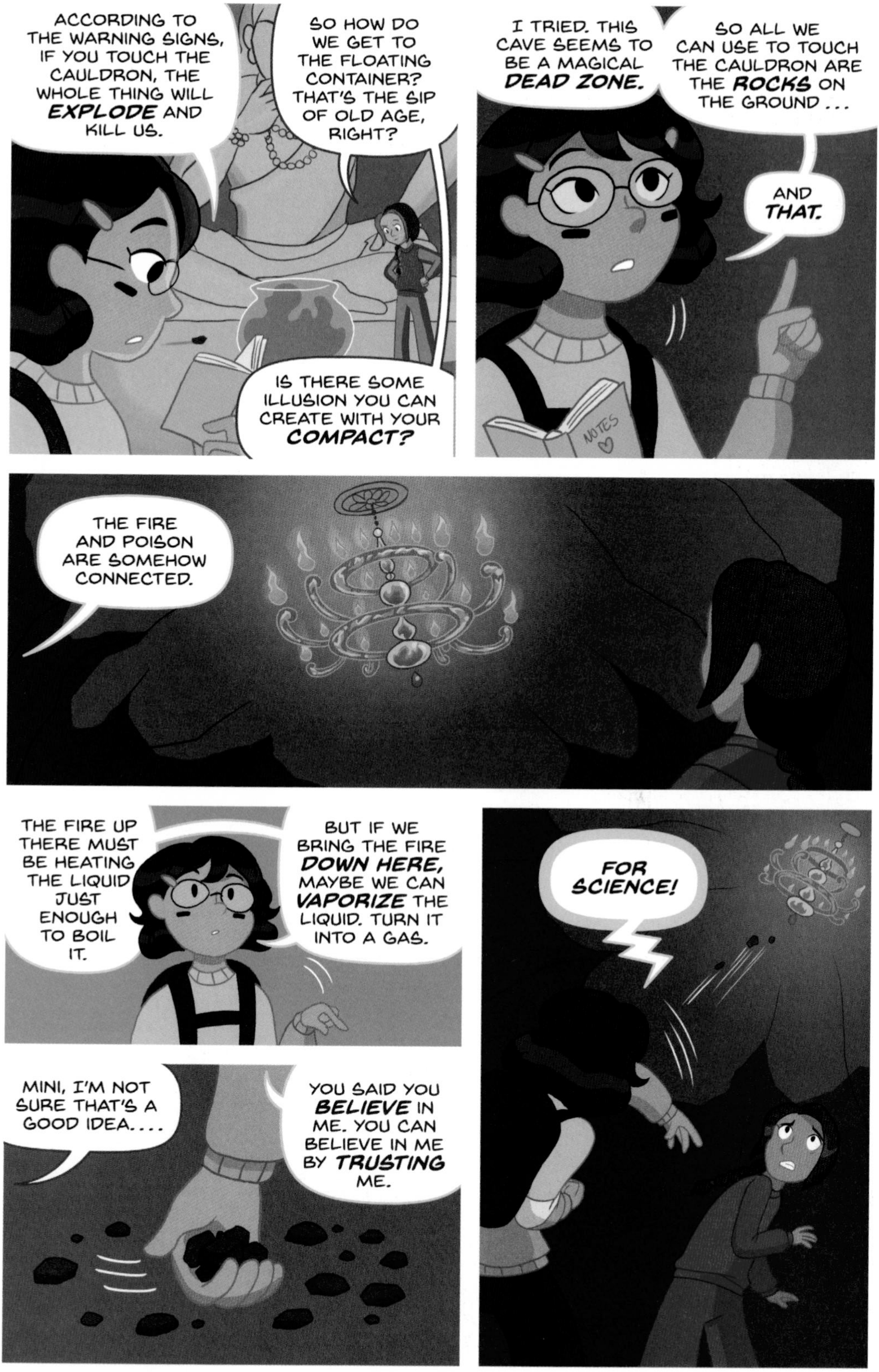
ACCORDING TO THE WARNING SIGNS, IF YOU TOUCH THE CAULDRON, THE WHOLE THING WILL **EXPLODE** AND KILL US.
SO HOW DO WE GET TO THE FLOATING CONTAINER? THAT'S THE SIP OF OLD AGE, RIGHT?
IS THERE SOME ILLUSION YOU CAN CREATE WITH YOUR **COMPACT?**
I TRIED. THIS CAVE SEEMS TO BE A MAGICAL **DEAD ZONE.**
SO ALL WE CAN USE TO TOUCH THE CAULDRON ARE THE **ROCKS** ON THE GROUND . . .
AND **THAT.**
NOTES
THE FIRE AND POISON ARE SOMEHOW CONNECTED.
THE FIRE UP THERE MUST BE HEATING THE LIQUID JUST ENOUGH TO BOIL IT.
BUT IF WE BRING THE FIRE **DOWN HERE,** MAYBE WE CAN **VAPORIZE** THE LIQUID. TURN IT INTO A GAS.
MINI, I'M NOT SURE THAT'S A GOOD IDEA. . . .
YOU SAID YOU **BELIEVE** IN ME. YOU CAN BELIEVE IN ME BY **TRUSTING** ME.
FOR SCIENCE!

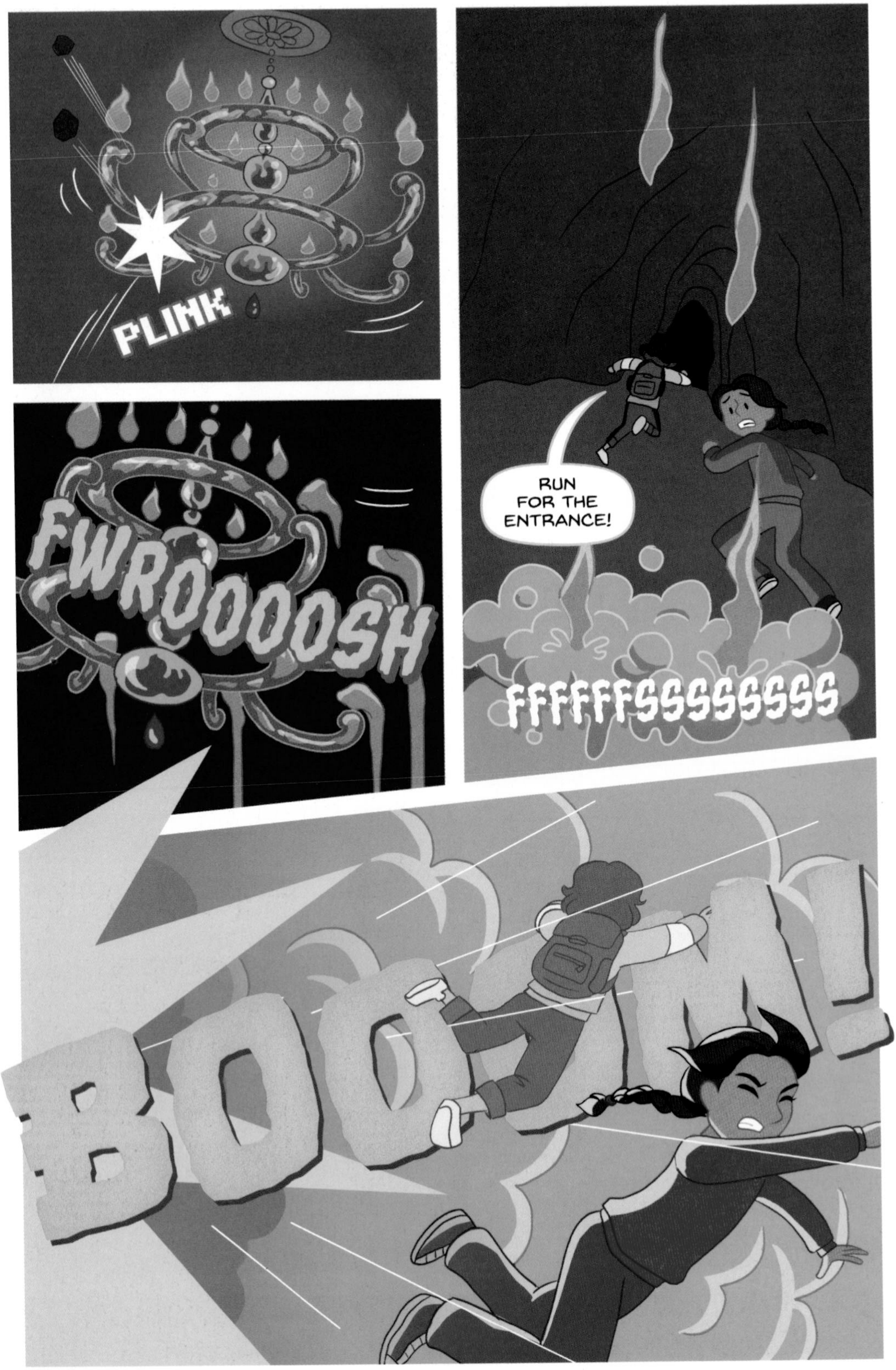
PLINK
FWROOOOOSH
RUN FOR THE ENTRANCE!
FFFFFFSSSSSSSSS
BOOM!

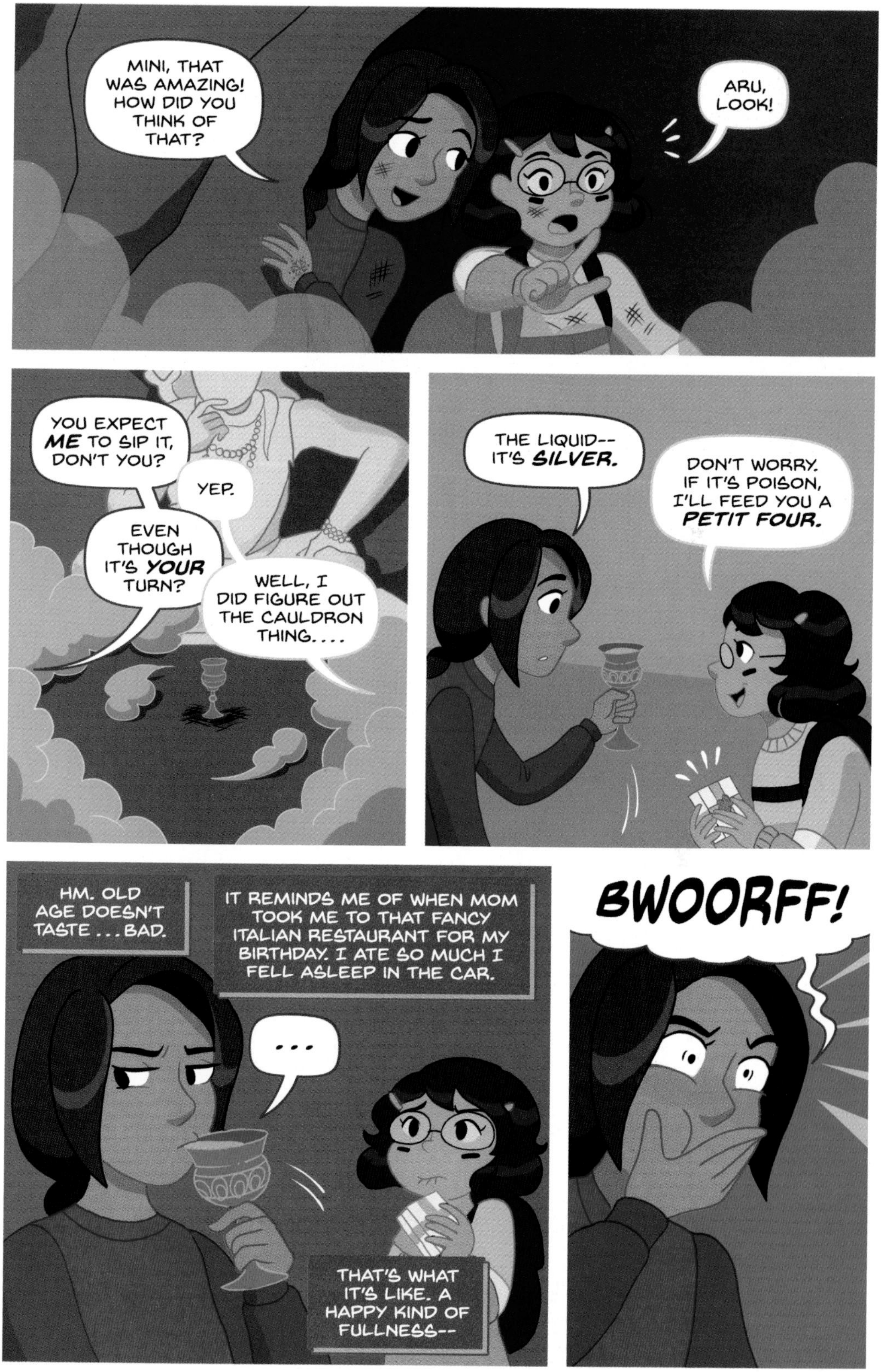
MINI, THAT WAS AMAZING! HOW DID YOU THINK OF THAT?
ARU, LOOK!
YOU EXPECT **ME** TO SIP IT, DON'T YOU?
YEP.
EVEN THOUGH IT'S ***YOUR*** TURN?
WELL, I DID FIGURE OUT THE CAULDRON THING....
THE LIQUID-- IT'S ***SILVER.***
DON'T WORRY. IF IT'S POISON, I'LL FEED YOU A ***PETIT FOUR.***
HM. OLD AGE DOESN'T TASTE...BAD.
IT REMINDS ME OF WHEN MOM TOOK ME TO THAT FANCY ITALIAN RESTAURANT FOR MY BIRTHDAY. I ATE SO MUCH I FELL ASLEEP IN THE CAR.
...
THAT'S WHAT IT'S LIKE. A HAPPY KIND OF FULLNESS--
BWOORFF!

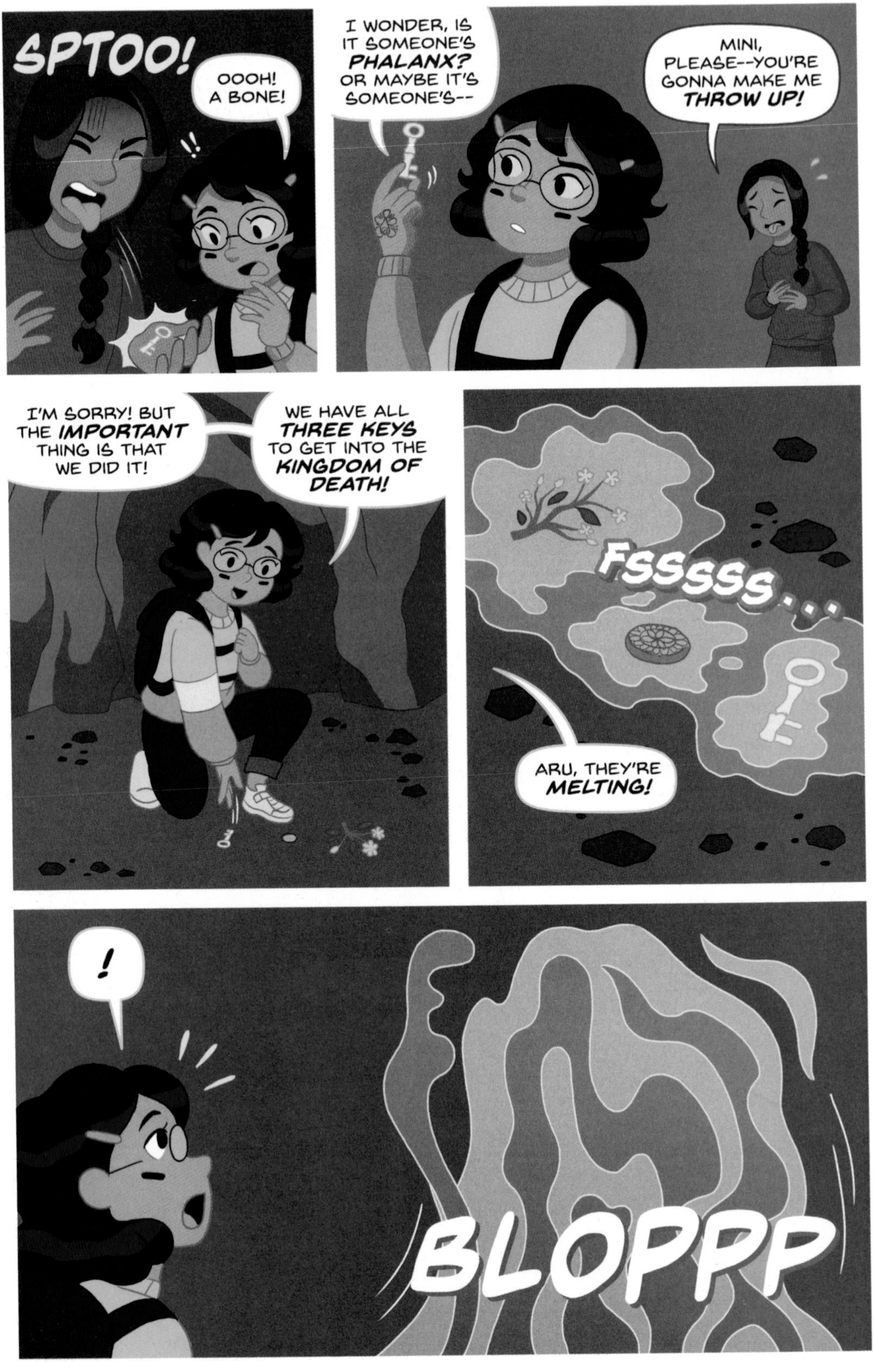
SPTOO!
OOOH! A BONE!
!!
I WONDER, IS IT SOMEONE'S **PHALANX?** OR MAYBE IT'S SOMEONE'S--
MINI, PLEASE--YOU'RE GONNA MAKE ME **THROW UP!**
I'M SORRY! BUT THE **IMPORTANT** THING IS THAT WE DID IT!
WE HAVE ALL **THREE KEYS** TO GET INTO THE **KINGDOM OF DEATH!**
FSSSSS...
ARU, THEY'RE **MELTING!**
!
BLOPPP

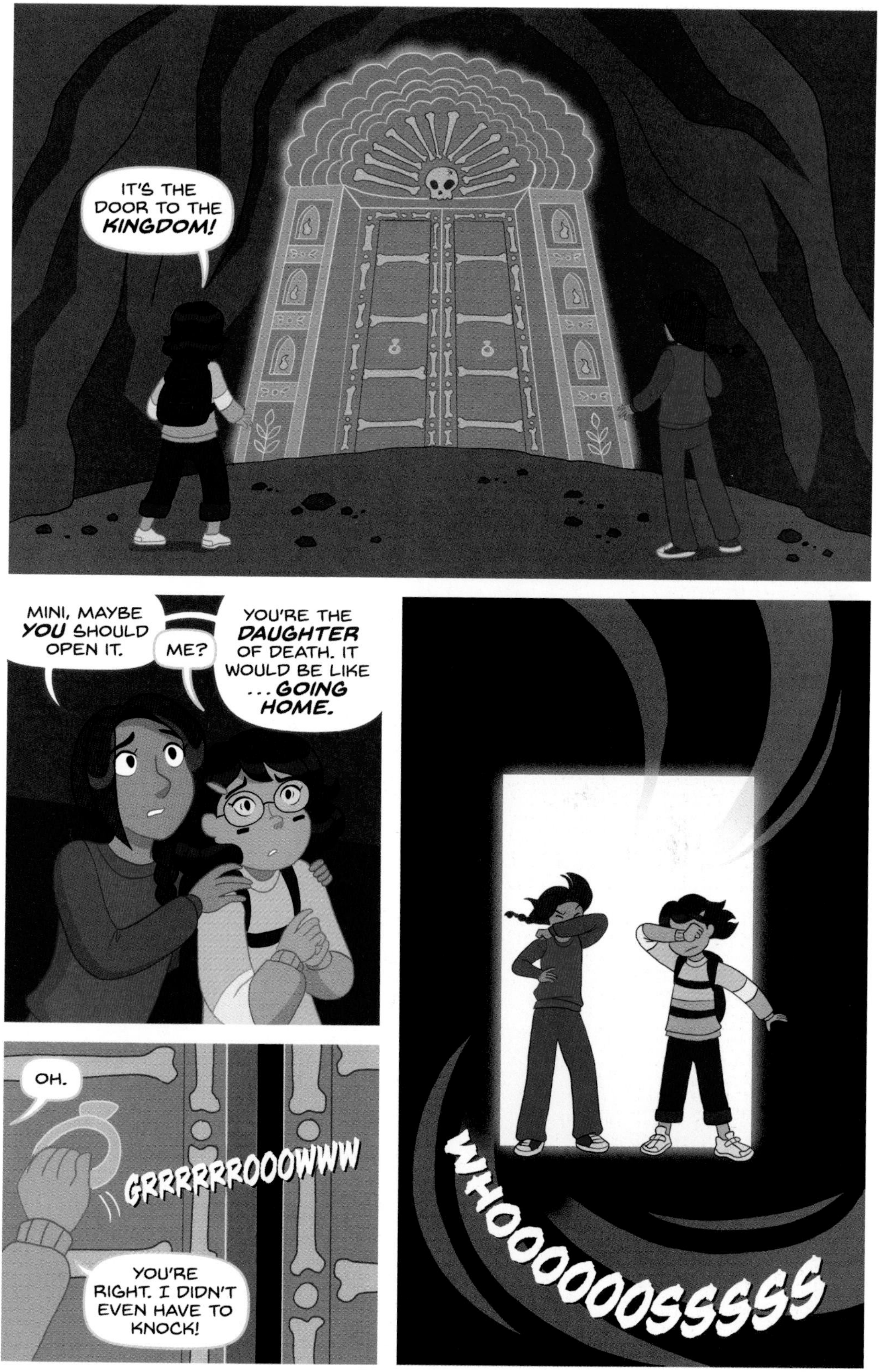
IT'S THE DOOR TO THE **KINGDOM!**
MINI, MAYBE **YOU** SHOULD OPEN IT.
ME?
YOU'RE THE **DAUGHTER** OF DEATH. IT WOULD BE LIKE . . . **GOING HOME.**
OH.
GRRRRRROOOWWW
YOU'RE RIGHT. I DIDN'T EVEN HAVE TO KNOCK!
WHOOOOOOOSSSSS

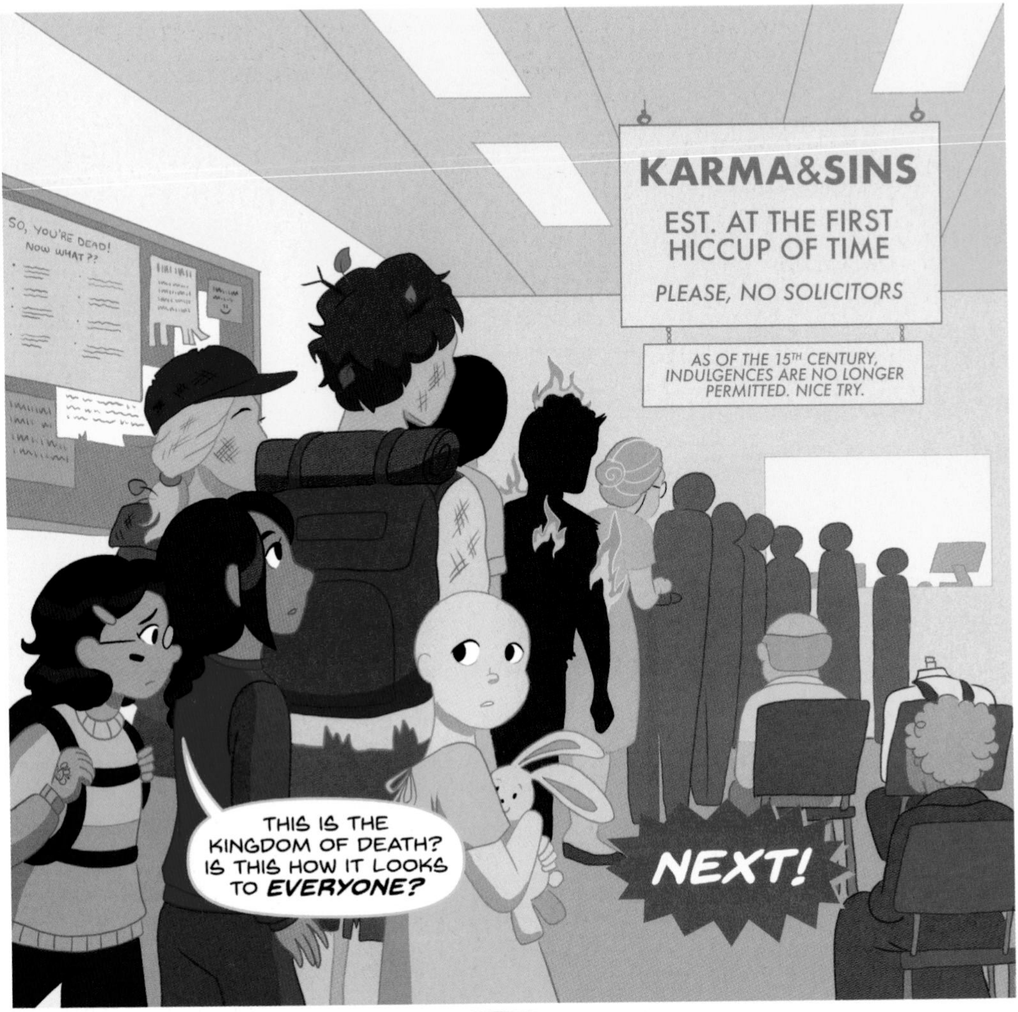
SO, YOU'RE DEAD! NOW WHAT??
KARMA&SINS
EST. AT THE FIRST HICCUP OF TIME
PLEASE, NO SOLICITORS
AS OF THE 15TH CENTURY, INDULGENCES ARE NO LONGER PERMITTED. NICE TRY.
THIS IS THE KINGDOM OF DEATH? IS THIS HOW IT LOOKS TO EVERYONE?
NEXT!

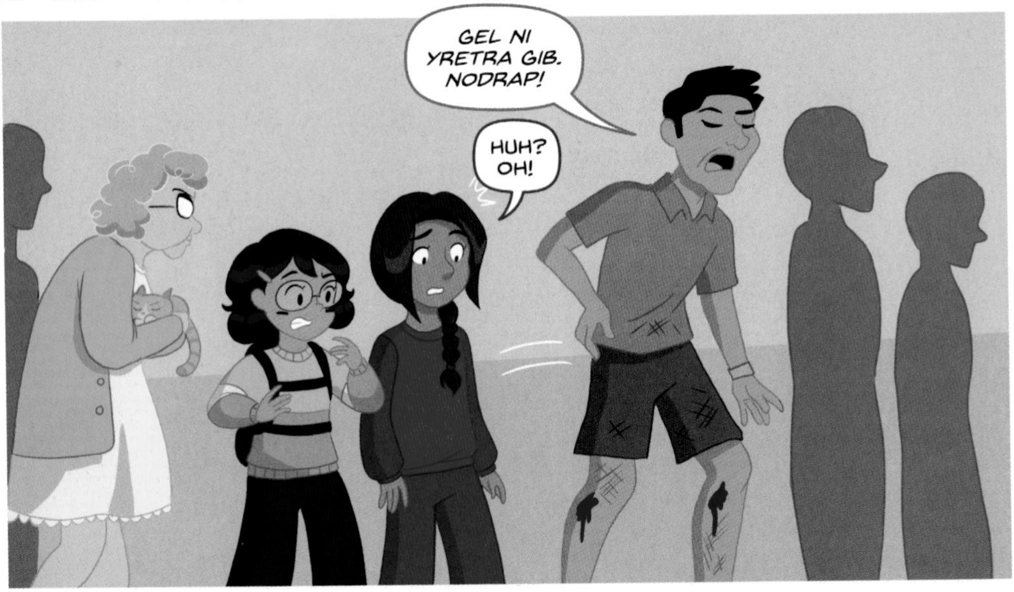
GEL NI YRETRA GIB. NODRAP!
HUH? OH!

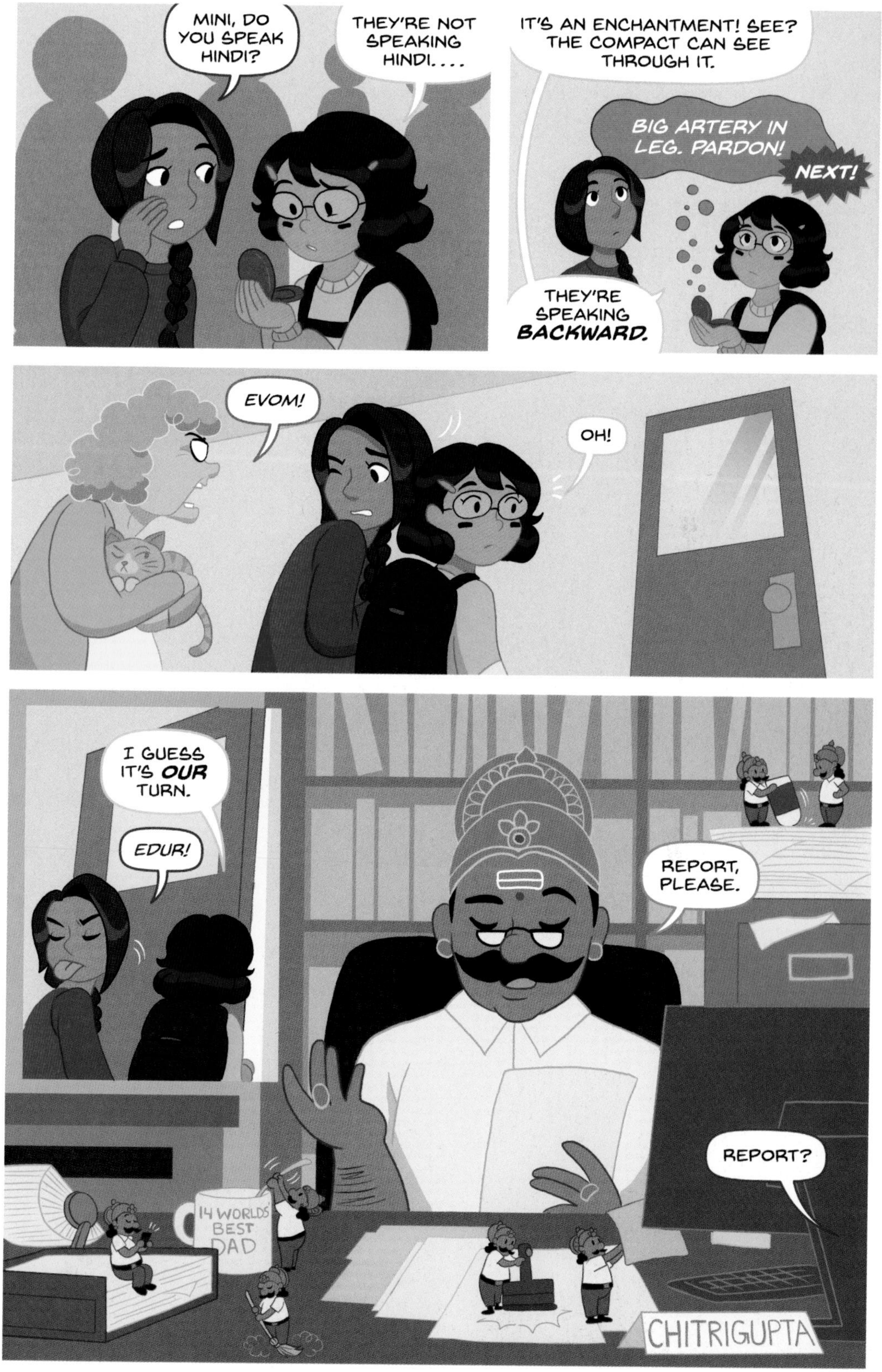
MINI, DO YOU SPEAK HINDI?
THEY'RE NOT SPEAKING HINDI. . . .
IT'S AN ENCHANTMENT! SEE? THE COMPACT CAN SEE THROUGH IT.
BIG ARTERY IN LEG. PARDON!
NEXT!
THEY'RE SPEAKING BACKWARD.
EVOM!
OH!
I GUESS IT'S OUR TURN.
EDUR!
REPORT, PLEASE.
REPORT?
#1 WORLDS' BEST DAD
CHITRIGUPTA

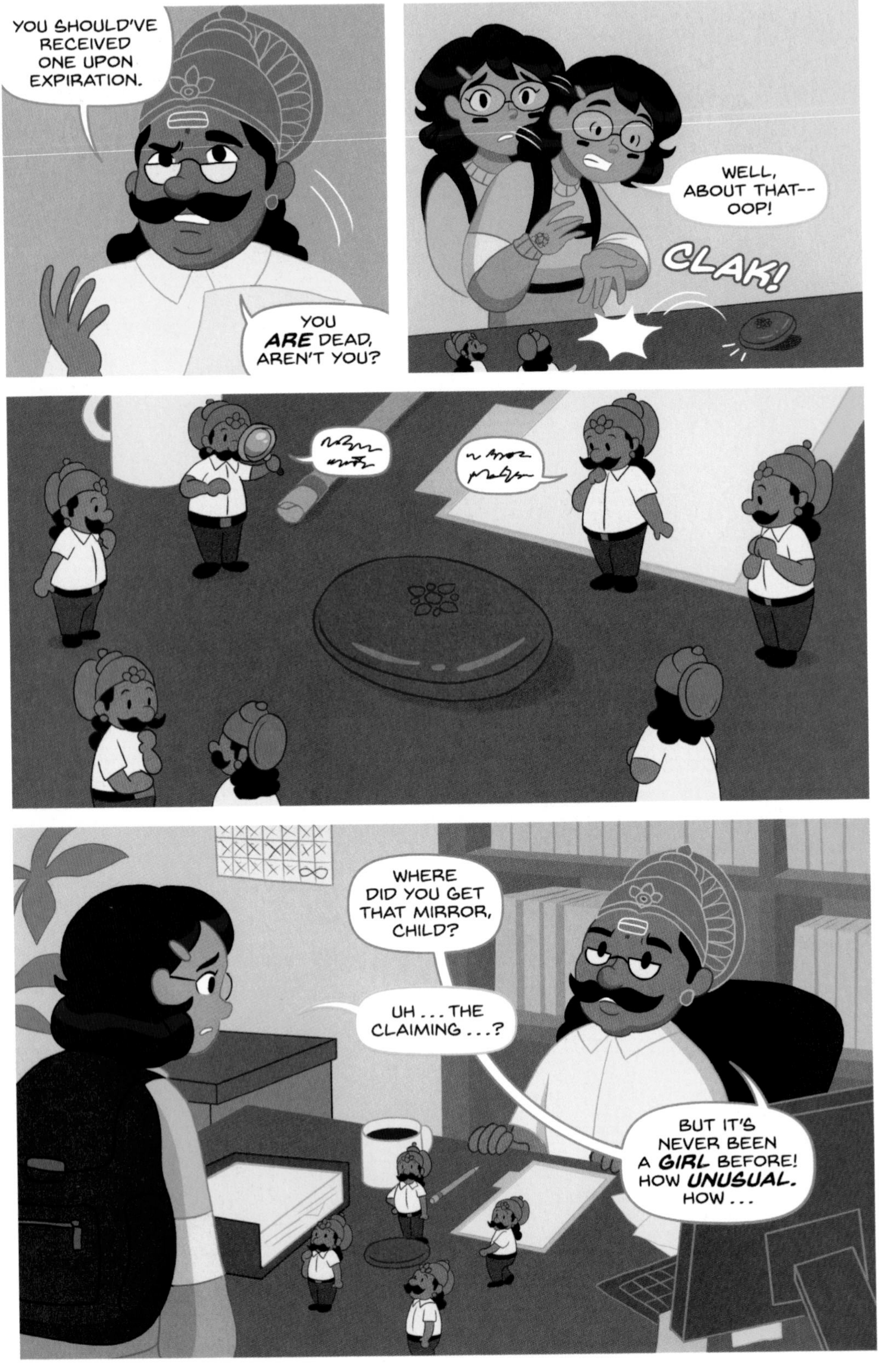
YOU SHOULD'VE RECEIVED ONE UPON EXPIRATION.
YOU **ARE** DEAD, AREN'T YOU?
WELL, ABOUT THAT-- OOP!
CLAK!
WHERE DID YOU GET THAT MIRROR, CHILD?
UH . . . THE CLAIMING . . .?
BUT IT'S NEVER BEEN A **GIRL** BEFORE! HOW **UNUSUAL.** HOW . . .

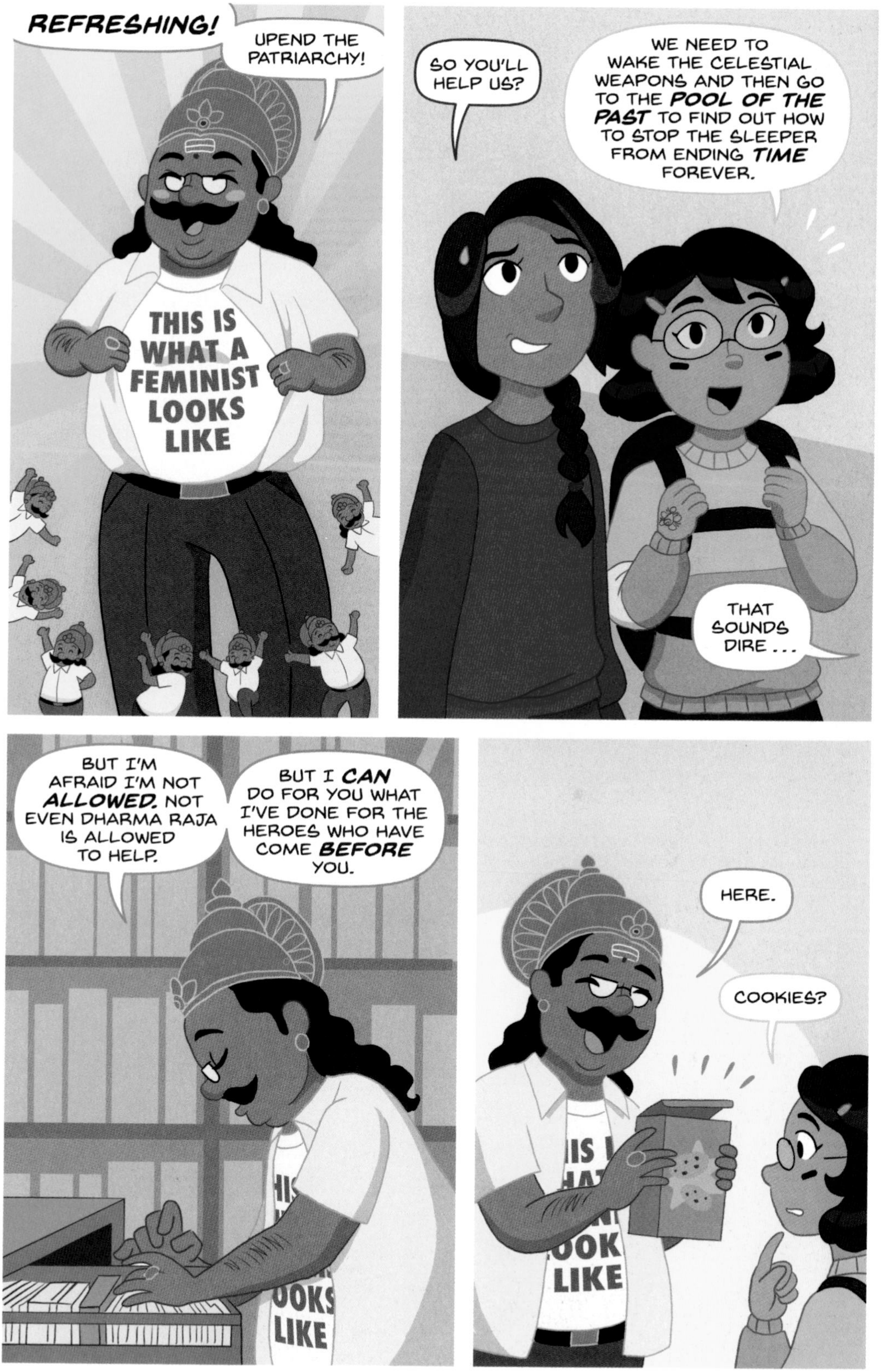

REFRESHING!
UPEND THE PATRIARCHY!
THIS IS WHAT A FEMINIST LOOKS LIKE
SO YOU'LL HELP US?
WE NEED TO WAKE THE CELESTIAL WEAPONS AND THEN GO TO THE POOL OF THE PAST TO FIND OUT HOW TO STOP THE SLEEPER FROM ENDING TIME FOREVER.
THAT SOUNDS DIRE . . .
BUT I'M AFRAID I'M NOT ALLOWED. NOT EVEN DHARMA RAJA IS ALLOWED TO HELP.
BUT I CAN DO FOR YOU WHAT I'VE DONE FOR THE HEROES WHO HAVE COME BEFORE YOU.
HERE.
COOKIES?

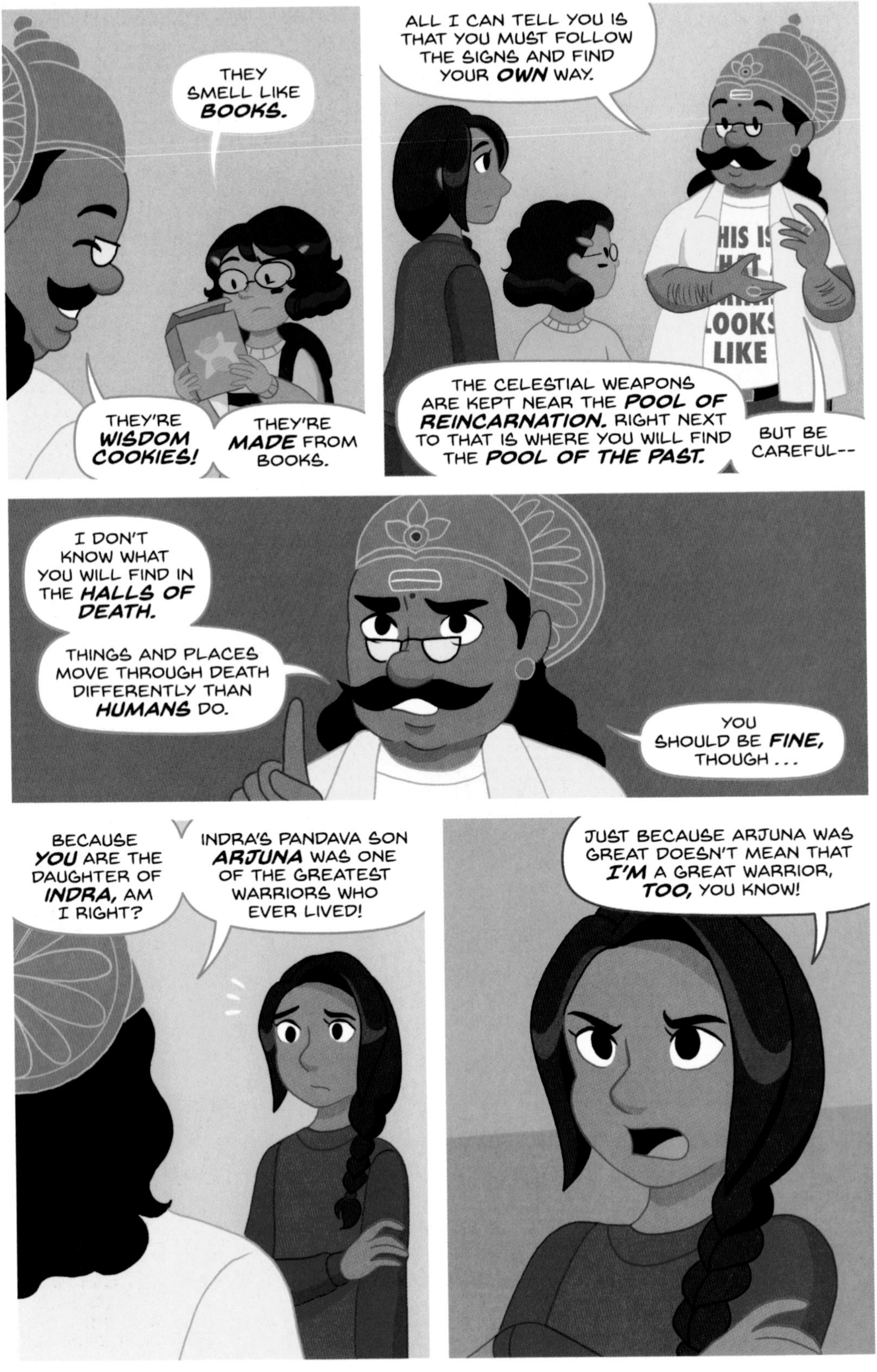
THEY SMELL LIKE BOOKS.
THEY'RE WISDOM COOKIES!
THEY'RE MADE FROM BOOKS.
ALL I CAN TELL YOU IS THAT YOU MUST FOLLOW THE SIGNS AND FIND YOUR OWN WAY.
THE CELESTIAL WEAPONS ARE KEPT NEAR THE POOL OF REINCARNATION. RIGHT NEXT TO THAT IS WHERE YOU WILL FIND THE POOL OF THE PAST.
BUT BE CAREFUL--
I DON'T KNOW WHAT YOU WILL FIND IN THE HALLS OF DEATH.
THINGS AND PLACES MOVE THROUGH DEATH DIFFERENTLY THAN HUMANS DO.
YOU SHOULD BE FINE, THOUGH . . .
BECAUSE YOU ARE THE DAUGHTER OF INDRA, AM I RIGHT?
INDRA'S PANDAVA SON ARJUNA WAS ONE OF THE GREATEST WARRIORS WHO EVER LIVED!
JUST BECAUSE ARJUNA WAS GREAT DOESN'T MEAN THAT I'M A GREAT WARRIOR, TOO, YOU KNOW!

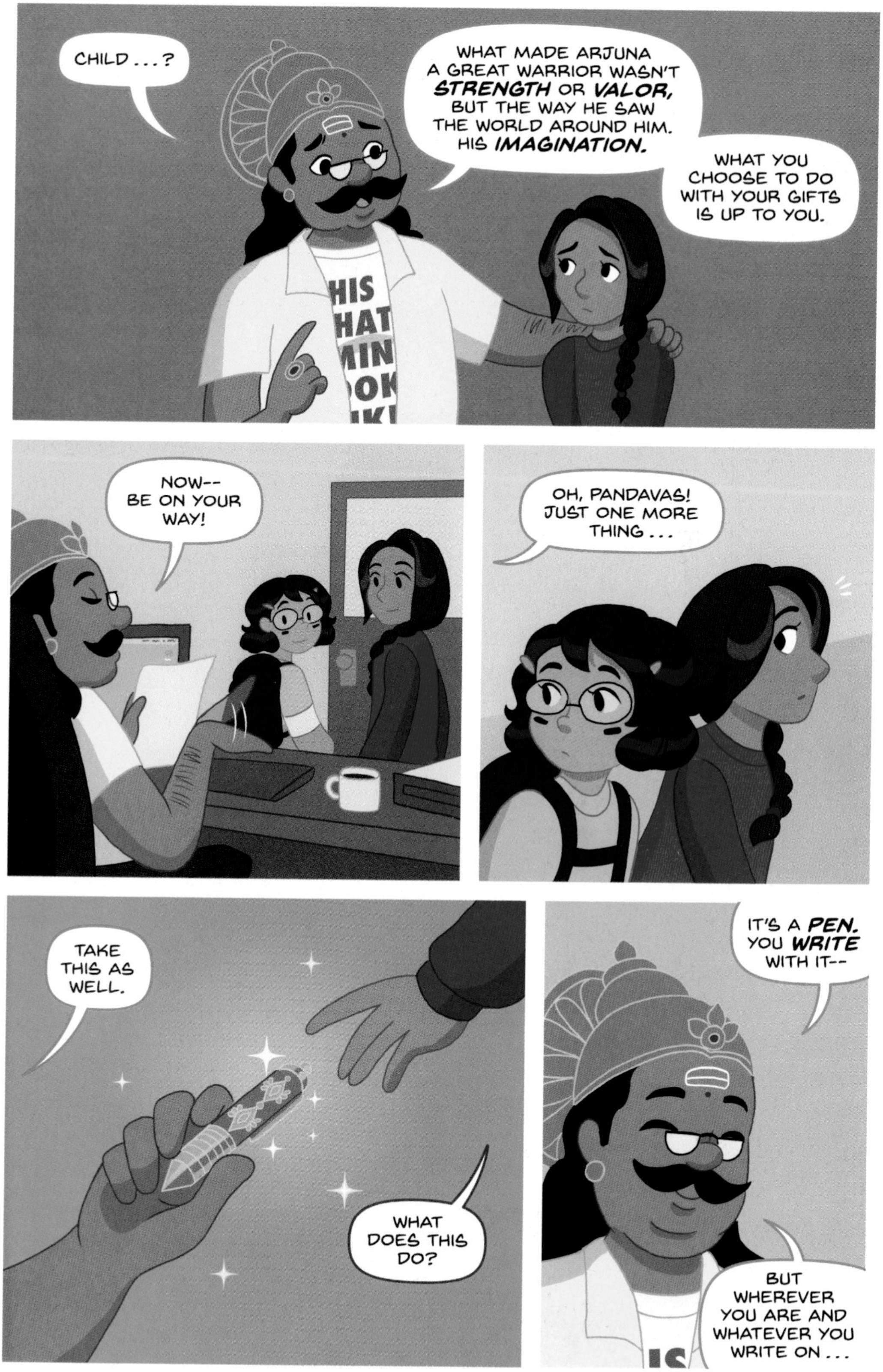
CHILD . . . ?
WHAT MADE ARJUNA A GREAT WARRIOR WASN'T ***STRENGTH*** OR ***VALOR,*** BUT THE WAY HE SAW THE WORLD AROUND HIM. HIS ***IMAGINATION.***
WHAT YOU CHOOSE TO DO WITH YOUR GIFTS IS UP TO YOU.
NOW-- BE ON YOUR WAY!
OH, PANDAVAS! JUST ONE MORE THING . . .
TAKE THIS AS WELL.
WHAT DOES THIS DO?
IT'S A ***PEN.*** YOU ***WRITE*** WITH IT--
BUT WHEREVER YOU ARE AND WHATEVER YOU WRITE ON . . .

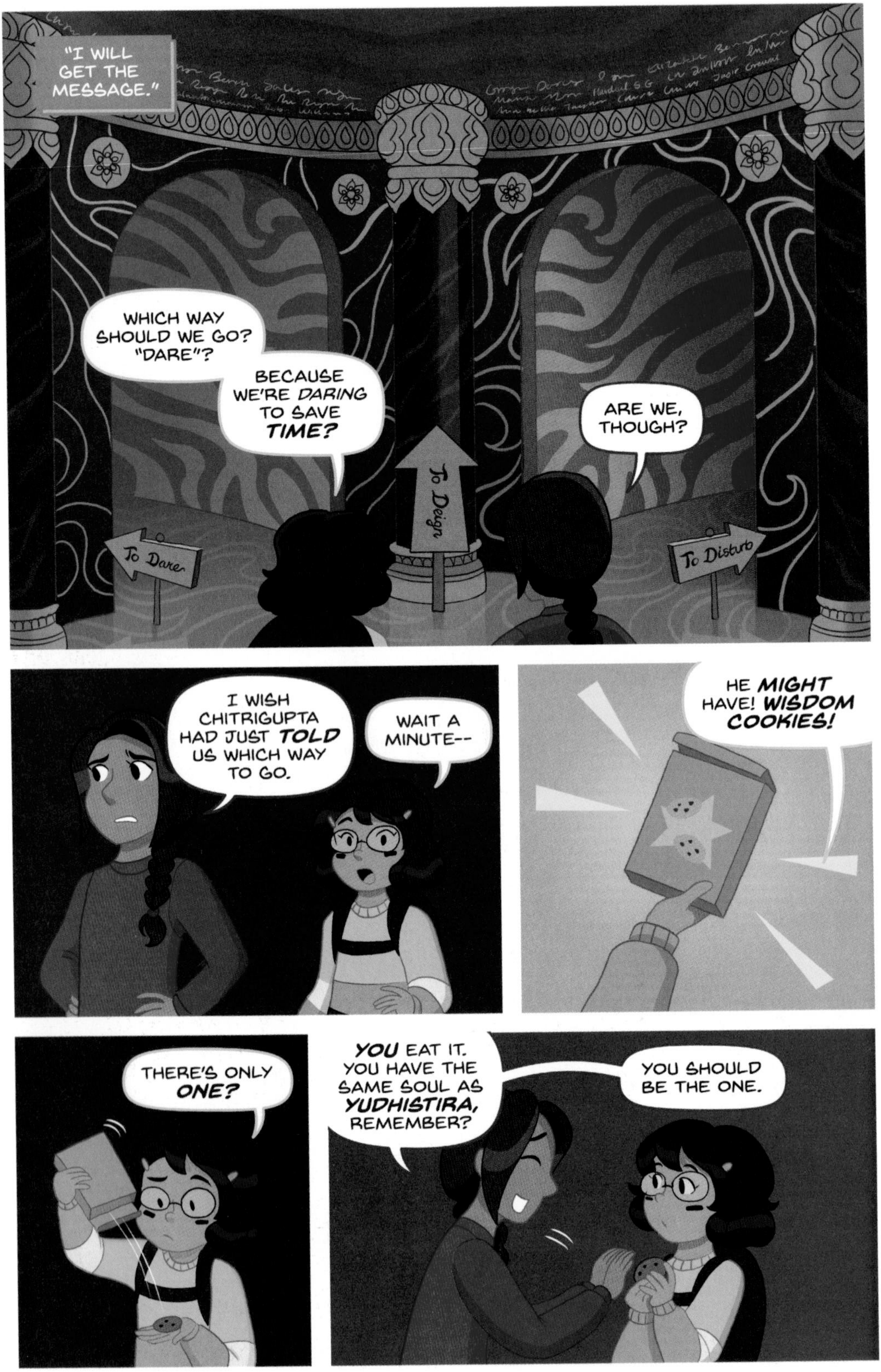
"I WILL GET THE MESSAGE."
WHICH WAY SHOULD WE GO? "DARE"?
BECAUSE WE'RE *DARING* TO SAVE ***TIME?***
ARE WE, THOUGH?
To Dare
To Deign
To Disturb
I WISH CHITRIGUPTA HAD JUST ***TOLD*** US WHICH WAY TO GO.
WAIT A MINUTE--
HE ***MIGHT*** HAVE! ***WISDOM COOKIES!***
THERE'S ONLY ***ONE?***
YOU EAT IT. YOU HAVE THE SAME SOUL AS ***YUDHISTIRA,*** REMEMBER?
YOU SHOULD BE THE ONE.

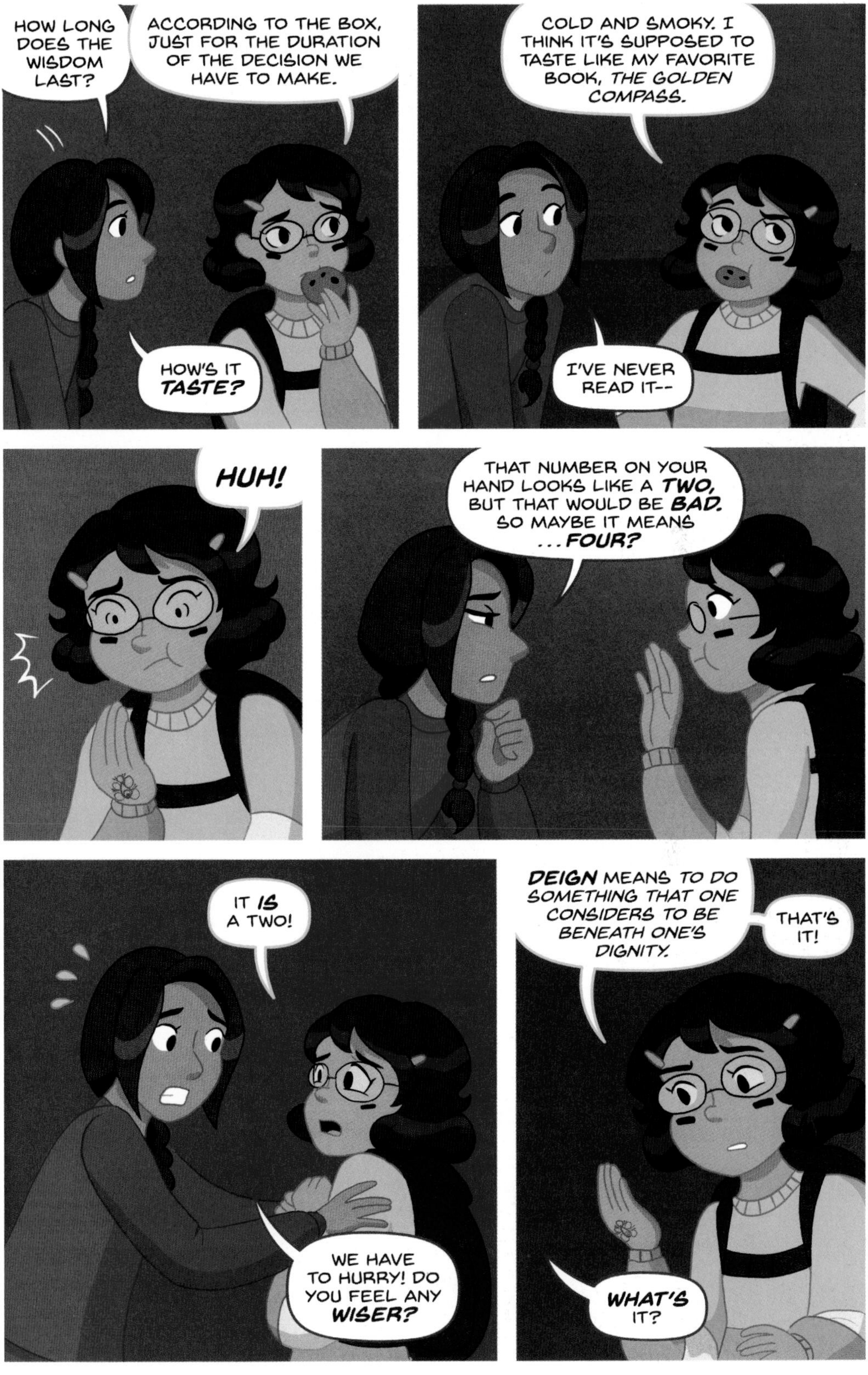
HOW LONG DOES THE WISDOM LAST?
ACCORDING TO THE BOX, JUST FOR THE DURATION OF THE DECISION WE HAVE TO MAKE.
HOW'S IT **TASTE?**
COLD AND SMOKY. I THINK IT'S SUPPOSED TO TASTE LIKE MY FAVORITE BOOK, *THE GOLDEN COMPASS.*
I'VE NEVER READ IT--
HUH!
THAT NUMBER ON YOUR HAND LOOKS LIKE A **TWO,** BUT THAT WOULD BE **BAD.** SO MAYBE IT MEANS ...**FOUR?**
IT **IS** A TWO!
WE HAVE TO HURRY! DO YOU FEEL ANY **WISER?**
DEIGN *MEANS TO DO SOMETHING THAT ONE CONSIDERS TO BE BENEATH ONE'S DIGNITY.*
THAT'S IT!
WHAT'S IT?

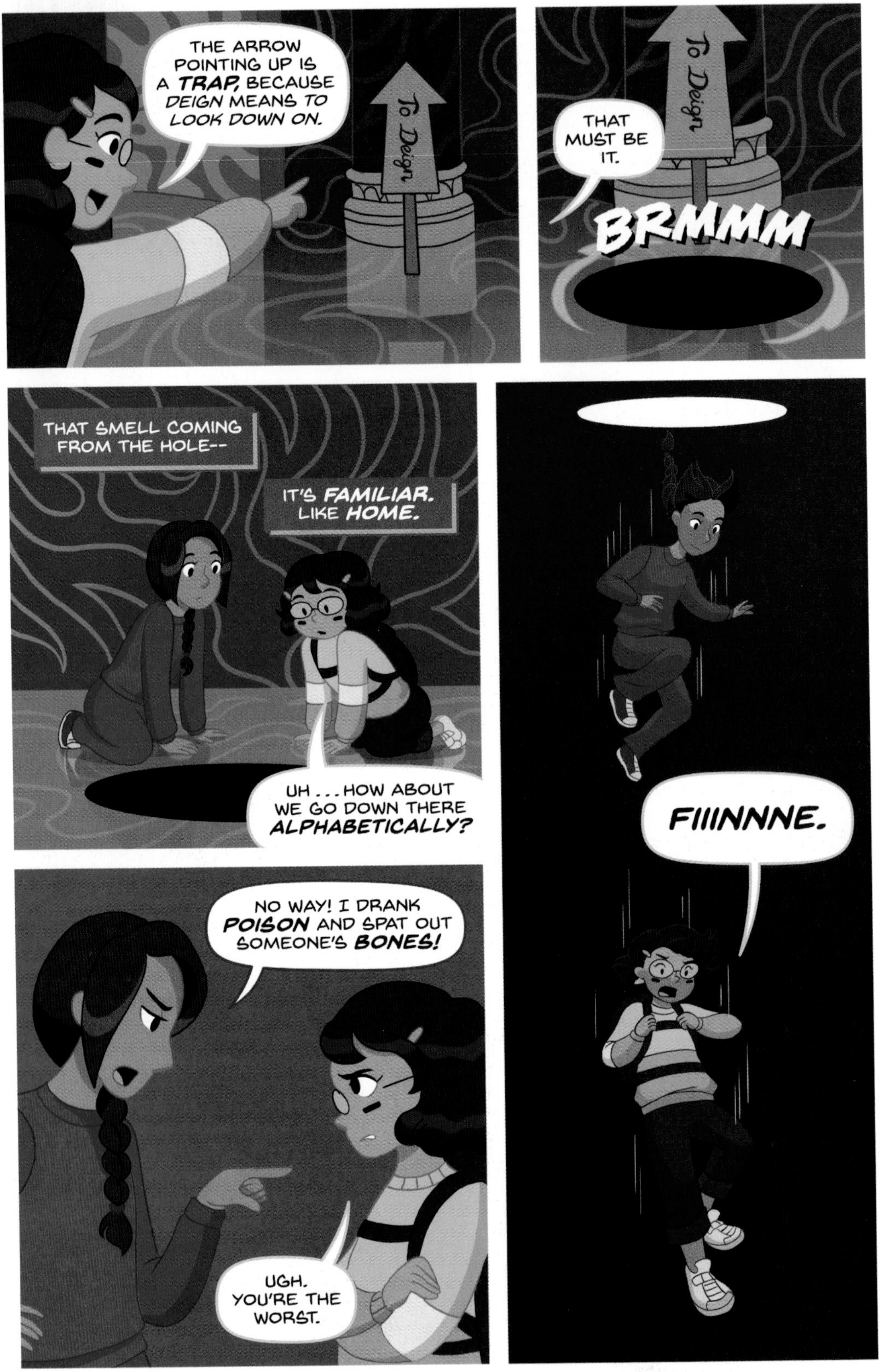
THE ARROW POINTING UP IS A TRAP, BECAUSE DEIGN MEANS TO LOOK DOWN ON.
To Deign
To Deign
THAT MUST BE IT.
BRMMM
THAT SMELL COMING FROM THE HOLE--
IT'S FAMILIAR. LIKE HOME.
UH . . . HOW ABOUT WE GO DOWN THERE ALPHABETICALLY?
NO WAY! I DRANK POISON AND SPAT OUT SOMEONE'S BONES!
UGH. YOU'RE THE WORST.
FIIINNNE.

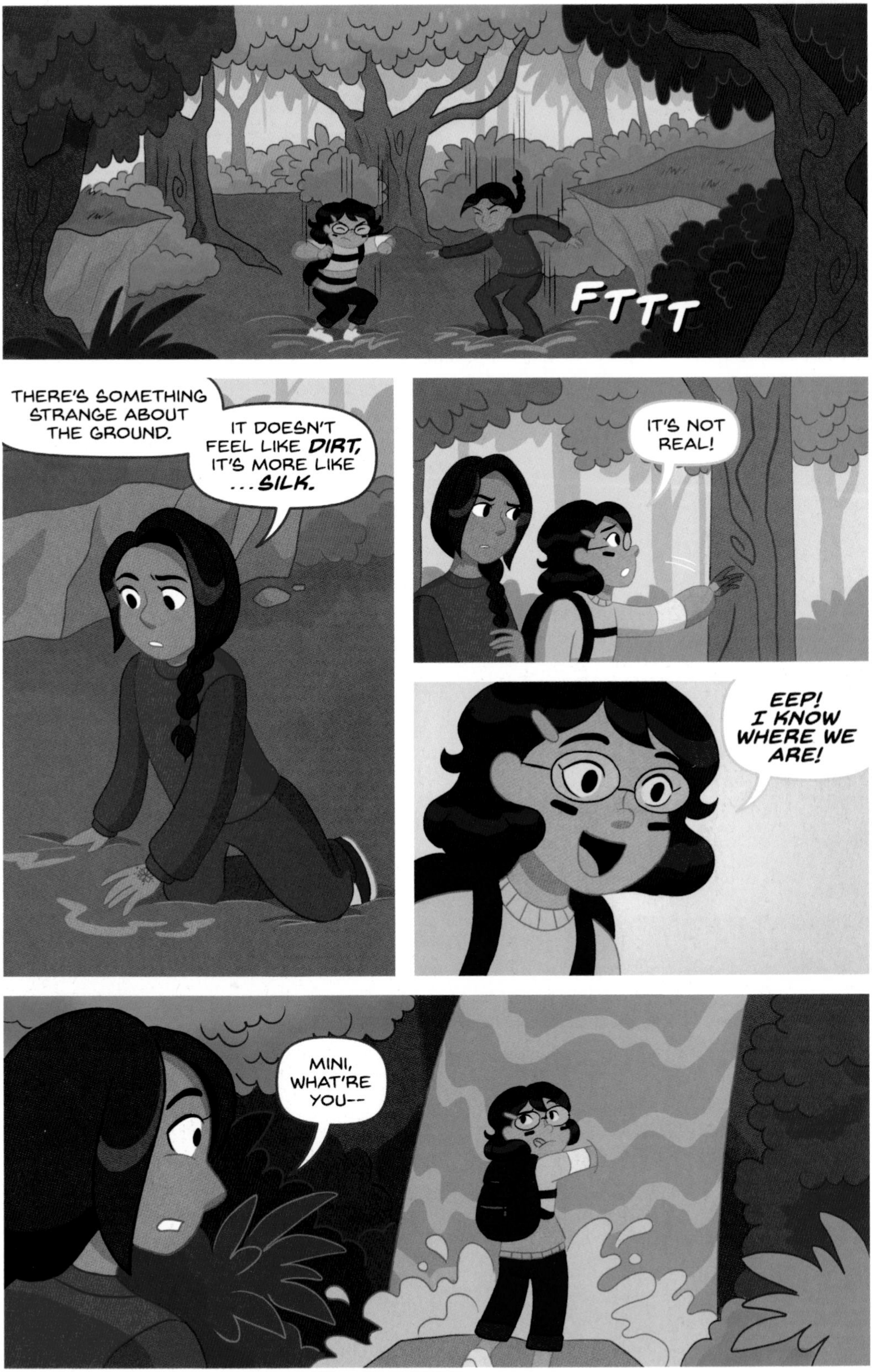
FTTTT
THERE'S SOMETHING STRANGE ABOUT THE GROUND.
IT DOESN'T FEEL LIKE DIRT, IT'S MORE LIKE ...SILK.
IT'S NOT REAL!
EEP! I KNOW WHERE WE ARE!
MINI, WHAT'RE YOU--

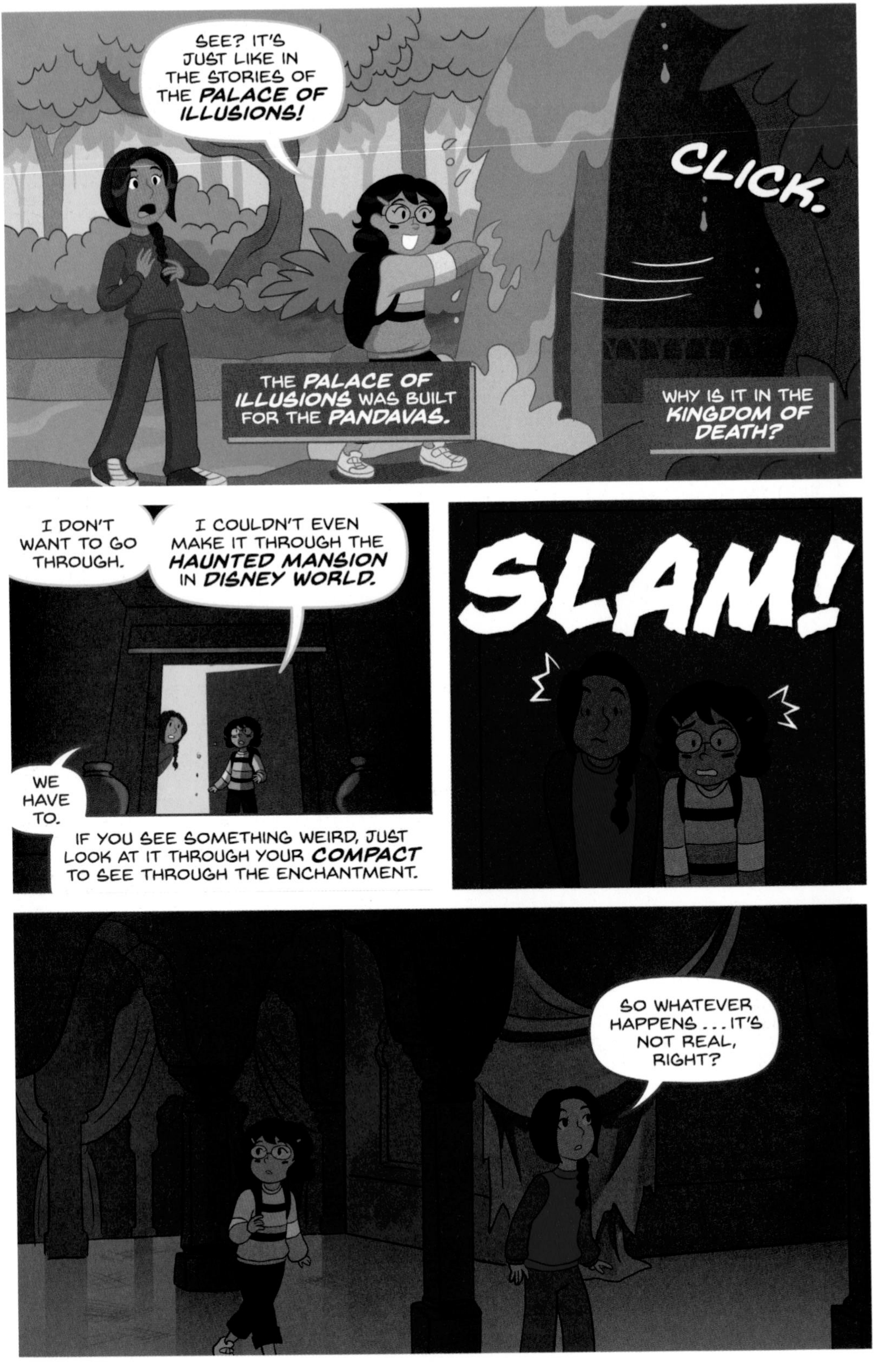
SEE? IT'S JUST LIKE IN THE STORIES OF THE *PALACE OF ILLUSIONS!*
CLICK.
THE *PALACE OF ILLUSIONS* WAS BUILT FOR THE *PANDAVAS.*
WHY IS IT IN THE *KINGDOM OF DEATH?*
I DON'T WANT TO GO THROUGH.
I COULDN'T EVEN MAKE IT THROUGH THE *HAUNTED MANSION* IN *DISNEY WORLD.*
WE HAVE TO.
IF YOU SEE SOMETHING WEIRD, JUST LOOK AT IT THROUGH YOUR *COMPACT* TO SEE THROUGH THE ENCHANTMENT.
SLAM!
SO WHATEVER HAPPENS . . . IT'S NOT REAL, RIGHT?

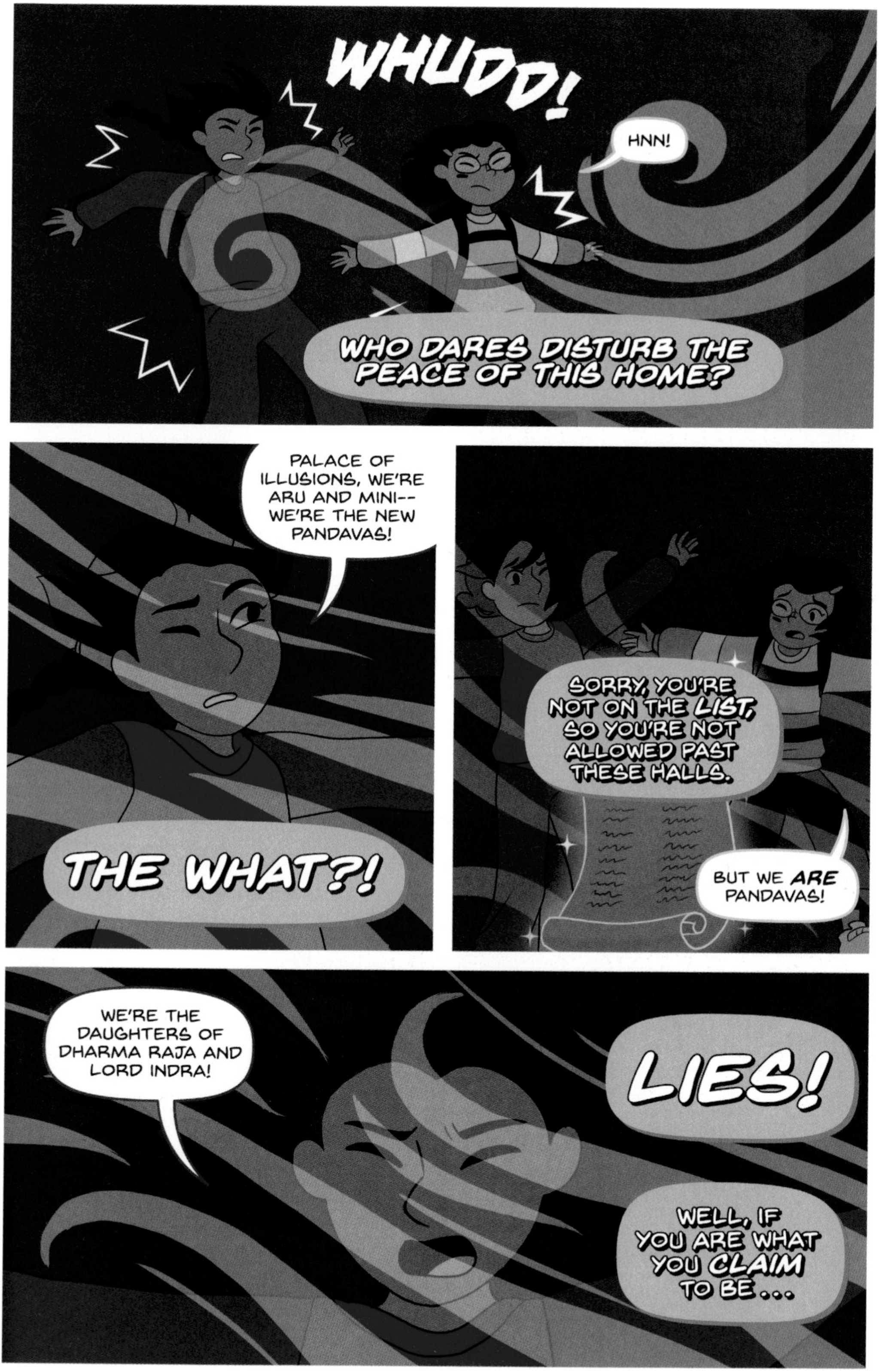
WHUDD!
HNN!
WHO DARES DISTURB THE PEACE OF THIS HOME?
PALACE OF ILLUSIONS, WE'RE ARU AND MINI-- WE'RE THE NEW PANDAVAS!
THE WHAT?!
SORRY, YOU'RE NOT ON THE LIST, SO YOU'RE NOT ALLOWED PAST THESE HALLS.
BUT WE ARE PANDAVAS!
WE'RE THE DAUGHTERS OF DHARMA RAJA AND LORD INDRA!
LIES!
WELL, IF YOU ARE WHAT YOU CLAIM TO BE . . .

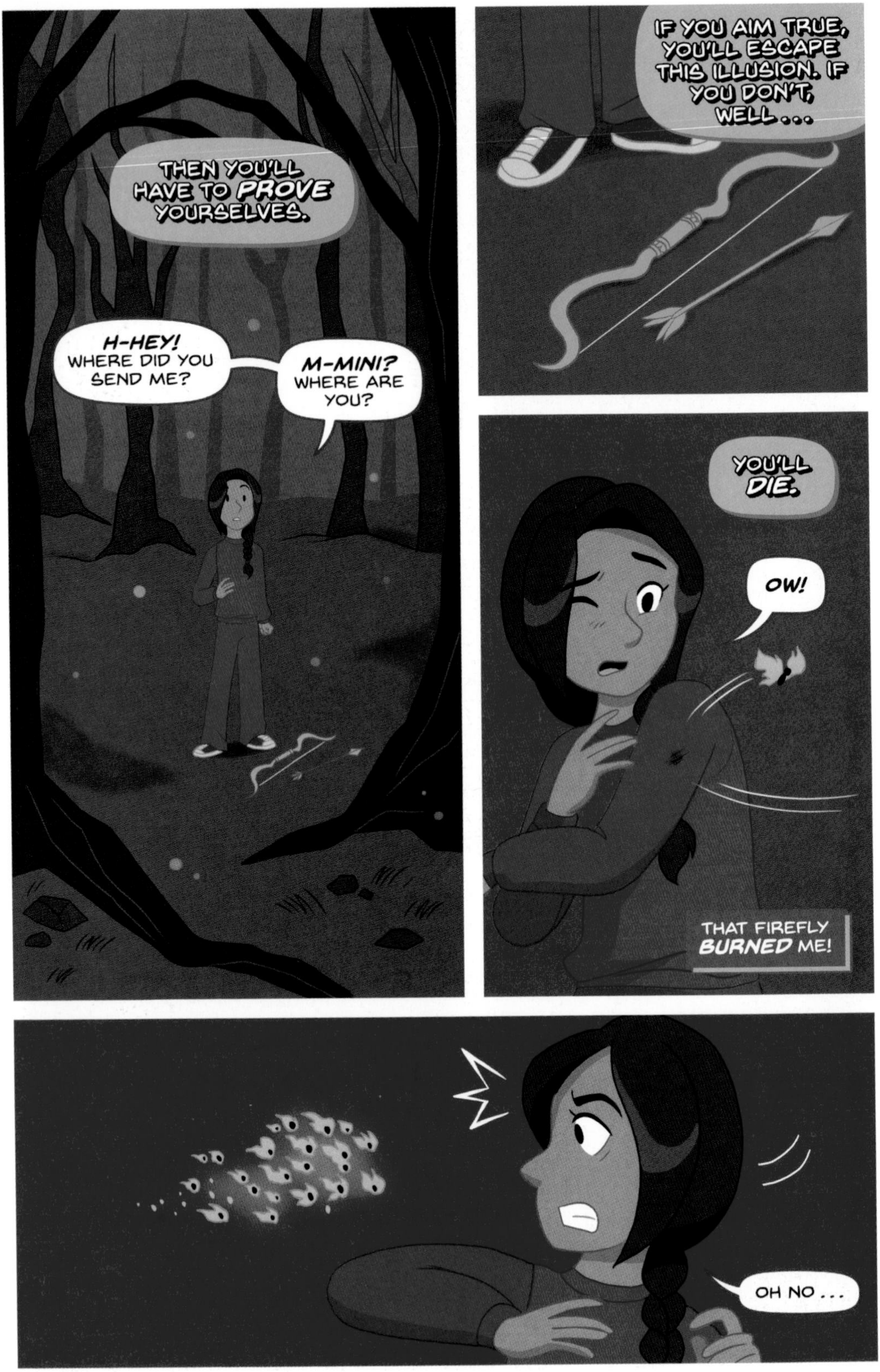
THEN YOU'LL HAVE TO PROVE YOURSELVES.
H-HEY! WHERE DID YOU SEND ME?
M-MINI? WHERE ARE YOU?
IF YOU AIM TRUE, YOU'LL ESCAPE THIS ILLUSION. IF YOU DON'T, WELL . . .
YOU'LL DIE.
OW!
THAT FIREFLY BURNED ME!
OH NO . . .

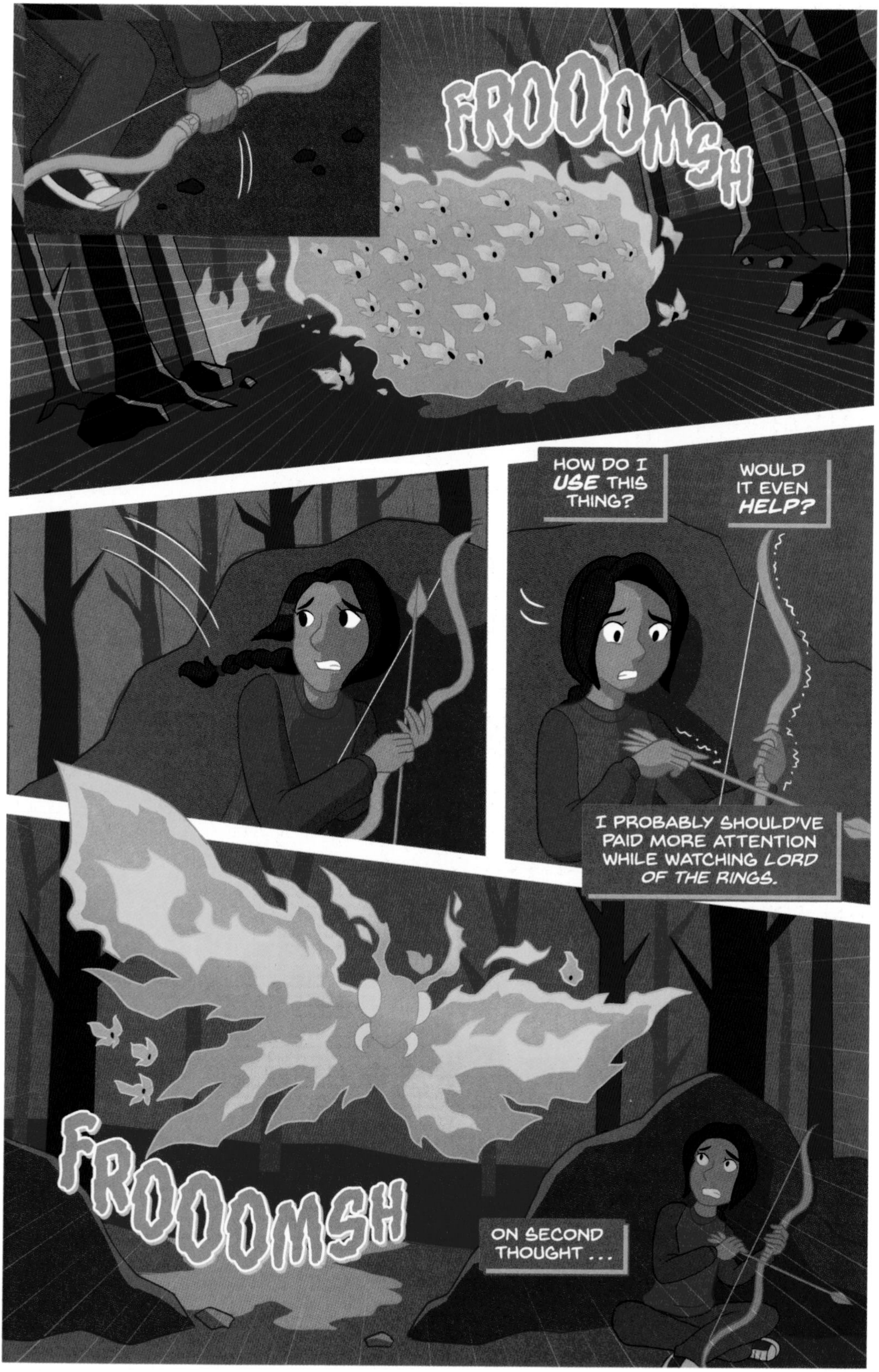
FROOOMSH
HOW DO I USE THIS THING?
WOULD IT EVEN HELP?
I PROBABLY SHOULD'VE PAID MORE ATTENTION WHILE WATCHING LORD OF THE RINGS.
FROOOMSH
ON SECOND THOUGHT . . .

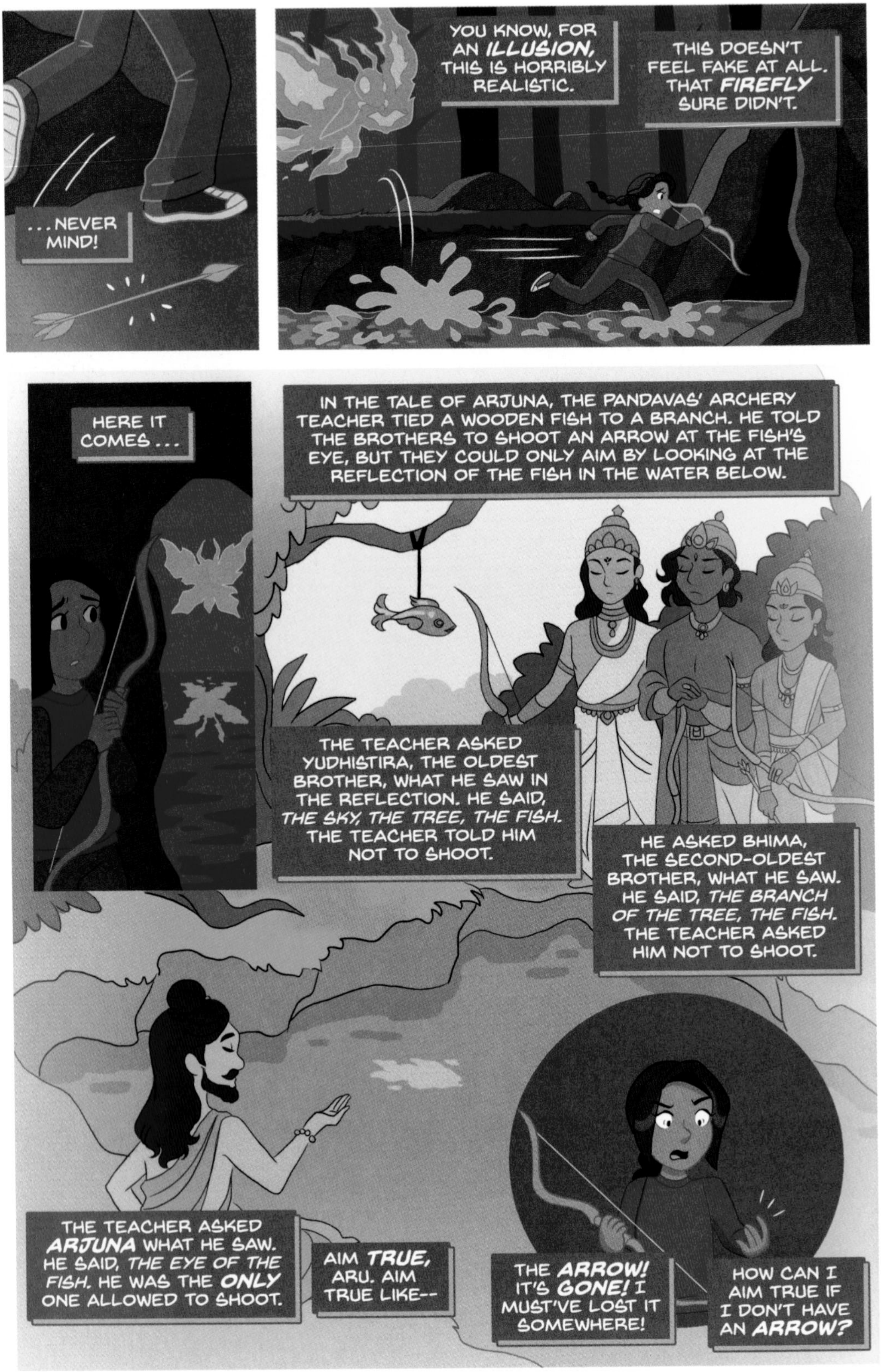
...NEVER MIND!
YOU KNOW, FOR AN ILLUSION, THIS IS HORRIBLY REALISTIC.
THIS DOESN'T FEEL FAKE AT ALL. THAT FIREFLY SURE DIDN'T.
HERE IT COMES...
IN THE TALE OF ARJUNA, THE PANDAVAS' ARCHERY TEACHER TIED A WOODEN FISH TO A BRANCH. HE TOLD THE BROTHERS TO SHOOT AN ARROW AT THE FISH'S EYE, BUT THEY COULD ONLY AIM BY LOOKING AT THE REFLECTION OF THE FISH IN THE WATER BELOW.
THE TEACHER ASKED YUDHISTIRA, THE OLDEST BROTHER, WHAT HE SAW IN THE REFLECTION. HE SAID, THE SKY, THE TREE, THE FISH. THE TEACHER TOLD HIM NOT TO SHOOT.
HE ASKED BHIMA, THE SECOND-OLDEST BROTHER, WHAT HE SAW. HE SAID, THE BRANCH OF THE TREE, THE FISH. THE TEACHER ASKED HIM NOT TO SHOOT.
THE TEACHER ASKED ARJUNA WHAT HE SAW. HE SAID, THE EYE OF THE FISH. HE WAS THE ONLY ONE ALLOWED TO SHOOT.
AIM TRUE, ARU. AIM TRUE LIKE--
THE ARROW! IT'S GONE! I MUST'VE LOST IT SOMEWHERE!
HOW CAN I AIM TRUE IF I DON'T HAVE AN ARROW?

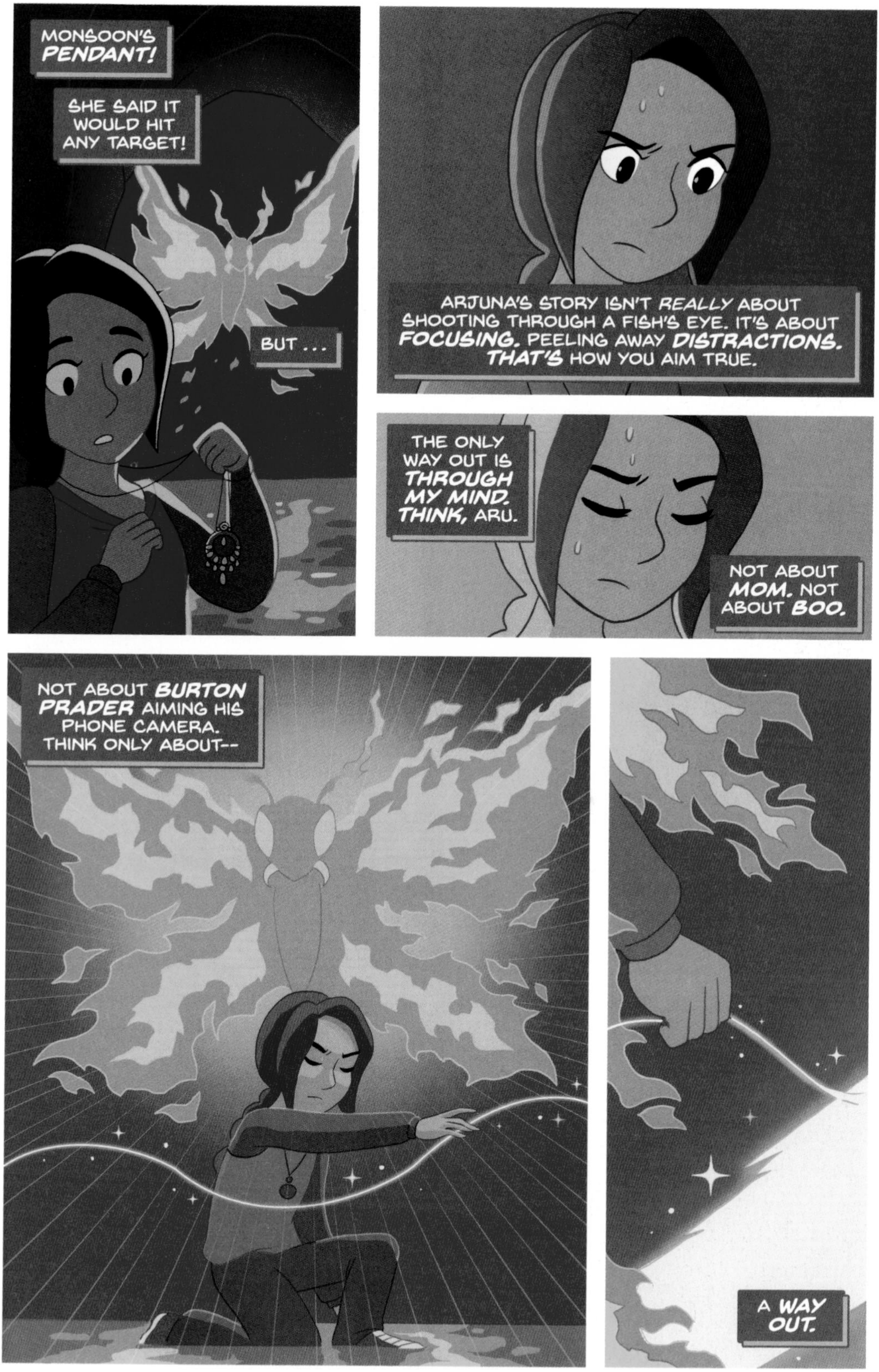
MONSOON'S **PENDANT!**
SHE SAID IT WOULD HIT ANY TARGET!
BUT . . .
ARJUNA'S STORY ISN'T *REALLY* ABOUT SHOOTING THROUGH A FISH'S EYE. IT'S ABOUT **FOCUSING.** PEELING AWAY **DISTRACTIONS. THAT'S** HOW YOU AIM TRUE.
THE ONLY WAY OUT IS **THROUGH MY MIND. THINK,** ARU.
NOT ABOUT **MOM.** NOT ABOUT **BOO.**
NOT ABOUT **BURTON PRADER** AIMING HIS PHONE CAMERA. THINK ONLY ABOUT--
A **WAY OUT.**

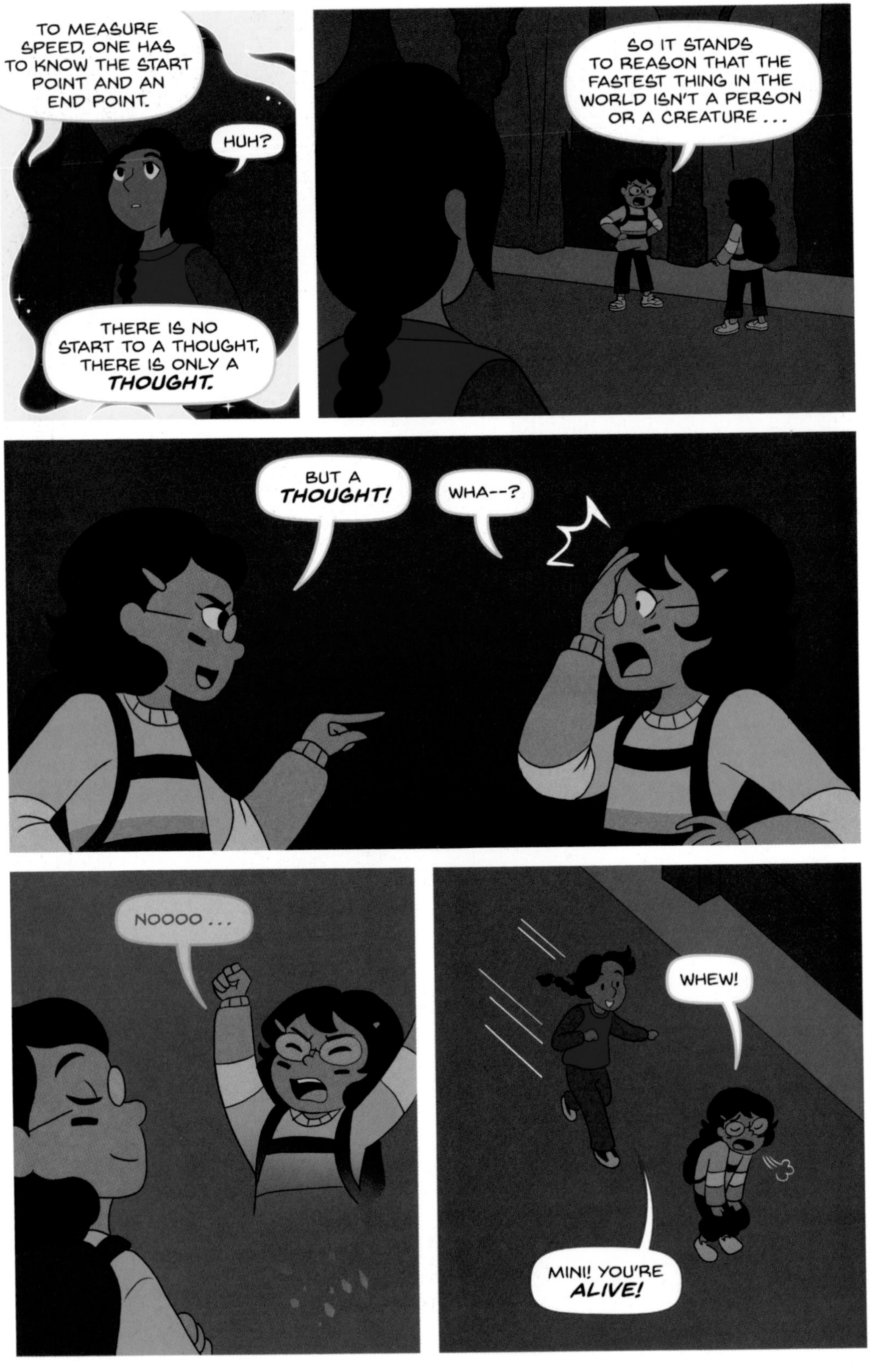
TO MEASURE SPEED, ONE HAS TO KNOW THE START POINT AND AN END POINT.
HUH?
THERE IS NO START TO A THOUGHT, THERE IS ONLY A ***THOUGHT.***
SO IT STANDS TO REASON THAT THE FASTEST THING IN THE WORLD ISN'T A PERSON OR A CREATURE . . .
BUT A ***THOUGHT!***
WHA--?
NOOOO . . .
WHEW!
MINI! YOU'RE ***ALIVE!***

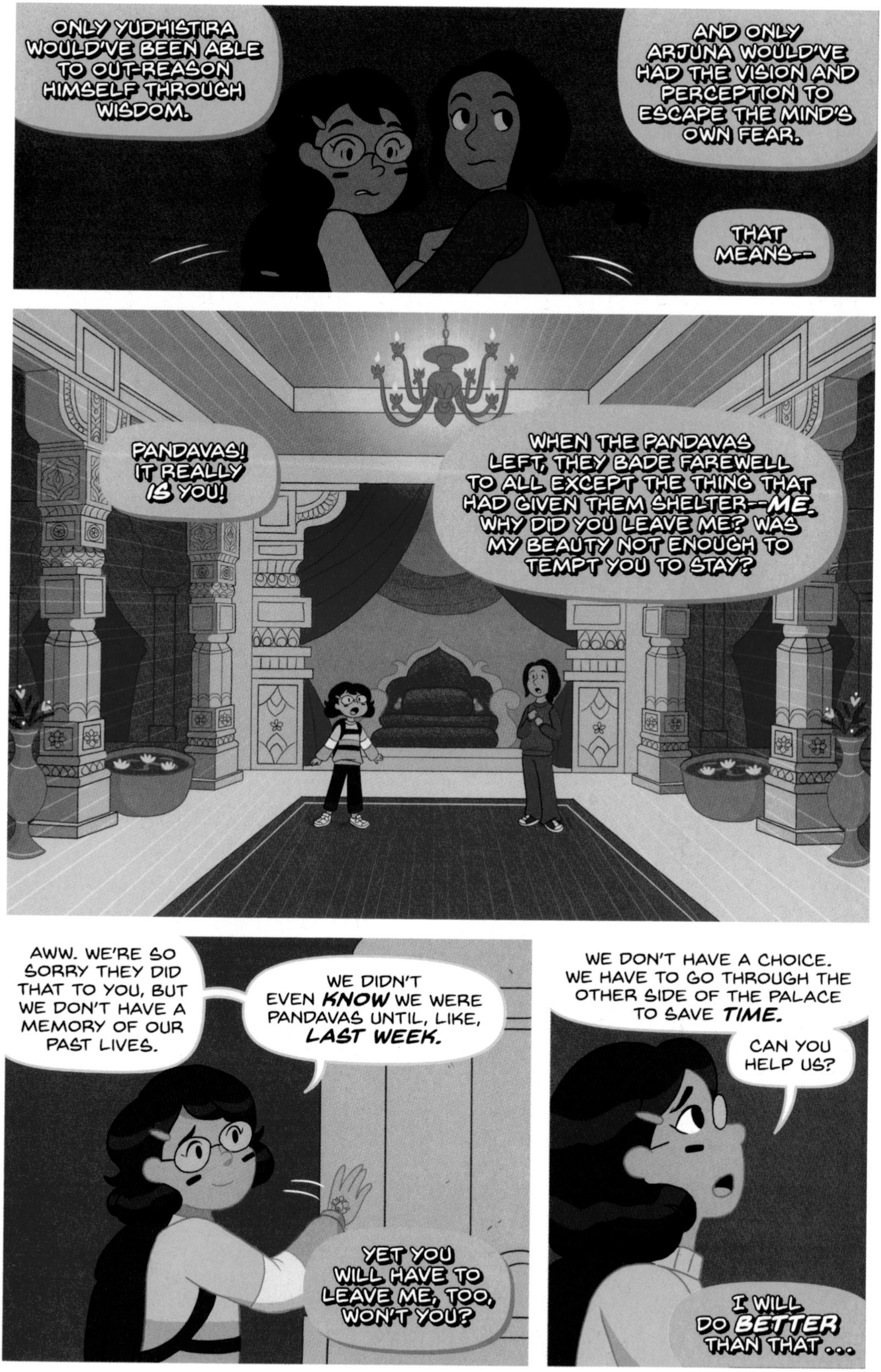
ONLY YUDHISTIRA WOULD'VE BEEN ABLE TO OUT-REASON HIMSELF THROUGH WISDOM.
AND ONLY ARJUNA WOULD'VE HAD THE VISION AND PERCEPTION TO ESCAPE THE MIND'S OWN FEAR.
THAT MEANS--
PANDAVAS! IT REALLY IS YOU!
WHEN THE PANDAVAS LEFT, THEY BADE FAREWELL TO ALL EXCEPT THE THING THAT HAD GIVEN THEM SHELTER--ME. WHY DID YOU LEAVE ME? WAS MY BEAUTY NOT ENOUGH TO TEMPT YOU TO STAY?
AWW. WE'RE SO SORRY THEY DID THAT TO YOU, BUT WE DON'T HAVE A MEMORY OF OUR PAST LIVES.
WE DIDN'T EVEN KNOW WE WERE PANDAVAS UNTIL, LIKE, LAST WEEK.
YET YOU WILL HAVE TO LEAVE ME, TOO, WON'T YOU?
WE DON'T HAVE A CHOICE. WE HAVE TO GO THROUGH THE OTHER SIDE OF THE PALACE TO SAVE TIME.
CAN YOU HELP US?
I WILL DO BETTER THAN THAT...

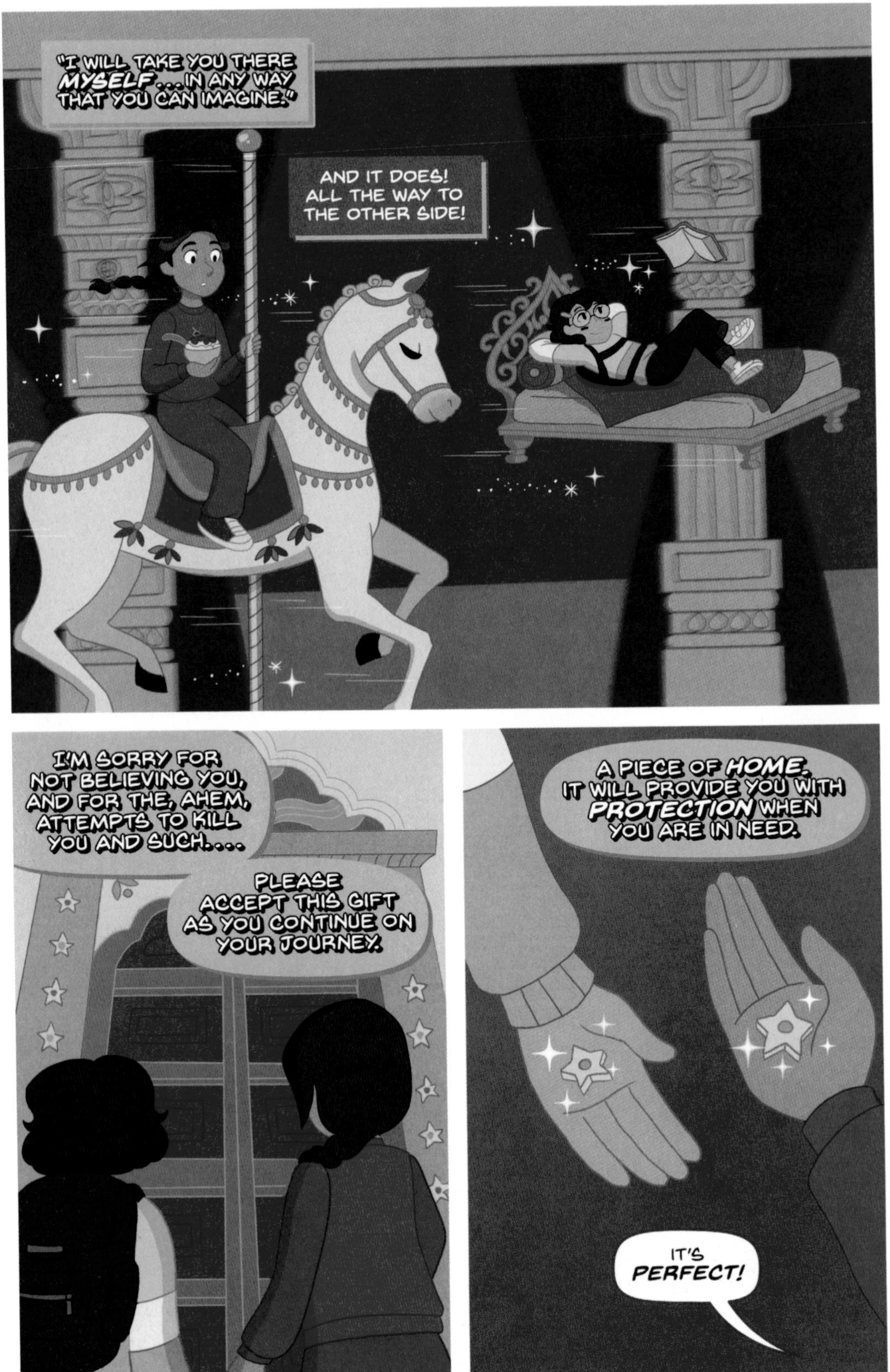
"I WILL TAKE YOU THERE MYSELF...IN ANY WAY THAT YOU CAN IMAGINE."
AND IT DOES! ALL THE WAY TO THE OTHER SIDE!
I'M SORRY FOR NOT BELIEVING YOU, AND FOR THE, AHEM, ATTEMPTS TO KILL YOU AND SUCH....
PLEASE ACCEPT THIS GIFT AS YOU CONTINUE ON YOUR JOURNEY.
A PIECE OF HOME. IT WILL PROVIDE YOU WITH PROTECTION WHEN YOU ARE IN NEED.
IT'S PERFECT!

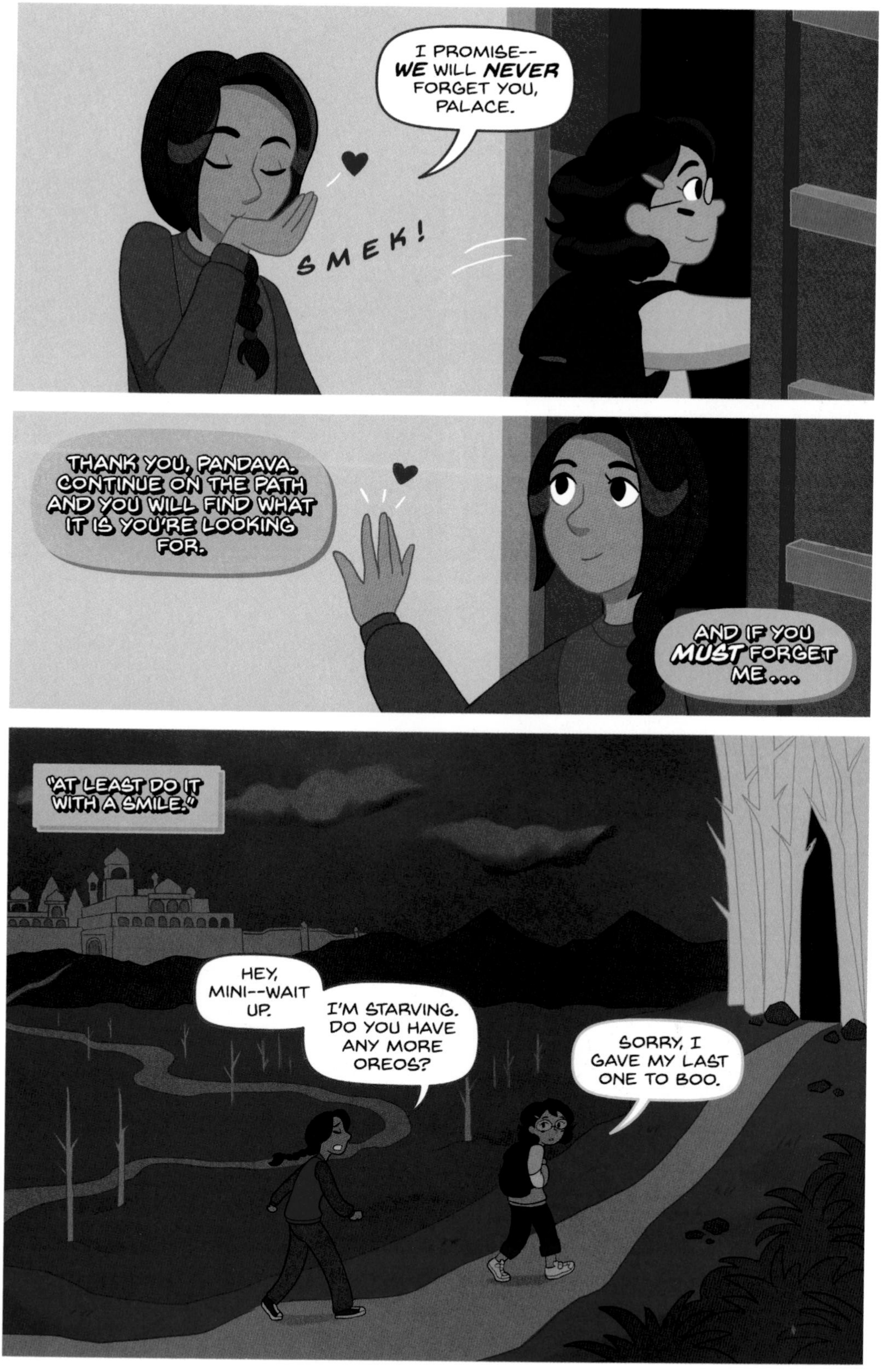
I PROMISE-- WE WILL NEVER FORGET YOU, PALACE.
SMEK!
THANK YOU, PANDAVA. CONTINUE ON THE PATH AND YOU WILL FIND WHAT IT IS YOU'RE LOOKING FOR.
AND IF YOU MUST FORGET ME...
"AT LEAST DO IT WITH A SMILE."
HEY, MINI--WAIT UP.
I'M STARVING. DO YOU HAVE ANY MORE OREOS?
SORRY, I GAVE MY LAST ONE TO BOO.

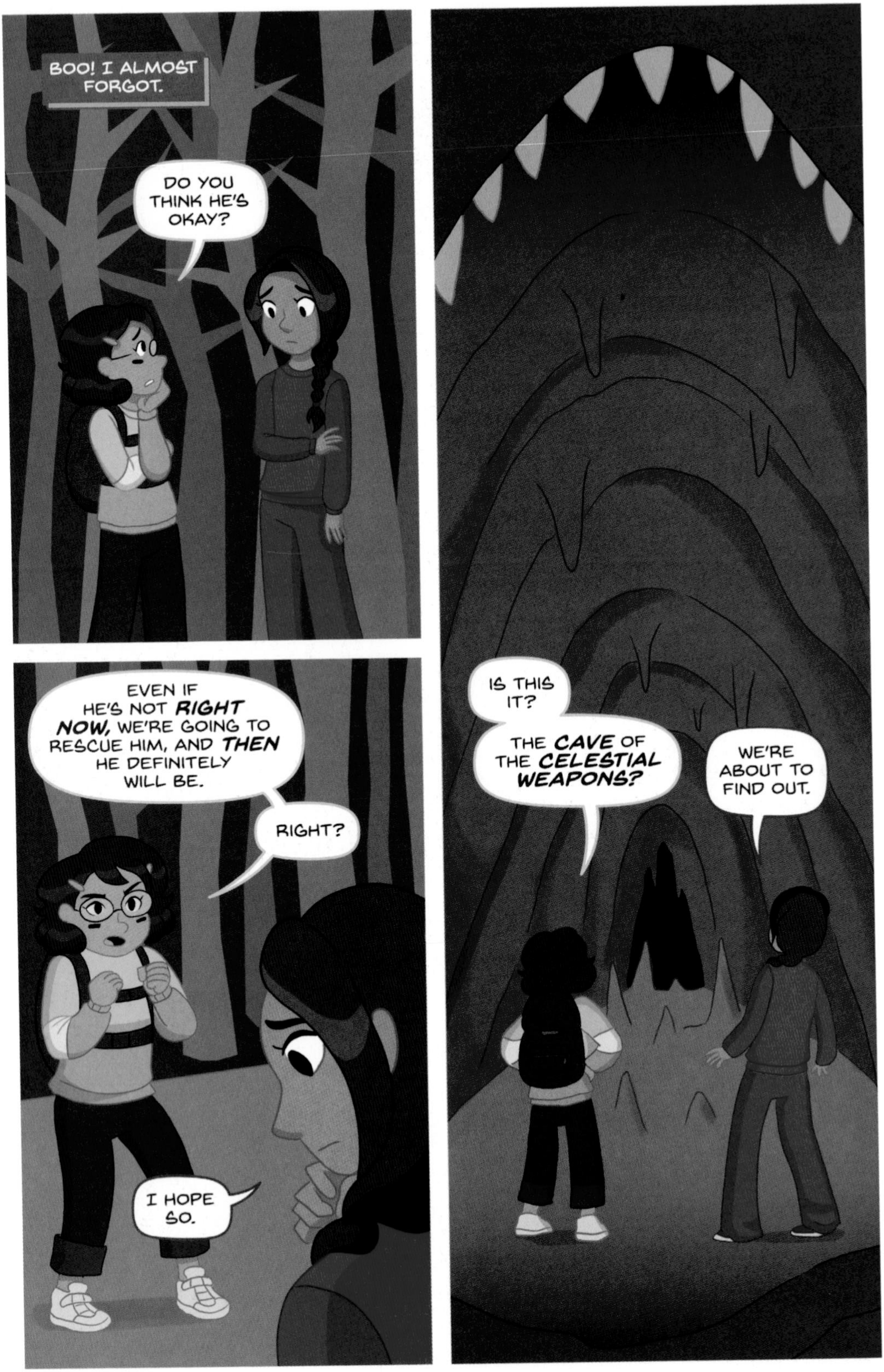
BOO! I ALMOST FORGOT.
DO YOU THINK HE'S OKAY?
EVEN IF HE'S NOT **RIGHT NOW,** WE'RE GOING TO RESCUE HIM, AND **THEN** HE DEFINITELY WILL BE.
RIGHT?
I HOPE SO.
IS THIS IT?
THE **CAVE** OF THE **CELESTIAL WEAPONS?**
WE'RE ABOUT TO FIND OUT.

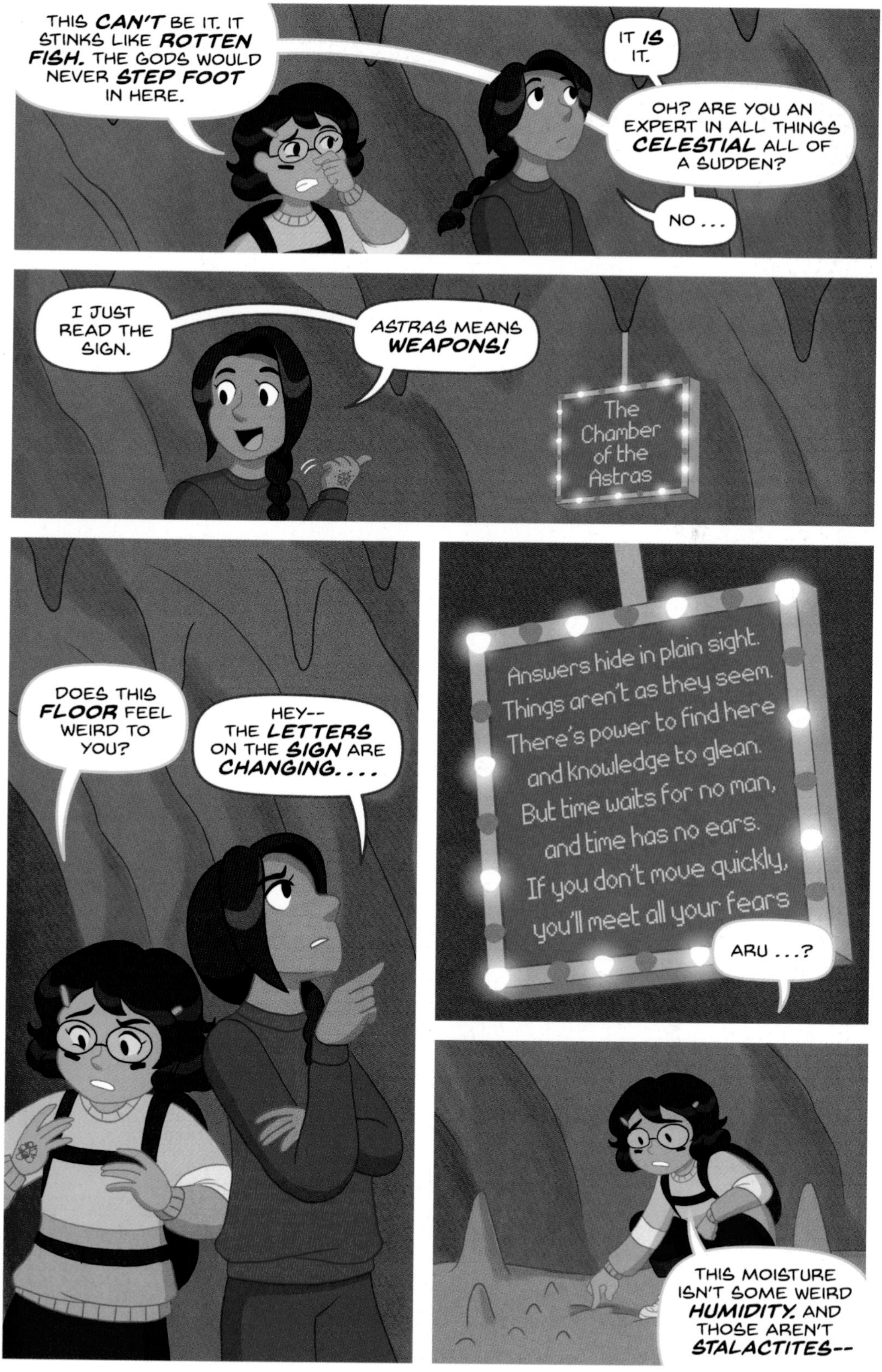

THIS CAN'T BE IT. IT STINKS LIKE ROTTEN FISH. THE GODS WOULD NEVER STEP FOOT IN HERE.
IT IS IT.
OH? ARE YOU AN EXPERT IN ALL THINGS CELESTIAL ALL OF A SUDDEN?
NO . . .
I JUST READ THE SIGN.
ASTRAS MEANS WEAPONS!
The Chamber of the Astras
DOES THIS FLOOR FEEL WEIRD TO YOU?
HEY-- THE LETTERS ON THE SIGN ARE CHANGING. . . .
Answers hide in plain sight.
Things aren't as they seem.
There's power to find here
and knowledge to glean.
But time waits for no man,
and time has no ears.
If you don't move quickly,
you'll meet all your fears
ARU . . .?
THIS MOISTURE ISN'T SOME WEIRD HUMIDITY. AND THOSE AREN'T STALACTITES--

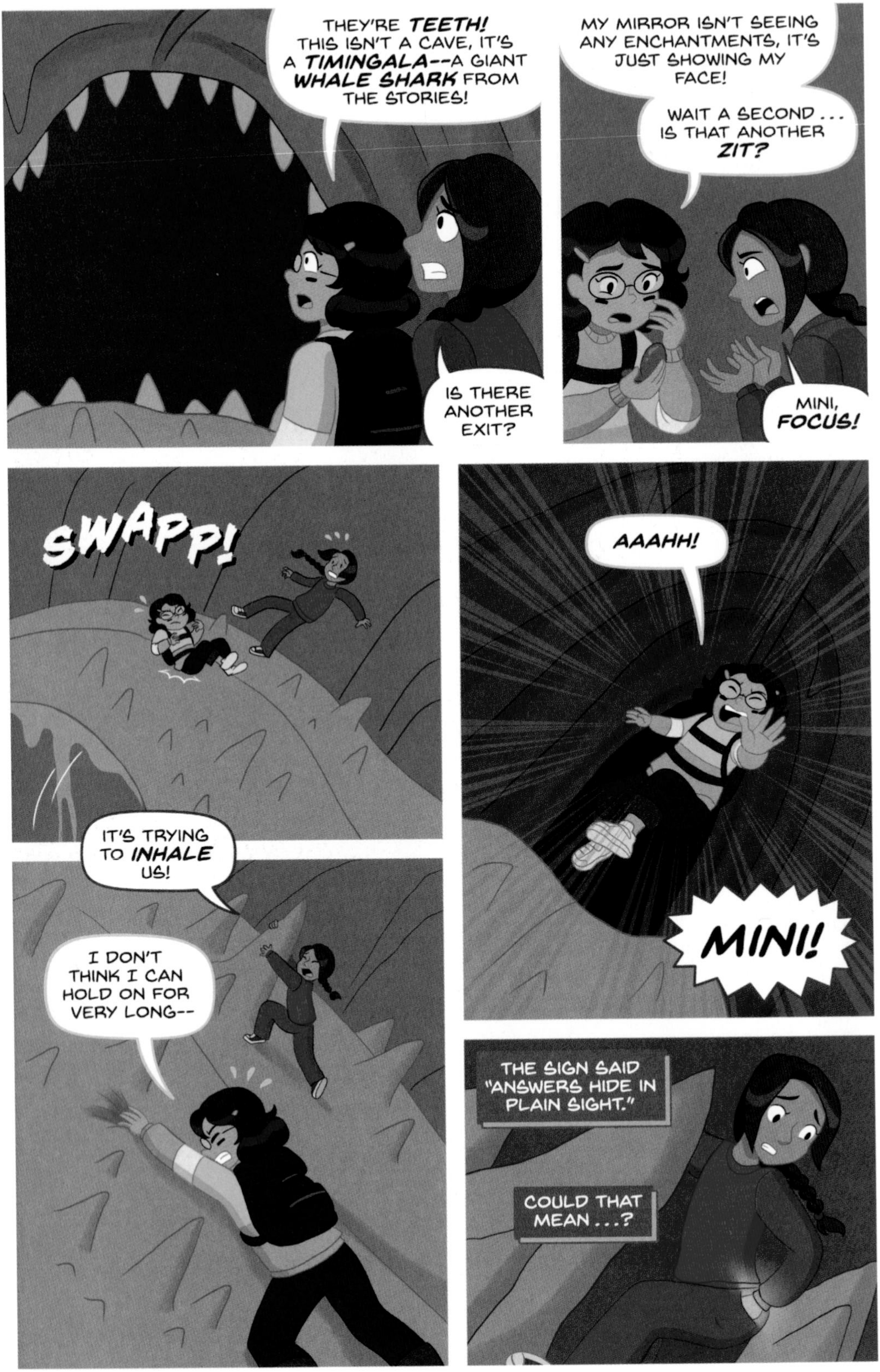
THEY'RE TEETH! THIS ISN'T A CAVE, IT'S A TIMINGALA--A GIANT WHALE SHARK FROM THE STORIES!
IS THERE ANOTHER EXIT?
MY MIRROR ISN'T SEEING ANY ENCHANTMENTS, IT'S JUST SHOWING MY FACE!
WAIT A SECOND . . . IS THAT ANOTHER ZIT?
MINI, FOCUS!
SWAPP!
IT'S TRYING TO INHALE US!
I DON'T THINK I CAN HOLD ON FOR VERY LONG--
AAAHH!
MINI!
THE SIGN SAID "ANSWERS HIDE IN PLAIN SIGHT."
COULD THAT MEAN . . .?

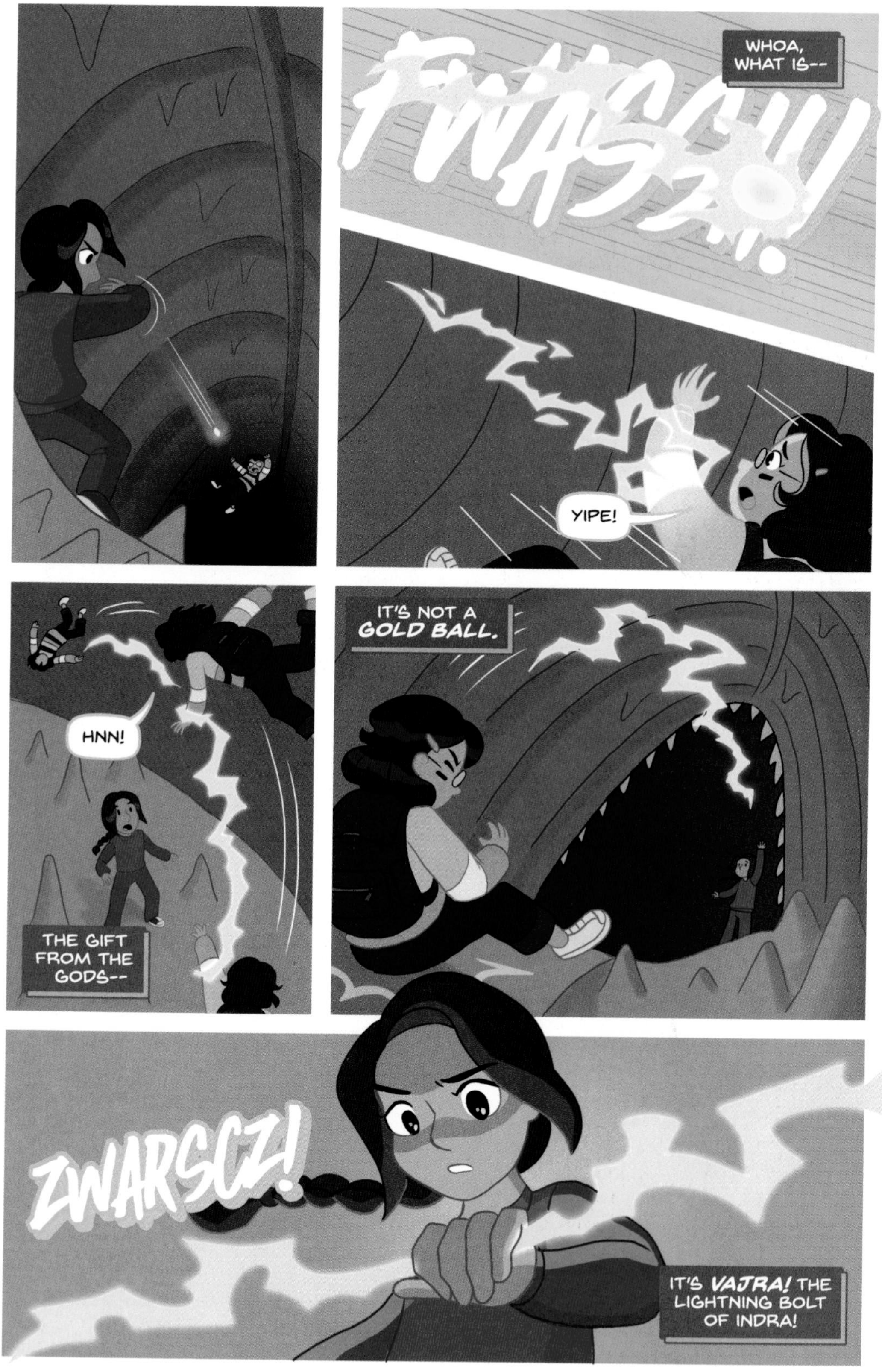
WHOA, WHAT IS--
YIPE!
HNN!
THE GIFT FROM THE GODS--
IT'S NOT A GOLD BALL.
ZWARSCZ!
IT'S VAJRA! THE LIGHTNING BOLT OF INDRA!

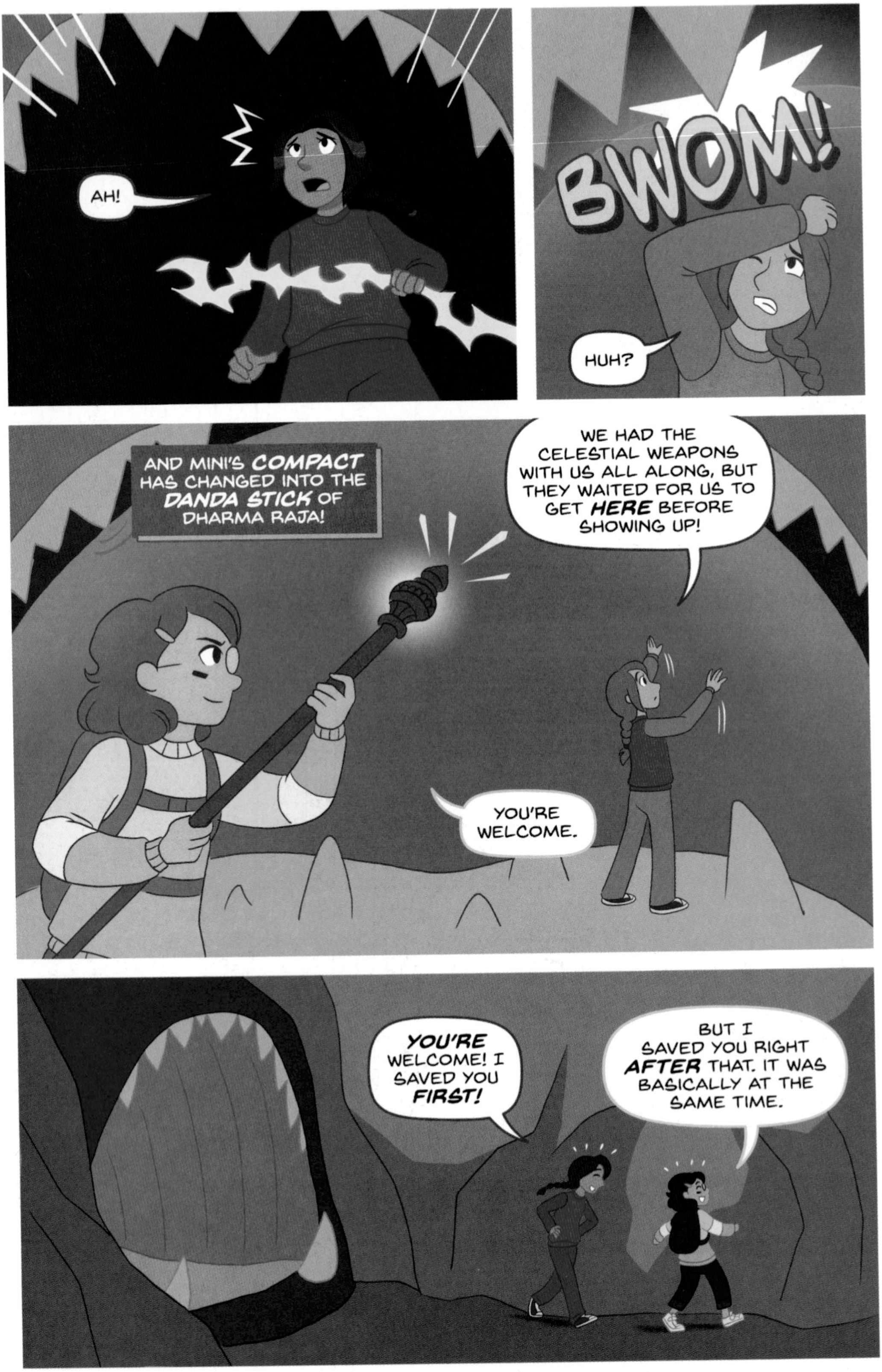
AH!
BWOM!
HUH?
AND MINI'S COMPACT HAS CHANGED INTO THE DANDA STICK OF DHARMA RAJA!
WE HAD THE CELESTIAL WEAPONS WITH US ALL ALONG, BUT THEY WAITED FOR US TO GET HERE BEFORE SHOWING UP!
YOU'RE WELCOME.
YOU'RE WELCOME! I SAVED YOU FIRST!
BUT I SAVED YOU RIGHT AFTER THAT. IT WAS BASICALLY AT THE SAME TIME.

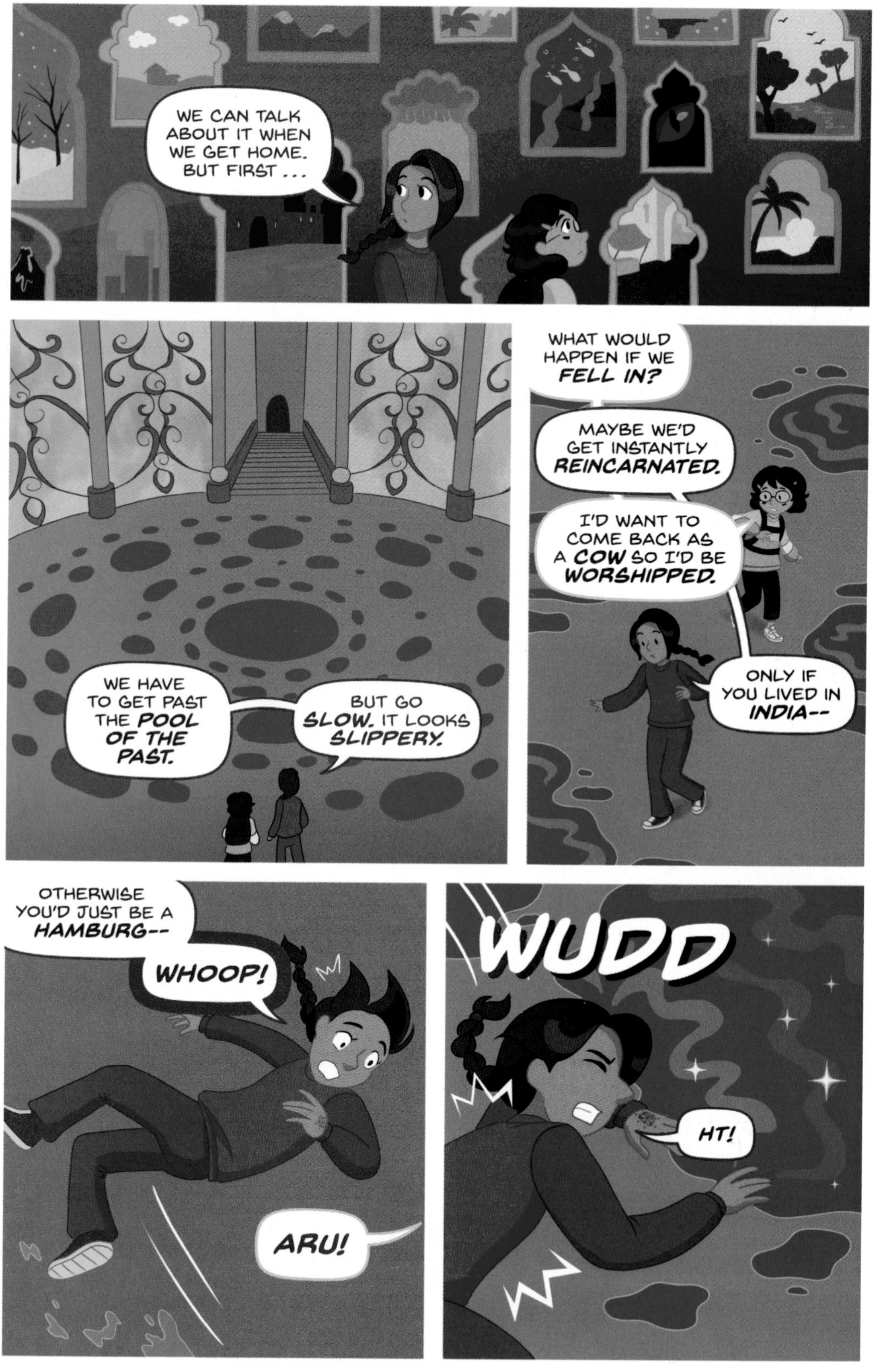
WE CAN TALK ABOUT IT WHEN WE GET HOME. BUT FIRST . . .
WE HAVE TO GET PAST THE POOL OF THE PAST.
BUT GO SLOW. IT LOOKS SLIPPERY.
WHAT WOULD HAPPEN IF WE FELL IN?
MAYBE WE'D GET INSTANTLY REINCARNATED.
I'D WANT TO COME BACK AS A COW SO I'D BE WORSHIPPED.
ONLY IF YOU LIVED IN INDIA--
OTHERWISE YOU'D JUST BE A HAMBURG--
WHOOP!
ARU!
WUDD
HT!

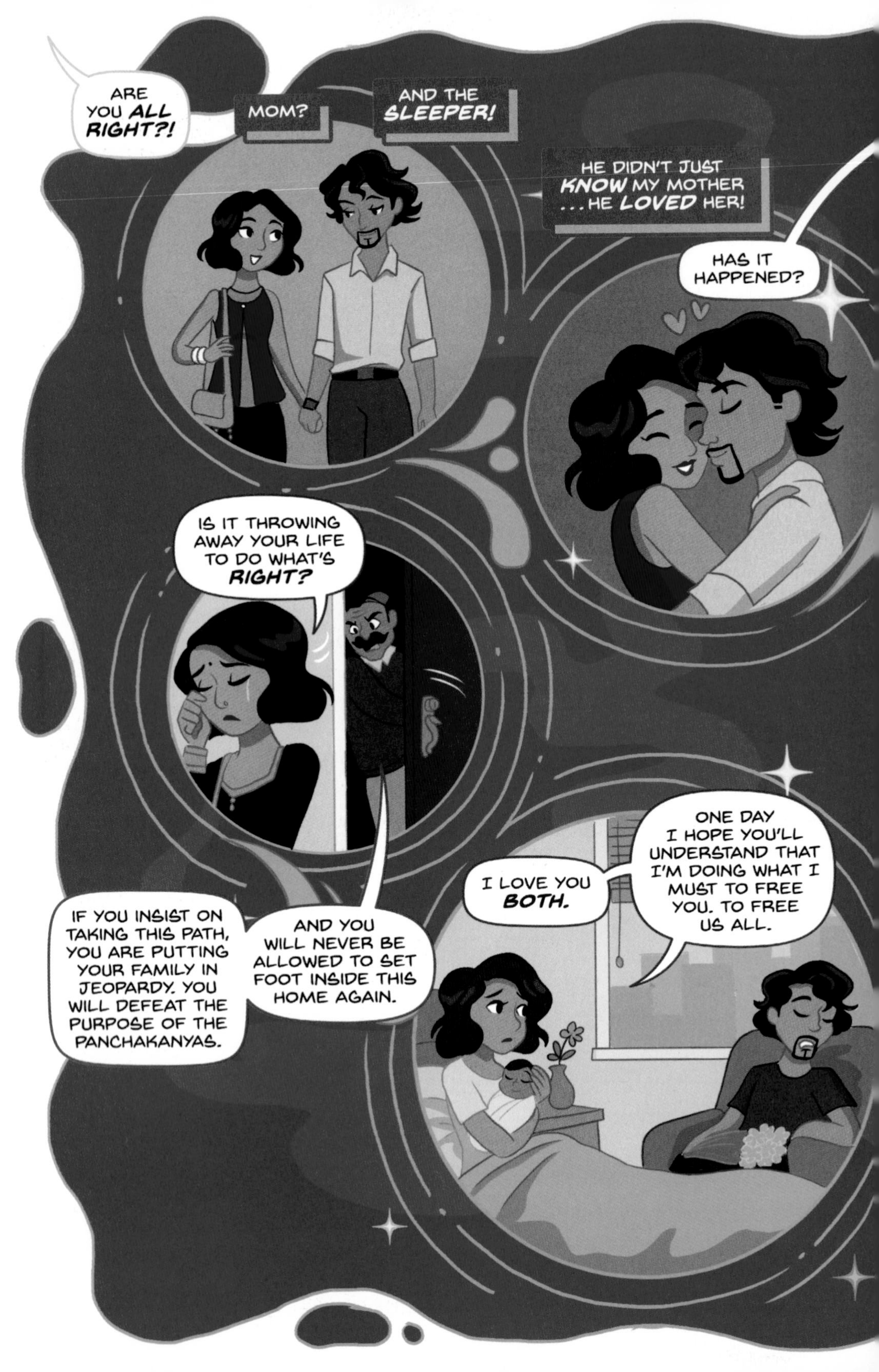

ARE YOU ALL RIGHT?!
MOM?
AND THE SLEEPER!
HE DIDN'T JUST KNOW MY MOTHER ...HE LOVED HER!
HAS IT HAPPENED?
IS IT THROWING AWAY YOUR LIFE TO DO WHAT'S RIGHT?
IF YOU INSIST ON TAKING THIS PATH, YOU ARE PUTTING YOUR FAMILY IN JEOPARDY. YOU WILL DEFEAT THE PURPOSE OF THE PANCHAKANYAS.
AND YOU WILL NEVER BE ALLOWED TO SET FOOT INSIDE THIS HOME AGAIN.
I LOVE YOU BOTH.
ONE DAY I HOPE YOU'LL UNDERSTAND THAT I'M DOING WHAT I MUST TO FREE YOU. TO FREE US ALL.

YOU KNOW AS WELL AS I DO THAT THE MOMENT THE CHILD COMES OF AGE, **SUYODHANA** IS DESTINED TO BECOME THE **SLEEPER!**
HE IS **AWARE** OF HIS OWN PROPHECY AND PROMISES HE WON'T LOSE HIMSELF TO IT.
MY DAUGHTER COULD HAVE A **FATHER.** WE COULD BE A **FAMILY.**
NO ONE CAN ESCAPE THEIR FATE. YOU MUST **CHOOSE**--YOUR CHILD OR YOUR LOVER. DON'T THROW AWAY YOUR LIFE.
I BIND YOU WITH MY HEART, THE SAME HEART THAT I GAVE TO YOU WILLINGLY.
I BIND YOU WITH SOMETHING THAT IS NOT MADE OF METAL, WOOD, OR STONE.
I BIND YOU WITH SOMETHING THAT IS NEITHER DRY NOR WET.
I NEVER WANTED THIS TO HAPPEN. BUT KNOW THAT I USED YOUR SECRETS NOT TO DESTROY YOU LIKE I WAS SUPPOSED TO, BUT TO **HOLD** YOU.
I'LL FIND AN ANSWER. I'LL FIND A WAY TO FREE BOTH YOU **AND** ARU.
I PROMISE.

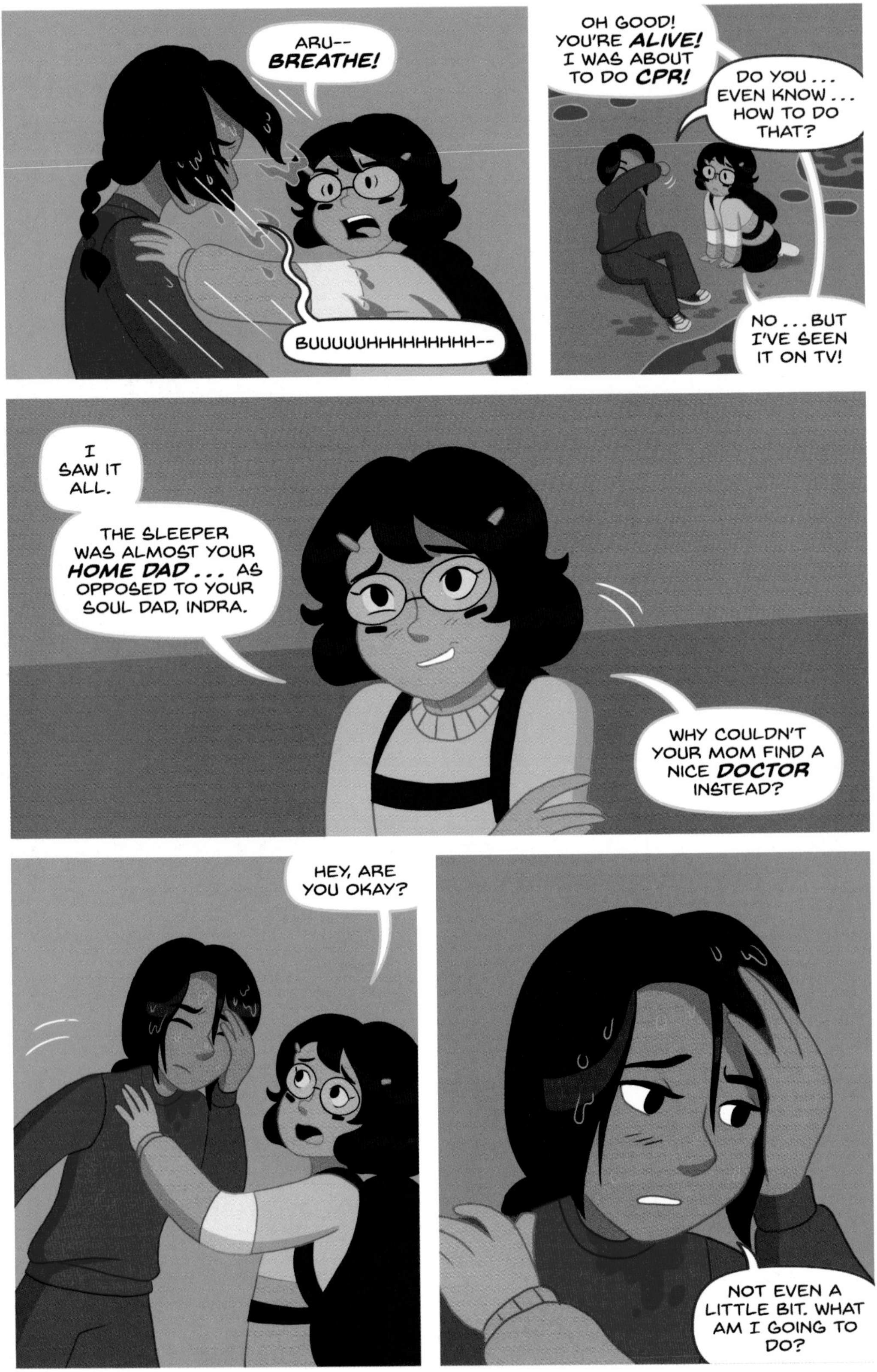
ARU-- **BREATHE!**
BUUUUUHHHHHHHHH--
OH GOOD! YOU'RE **ALIVE!** I WAS ABOUT TO DO **CPR!**
DO YOU . . . EVEN KNOW . . . HOW TO DO THAT?
NO . . . BUT I'VE SEEN IT ON TV!
I SAW IT ALL.
THE SLEEPER WAS ALMOST YOUR **HOME DAD . . .** AS OPPOSED TO YOUR SOUL DAD, INDRA.
WHY COULDN'T YOUR MOM FIND A NICE **DOCTOR** INSTEAD?
HEY, ARE YOU OKAY?
NOT EVEN A LITTLE BIT. WHAT AM I GOING TO DO?

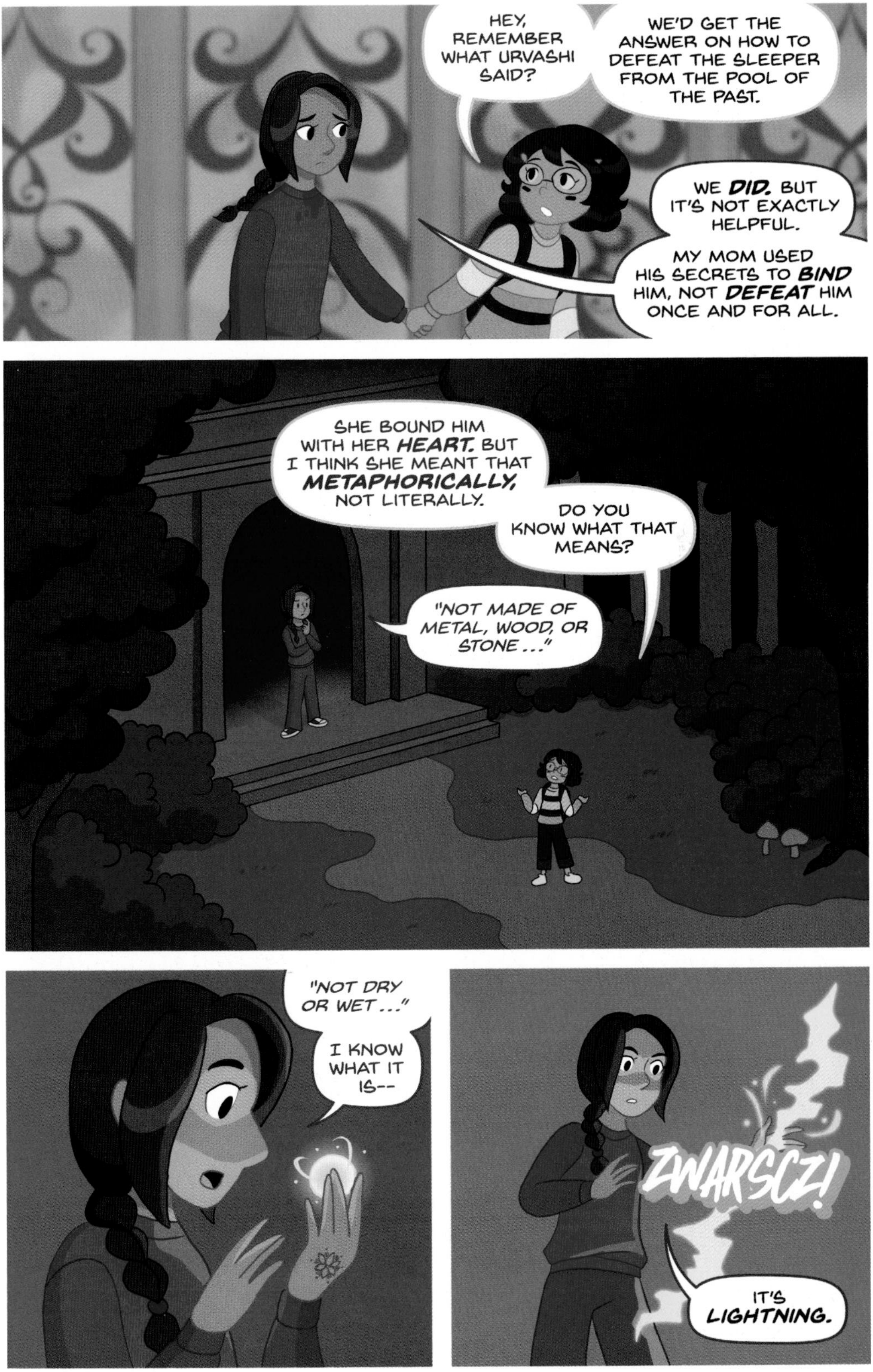
HEY, REMEMBER WHAT URVASHI SAID?
WE'D GET THE ANSWER ON HOW TO DEFEAT THE SLEEPER FROM THE POOL OF THE PAST.
WE **DID.** BUT IT'S NOT EXACTLY HELPFUL.
MY MOM USED HIS SECRETS TO **BIND** HIM, NOT **DEFEAT** HIM ONCE AND FOR ALL.
SHE BOUND HIM WITH HER **HEART.** BUT I THINK SHE MEANT THAT **METAPHORICALLY,** NOT LITERALLY.
DO YOU KNOW WHAT THAT MEANS?
"NOT MADE OF METAL, WOOD, OR STONE . . ."
"NOT DRY OR WET . . ."
I KNOW WHAT IT IS--
ZWARSCZ!
IT'S **LIGHTNING.**

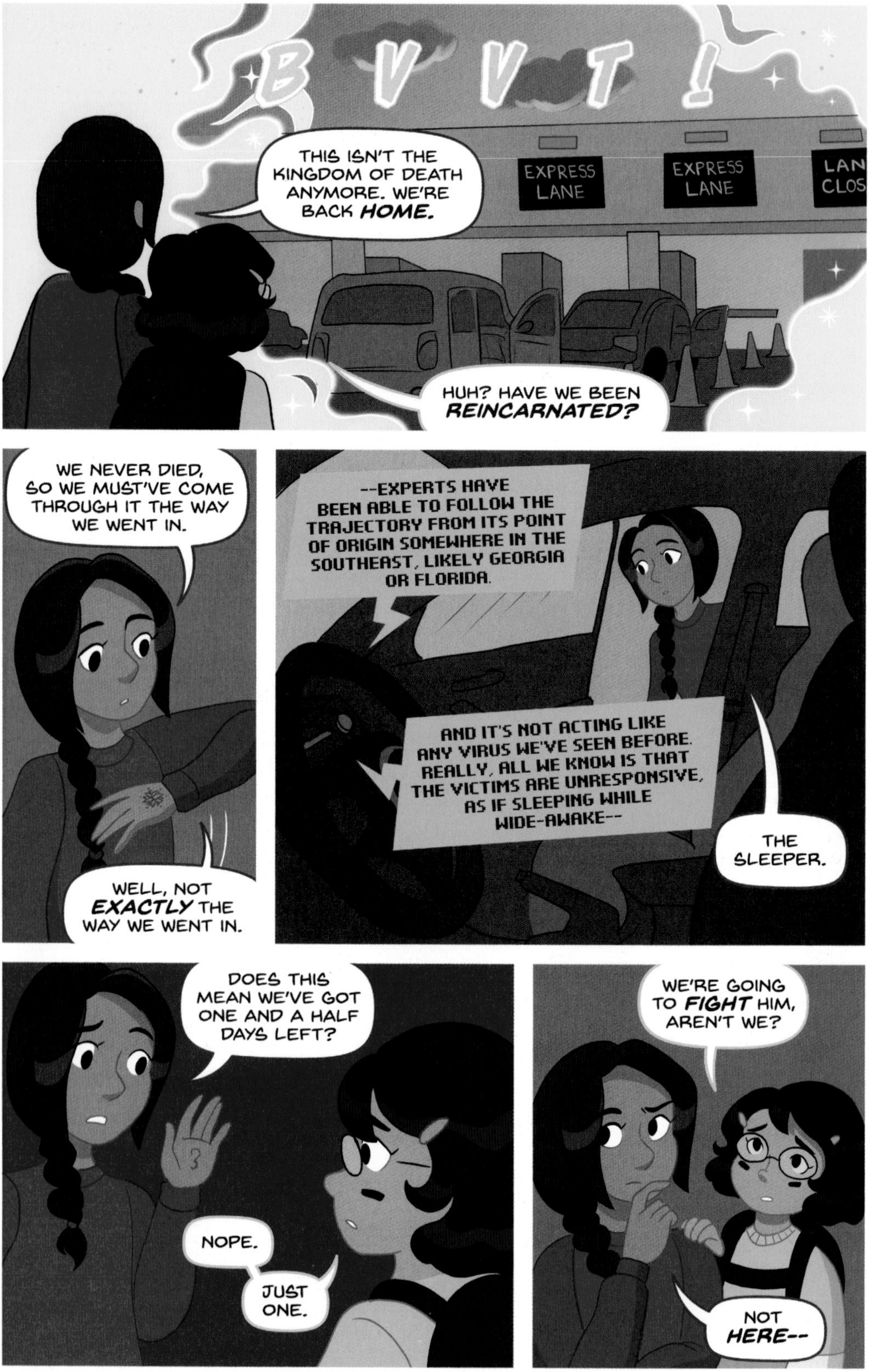
BVVT!
THIS ISN'T THE KINGDOM OF DEATH ANYMORE. WE'RE BACK HOME.
EXPRESS LANE
EXPRESS LANE
HUH? HAVE WE BEEN REINCARNATED?
WE NEVER DIED, SO WE MUST'VE COME THROUGH IT THE WAY WE WENT IN.
WELL, NOT EXACTLY THE WAY WE WENT IN.
--EXPERTS HAVE BEEN ABLE TO FOLLOW THE TRAJECTORY FROM ITS POINT OF ORIGIN SOMEWHERE IN THE SOUTHEAST, LIKELY GEORGIA OR FLORIDA.
AND IT'S NOT ACTING LIKE ANY VIRUS WE'VE SEEN BEFORE. REALLY, ALL WE KNOW IS THAT THE VICTIMS ARE UNRESPONSIVE, AS IF SLEEPING WHILE WIDE-AWAKE--
THE SLEEPER.
DOES THIS MEAN WE'VE GOT ONE AND A HALF DAYS LEFT?
NOPE.
JUST ONE.
WE'RE GOING TO FIGHT HIM, AREN'T WE?
NOT HERE--

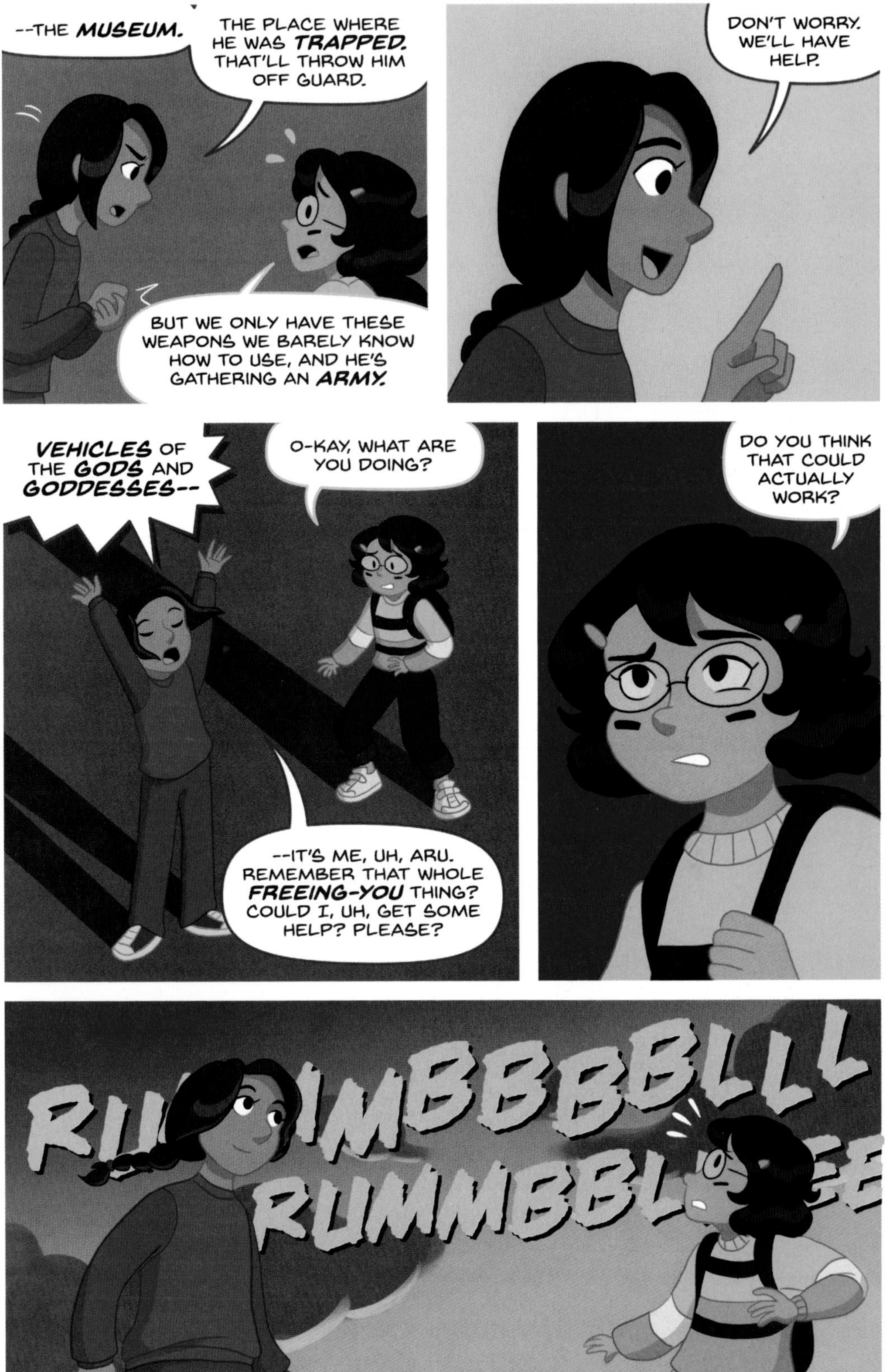

--THE MUSEUM.
THE PLACE WHERE HE WAS TRAPPED. THAT'LL THROW HIM OFF GUARD.
BUT WE ONLY HAVE THESE WEAPONS WE BARELY KNOW HOW TO USE, AND HE'S GATHERING AN ARMY.
DON'T WORRY. WE'LL HAVE HELP.
VEHICLES OF THE GODS AND GODDESSES--
O-KAY, WHAT ARE YOU DOING?
--IT'S ME, UH, ARU. REMEMBER THAT WHOLE FREEING-YOU THING? COULD I, UH, GET SOME HELP? PLEASE?
DO YOU THINK THAT COULD ACTUALLY WORK?

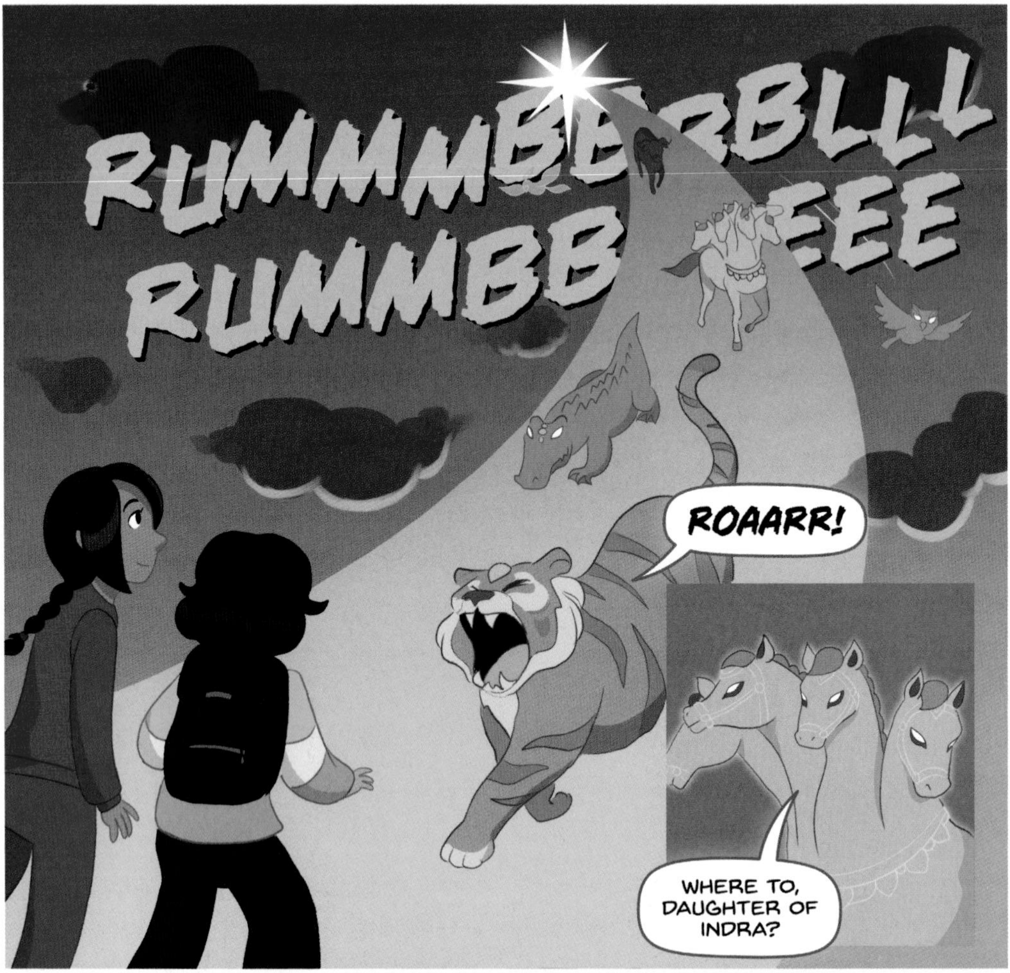
RUMMMBBRBLLL
RUMMBBEEE
ROAARR!
WHERE TO, DAUGHTER OF INDRA?

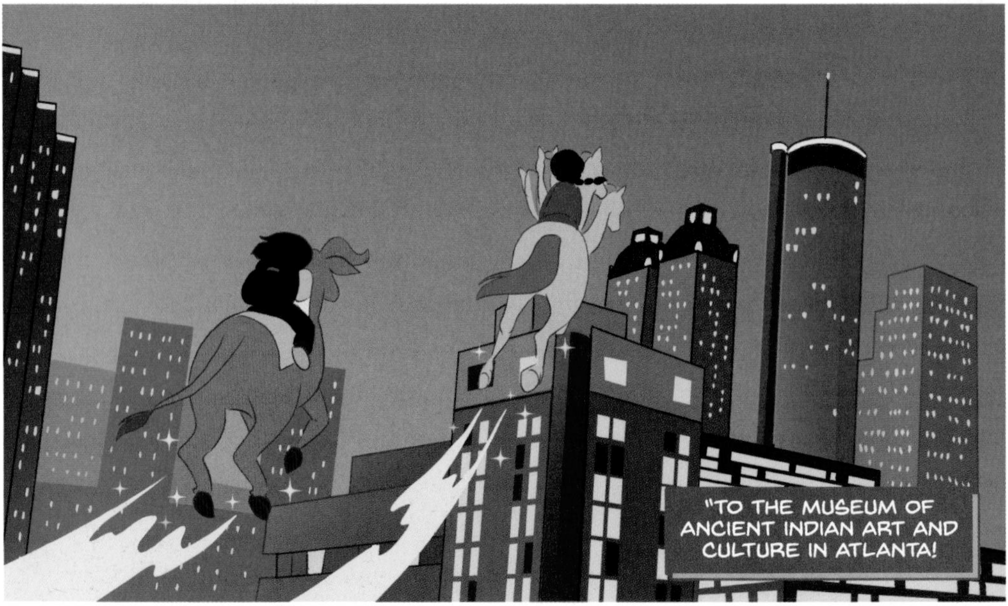
"TO THE MUSEUM OF ANCIENT INDIAN ART AND CULTURE IN ATLANTA!

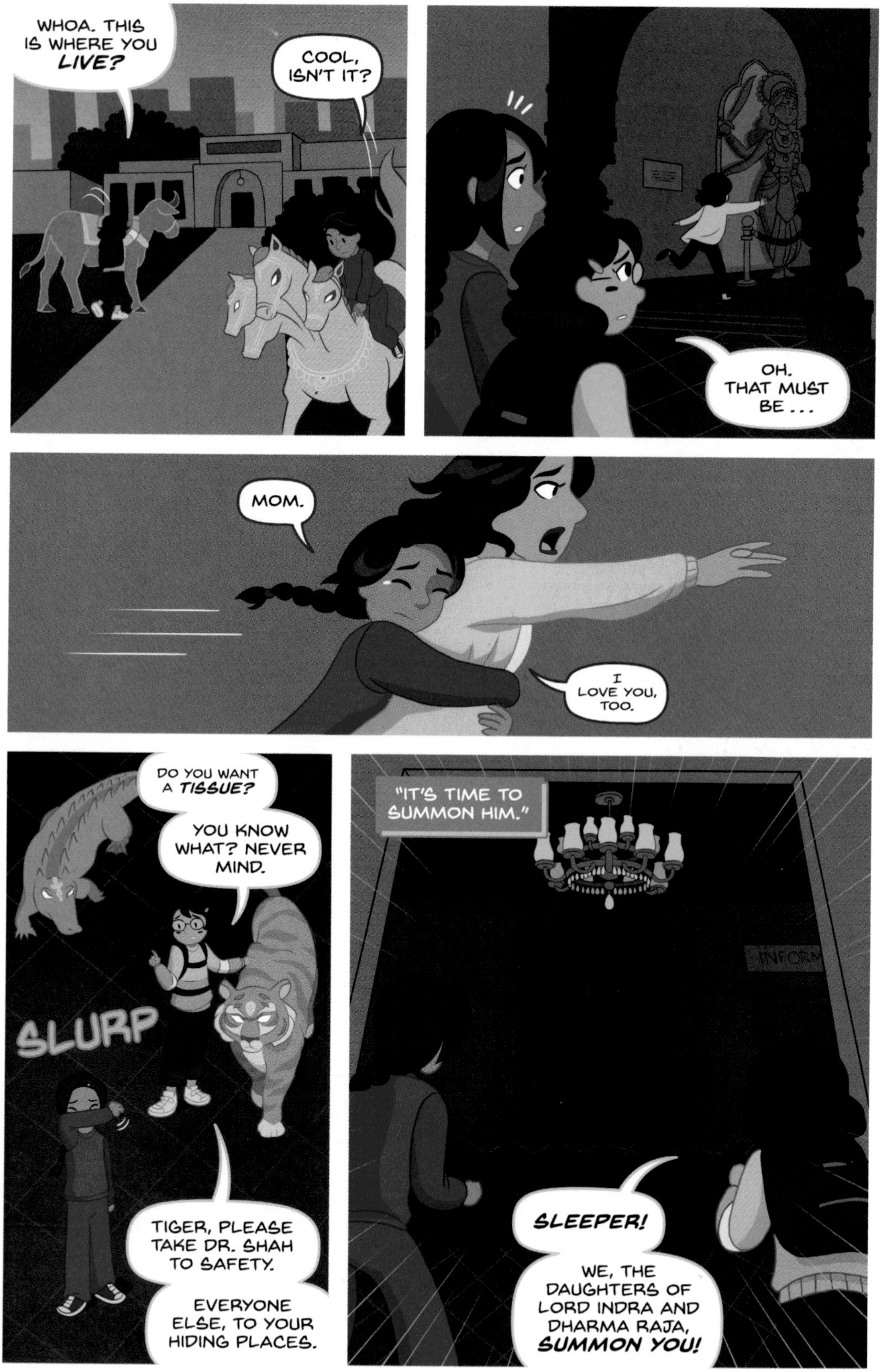
WHOA. THIS IS WHERE YOU *LIVE?*
COOL, ISN'T IT?
OH. THAT MUST BE . . .
MOM.
I LOVE YOU, TOO.
DO YOU WANT A *TISSUE?*
YOU KNOW WHAT? NEVER MIND.
SLURP
TIGER, PLEASE TAKE DR. SHAH TO SAFETY.
EVERYONE ELSE, TO YOUR HIDING PLACES.
"IT'S TIME TO SUMMON HIM."
SLEEPER!
WE, THE DAUGHTERS OF LORD INDRA AND DHARMA RAJA, *SUMMON YOU!*

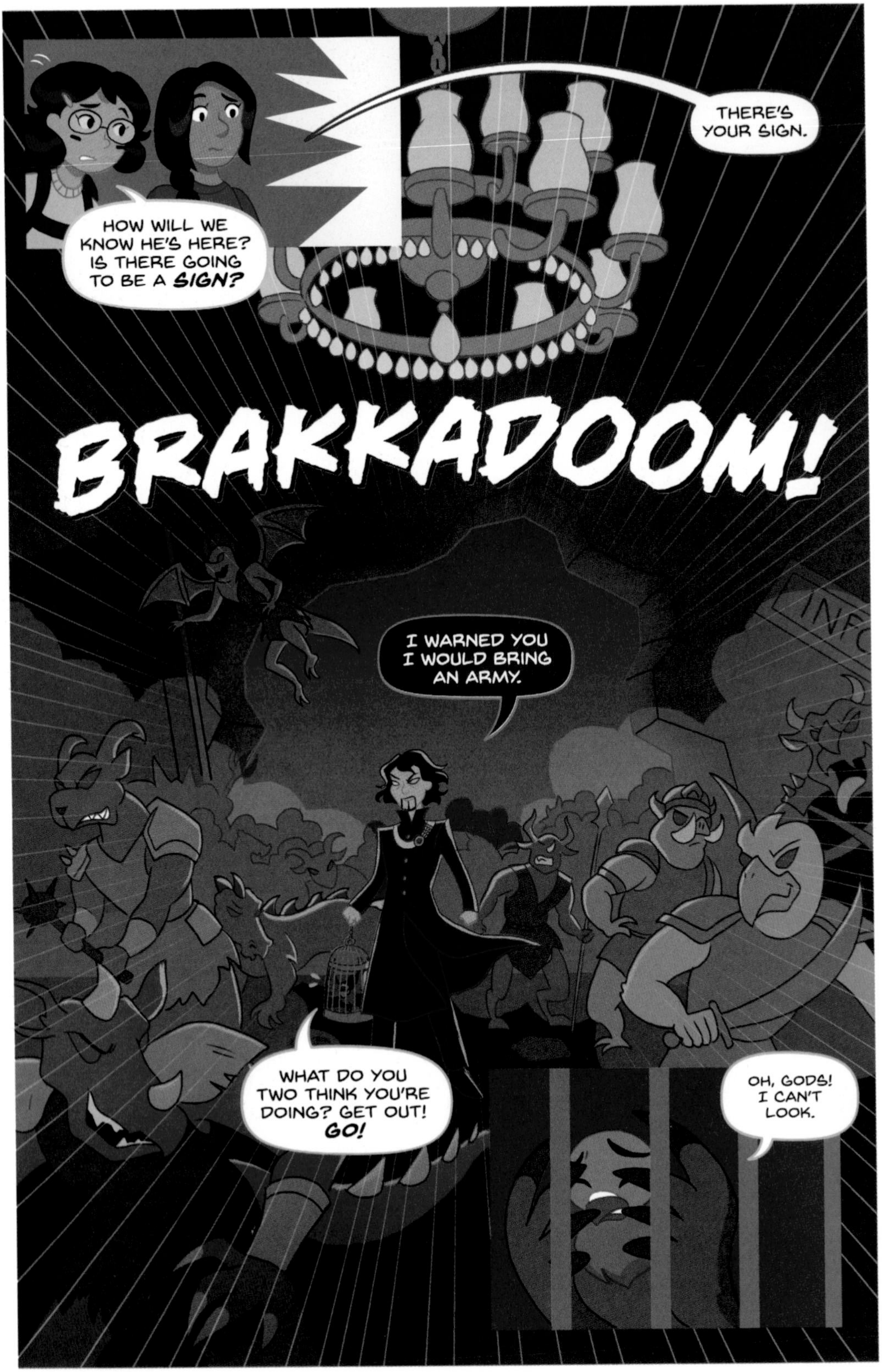
HOW WILL WE KNOW HE'S HERE? IS THERE GOING TO BE A SIGN?
THERE'S YOUR SIGN.
BRAKKADOOM!
I WARNED YOU I WOULD BRING AN ARMY.
WHAT DO YOU TWO THINK YOU'RE DOING? GET OUT! GO!
OH, GODS! I CAN'T LOOK.

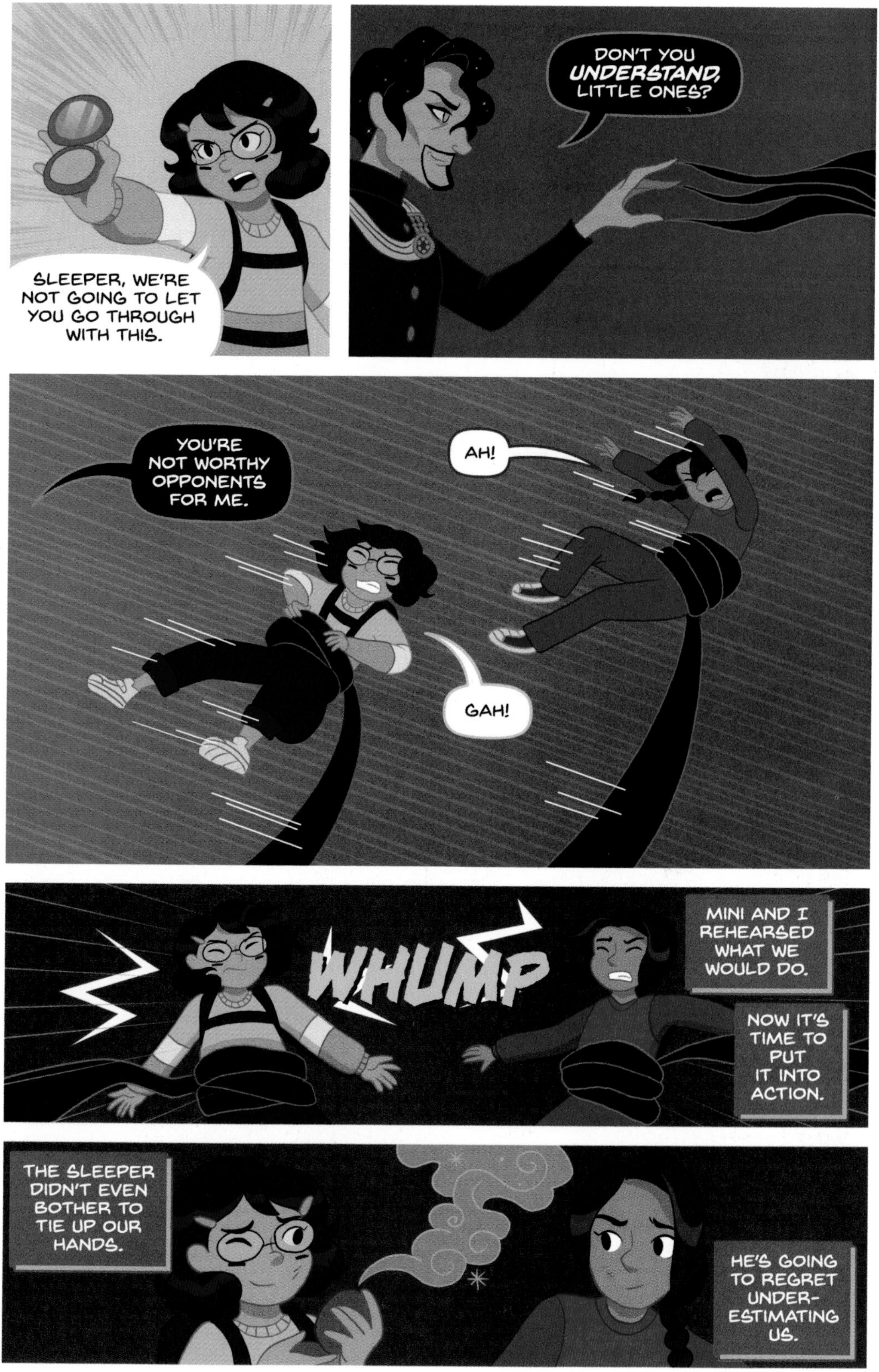

SLEEPER, WE'RE NOT GOING TO LET YOU GO THROUGH WITH THIS.
DON'T YOU *UNDERSTAND,* LITTLE ONES?
YOU'RE NOT WORTHY OPPONENTS FOR ME.
AH!
GAH!
WHUMP
MINI AND I REHEARSED WHAT WE WOULD DO.
NOW IT'S TIME TO PUT IT INTO ACTION.
THE SLEEPER DIDN'T EVEN BOTHER TO TIE UP OUR HANDS.
HE'S GOING TO REGRET UNDER-ESTIMATING US.

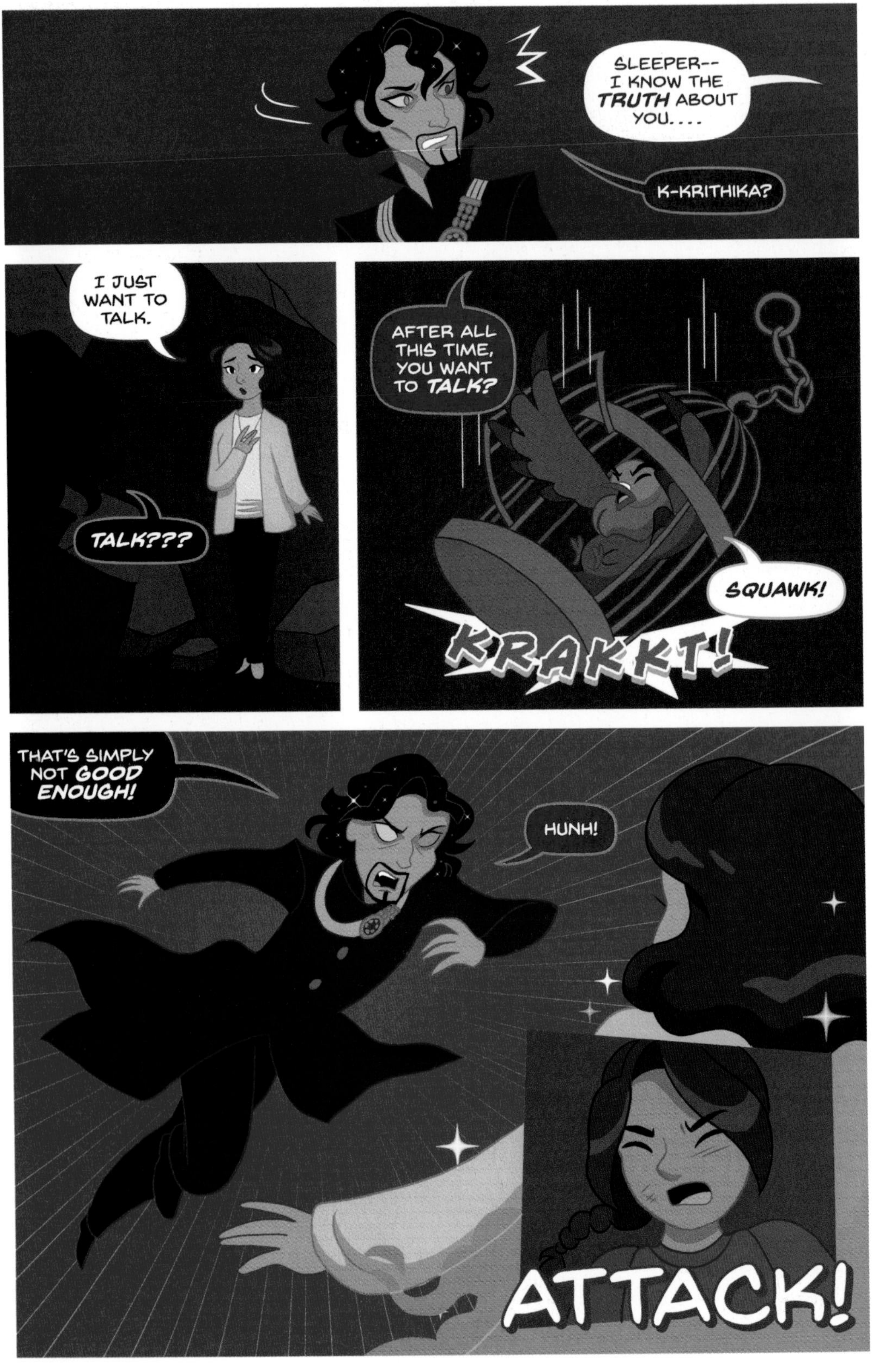
SLEEPER--
I KNOW THE
TRUTH ABOUT
YOU. . . .
K-KRITHIKA?
I JUST
WANT TO
TALK.
TALK???
AFTER ALL
THIS TIME,
YOU WANT
TO TALK?
SQUAWK!
KRAKKT!
THAT'S SIMPLY
NOT GOOD
ENOUGH!
HUNH!
ATTACK!

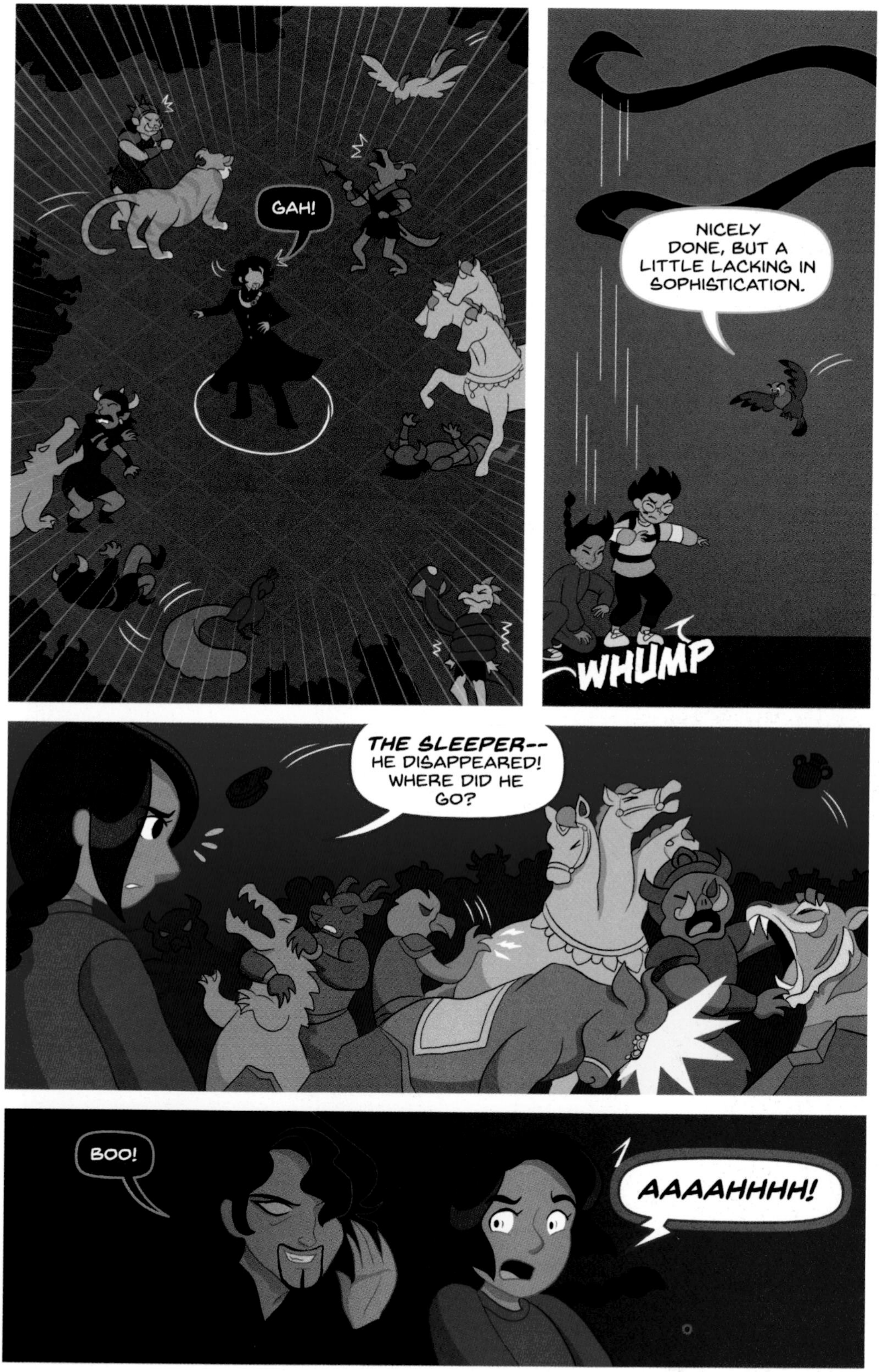
GAH!
NICELY DONE, BUT A LITTLE LACKING IN SOPHISTICATION.
WHUMP
THE SLEEPER-- HE DISAPPEARED! WHERE DID HE GO?
BOO!
AAAAHHHH!

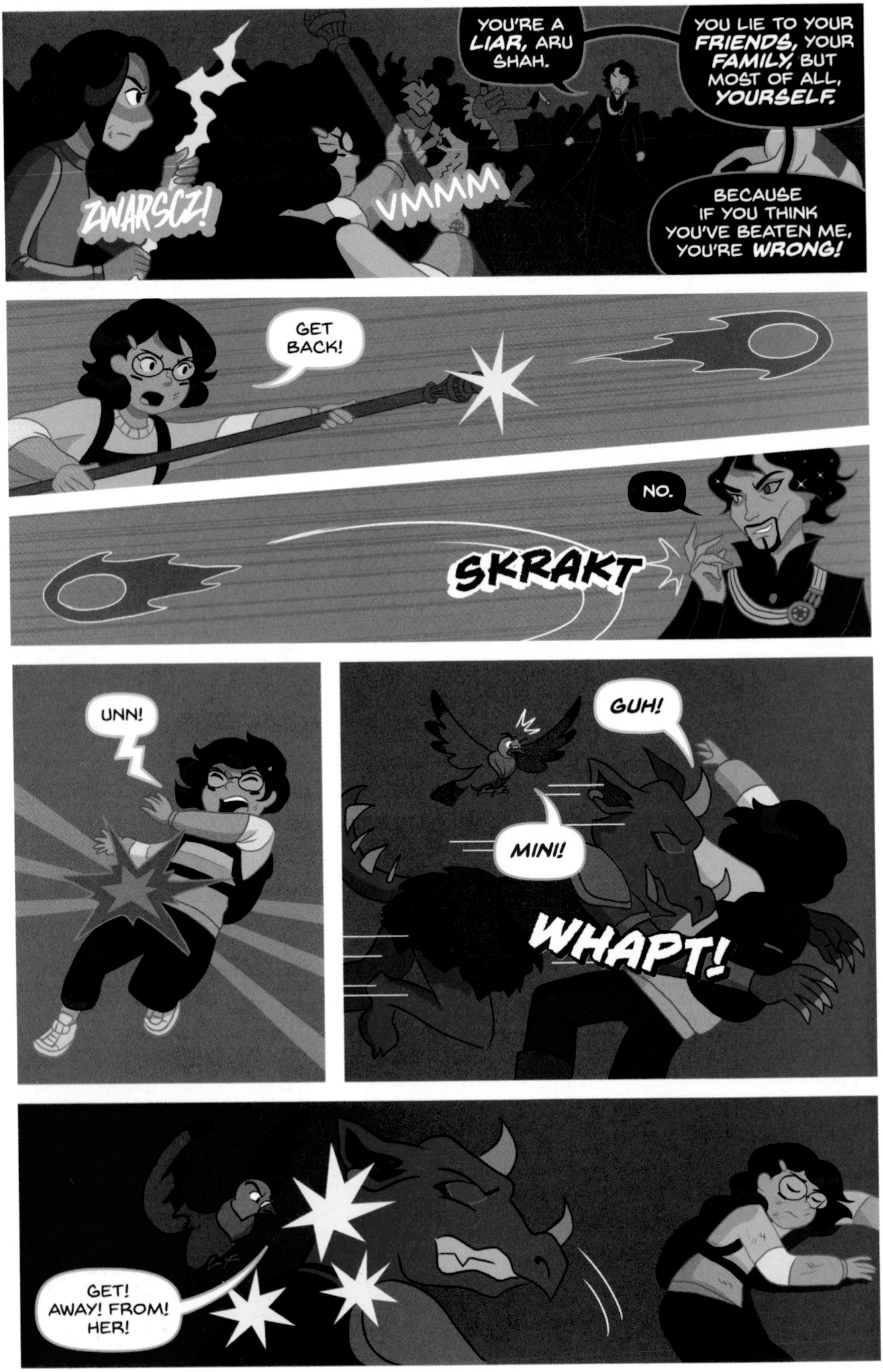
YOU'RE A LIAR, ARU SHAH.
YOU LIE TO YOUR FRIENDS, YOUR FAMILY, BUT MOST OF ALL, YOURSELF.
ZWARSCZ!
VMMM
BECAUSE IF YOU THINK YOU'VE BEATEN ME, YOU'RE WRONG!
GET BACK!
NO.
SKRAKT
UNN!
GUH!
MINI!
WHAPT!
GET! AWAY! FROM! HER!

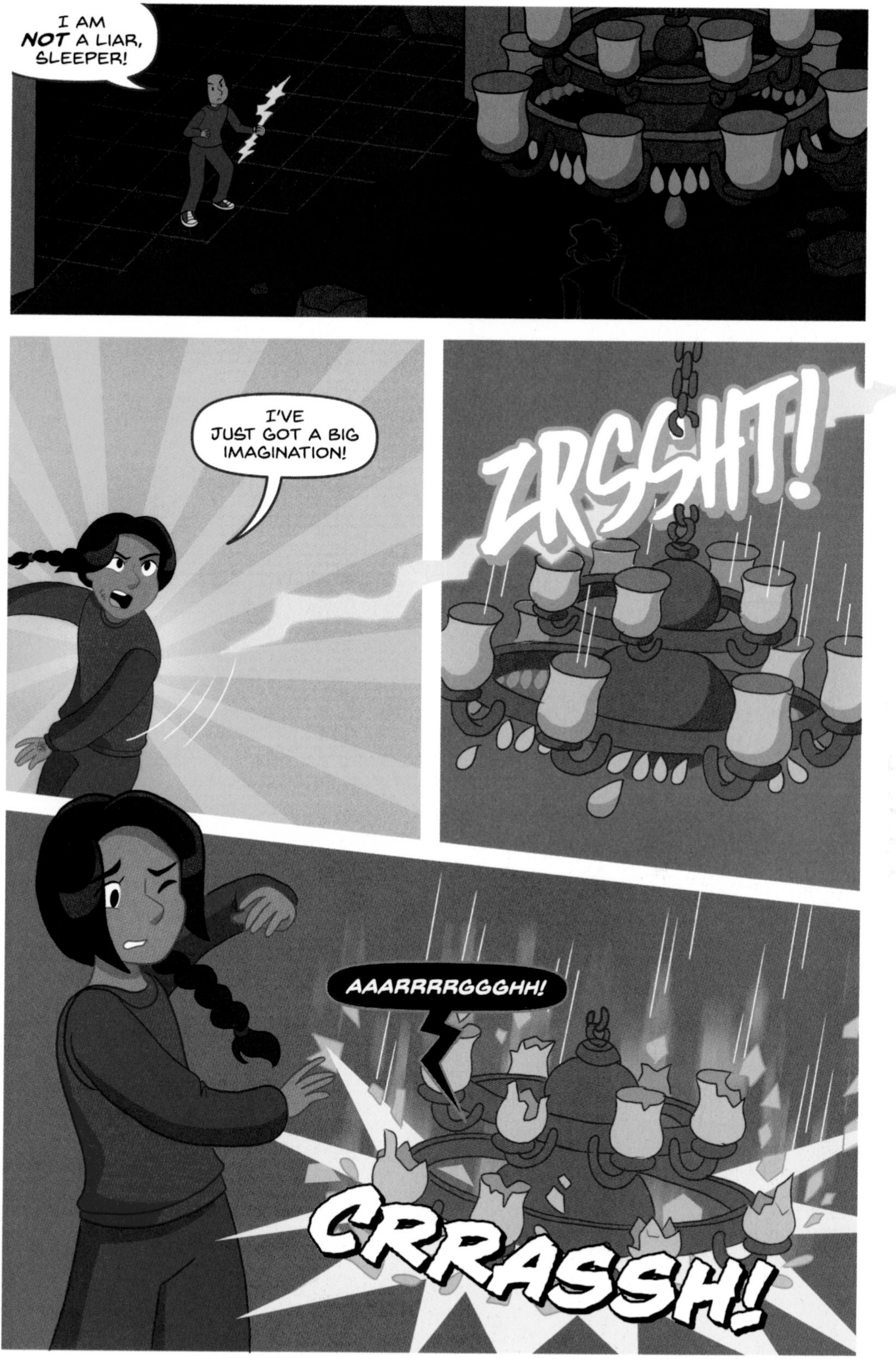
I AM NOT A LIAR, SLEEPER!
I'VE JUST GOT A BIG IMAGINATION!
ZRSSHT!
AAARRRRGGGHH!
CRRASSH!

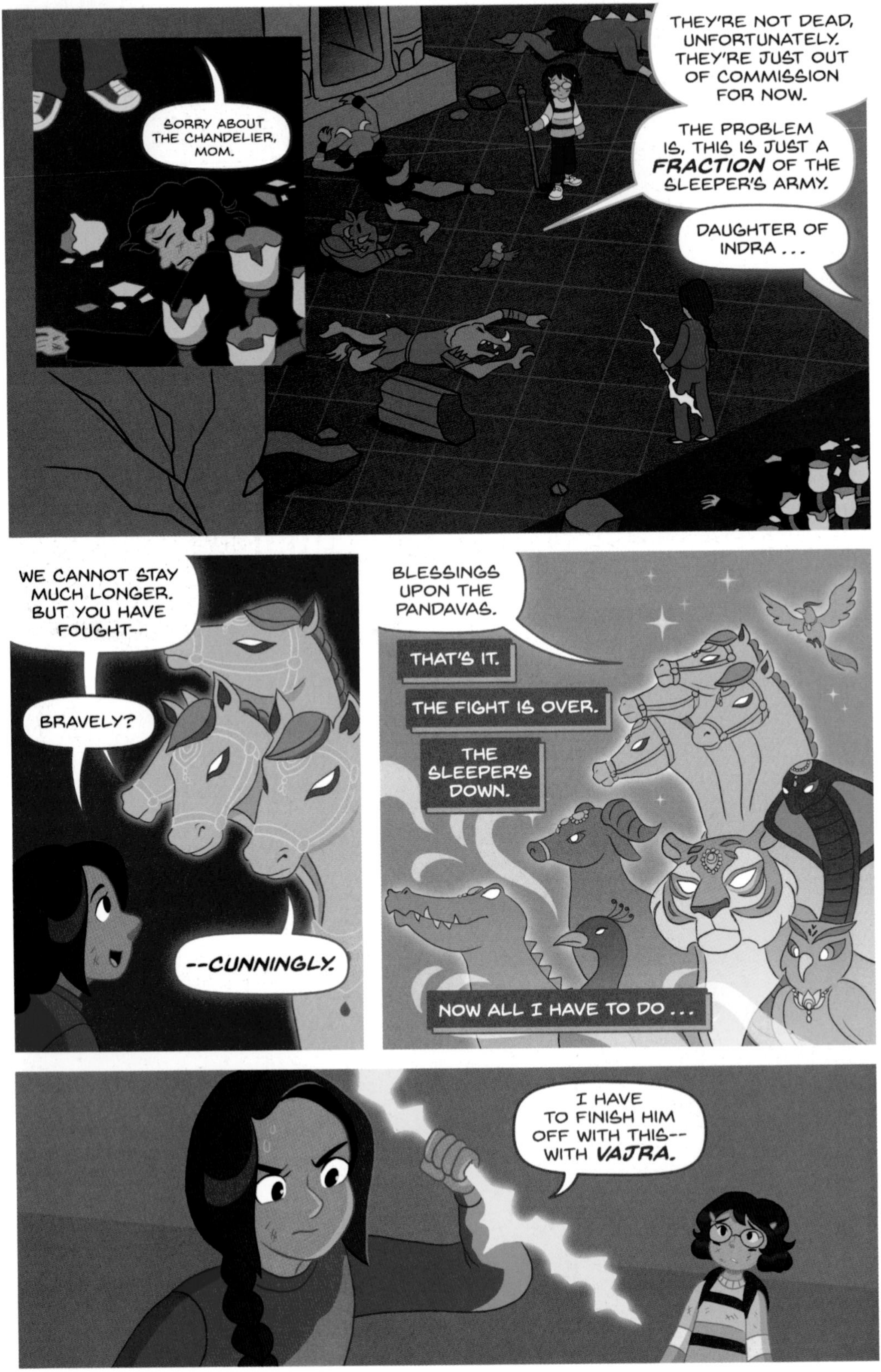
SORRY ABOUT THE CHANDELIER, MOM.
THEY'RE NOT DEAD, UNFORTUNATELY. THEY'RE JUST OUT OF COMMISSION FOR NOW.
THE PROBLEM IS, THIS IS JUST A FRACTION OF THE SLEEPER'S ARMY.
DAUGHTER OF INDRA . . .
WE CANNOT STAY MUCH LONGER. BUT YOU HAVE FOUGHT--
BRAVELY?
--CUNNINGLY.
BLESSINGS UPON THE PANDAVAS.
THAT'S IT.
THE FIGHT IS OVER.
THE SLEEPER'S DOWN.
NOW ALL I HAVE TO DO . . .
I HAVE TO FINISH HIM OFF WITH THIS-- WITH VAJRA.

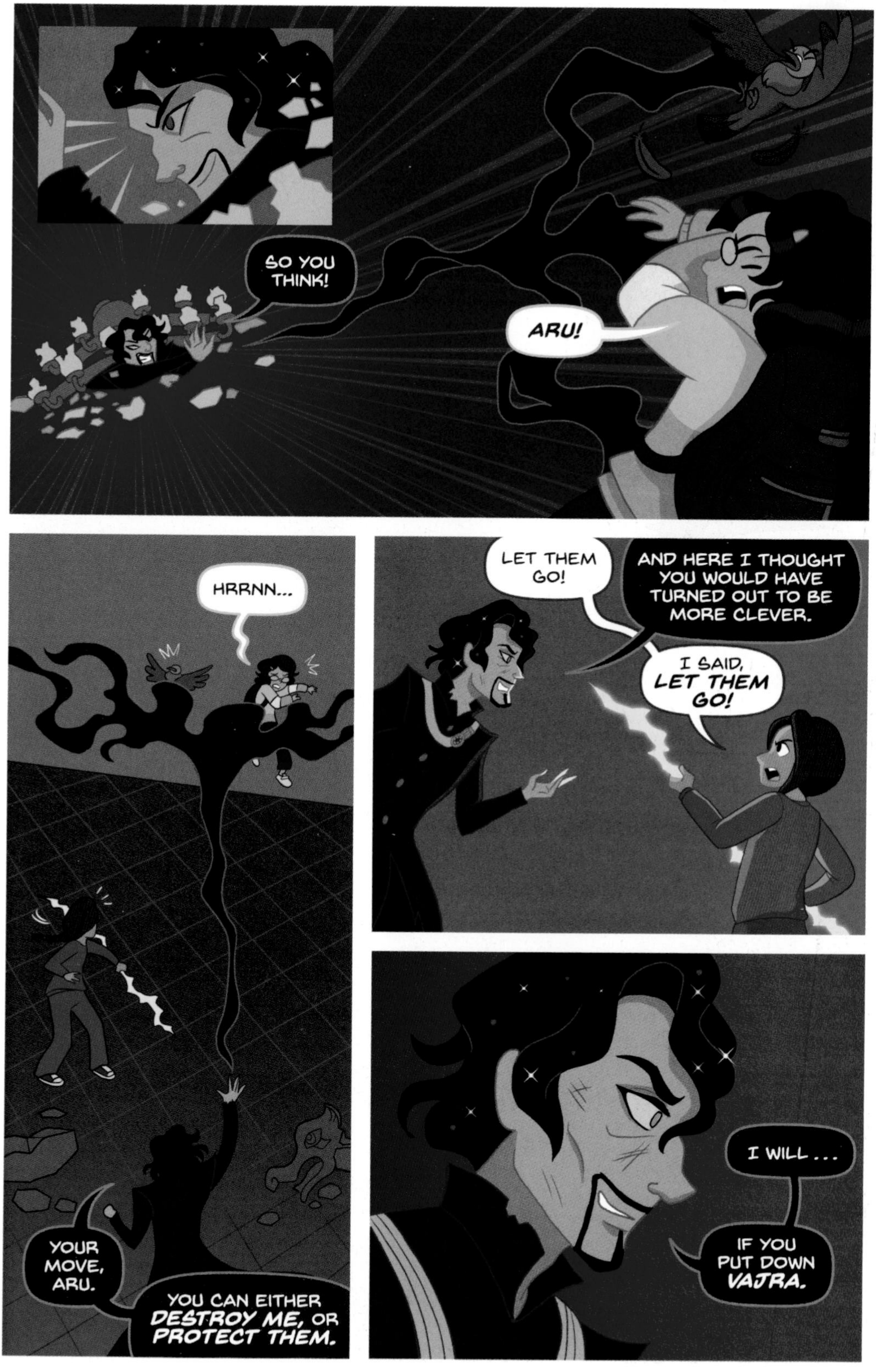
SO YOU THINK!
ARU!
HRRNN...
YOUR MOVE, ARU.
YOU CAN EITHER DESTROY ME, OR PROTECT THEM.
LET THEM GO!
AND HERE I THOUGHT YOU WOULD HAVE TURNED OUT TO BE MORE CLEVER.
I SAID, LET THEM GO!
I WILL . . .
IF YOU PUT DOWN VAJRA.

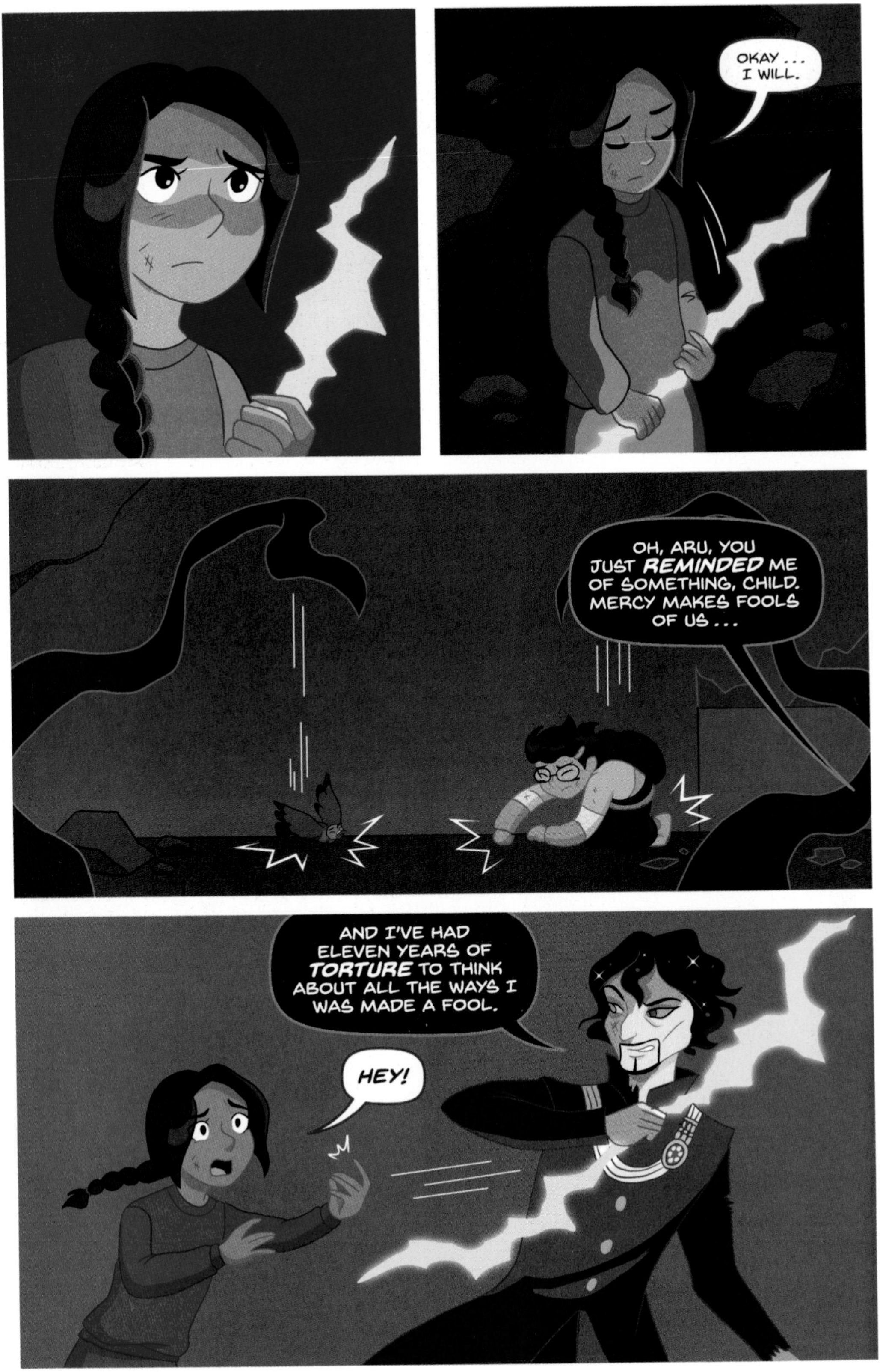
OKAY . . . I WILL.
OH, ARU, YOU JUST REMINDED ME OF SOMETHING, CHILD. MERCY MAKES FOOLS OF US . . .
AND I'VE HAD ELEVEN YEARS OF TORTURE TO THINK ABOUT ALL THE WAYS I WAS MADE A FOOL.
HEY!

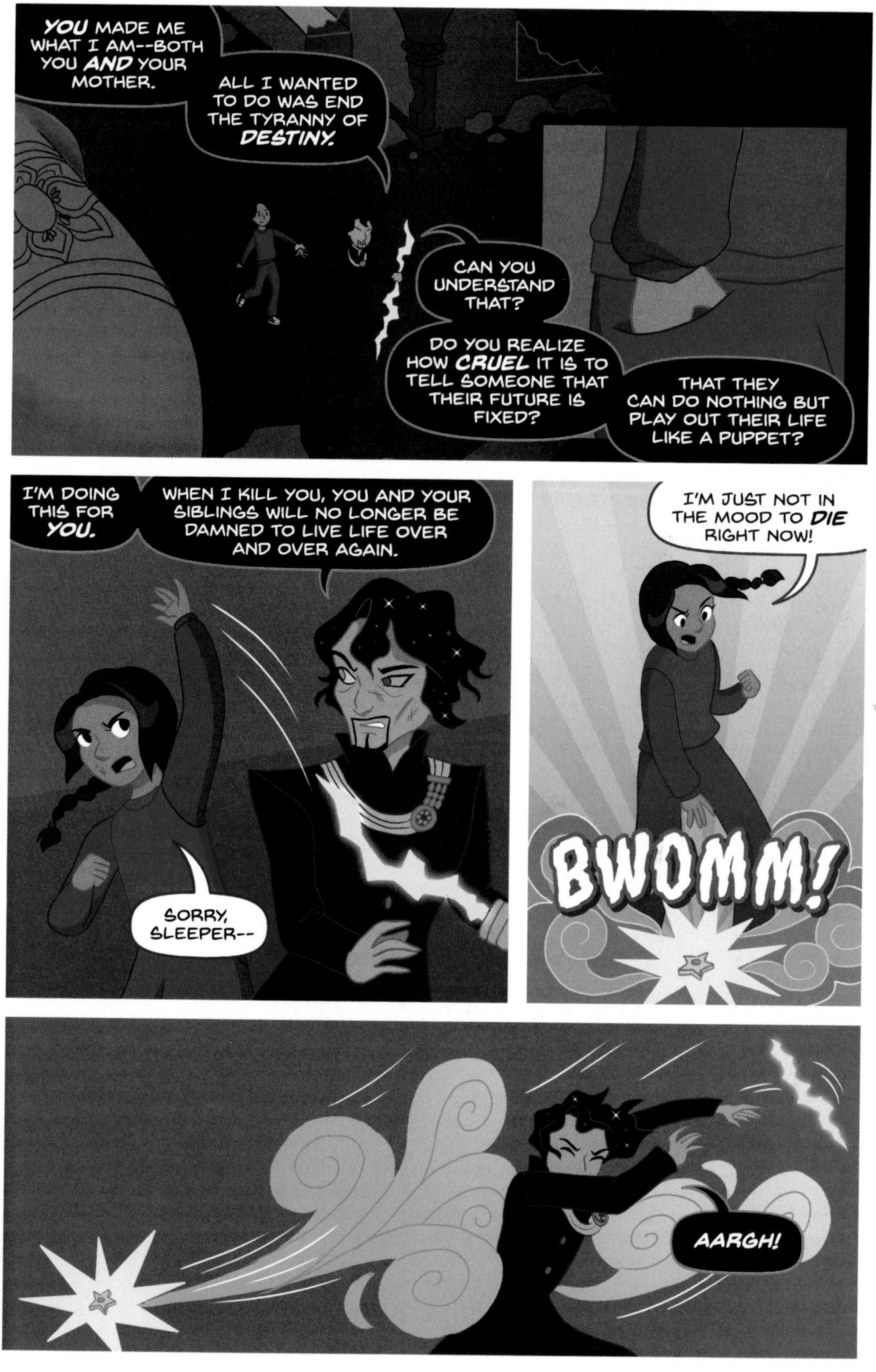
YOU MADE ME WHAT I AM--BOTH YOU AND YOUR MOTHER.
ALL I WANTED TO DO WAS END THE TYRANNY OF DESTINY.
CAN YOU UNDERSTAND THAT?
DO YOU REALIZE HOW CRUEL IT IS TO TELL SOMEONE THAT THEIR FUTURE IS FIXED?
THAT THEY CAN DO NOTHING BUT PLAY OUT THEIR LIFE LIKE A PUPPET?
I'M DOING THIS FOR YOU.
WHEN I KILL YOU, YOU AND YOUR SIBLINGS WILL NO LONGER BE DAMNED TO LIVE LIFE OVER AND OVER AGAIN.
SORRY, SLEEPER--
I'M JUST NOT IN THE MOOD TO DIE RIGHT NOW!
BWOMM!
AARGH!

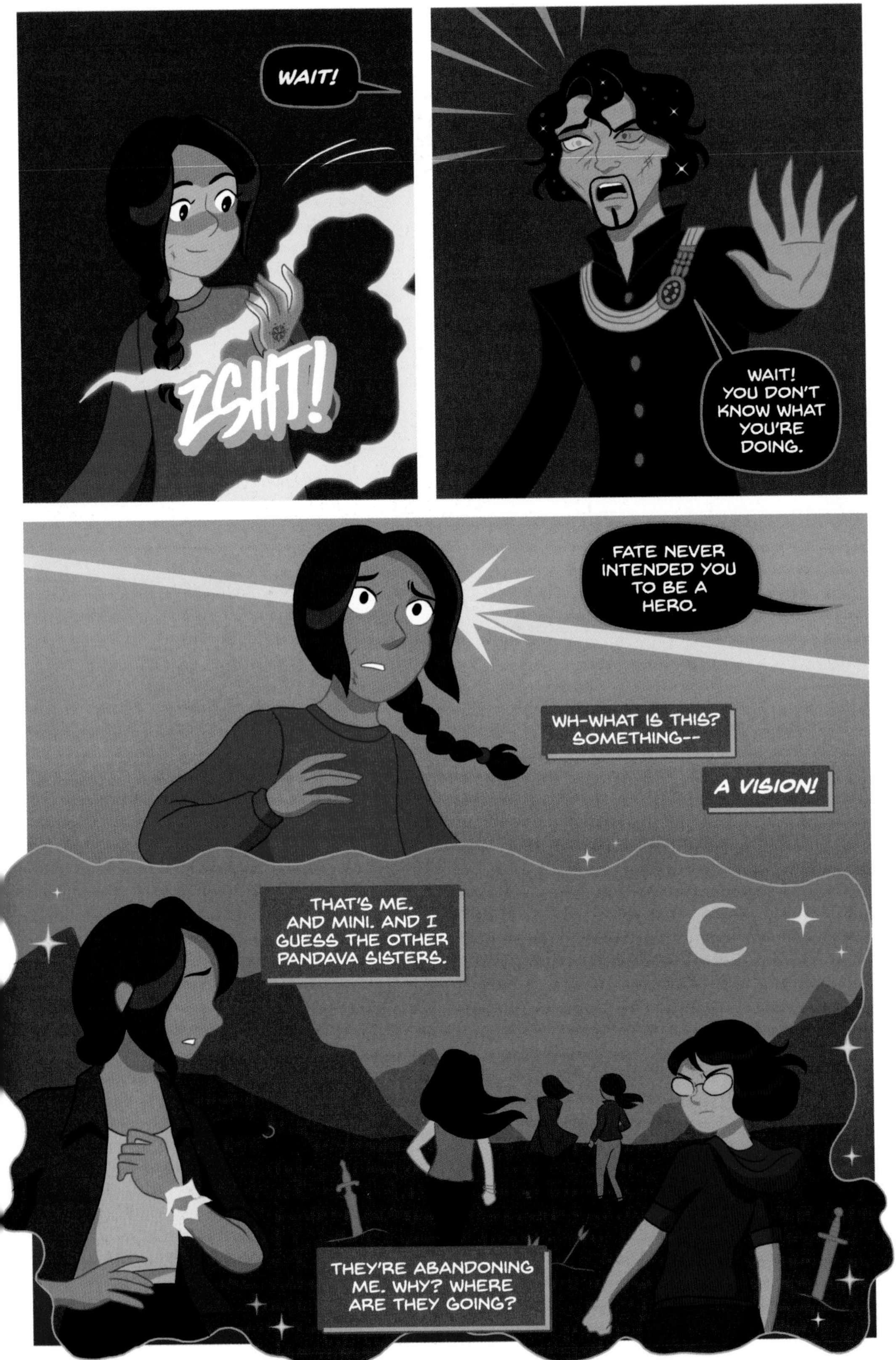
WAIT!
ZSHT!
WAIT! YOU DON'T KNOW WHAT YOU'RE DOING.
FATE NEVER INTENDED YOU TO BE A HERO.
WH-WHAT IS THIS? SOMETHING--
A VISION!
THAT'S ME. AND MINI. AND I GUESS THE OTHER PANDAVA SISTERS.
THEY'RE ABANDONING ME. WHY? WHERE ARE THEY GOING?

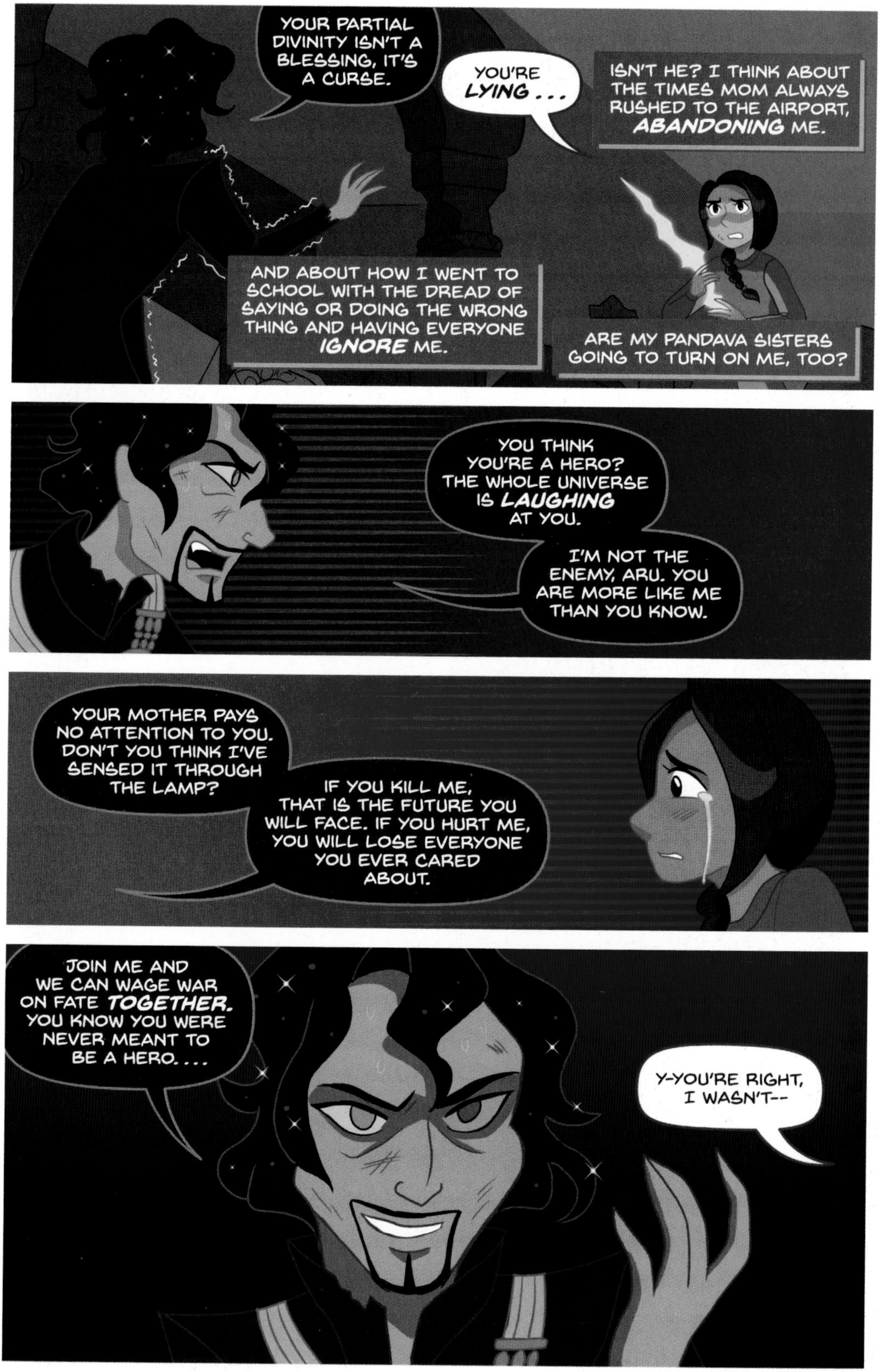
YOUR PARTIAL DIVINITY ISN'T A BLESSING, IT'S A CURSE.
YOU'RE *LYING* . . .
ISN'T HE? I THINK ABOUT THE TIMES MOM ALWAYS RUSHED TO THE AIRPORT, *ABANDONING* ME.
AND ABOUT HOW I WENT TO SCHOOL WITH THE DREAD OF SAYING OR DOING THE WRONG THING AND HAVING EVERYONE *IGNORE* ME.
ARE MY PANDAVA SISTERS GOING TO TURN ON ME, TOO?
YOU THINK YOU'RE A HERO? THE WHOLE UNIVERSE IS *LAUGHING* AT YOU.
I'M NOT THE ENEMY, ARU. YOU ARE MORE LIKE ME THAN YOU KNOW.
YOUR MOTHER PAYS NO ATTENTION TO YOU. DON'T YOU THINK I'VE SENSED IT THROUGH THE LAMP?
IF YOU KILL ME, THAT IS THE FUTURE YOU WILL FACE. IF YOU HURT ME, YOU WILL LOSE EVERYONE YOU EVER CARED ABOUT.
JOIN ME AND WE CAN WAGE WAR ON FATE *TOGETHER.* YOU KNOW YOU WERE NEVER MEANT TO BE A HERO. . . .
Y-YOU'RE RIGHT, I WASN'T--

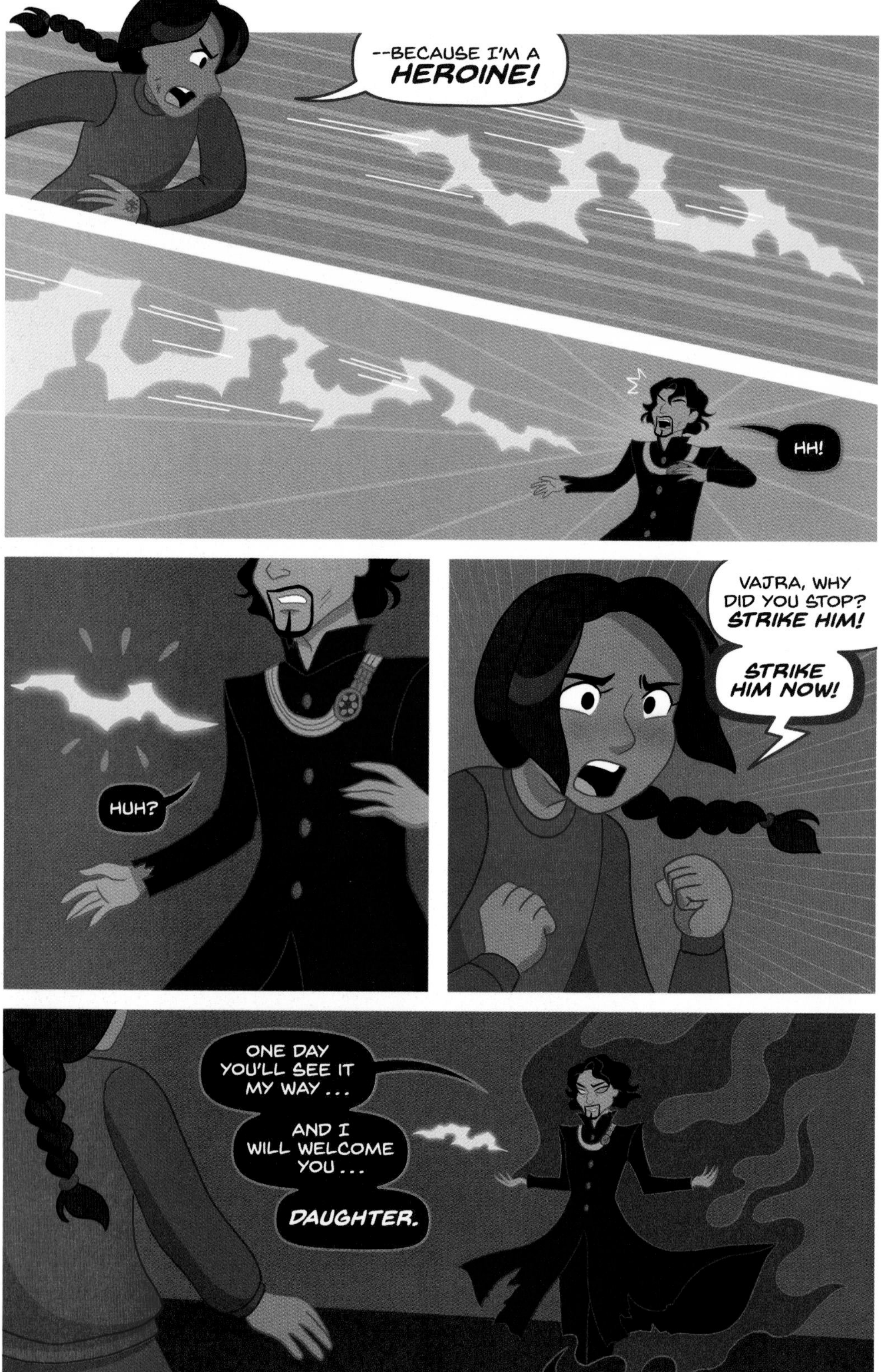
--BECAUSE I'M A HEROINE!
HH!
HUH?
VAJRA, WHY DID YOU STOP? STRIKE HIM!
STRIKE HIM NOW!
ONE DAY YOU'LL SEE IT MY WAY . . .
AND I WILL WELCOME YOU . . .
DAUGHTER.

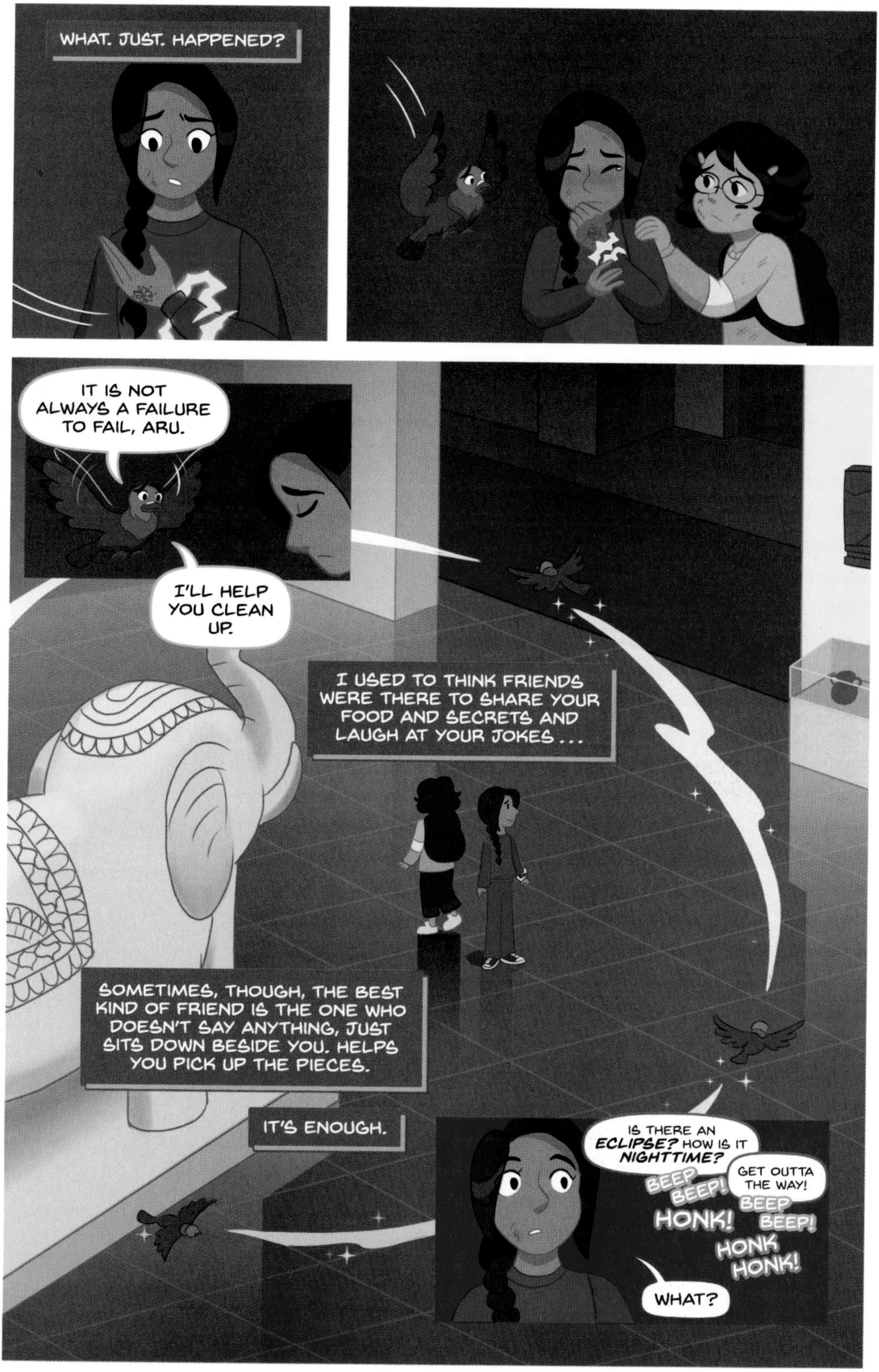

WHAT. JUST. HAPPENED?
IT IS NOT ALWAYS A FAILURE TO FAIL, ARU.
I'LL HELP YOU CLEAN UP.
I USED TO THINK FRIENDS WERE THERE TO SHARE YOUR FOOD AND SECRETS AND LAUGH AT YOUR JOKES . . .
SOMETIMES, THOUGH, THE BEST KIND OF FRIEND IS THE ONE WHO DOESN'T SAY ANYTHING, JUST SITS DOWN BESIDE YOU. HELPS YOU PICK UP THE PIECES.
IT'S ENOUGH.
IS THERE AN *ECLIPSE?* HOW IS IT *NIGHTTIME?*
BEEP BEEP!
GET OUTTA THE WAY!
BEEP BEEP!
HONK!
HONK HONK!
WHAT?

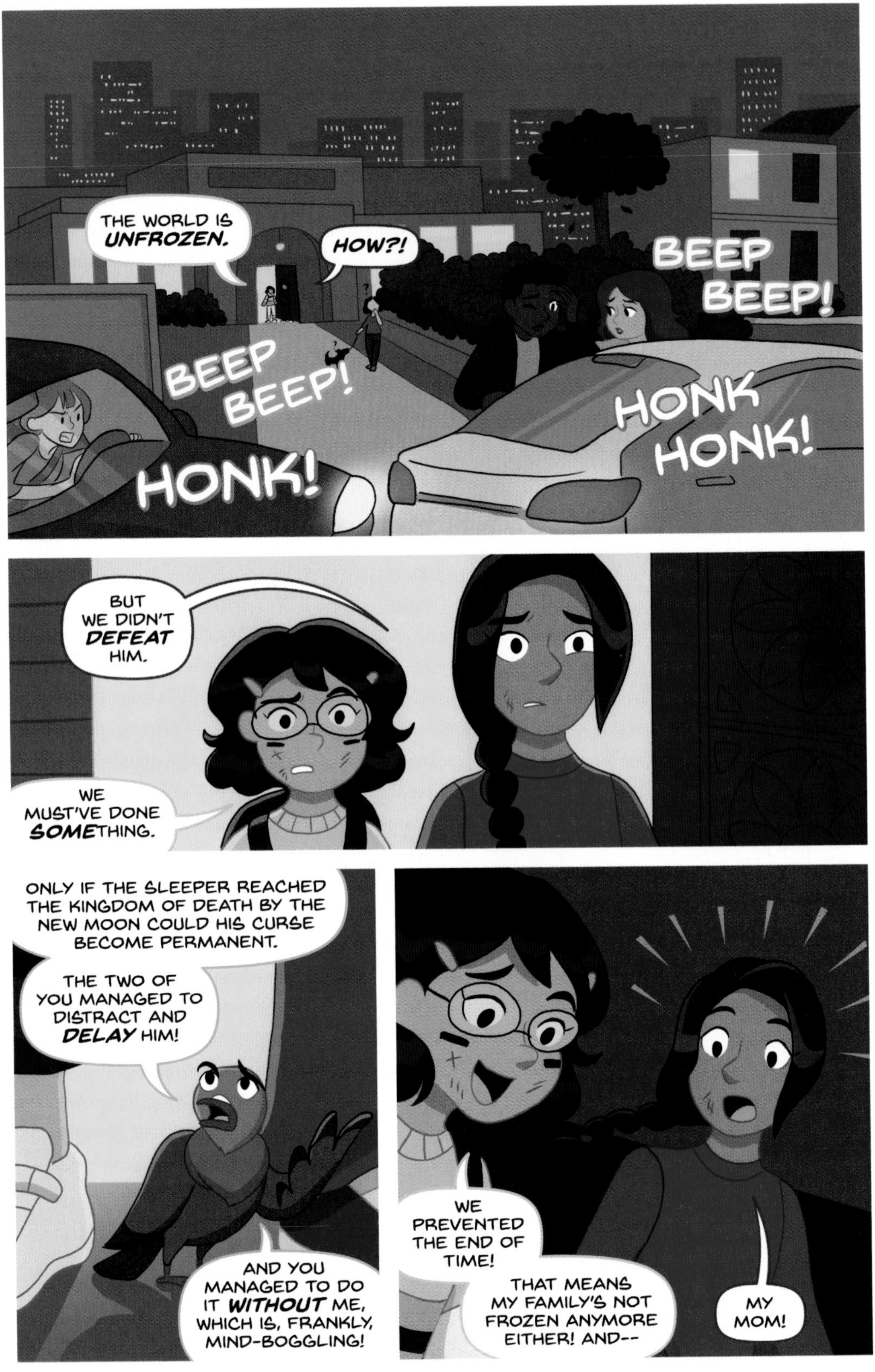
THE WORLD IS UNFROZEN.
HOW?!
BEEP BEEP!
BEEP BEEP!
HONK!
HONK HONK!
BUT WE DIDN'T DEFEAT HIM.
WE MUST'VE DONE SOMETHING.
ONLY IF THE SLEEPER REACHED THE KINGDOM OF DEATH BY THE NEW MOON COULD HIS CURSE BECOME PERMANENT.
THE TWO OF YOU MANAGED TO DISTRACT AND DELAY HIM!
AND YOU MANAGED TO DO IT WITHOUT ME, WHICH IS, FRANKLY, MIND-BOGGLING!
WE PREVENTED THE END OF TIME!
THAT MEANS MY FAMILY'S NOT FROZEN ANYMORE EITHER! AND--
MY MOM!

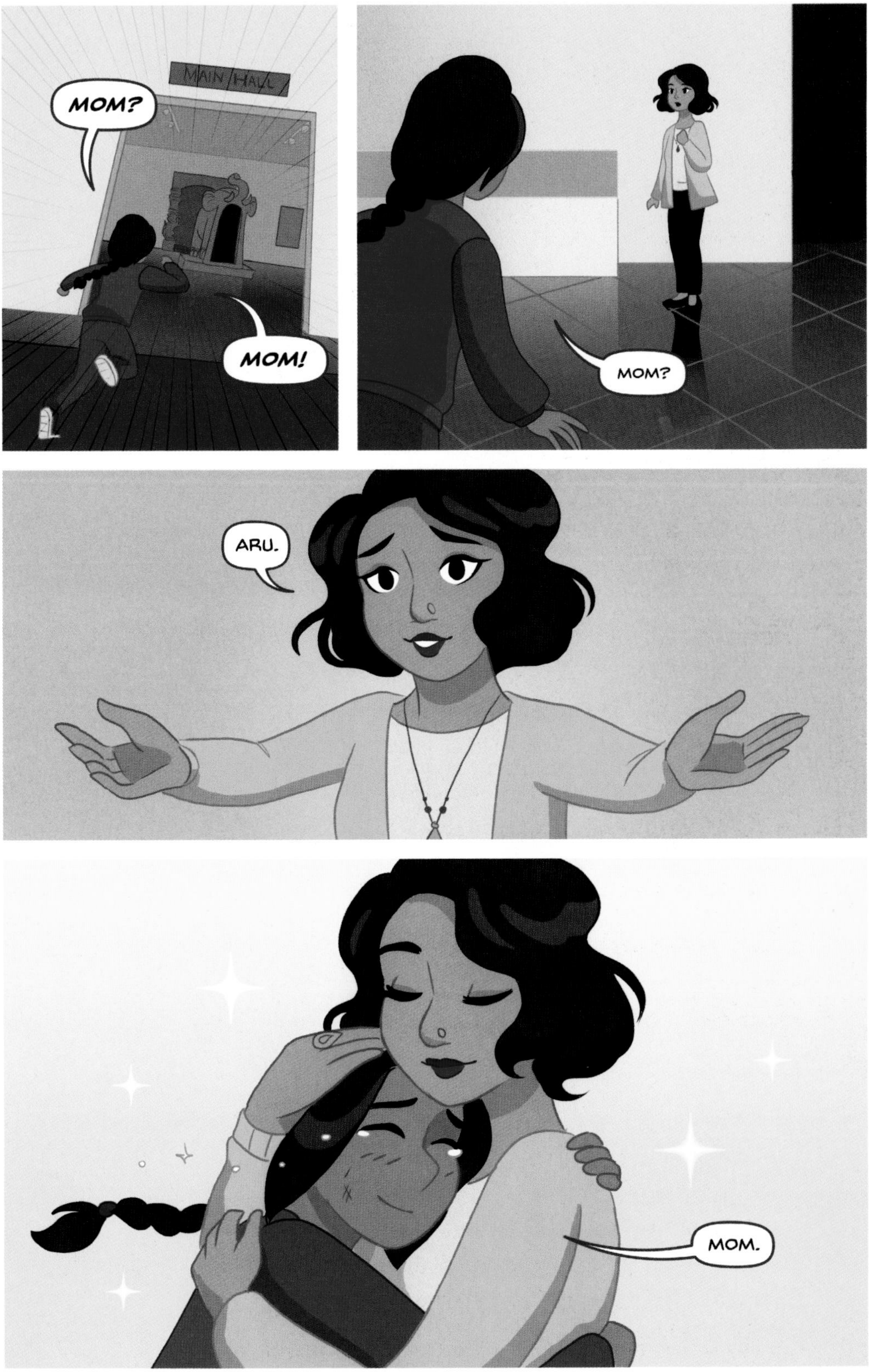
MAIN HALL
MOM?
MOM!
MOM?
ARU.
MOM.

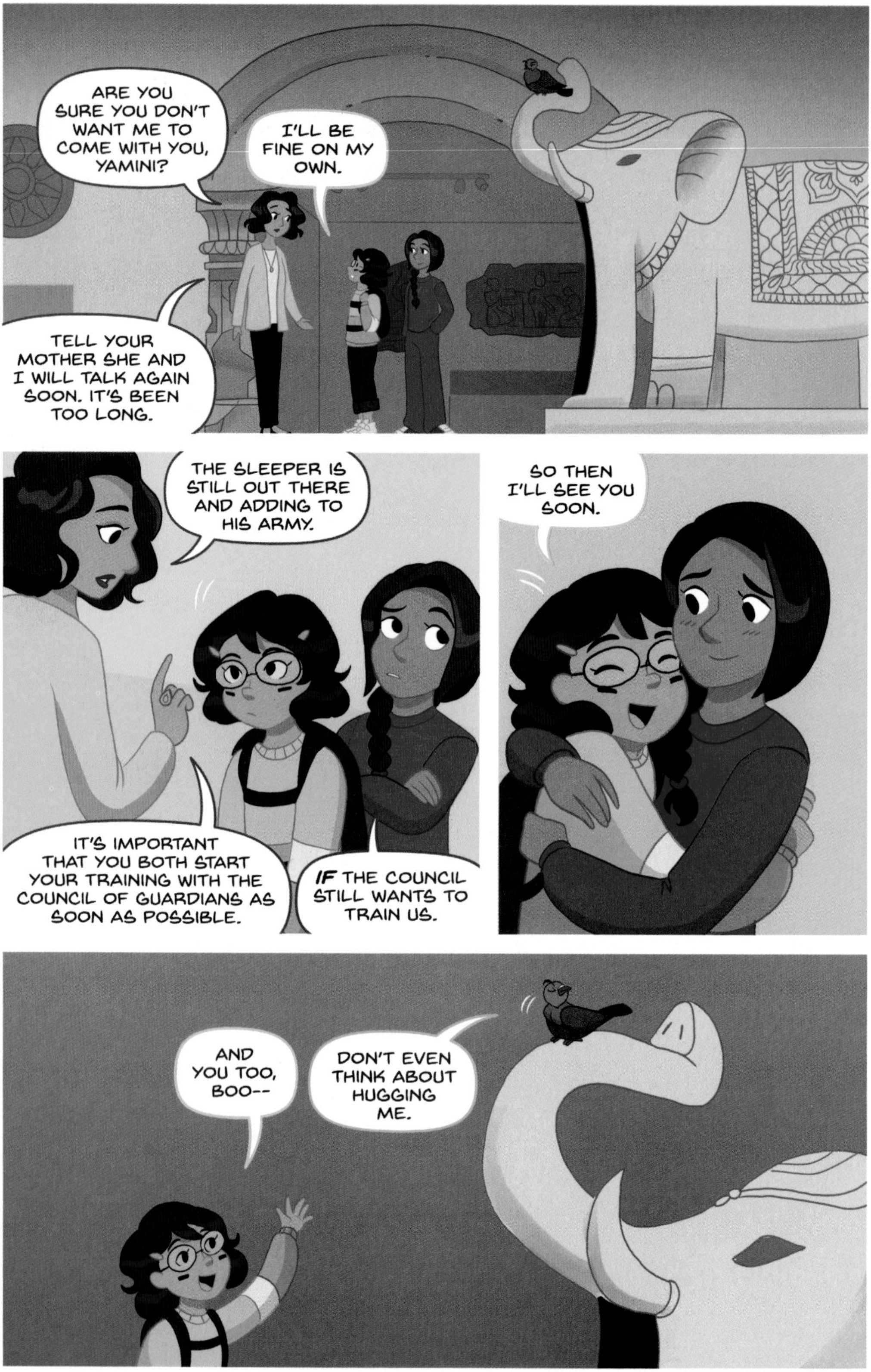
ARE YOU SURE YOU DON'T WANT ME TO COME WITH YOU, YAMINI?
I'LL BE FINE ON MY OWN.
TELL YOUR MOTHER SHE AND I WILL TALK AGAIN SOON. IT'S BEEN TOO LONG.
THE SLEEPER IS STILL OUT THERE AND ADDING TO HIS ARMY.
IT'S IMPORTANT THAT YOU BOTH START YOUR TRAINING WITH THE COUNCIL OF GUARDIANS AS SOON AS POSSIBLE.
IF THE COUNCIL STILL WANTS TO TRAIN US.
SO THEN I'LL SEE YOU SOON.
AND YOU TOO, BOO--
DON'T EVEN THINK ABOUT HUGGING ME.

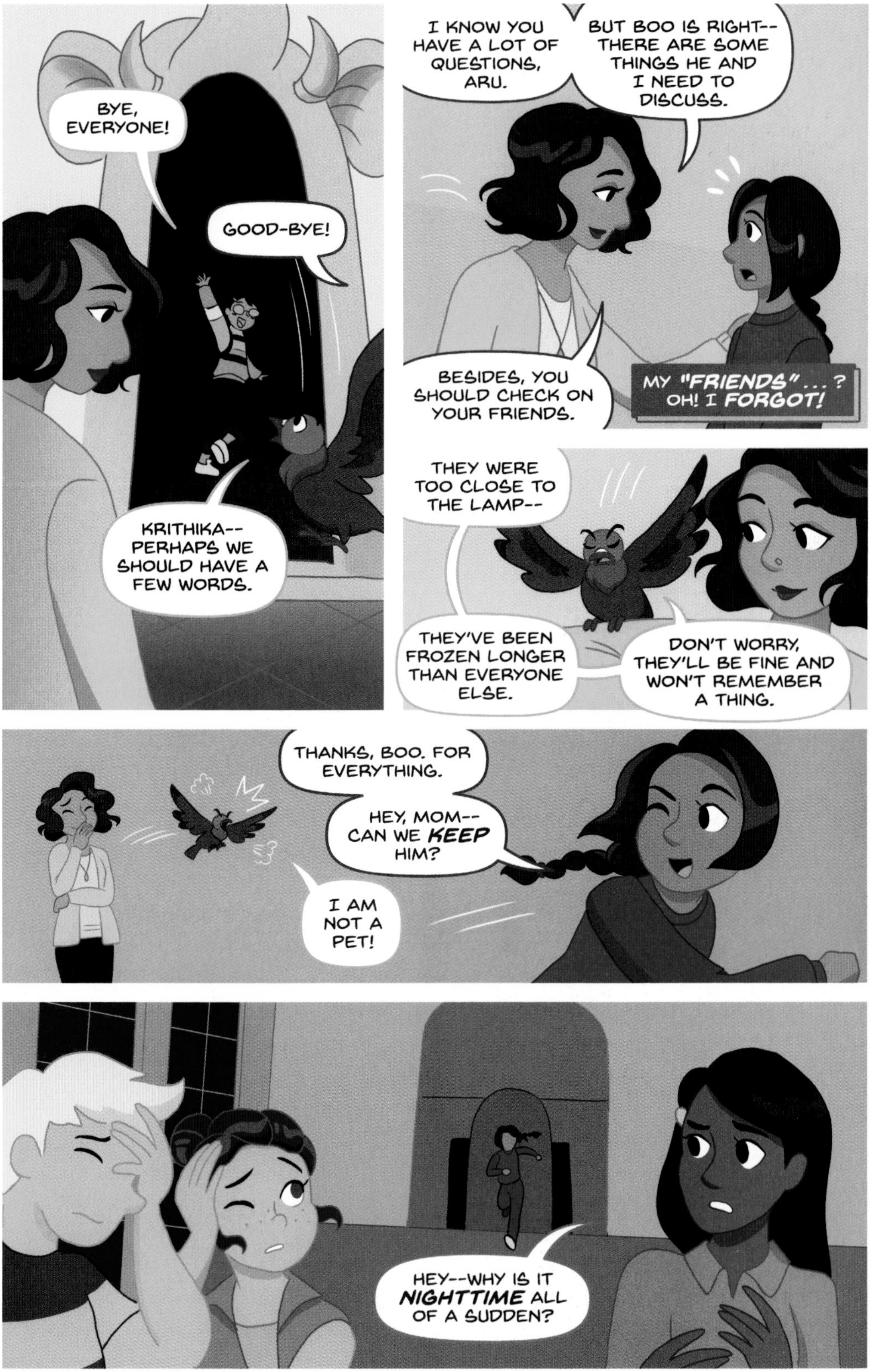
BYE, EVERYONE!
GOOD-BYE!
KRITHIKA-- PERHAPS WE SHOULD HAVE A FEW WORDS.
I KNOW YOU HAVE A LOT OF QUESTIONS, ARU.
BUT BOO IS RIGHT-- THERE ARE SOME THINGS HE AND I NEED TO DISCUSS.
BESIDES, YOU SHOULD CHECK ON YOUR FRIENDS.
MY "FRIENDS"...? OH! I FORGOT!
THEY WERE TOO CLOSE TO THE LAMP--
THEY'VE BEEN FROZEN LONGER THAN EVERYONE ELSE.
DON'T WORRY, THEY'LL BE FINE AND WON'T REMEMBER A THING.
THANKS, BOO. FOR EVERYTHING.
HEY, MOM-- CAN WE KEEP HIM?
I AM NOT A PET!
HEY--WHY IS IT NIGHTTIME ALL OF A SUDDEN?

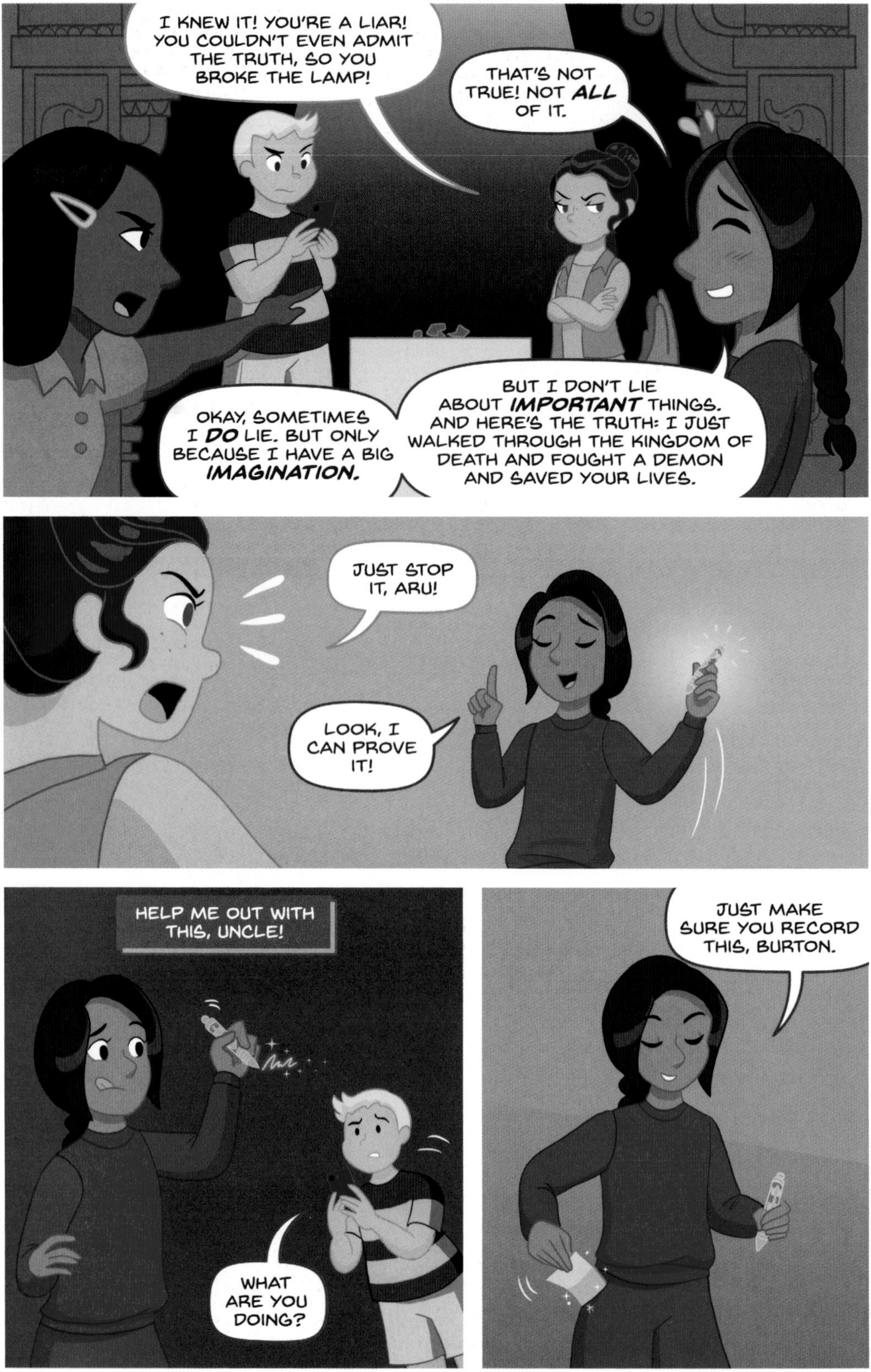
I KNEW IT! YOU'RE A LIAR! YOU COULDN'T EVEN ADMIT THE TRUTH, SO YOU BROKE THE LAMP!
THAT'S NOT TRUE! NOT ALL OF IT.
OKAY, SOMETIMES I DO LIE. BUT ONLY BECAUSE I HAVE A BIG IMAGINATION.
BUT I DON'T LIE ABOUT IMPORTANT THINGS. AND HERE'S THE TRUTH: I JUST WALKED THROUGH THE KINGDOM OF DEATH AND FOUGHT A DEMON AND SAVED YOUR LIVES.
JUST STOP IT, ARU!
LOOK, I CAN PROVE IT!
HELP ME OUT WITH THIS, UNCLE!
WHAT ARE YOU DOING?
JUST MAKE SURE YOU RECORD THIS, BURTON.

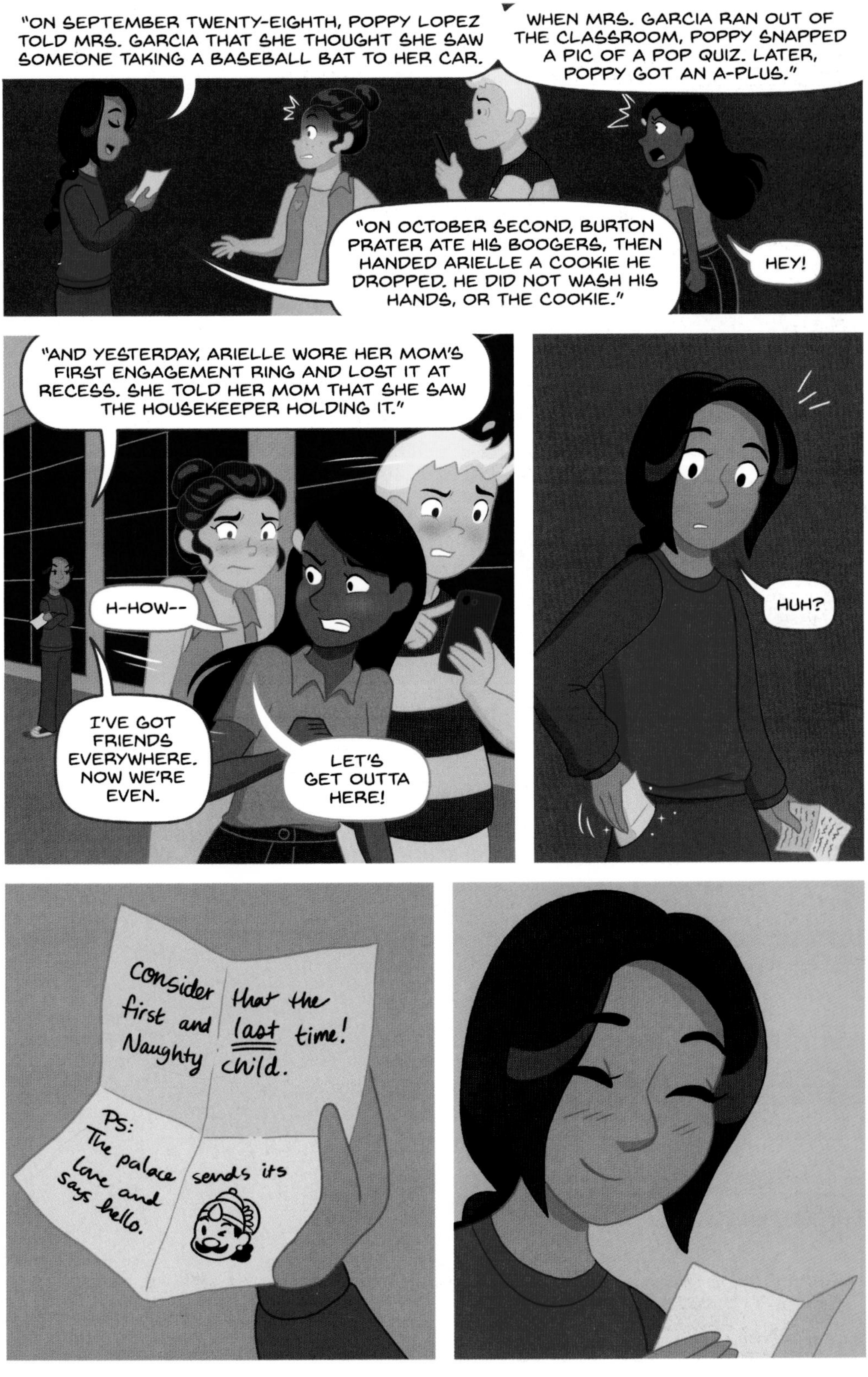
"ON SEPTEMBER TWENTY-EIGHTH, POPPY LOPEZ TOLD MRS. GARCIA THAT SHE THOUGHT SHE SAW SOMEONE TAKING A BASEBALL BAT TO HER CAR.
WHEN MRS. GARCIA RAN OUT OF THE CLASSROOM, POPPY SNAPPED A PIC OF A POP QUIZ. LATER, POPPY GOT AN A-PLUS."
"ON OCTOBER SECOND, BURTON PRATER ATE HIS BOOGERS, THEN HANDED ARIELLE A COOKIE HE DROPPED. HE DID NOT WASH HIS HANDS, OR THE COOKIE."
HEY!
"AND YESTERDAY, ARIELLE WORE HER MOM'S FIRST ENGAGEMENT RING AND LOST IT AT RECESS. SHE TOLD HER MOM THAT SHE SAW THE HOUSEKEEPER HOLDING IT."
H-HOW--
I'VE GOT FRIENDS EVERYWHERE. NOW WE'RE EVEN.
LET'S GET OUTTA HERE!
HUH?
Consider that the first and last time! Naughty child.
PS: The palace sends its love and says hello.

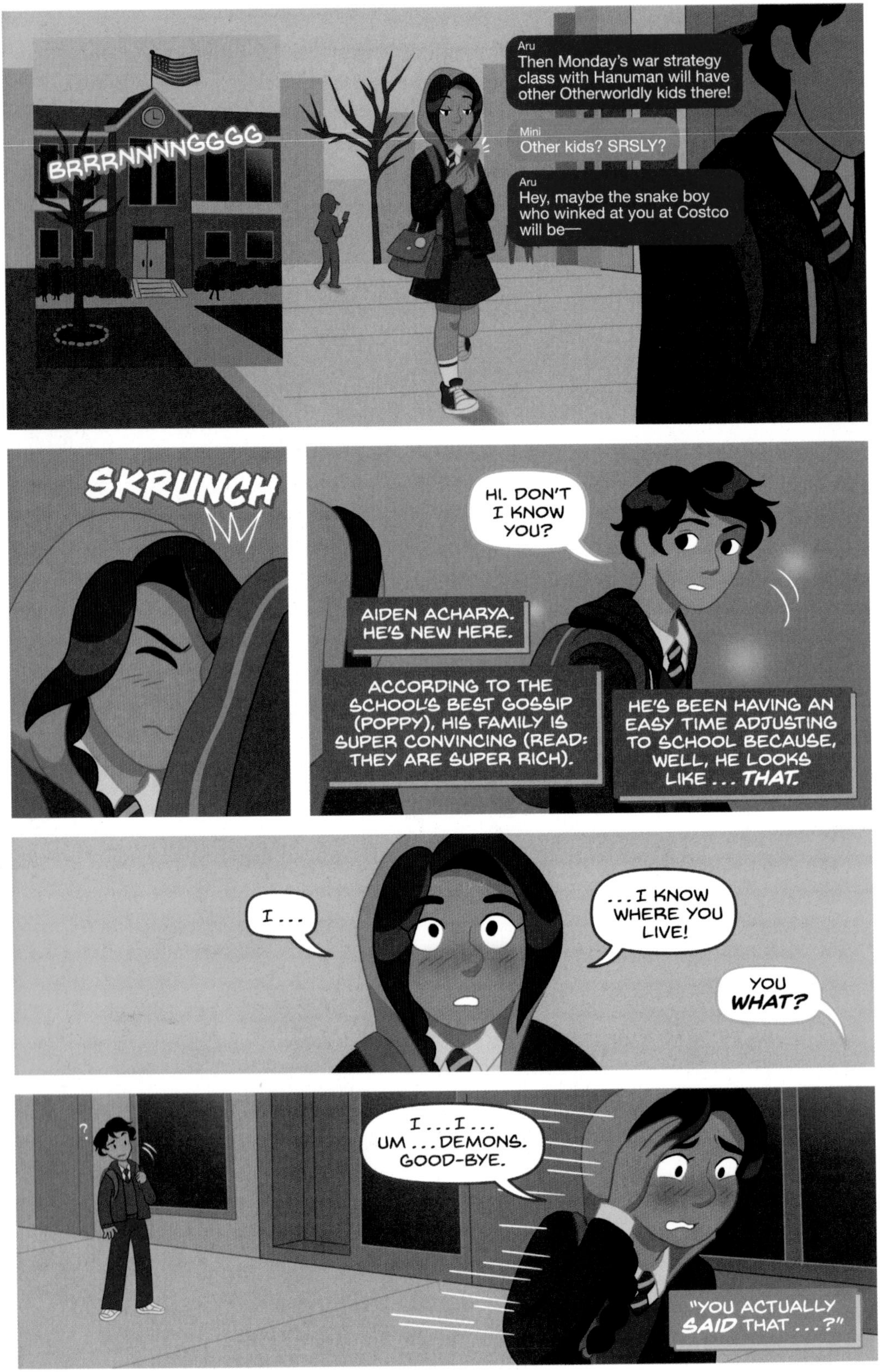
BRRRNNNNGGGG
Aru
Then Monday's war strategy class with Hanuman will have other Otherworldly kids there!
Mini
Other kids? SRSLY?
Aru
Hey, maybe the snake boy who winked at you at Costco will be—
SKRUNCH
HI. DON'T I KNOW YOU?
AIDEN ACHARYA. HE'S NEW HERE.
ACCORDING TO THE SCHOOL'S BEST GOSSIP (POPPY), HIS FAMILY IS SUPER CONVINCING (READ: THEY ARE SUPER RICH).
HE'S BEEN HAVING AN EASY TIME ADJUSTING TO SCHOOL BECAUSE, WELL, HE LOOKS LIKE . . . THAT.
I . . .
. . . I KNOW WHERE YOU LIVE!
YOU WHAT?
?
I . . . I . . . UM . . . DEMONS. GOOD-BYE.
"YOU ACTUALLY SAID THAT . . . ?"

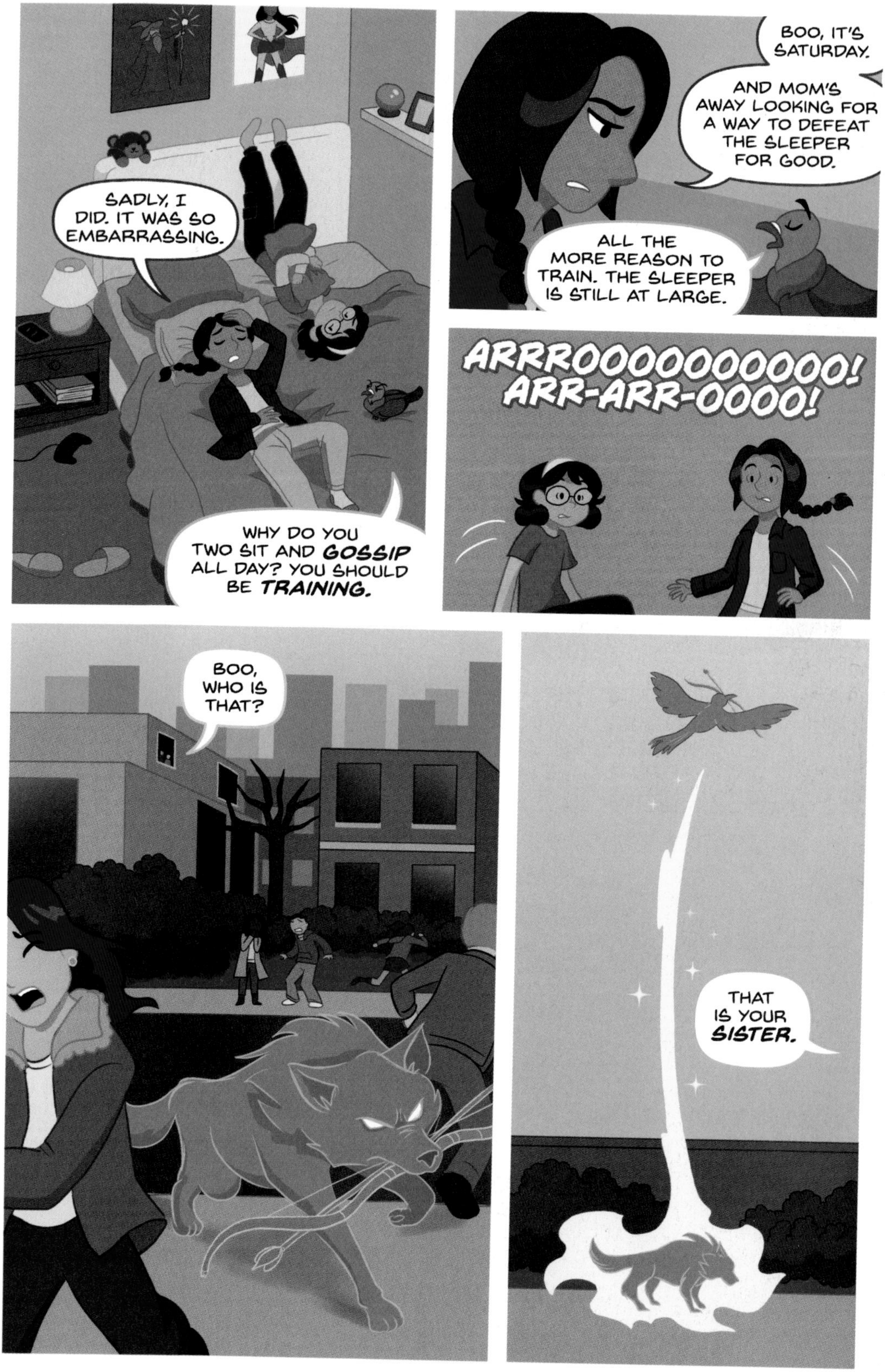
SADLY, I DID. IT WAS SO EMBARRASSING.
WHY DO YOU TWO SIT AND GOSSIP ALL DAY? YOU SHOULD BE TRAINING.
BOO, IT'S SATURDAY.
AND MOM'S AWAY LOOKING FOR A WAY TO DEFEAT THE SLEEPER FOR GOOD.
ALL THE MORE REASON TO TRAIN. THE SLEEPER IS STILL AT LARGE.
ARRROOOOOOOOOOO! ARR-ARR-OOOO!
BOO, WHO IS THAT?
THAT IS YOUR SISTER.

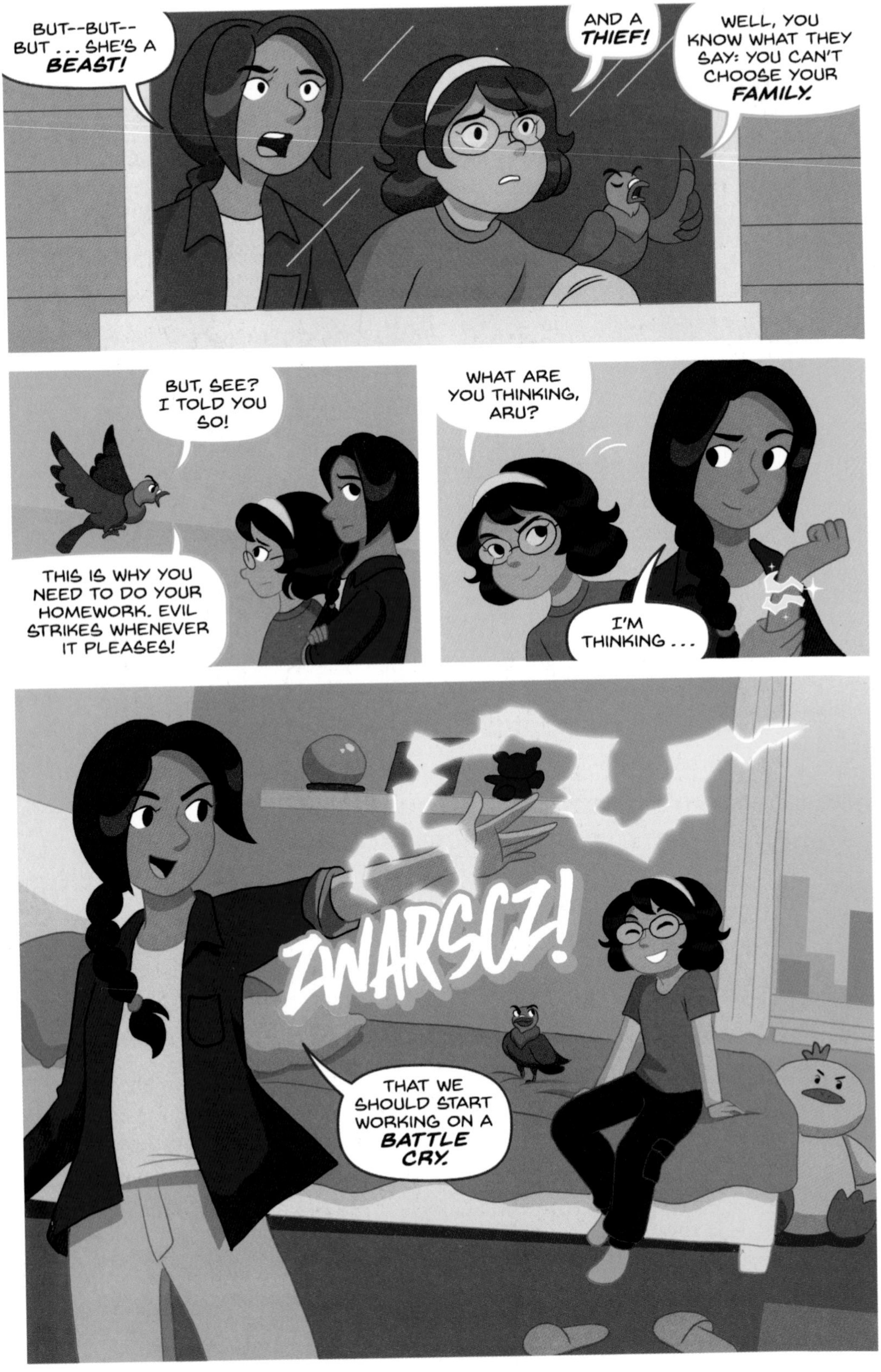
BUT--BUT--
BUT . . . SHE'S A
BEAST!
AND A
THIEF!
WELL, YOU
KNOW WHAT THEY
SAY: YOU CAN'T
CHOOSE YOUR
FAMILY.
BUT, SEE?
I TOLD YOU
SO!
THIS IS WHY YOU
NEED TO DO YOUR
HOMEWORK. EVIL
STRIKES WHENEVER
IT PLEASES!
WHAT ARE
YOU THINKING,
ARU?
I'M
THINKING . . .
ZWARSCZ!
THAT WE
SHOULD START
WORKING ON A
BATTLE
CRY.